W9-AEZ-027

WITHDRAWN

NEFERTITI
THE BOOK OF THE DEAD

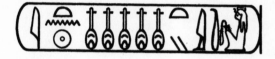

ALSO BY NICK DRAKE

The Man in the White Suit

NEFERTITI
THE BOOK OF THE DEAD

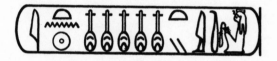

Nick Drake

🔥 HarperCollins*Publishers*

HarperCollins books may be purchased for educational, business, or sales promotional use. For information, please write: Special Markets Department, HarperCollins Publishers, 10 East 53rd Street, New York, NY 10022.

First published in Great Britain in 2006 by Bantam Press, a division of Transworld Publishers.

FIRST U.S. EDITION

Library of Congress Cataloging-in-Publication Data is available upon request.

ISBN: 978-0-06-076589-7
ISBN-10: 0-06-076589-5

07 08 09 10 11   UK OFF/RRD   10 9 8 7 6 5 4 3 2 1

To my father,
Miles Drake

AUTHOR'S NOTE

Three and a half thousand years ago Akhenaten inherited an empire at the peak of its international power and wealth. It was a time of astonishing sophistication and beauty, but also of vanity and brutality. The Empire had a police force – the Medjay – and extensive papyrus archives to keep tabs on its citizens. The affluent worried about going grey, enjoyed their hunts and love affairs, and spent large amounts of money on their tombs in preparation for the afterlife. There were career bureaucracies and an enormous workforce, both local and immigrant. This complex society depended on the waters of the Nile that weaved like a great snake through the desert, dividing the Egyptian world into the fertile Black Land and the barren Red.

Akhenaten chose to do something extraordinary with his riches. He and his Great Royal Wife, Nefertiti – 'the Perfect One' – initiated a period of revolution in religion, politics and art. Rejecting and abolishing Egypt's traditional institutions and gods, and challenging the powerful priesthoods, they built an extraordinary new city, Akhetaten, as a centre for the celebration of their new faith. At the heart of this was the worship of the Aten, now the only god, represented by the disc of the Sun.

Today little remains of the city. Outside the modern Amarna you can trace the line of the Royal Road, and the palaces and Aten Temples. You can visit the cliff tombs of the great men who worked for Akhenaten and Nefertiti: Mahu, the chief of police, Meryra, the High Priest, Parennefer, the architect of the Amarna style, and Ay, 'God's father' and influential adviser to the King. You can descend the many steps into Akhenaten's empty burial chambers.

But you cannot visit Nefertiti's tomb, for she, the most powerful and charismatic woman of the ancient world, mysteriously vanished in year 12 of Akhenaten's seventeen-year reign. Why she vanished when she did, and what happened to her, is the mystery this story explores.

O my heart which I had from my mother, O my heart which I had upon earth, do not rise up against me as witness in the presence of the Lord of Things

The Book of the Dead

NEFERTITI

THE BOOK OF THE DEAD

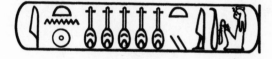

1

Year 12 of the Reign of King Akhenaten, Glory of the Sun Disc.

Thebes, Egypt

I had dreamed of snow. I was lost in a dark place, and snow was falling slowly and silently, each flake a puzzle I could never solve before it disappeared. I awoke with the feeling of its fleeting, cryptic lightness on my face. It made me feel surprisingly sad, as if I had lost something, or someone, for ever.

I lay still for a moment, listening to Tanefert breathing quietly at my side, the heat of the day already rising. I have never seen snow, of course, but I remember reading the report of a box of it carried from the furthest north, like treasure, packed in straw. And one hears the stories brought back from beyond the horizon. A freezing world. Deserts of snow. Rivers of ice. White and weightless, it may be held in the hand if one can endure the pain of its cold fire. Yet it is nothing but water. Water, which cannot be held in the hand. Only its incarnation has been changed, and I believe it changes back again depending on the world in which it finds itself. I also heard that when they finally opened the box, it was empty. This mysterious snow had vanished. Someone no doubt died for the disappointment. Such is treasure.

Maybe this is also death. That is not what we hear from the Priests. We all learned the prayer: 'when the tomb is opened may the body be perfect for the perfect life after life'. But have they seen the heat of the sun god rot and putrefy the charming flesh of the living, the young and the beautiful, with their nonsensical hopes and point-less dreams, into the contorted shapes of horror and monstrosity and petrified agony? Have they seen lovely faces cut apart, holes ripped open through muscle, heads smashed to bony fragments, the strange puckering of burned flesh where the fat has boiled? I doubt it.

Such thoughts are the torment of my work. I, Rahotep, youngest chief detective of the Thebes Medjay division, see my children playing or struggling to concentrate on their musical instruments. And I know their skin, which we caress and kiss, and care for with almond and moringa oils, and perfume with persea and myrrh, and dress with linens and gold, is merely a bag containing organs and bones and jars of blood; the hopes of being alive and in love depend on this butcher's business. I keep this to myself, even when I make love to my wife and for an instant her elegant body as it turns to me by the light of the oil lamp blurs from perfection into death. Apparently this is a rather famous thought. I should be grateful, perhaps, to have such thoughts. I should be more poetic, more philosophical, more often, if only to amuse during my private hours. Well, I have no private hours. And then again, as I stand over yet another corpse, a life – a little history of love and time – ended in a moment of frenzy or hatred or madness or panic, I feel it is the only time I know where in the world I am.

Of course, as Tanefert says whenever she finds the opportunity – which these days is too often – it is typical of me to think the worst of any given situation. But in these impossible times of the reign of Akhenaten I am confronted daily with justifications for this attitude. Things grow worse. I see it in my work: in the ever-increasing numbers of tormented and mutilated bodies of murder victims, and in the

14

robbed and desecrated tombs of the rich and powerful, with the Nubian security guards grinning from ear to ear through their slit throats. I see it in the ostentation of the rich and the endless misery of the poor. I see it in the greater world in the shaking news of the Great Changes: the King's banishment of the Karnak Temple Priesthood from their ancient places and rights; the denial and sometimes the desecration of Amun and all the lesser, older, popular gods; the imposition of the strange new god we are now supposed to celebrate and worship. I see it in the eccentric conception and extravagant expense of the mysterious new temple city of Akhetaten, under construction these last years in the desert, midway between here and Memphis and therefore so deliberately far from everyone. And I see all this imposed upon a perilous economy at a time of turbulence and uncertainty in our Empire. So, indeed, how else should I think? She says it is not normal, and she is right. But I passed through that portal long ago, when I understood that shadows and darkness live inside each one of us, and how little it takes before they leach through the soul and the smile. Death is easy.

So when I returned home at noon with the news of my sudden calling to investigate a great mystery at the heart of the regime stuck alarmingly in my mind, Tanefert took one look at me and said, 'What has happened? Tell me.' She sat down on the bench in the front room, where we never sit. I reached out to her, but she knows this ploy. 'I don't need you to hold my hand. I've been through this before.'

So I told her. About Ahmose coming into my office that morning. He was relishing a pastry, as always, not noticing the crumbs that fell clumsily into the ample folds of his robe. His belly makes him slow, and a detective should be strong but trim (as I think my daily exercises have made me). About how, with his usual sullen manner, he communicated with more than usual reluctance and aggression the arrival of the command from on high ordering me immediately and without delay to Akhetaten, to attend the court of Akhenaten in pursuit of a great mystery.

We stared at each other.

'Why has this honour fallen to me?' I asked.

Ahmose shrugged, and then smiled like a yawning necropolis cat. 'That's your job to find out.'

'And what is the mystery?'

'You will be enlightened when you meet the head of the new Medjay there, Mahu. You know him by reputation?'

I nodded. Notorious for his zealous application of the letter of the law.

Ahmose noisily swallowed the last of his pastry, and leaned towards me. 'But I have contacts in the new capital. And I hear it is a question of a missing person.' And he grinned ominously again.

Tanefert held herself still, her expression tight with fear. She knows as I know that if I fail to solve this mystery, whatever it may be – and Ra knows it cannot be other than a great mystery involving great figures and great powers – there will be no mystery about my fate. I will be stripped of my position, my few honours, my belongings, and set to death. And yet I did not feel afraid. I felt something else I could not acknowledge at that moment.

'Say something.' I looked at her.

'What do you want me to say? Nothing will make you stay with us. You actually look excited.'

Which was true, though I still would not admit it.

'That's because I am trying not to look worried in front of the girls.'

She did not believe me.

'How long will you be away?'

I couldn't tell her the truth, which was that I had no idea. 'About fifteen days. Perhaps much less. It depends on how quickly I can solve the mystery. On the state of the evidence, the existence of the clues, the circumstances . . .'

But she had turned her head away and was staring without seeing out of the window. Suddenly, the way the afternoon light struck her face pushed my heart into my mouth, and silenced me.

We sat like that for a little while, not speaking.

Then she said, 'I don't understand. Surely the city Medjay there should investigate the mystery? It's an internal issue. Why do they want you? You're a stranger, you have no contacts, no-one you can trust . . . and if it's supposed to be so secret why are they commanding an outsider? The local police will resent you for trespassing on their territory.'

Everything she said was true, as usual; her nose for the simple truth is smart and infallible. I smiled.

'There's nothing to smile about,' she said.

'I love you.'

'I don't want you to go.'

Her words caught me out.

'You know I have no choice.'

'You have a choice. There is always a choice.'

I embraced her, felt her shaking, and tried to soothe her. She calmed herself, and gently placed her hands on my face.

'I never know, every morning, whether this is the last time I will see you. So I memorize your face. I know it so well, now, that I could carry it perfectly to my grave.'

'Let's not talk about graves. Let's talk about what we'll do with the Lord's gift I will receive when I solve this mystery and become the most famous detective in the city.'

She smiled at last. 'Some gift would be welcome. You haven't been paid for months.'

The economy is a mess, the harvests have been poor for several years running, there are even reports of looting; and the waves of immigration from beyond our northern and southern borders, drawn by the promises of the great new constructions, have created a rootless and hopeless unemployed constituency with nothing to lose. Grain is scarce, they say, even in the royal granaries. No-one has been paid. It is the talk of the town. It has made everyone even more anxious. Everyone has mouths to feed. People fear the shortages. They wonder when they will be forced to barter their good city furniture on the black economy for a side of meat and a basket of vegetables from the countryside.

'I can take care of myself. And every moment I will be thinking only of coming back to you. I promise.'

17

She nodded, and wiped her eyes on her sleeve.

'I must say farewell to the children.'

'You're leaving *now*?'

'I must.'

She turned away from me.

As I came into their room, the girls stopped what they were doing. Sekhmet looked up at me from her scroll. Her topaz eyes under her black fringe. A hard choice between reading the next words of her story and a proper greeting. I stood her on a chair and put our faces together. I smelled the familiar sweet milkiness of her breath. She draped her weightless arms around my neck.

'I have to go away for a while. Work. Will you look after your mother and your sisters for me until I come home?'

She nodded, and whispered seriously into my ear that she would, that she loved me and would think of me every day.

'Write me a letter,' I asked.

She nodded again. My little sage. She is self-conscious this year: her voice has a new and careful refinement in it.

Next, Thuyu, grinning, her teeth all there now, making a silly face. She wanted to bite my nose, and I let her. 'Have fun!' she yelled, and dropped to the floor.

Nedjmet, the baby, 'the sweet one' as we call her, hopefully; a determined creature, her absoluteness so shockingly like mine. Her night weeping has given way to an utterly serious consideration of the world around her. I can no longer fool her at breakfast, when I try to persuade her a sweet roll is fresh when it is left over from yesterday's bake.

And lastly my Tanefert, my heart, with your hair the black of a moonless night, and your strong nose and long eyes. Forgive me for leaving you. If I have done nothing else with my life I have at least made this family. My bright girls. May they be given back to me at the end of this story. I will lay anything on the libation table for this. One knows the things one loves when one must leave them.

18

As is my habit and working method, I will keep a journal through the time to come. I shall record at the end of each day or night what I know I know, and also what I do not. I shall record clues and questions and conundrums and enigmas. I shall write what I please and what I think, not what I ought to write. In case something happens to me, perhaps this journal may survive as a testament, and return to its home like a lost dog. And perhaps the mystery will unfold from the bits and pieces, the shards and apparent irrelevances, the dreams and chances and impossibilities that make up the evidence and the history of a crime, into a successful, well-ordered and, who knows, sensible, logical, brilliantly deduced conclusion. But it would not be true. In my experience, things do not add up so easily. Things are, in my experience, a mess. So in this journal I will record the digressions, the thoughts that do not fit, the unrefined, the nonsensical and the inscrutable. And see what they tell me. And see if, from the broken evidence (for I normally deal in what is unredeemable), the outline of truth will emerge.

And then I did the hardest thing I have ever done. Dressed in my finest linens, and with my authorizations in my case, I made a brief libation to the household god. I prayed, with unusual sincerity (for he knows I do not believe in him), for his protection, and for the protection of my family. Then I embraced my girls, kissed Tanefert, who touched my face with her hands, put my feet into my old leather sandals and, with shaking hands, closed the door on my home and my life. I walked away towards a future where nothing was certain, everything at risk. And I am ashamed to write here that I felt more alive than ever, even though my heart was broken glass in my chest.

2

Great Thebes, your lights and shadows, your corrupt businesses and your chattering parties, your shops and your luxuries; your rotten, squalid quarters and your youthful, fashionable beauties; your crimes and miseries and murders. I never know whether I hate or love you. But at least I know you. Above the low rooftops of my neighbourhood I can see the blue, gold, red and green of the temple façades, their colonnades and pylons standing to the sun. The holy sycamore groves around them like dark green candles. Orchards and hidden gardens. And next to them rubbish in piles between dark shacks, and in dangerous passageways. Behind the costly villas and great palaces and temples lie the shanties made from the cast-offs and detritus of the rich where the multitudes scrape meagre livings. The niches of the household gods, each dish with its daily offering. They say there are more gods than mortals in the city, yet I have never seen one that was not shaped from the materials of this world. No, I do not hold with gods. They are selfish, in their temples and heavens. They have too much to answer for, in their relish of our sufferings and misfortunes, and their neglect of the petitions of our hearts. But this is sacrilege, and I must silence my thought – although I will write it here, and who reads this must honour my stupid trust.

I walked down the streets towards the docks, beneath the dusty white awnings that protect us from the noon sun. I saw the local kids running along the rooftops, shouting and darting between the piles of drying crops and fruit, jostling the cages of birds causing tiny uproars of shrieks and songs, jumping over the afternoon sleepers and leaping the crazy gaps between the buildings. I passed by the stalls piled with colourful produce and walked down the Alley of Fruit and then into the shadowy passages under the patterned awnings where the expensive shops sell rare clever monkeys, giraffe skins, ostrich eggs and tusks engraved with prayers. The whole world brings its tributes and its wonders to us: the remarkable fruits of its endless labours are presented at our doors. Or, at least, the doors of those who do not have to wait so many months for their gift of pay (note to self: reapply to treasurer for unpaid salary gifts).

I prefer this great chaos of the living streets to the hushed and ordered temples, courts and sanctuaries of the gods and the hierarchies of the Priests. I prefer noise and mess and dirt, even the workers' suburbs in the east, and the smelly pig yards, and the dogs on chains in the miserable dark hovels these people must call home. Those are the places we enter with the caution of experience, knowing we are hated and in danger. The law of the Medjay, whose authority to maintain order stretches through all the Provinces of the Two Lands, has no power there, although few of us would admit it. When we approach, kites, their stretched canvases painted with the eyes of angry gods, rise, dart and swoop in the sky, to warn of our approach. But then I think our law has no sway in the palaces and temples either. They too have their definitive powers. I will no doubt find this where I am bound.

I arrived, finally, at the docks, and found among the thousands of vessels the boat which was to carry me on the first stage of this journey.

I was the last to board, and as soon as I was installed the sailors pushed off, the oars came out, and we began to merge into the life of the Great River, which now spread out wide with all its traffic of people and goods, as far as the eye can travel to the horizon where the Black Land meets the Red and holds it back for all time.

Lightland, our world of light. The triumph of time. Countless boats, sails bowed to the invisible wind: the fishing men, the larger transports of stones and cattle, the ferries that travel between the banks of the river, between the temples to the east and the tombs to the west, between the rising and the setting of the sun, with their mortal passengers. Flocks of ibis wading in the shallows. Votive blue lotus flowers bobbing in the waters beside the remains of everyday life: bits of food, clothing, rubbish, dead fish and dogs, and dog fish, and cat fish. The endless quiet creaking of the shadoufs. The ceaseless gifts of the Great River. Thebes survives for and by it. Or rather, the river grants the waters of life to the city. Where would we be without water? We would be nothing but the desert that fears the river.

They say the gods possess the river, and that the river is a god, but I think its owners are the Priests in the offices, and the rich with their villas and terraces where the cool water laps at their soft and lazy feet. And he who owns the water, owns the city – indeed owns life itself. But no-one in truth owns the river. It is greater, more enduring and more powerful than any of us, almost more than any god. It can tear us apart with its force or starve us by withholding its yearly inundation. It is full of death. It carries corpses of beasts and men and children whose dwelling time in its depths has shocked them green. Sometimes I believe I sense their hopeless and unfinished spirits as they touch upon the water, sending out silent concentric rings as signs to tell us they were here and are gone without rest. And yet it sustains our rich black earth from which spring our green crops, our barley and emmer wheat.

As the city of my birth and life dwindled in our wake, I left the world I know, where we live out our brief stories between the Black and the Red, between the land of the living and the rising sun and the land of long shadows and death, between the little moments and luxuries of our life and the western desert, that wilderness where we send our criminals to die only for them to return as demons to haunt us as we sleep. Once, they say, before time began the whole of the land was green, with herds of water buffalo, gazelles and elephants. And suddenly I remembered years ago, when my father and I rode into the desert. A great storm had changed again the landscape of the dunes. We found revealed the skeleton of a crocodile, so far from any kind of water. What else lies hidden there? Great cities, strange statues, lost peoples, their ships built to sail the Otherworld's eternal sea of sand.

Alas, I am carried away again. I must be sober as the great serpent of water carries me away from all I know, and all I love, on its blackness, its perpetual glittering scales, with its sightless memory of a long journey from high in the unknown stones of Nubia, down through the great cataracts, and into the fields, into the fruit and the vegetables, into the wine, into the sea; and somewhere into snow.

3

I admire the neatness of a boat. The simplicity of necessity. Blankets folded in the morning and stowed. Objects made small and precise for their purpose. Everything in its place. The captain has blue eyes, a handful of crooked white teeth, a confident belly and the hands-on look of an intelligence at home on the water; an intelligence that can look through people of the land and discern their motives and thoughts as if they were as easy to read as small fish in the shallows. Then there is the boat itself, a wonderful construction, an equation between wind and water that results in sails filling to perfect curves, drawing out the ropes to an immaculate geometrical tension that brings about the miraculous power to draw the vessel and its temporary passengers through the water. Look: the perfect cut of the prow through the skin of the water that heals as we pass. The wake – blind white fingers feeling their way along the edge of some unknown material, then relenting, with little shrugs and gestures of farewell, and sinking back into the blackness whence they so briefly appeared.

24

Here I am, a senior detective of the Medjay, spending my time pondering the inscrutable puzzles of the passing water as we are carried with the current of the river past Coptos, Dendera and the Temple of Hathor, and the Temple of Osiris at Abydos. My mind like a water fly, thinking of nothing, when I should be preparing myself for the urgent mystery at hand.

The captain invited the passengers to dine together this evening, around the brazier, for it is cold on the water once the sun has descended. I hate dinner parties, and I annoy Tanefert by making sure work prevents me from attending the invitations we receive. In part, this is because I cannot talk, at the table or even anywhere else, about my work: who wants to hear about murder when they are enjoying their meat? And in part because I just cannot discuss the perils and evils of the world from the point of view of luxury, around a table set with good things, as if it were all just matter for debate.

We greeted each other politely as we took our places, and then fell into an uneasy silence. It is true that the Great Changes have brought about more caution, and sometimes almost suspicion, into daily life. Once we spoke freely; now people think twice before they express an opinion. Once one provoked laughter and amusement for expressing a heretical point of view; now such things are met with silence and discomfort.

I was seated next to a portly gentleman whose belly was the most notable part of his anatomy; it was like a great globe with a white moony head gazing down in constant surprise at itself. The food, which was simple and plentiful, drew from him gestures of approval and delight: his polished little hands wafted in the air to describe his pleasure. He leaned over to me, and broke the silence: 'And what, sir, is your purpose in our new City of the Horizon of the Aten?'

I could tell he was pleased with himself for calling the new capital by its rather pompous proper name. I like to engage in the amateur drama of an assumed identity in these circumstances.

'I am an official in the Office of Accounts,' I replied.

'So we should make friends with you, as otherwise we shall never be paid!' He looked around the table for approval of his little quip.

'Indeed, our Lord's finances are a great mystery, but the greatest is that they are never-ending, and ever bountiful.'

He appraised me and the conformity of my reply with a cool eye. Before he could get further into this, I quickly asked, 'And what are your own affairs in Akhetaten?'

'I am director of the court orchestra and dancers. It is a position enjoying considerable status, and I believe there was great competition for it. I shall be directing the opening drama for the city's inauguration. Did you know, all the members of the court orchestra are women?'

'Do you mean, sir, that women are less capable than men in the expertise of dance and music?'

A handsome, intelligent woman had spoken from the opposite side of the table. Her husband, a smaller and somehow diminished middle-aged man with the appearance of a born bureaucrat, glanced at her as if to say: it is not your place to speak of this. But she gazed calmly on the Great White Moon.

He sniffed and said, 'Dancing will always be the woman's art. But music makes great technical and spiritual demands. I am not speaking of mere decoration but of the deep soul.' He picked out the morsel of a prawn from its pink sheath and popped it between his fastidious and ambitious lips.

'I see. And is our Queen Nefertiti decoration? Or is she of deep soul?' She smiled at me, an invitation to share her amusement.

'We know too little of her,' he said.

'Oh no, sir,' she responded. 'We know she is beautiful. We know she is clever. And we know she is the most powerful woman alive today. She drives her own chariot, and she wears her hair as she wishes, not as tradition would dictate. She smites her enemies as a King. And no-one tells her what to do. She is, in fact, the epitome of the modern woman.'

A small silence ensued around the table. Finally, the Moon spoke: 'Indeed, and that may very well be why we find ourselves in a world which is changing faster than perhaps everyone would like.'

The conversation was becoming more charged; the stakes of the game increased. She answered him with a counter-play.

'Do you not, then, approve of the new religion?'

This was a subject not to be carelessly discussed among strangers. Moon Man squirmed with discomfort and uncertainty, caught between speaking his mind and fearing for his future. 'I approve it with all my heart. Of course I do. I am merely a music-maker. It is not my business to ask questions, merely to do what is asked of me and make it sound as tuneful as possible. I only wonder, privately, and I am not alone in this, whether our Lord and his Lady, she-who-will-not-be-told-what-to-do, have not bitten off more than they can chew.' And with that, he placed a fried sprat between his lips and teased off the flesh from the bones as if he were playing a tune on a small reed pipe.

The handsome woman's eyes were alive with amusement at the absurdity of his turn of phrase, which she seemed to want to share with me.

'We live in a time of great turbulence,' said her husband. 'Can we know whether we are blessed or cursed? Will the people miss their old gods, and the Priests their easy riches? Or are we moving forward, together, as a society, towards a higher and greater truth, however challenging?'

Moon Man spoke again: 'Higher truths need proper financing. Enlightenment is expensive. So I am pleased to hear you' – here he pointed a greasy finger at me – 'can confirm the finances of our Lord are drawn from so perpetual a spring of plenty. I hear the harvest is poor again this year. And I hear salaries are in arrears, sometimes by several years. Indeed, it is the guarantee of regular gifts from Akhenaten that has persuaded me to uproot my life and cast my fortune on the success of the new capital.'

I did not respond. Instead, the handsome woman gracefully

changed the subject. She turned to the young man to her left, who had remained silent throughout these exchanges. He was an apprentice architect.

'So, what can you tell us about the construction of the city?' she asked. 'And more importantly whether the bigger houses have gardens, for little else would have persuaded me to sacrifice my own home and friends for the desert.'

'I believe the villas are luxurious. And the supply of water to the gardens is prodigious. So although the city is surrounded by the desert, and would seem an arid and unpropitious place to build a new world, yet it is now green and fertile. But alas, I am working only in a minor capacity.' He paused, embarrassed.

'And what is that?' I asked.

'I am designing the toilet area near the Great Aten Temple.' Everyone laughed at that. Encouraged, he added, 'Even Priests must take their libatory shits in sacred surroundings!'

'Don't talk to me about the Priests,' Moon Man said. 'Their calling is riches. And that's all there is to it. The least Akhenaten will have achieved is the destruction of their great temples to the gods of profit!'

We all fell into silence. It is dangerous to criticize the Priests, or let us say the Old Families who have commanded so much inherited power for so many generations and are now in turmoil, like an enraged monster, at their losses of status, land and income. Likewise the Medjay: many believe that elements within the force are compelling the less orthodox members of society to accept and conform to the new religion by the use of the old techniques – intimidation, violence and suffering. I have heard stories of people disappearing, of unidentifiable bodies washing up in the river, their hands chopped off, their eyes plucked out. But it is hearsay. We are a force for order over chaos, for the harmony of *maat* and the rightness of things. It is how things must be.

We retired, with bids and nods of goodnight, to our hammocks and blankets. I found some solitude in my couch in the stern of the boat, among the coils of rope, beneath the great guiding oars now driven

28

into the mud of the riverbed. The captain lay in the prow in a hammock, with a candle. Soon all the passengers were snoring beneath tents of cloth and insect nets.

And so I sit here now with this journal and think about what I may encounter in the city of Akhetaten. Essentially, I have no idea. It is a blank. Akhenaten's so-called great idea, to initiate a new religion and to forbid the old, strikes me as insane. It is a revolution against sense. This is not an original thought: I doubt if there are more than a handful of people – the close circle of the King, and those like the builders and architects who have jobs for life – who think he has not lost his mind. A new religion, based upon himself and Nefertiti as the incarnations and only intermediaries of the Aten, the sun disc? Akhenaten has banished the minor gods the people have worshipped all their lives, as well as the major deities of the Otherworld, the World and the Sky. These days I only believe what I can see with my own eyes, or glean from the clues available to me here in this world, so he may well be right to disclaim the power of the invisible. And indeed he may be right to play the Priests at their own game, which they have been winning, at enormous personal gain, for generations. But then to take all power from them unto himself at one stroke, to drive them from their ancient temples at Karnak, and (worst of all) to leave them at large in the country wandering without employment or purpose other than inventing revenge? How is this possible? How can it end but in disaster? We hear he is hardly a god to look at. They say he is as unusual in body as he is curious in mind. His limbs long and spindly as a grasshopper, his belly like a water butt. But this is from those who have not seen the man himself. The only thing he has done right is come from a powerful mother and father, and marry well. Nefertiti. The Perfect One. They say her ancestry is mysterious, but that she is greatly admired.

Perhaps I will see all this for myself. What is clear is that these are changing times, and we must change with them or perish – at least until the powers-that-be bring about a reversal of all this, and what has come to pass crumbles back into the dust of its making. For surely

Akhenaten cannot survive long. The Priests will not allow their riches and their earthly powers to be taken away from them.

But what all this has to do with the mystery to which I am called, I cannot tell.

4

I lay beneath the moon and observed the many serene and imperishable stars of the Otherworld. But the night always stirs with hidden struggles. From the bank came the sounds of birds and beasts busy with their nocturnal lives. I remembered how, when we first met, at that party, Tanefert and I stepped out from the lights and noise and walked along the water's edge, our hands just beginning to risk a touch here and there, each apparently casual brushing of skin on skin sending shivers through my whole body. It was as if we could finish each other's thoughts, without speaking. We sat on a bench and watched the moon. I said it was a mad old woman left alone in the sky, but Tanefert said, 'No, she is a great lady in mourning for her lost love. Look how she calls to him.' We talked more. She told me the truth about everything in her heart, the good and the bad, with the risks attending her confession, and I knew then, from her honesty, that she would change my life with love. Of course, it hasn't all been easy. The gods know how I can be: moody, selfish, sad.

A pang of loss flashed through me. I stood up and stared out across the dark waters. I felt alarmed, in the wrong place. I wanted to turn the boat around and return to her at once. Then suddenly, whirring out of the darkness faster than a diving hawk, an arrow. I saw it after I felt the cold needle of its passage through the air by my left eye. I felt – or did I imagine it? – hot feathers brushing past my face, bright with some furious point of light. And then I saw flames racing up and out from the point where the arrow had embedded itself in the wood of the mast, below the Eye of Horus, nailed there for safe passage. The mind is slower than time, slower than fire and air. Then a noise, like enthusiastic applause, brought me out of this trance. I shouted like a fool. The fire was feasting on the sail, its many greedy mouths moving out from the mast, by now a tree of flame. And the captain arrived, pulling on ropes, while the sailors hurried buckets of water out of the river, which they cast into the roaring throat of the blaze. And this interested, then gradually placated, and finally subdued the god.

I slowly came back to myself. All the passengers were gathered now on the deck, huddled in their night attire, holding each other, or weeping, or staring at the now-threatening darkness that surrounded this frail and damaged vessel. I could hear the drip-drip-drip of the water that saved us from extinction, as each drop fell from the charred wood. Everyone knew the arrow was aimed at me. They also knew their own brush with mortality was because of my presence on the boat. And they knew I was not who I said I was.

The Moon Man spoke: 'You, sir, have not been honest with us. An official in the Treasury does not earn this kind of attention.'

I shrugged. The handsome woman glanced at me with more interest, a question in her eye. And the captain, his face struck with humiliation and anger, looked at the wizened and blackened remains of the arrow. 'You owe me a ship,' he said.

He was about to pull it out when I shouted at him to stop. This was evidence. I pushed him to one side and examined it. I could not draw the point from the wood. It had been made so delicate by fire that it could have collapsed to ash at any moment. But although it was damaged, I could see immediately two things that interested me. One: the tip, although blackened, was metal, probably silver. Not flint. Not, then, a casual act of violence, but one in which there had been considerable investment of skill, quality and expense. And two: still visible in the wood, two hieroglyphs. Cobra. The Snake, Great of Magic, Poised on the Crown of Pharaoh, Protector of Ra in his passage through the Underworld of the Night. And Seth with his forked tail, god of chaos and confusion, of the Red Land and war. This was the work of an expert, and I was lucky, strangely, to be alive. Equally strangely, I did not feel lucky. I felt warned. Either I had survived by the merest chance, or I was meant to survive. Either the unknown assassin had missed by the smallest degree – the lucky drift of the night breeze, the sudden cry of a bird distracting the arrow from its true course – or he had hit the mark exactly.

And then he had signed his work.

5

The rest of the journey passed in an uncomfortable silence. I was under the suspicion of all the passengers and crew, and they kept well away from me. The captain had had the charred damage patched but our pace was slowed, and it made us seem ugly and noticeable, now, among the busy ordinary traffic on the river. Even the children of the river villages, always ready to laugh and wave and call, watched us pass in silence. I offered the captain compensation through the Medjay office. But we both know the chances of his receiving anything are remote. If we are not paid our salaries, how are such unusual claims to be honoured? But I gave him my word, and it was all I had to give. He was not impressed. Somehow I must make this good. And I must consider the obvious fact: someone powerful knows I am coming, and does not want me in Akhetaten, this city that I had not seen – until now.

As we rounded a bend in the river, suddenly, after nothing but fields and hamlets and beyond them always the endless shape-shifting and broken stones of the Red Land, there appeared a vision: a bright white city laid out in a great crescent along the eastern curve of the river, and defended at its back by a range of red and grey cliffs that encircled and delineated the eastern edges of the territory, marked in the centre by a deep and narrow valley, like a large notch in a length of wood. The cliffs met the river at their north-westernmost tip. Thus the city was held – cupped, almost – in the vast palm of the land. It appeared nothing like the other cities of our world, not as a chaotic improvisation of ancient and temporary buildings. Rather, it seemed a vast ordered garden from which rose towers, temples, offices and villas, spreading from the shores of the river towards the edges of the desert behind. Great flocks of birds wheeled in the sky, and the sound of their singing and their cries reached me even from some distance.

All the passengers stood in awe together at the prow of the boat gazing at this impossible paradise in the desert, the place that held all our futures in its grasp. The young architect was able to point out the various sections of the city as well as the northern palace and its related buildings, all set, he said, within a novel system, a regulated grid of thoroughfares and streets so that all the buildings conformed to its consistent pattern. Why there should be a separation of sites he did not know. The workmen's village was behind the main city, as one would expect. Apparently it is a model of its kind. Conceived, I am sure, not out of enlightenment but the simple fact that healthy and well-fed artisans and workers constitute a properly economical means of achieving the fastest and most competent construction. And run, as the world runs, on lines to suit the overseers and the heads of construction gangs.

At the landing stage a small Medjay retinue waited at attention to meet me. As I descended the gangplank, one stepped forward to offer the formal greeting. He introduced himself as the assistant to Mahu, and said he would be honoured to accompany me to my first meeting with him. Two guards before me, and two behind, we marched from the dock, leaving behind my astonished fellow passengers. The young architect bowed, as if caught out by the possibility that his indiscretions were naive and careless. I acknowledged him, in an attempt to reassure him that we both know this is a world in which Priests shit. The Moon gentleman merely raised a supercilious eyebrow, as if to say: you played us like fools, and now you assume your true identity. Good luck to you. The bureaucrat looked annoyed. And his handsome wife sent me a quick, bright glance, as if to say: perhaps I will see you in a crowded room some day, at an official function. And we will know each other . . . I bowed respectfully to her.

I was surprised at the absence on the streets of crowds, of bustle, of people with the usual variety of casual business. It seemed to be a place of single purpose. Its industry was the focus of its activities, in the service and celebration of Akhenaten and the royal family. All of which gave to the city a conscious and conspicuous strangeness, as if the confusion and colour of street life in Thebes had been reduced, calculated away almost; a place in which everyone was aware of the status and power of everyone else. It seemed less a city, more like a vast temple and palace complex with additions for the necessities of daily life. A beautiful place of enormous and overwhelming artifice.

But as we walked further into the city it began to seem less organized and complete than it had at first appeared. The newness of it all meant the courtyards' pylons and sacred buildings dazzled because they were whitewashed but in many places undecorated. The hieroglyphs on the walls were unfinished. Whole sections of the city centre were still under construction. Ugly scaffolding hid what will surely be offices and temple complexes. Thousands of workmen laboured at every level of the constructions. Wide pathways and processionals petered out into desert tracks, or lost themselves in stones and dust. In the suburbs to the north and the south I was puzzled to note fine villas set next to poor shacks. The first tombs and chapels raised on an empty, stony arena at the edge of the cultivation, near the workmen's village, suggested the city's necropolis. At the heart of it all lay the central city, with the temple complexes to Aten and the bureaucracies. The extensive nature of these headquarters – indeed they seem as massive and as dominating as the temples themselves – is a signal of the true

36

nature of the city, and I have heard they contain the largest secret papyrus archive assembled anywhere. I am keen to inspect this palace of secrets, and carry with me a letter of introduction. The purpose of collecting so much information can only be power. Perhaps, for all its impressive appearance, this is a city predicated on making its people afraid.

The other overwhelming impression – and one is glad of this for the heat, even for me, is shocking – was of water, everywhere. Normally one steps from the coolness of the river into chaos and dust. Not so here. The very stones of the walkways and the walls seemed fresh and clean, shining almost as if they too were fed on water. Firstly one became aware of the sound of it, constantly running in secret, under your feet, just out of sight. Then of the greenery and freshness of the gardens, and of the new trees planted along the avenues: I saw figs, date palms, persea, carobs and pomegranates. It may be that in this impossible capital it is always the season of fruit.

I boldly plucked a fig as I passed a garden wall; the branch was hanging down before me. Looking as I did so over the wall and into the garden I saw a tiled pool, and a woman who looked up in surprise and annoyance as the branch from which I had stolen my fig brushed back into place. The water was as clear as glass, the pool tiled in complex patterns of blue and gold. Such is the work of wealth. I would have to labour ten years to build such a pleasure palace. She was nearly naked as well, her skin the colour of the gold running through the tiles and the water. Here it seems women have leisure to sit in the shade while their husbands, presumably officers or diplomats, work at the business of creating the new world.

As we moved on, in strange contrast, we passed herds of labourers struggling among the rickety supports that were placed, ramshackle, along the high walls of the buildings. It is a wonder to me that such in-adequate scaffolding does not collapse on a daily basis. Great stacks of dry mud-bricks stood everywhere like miniature desert cities for populations of tiny citizens. And I noticed, hidden in some of the shadowy alleys, broken, collapsed figures, looking as though they had not stirred for some time, and might not do so again.

I was marched directly to the offices of the Medjay. New quarters. Marble and limestone cladding on the walls, fresh decorations, efficient, elegantly stylish furniture, crates of documents and who knows what unnecessary junk half-unpacked or still unopened. Is this how our power is to be accommodated now? Such a contrast with our own dark, dated and shabby offices in Thebes, and in all the other stations in the different nomes I have visited. We passed down corridor after corridor, past crowds of men going about their business, most casting brief curious glances at me, until finally we arrived at large and ornately gilded wooden doors inscribed with the insignia of power and surmounted by that new emblem of divine power the Aten sun disc, its many little hands reaching down to the adoring world.

A secretary sat to one side at a desk. Barely acknowledging me, this young officer then entered the Great Office, while I was left to stand. The guards shuffled a little, my guide looked embarrassed, and the seconds ticked by. We all listened to a bird singing in the courtyard. I cleared my throat, which had no discernible effect on anyone. The guards continued to stare at the doors. I began to feel more like a prisoner than an honoured fellow officer. Finally, the door scraped open again – the new wood has expanded in the frame; how absurd this affected display of power, and a door that sticks! – and the secretary bid me enter. I gave him a nod of the head, meant to be ironic, and walked forward into the next stage of the mystery. The doors closed behind me.

6

I found myself in a large, open, well-lit room. A great desk, its polished surface of some gorgeous hardwood unfamiliar to me, dominated. On it were a few objects of fine workmanship: a vase of blue lotus flowers, a statuette of Akhenaten, an alabaster decanter delicately formed in the shape of a bird rising from water, a collection of goblets, and two wooden trays. There was a strange panting sound coming from beneath the desk where a large man sat considering a document he had taken from the first tray. He ignored my presence. Mahu.

He was stocky, powerfully muscled, middle-aged. His seniority and power were evident in the manner and proportions of his body and the distinctively brutal, almost hewn shape of his head, with its strong grey hair cut close to the scalp; as well as in the elegant clothing of that body, which was rich and luxurious in every way. He wore an extraordinary collar. I had time to observe it. Six rows of rings carried a multitude of smaller gold rings strung on cords, held together by a heavy clasp decorated with a winged scarab and sun discs, and inlaid with lapis lazuli. He also wore a sleeved tunic of finest white linen and sandals.

But more interesting than all this theatrical regalia were his eyes. When he finally deigned to look up I saw that they were unusual, not in their topaz colouring, but in the way they shimmered with hunger. As cruel and apparently casual as a lion or a god. I felt he could gaze through to my very bones, to the weaknesses and vulnerabilities and destinies hidden within them. I wondered whether he ate breakfast; whether he had children, a wife, friends; whether his was a life in which such power can be harnessed to tenderness and care; or whether all humanity, all its dreams and ambitions and vanities of the heart, was so clear to him that he had no more feeling for it than a god has for the foolish mortals whom time wipes out in a moment, like a cloth across a speckled and misty mirror.

I returned his stare. He rose from the desk and moved towards me, accompanied by a slathering black dog – the source of the odd panting.

'I see you are interested in my collar,' he said. 'A gift from Akhenaten. It is important to dress as one believes oneself to be, don't you think?'

'Your attire is magnificent,' I acknowledged, hoping my slight irony would hit home. But his fastidious appraisal of my own rather travel-worn clothing seemed to indicate that any irony on my part would be cancelled out by the evident inadequacy, and therefore lack of self-belief, of my own appearance.

We waited a moment, considering what could be said next. I used to talk and talk; now I wait in silence for them to make the first move. But he seemed entirely undaunted by my poor ploy. As if reading my thoughts, he gestured to the couch. I had no choice but to sit while he remained standing. I still have a lot to learn about these games of power.

He stared down at me, and rubbed his chin. The silence was discomforting.

'So, you are chosen to investigate the mystery.'

'I have that honour.'

'What do you suppose you have done to deserve it?'

'I suppose nothing. Whatever gifts I have are in the service of our Lord.' I winced as I listened to these feeble platitudes.

'And your family . . . ?'

'My father was a scribe in the Office of Construction.'

My lack of elite status hung in the air between us.

'I am prepared to learn the nature of the mystery,' I added.

'Akhenaten himself wishes to apprise you of its known elements. He has granted me the task to introduce you to our new world here, to assist you as may seem appropriate, and above all to keep an eye on you.'

He paused meaningfully. I waited.

'Also we have assigned two of our best officers, one senior, one more junior but promising, to guide you as required, at all hours of the day and night. To help you to find your way around the place.'

Watchdogs running at my heels. A nuisance, and deliberately so.

'I'm sorry to say I do not support the choice of you,' he continued. 'You may as well know this now. Why bring in an outside man? A man who knows nothing of how things work here? A man whose experience of the real world consists of petty thieves and whores, whose *expertise* extends to examining the petty and minor clues scattered about in the muck and dirt of the pathetic scenes of the murders of the low-class scum and the criminal? A man who calls this the new science of investigation. However, the matter was not in my hands. This is a new world. It is not Thebes, and it will take you time you do not have to learn its ways. There are many forces at work; I am concerned that, mishandled or misunderstood, they could crush a man like stale bread.'

And those topaz eyes gazed right through me for a long moment.

'But please remember: I am here to help. Let me offer my hand in professional respect, Medjay to Medjay. I am the man with the keys to this city. I know it stone by stone. I know where the stones are from, and who placed them in their positions, and why.'

41

I maintained a level gaze throughout this soliloquy. And since it seemed we were making speeches to each other, after a respectful pause I stood up and began my reply.

'I agree with your assessment of the situation. And I gratefully accept your offer of professional support. But since Akhenaten himself has chosen me, I hope I can earn the unqualified support of all his servants. I believe he would wish it to be so. And if I fail, there will be no question of my fate.'

He inclined his head very slightly, and held my gaze for a little too long. 'We understand each other perfectly.' He then turned back to his desk, briefly scanned the papyrus document, looked up at me with an enigmatic expression somewhere between a smile and a warning, and almost negligently let the document drift back down into the empty tray on his desk. 'Your interview is destined for sunset,' he said, before sitting down and turning his attention to the window.

I walked out of the room with the feeling he was watching me through the back of that cruel skull, and closed the door behind me. I had to give it a little shove to close it fully, and the squeak and bang alerted the guards, the nasty little secretary and the assistant. The latter came forward and said, 'I will show you your accommodation. And then bring you to your appointment.' So he already knew all about it. I felt like an animal being prepared for the offering table.

Sunset, indeed. The hour of death.

7

I can do nothing but wait, and waiting is torture to me. I would rather eat sand. I have been given an office, with a couch and a desk, in a construction behind the main temples and the Medjay barracks. It looks on to an empty pool, with a fountain that does not work. It is surrounded by a terrace, and beyond that there is a view of a rock-strewn, red-earth plot. Someone has hurriedly tried to make the terrace look less derelict by placing some uncertain plants and little acacia bushes in pots. And a bench, as if I might have the leisure to sit in the shade and think of pleasure and poetry. But otherwise the building seems uninhabited. Above the head of the couch is a niche containing an icon of Akhenaten himself, the Great King into whose presence I am shortly to be ushered. Well, I will then be able to gauge the differences between the strange fellow in this niche, with his long neck, sagging belly and large sloping eyes, somewhere between a mule and a mother-in-law, and the reality of the divine incarnation.

I drank water from the jug. It was unusually sweet and clear. Then

I tested the couch for softness and was surprised by how comfortable it seemed, especially after the spine-bending experience of the ship's hammock. Too comfortable as it turned out. I awoke, suddenly, to banging. It was late, and someone was knocking on the door. I remembered nothing. My journal lay on the floor, its sheets somewhat creased, the flow of words stopped in mid-thought. The image of Akhenaten still stared down at me, as if I was already failing on the job. But I felt strangely rested. Had I been so tired to sleep like that? I checked the room. Nothing seemed changed. I examined the journal: no sheets torn out, no markings. Yet – something felt different. As if there were a trace of some other presence in the memory of the air. Had there been some potion in the water? I remembered then its unusual sweetness.

The knocking was repeated. I called out 'Enter!' in an authoritative way that I hoped disguised my afternoon sleepiness. The officer of the guard who had conducted me to the interview, and then to this office, appeared at the threshold. A man perhaps five years younger than me, with careful eyes and a well-learned expression of caution accommodated within a pleasant, alert and undistinguished face. He was followed by a younger man, more handsome, neat and smooth, with the eyes of a charmer and that deliberately slow leisure of movement common to our profession.

'What is your name?' I addressed the more senior of the pair.

'Khety, sir.'

'A wise name for a wise man?'

'My parents hoped so, sir.'

'We gain power from our names, don't you believe?'

'It is generally believed to be so, yes, sir.'

He held himself carefully. Unconfidently confident.

'How long have you been here, Khety?'

'Since the beginning, sir. With Mahu himself.'

'You mean since the city was built?'

'All my life. My father worked for him before me.'

This was common practice, of course. The generations of a low- or even middle-ranking family would have a great deal to gain by such an alliance, as well as a great deal to lose if they were in any way to fall from favour. But it told me quite candidly, and as I might easily have guessed, that I must deal carefully with this officer. Bring him in to my researches while knowing that every detail and every step will be reported to Mahu. All perfectly normal.

'And you?'

'Tjenry, sir.'

His tone lacked a touch of respect, but I liked his style, his hint of bravura.

'I look forward to the benefit of your experience and knowledge during the investigation of the mystery.'

'It's an honour, sir.' He allowed a touch of a smile to curve his lips.

'Good. I need you to assist me, to show me the ways and the secrets of this great city.'

'Yes, sir.'

'You have come to conduct me to my interview?'

'It is time.'

'Then let us go.'

And indeed, the sun was setting, the shadows lengthening, trees and buildings now illuminated sideways; not the blinding in-candescence of afternoon, but an evening world of gold, quicksilver and blue shades, accompanied by conferences of birds. We walked together up the wide thoroughfare and on to the neatly swept Royal Road as it ascended gradually towards the central precinct parallel to the river and the setting sun. Individuals were walking in the same direction accompanied by their obedient shadows, with an air of singular purpose, as if they must never be seen to be doing anything less than work vital to the survival of the state.

'Khety, what is the principle of the arrangement of this part of the city?'

'It is a grid, sir. The streets are all straight lines, and they intersect each other so that the buildings in their sections are all of the same size. It is perfect.'

'Perfect, but not finished.'

He ignored my comment, but Tjenry added, 'There's not much time left now until the Festival. They've brought in extra labour. Even so, it's going to be tough to meet the deadlines.'

Khety continued with his guided tour: 'To the right of us is the Records Office, and beyond that the House of Life.'

'The Records Office? I'll want to visit that.'

'It is an extensive library of information about everything and everyone.'

'It's the only one in the whole of the Two Lands,' chipped in Tjenry brightly, as if he thought it was a great idea.

'So we are all in there, reduced to information?'

'I believe so,' said Khety.

'It is amazing how a few marks on papyrus can be said to represent all our histories and secrets, and be stored, and read, and remembered.'

Khety nodded as if he was not sure what I was talking about.

'And what is that construction beyond?'

'The Small Aten Temple.'

'And that in the distance?' I could see ahead, opposite the sparkle and sails of the Great River, a low and immensely long building.

'The Great Aten Temple, which is kept for exceptional festivities.'

'Where am I to meet the King?'

'My instructions are to bring you to the Great Palace but to show you the Small Aten Temple first.'

'Houses, palaces, temples; great this, small that. It is confusing, isn't it? What's wrong with how things used to be?'

Khety nodded again, uncertain how to respond. Tjenry grinned. I grinned back.

Up ahead I could see the river of people and their shadows heading towards the great pylons of the temple, six of them arranged in pairs through the heart of the building, dazzlingly white. Streamers of multicoloured cloth drifted elegantly in the river breeze from their high poles as if they had all the time in the world. Unfinished hieroglyphs covered the stone façades of the pylons, illuminated gold by the setting sun. I struggled to read some of them, but I have never been good at this. Then we passed between the central pylons, jostled stiffly by the human stream that narrowed through the guard gate under another carving of the Aten, then bunched, hustled and distributed itself out into an open courtyard with colonnades on each side. The people dispersed expertly to their offices and appointments. Sunset is an important time of prayer, in these days more so than ever before.

But this was a temple unlike any other I had seen. The great dark stone temples at Karnak are labyrinths lit by a few spots of intense white light, leading to ever more obscure chambers, all ensuring the god is kept perpetually hidden deep in the shadowy heart of his House, away from the ordinary light of the world and its teeming temporal worshippers. This was deliberately designed to be exactly the opposite, wide open to the air and the sun. Vast walls were decorated with thousands of images in panels and sections, almost all of them, as far as I could see, depicting Akhenaten, Nefertiti and their children worshipping the Aten. And the whole space was filled with hundreds of altars, arranged in rows, and all around the walls. At the back were chapels, again filled with altars. In the centre a main raised altar, surrounded by lotus-shaped incense burners, was piled high with food and flowers from both Upper and Lower Egypt. How clever to unite the offerings of the Two Lands in the one altar, and how ostentatious in our time of trouble. And everywhere one looked were statues, in all sizes, of Akhenaten and Nefertiti, looking down at their subjects not with the distant stare of official power, but with lively human faces, perfectly carved in the limestone, their hands intertwined or raised, cupped, to receive the divine gifts of the sun that on this evening, as every evening, were streaming down to them from a real sky. And people stood still, eyes wide open, their hands holding up offerings to the light: flowers, food, even occasionally babies.

I looked down at my own hands and saw that they were gilded by the warm evening light.

'"Since he casts his rays on me, bestowing life and dominion for

47

ever and eternity, I shall make Akhetaten for the Aten, my father, in this place,"' Khety recited, and he smiled. 'The god is everywhere with us.'

'Except at night.'

'The god sails the darkness of the Otherworld, sir. But he always returns, reborn to a new day.'

'Speaking of which, should we not now continue to the appointment?' said Tjenry, amusingly bored by the spectacle of the worship.

They led, and I followed, through the crowds.

Whether or not this was the deliberate intention, I was disorientated by the experience of the new temple and its worshippers. Yes, one hears about the new religion, and how we must now worship the sun disc, with our arms raised. Yes, one discusses its pros and cons. Yes, one has to consider one's position and one's future. For some it is a matter of life and death while for most of us it is a question of doing what is required and getting on with our lives. But now I do not know what to think. Standing in the sun has never been a wise thing to do.

We turned back out of the temple, left onto the Royal Road, and soon found ourselves outside the Great Palace. Connecting that complex to the King's House was a great covered bridge, with square archways to allow traffic to pass beneath. And in the centre, above the crowds, a large balcony.

'The Window of Appearances.'

'Ah.'

'From where our Lord bestows gifts.'

'Have you received gifts, Khety?'

'This collar, sir. It is of fine workmanship. And the materials are excellent.'

He fingered the gold thread and azure beads. It wasn't nearly as fine as the one worn by Mahu, but nevertheless a piece of beauty and worth.

'You must have done great works to deserve such a gift.'

'He's very reliable, sir,' said Tjenry, who wore no such collar.

'I am faithful,' said Khety.

They glanced at each other.

'And here we are – the Great Palace,' said Tjenry expansively, as if he owned the place.

8

We passed through the guard gate and into a vast courtyard that spread out in the direction of the river. The sight of its flowing evening colours, and the feminine orchestra of the water birds, revived my spirits. And above me, looking out to the river, towered yet more statues of Akhenaten and Nefertiti. A man and a woman carved as gods.

We turned right into an enclosed courtyard, and then right again into an antechamber. Beneath my feet I noticed pavements of painted scenes: beautiful waterways with fish and flowers, and stones and butterflies. We were approaching the heart of the palace, for more and more officials, men of status in fine white linens, passed us. They quickly assessed me, curiously, dispassionately and without warmth, as a stranger in the city. Clearly this was a place where everyone knew everyone but none were friends.

Khety spoke to an officer of the court. Tjenry gave me a quick and inappropriate gesture of encouragement, and then I was ushered alone into a private courtyard as into the cage of a lion. It was exquisitely beautiful. Shuttered panels carved with filigree patterns ran around the edges until they opened on the side of the river. A fountain played in a translucent bowl balanced over a long pool. Flowers and river ferns flourished, nodding gently. The cool shade served only to sharpen the outline of a figure who stood, framed by the shutters, on a wide balcony giving on to the great panorama of the river and the greater one of the sunset, apparently gazing deeply into the dazzling consort of lights, the water's dance, that surrounded him. Then he turned to face me.

At first I could not make him out. 'Life, Prosperity, Health,' I said. 'I offer myself to my Lord and to Ra.' I kept my eyes lowered.

Finally he spoke: 'We have need of your offering.' His voice was clear and light. 'Look up.'

He seemed to gaze upon me for a little while. Then he stepped carefully down and out of the last red light of the setting sun.

Now I could look at him properly. He was both like and unlike his images. His face was still quite young; long, slender and almost beautiful, with precise lips and intelligent eyes that conveyed absolute power: it was both hard to look into them and impossible to look away. It was a fluid, alive face, but also one I could imagine hardening in an instant into ruthlessness. His body was disguised under his clothes, and a leopard skin was cast over one shoulder, but I had the impression of a slender, refined physique. Certainly his hands were fine. A beautifully wrought crutch was tucked under his right arm. He seemed at once brittle, as if with one light tap he would turn to dust, and immeasurably powerful, like someone who has been smashed to pieces and then restored, the stronger for the shattering. A rare creature, not quite of this world. Something of beauty and something of the beast.

Akhenaten, Lord of the Two Lands, Lord of the World, smiled. His lips revealed teeth that were thin and widely spaced. And then the smile vanished. He shuffled to a throne, his right foot dragging slightly, and lowered himself into it. A very ordinary, human sigh of relief.

'The work of creating the new world is challenging. But it is the way we will return to our ancestors and the great truth. Akhetaten, the City of the Great Horizon, is the portal to the eternal, and I am rebuilding the way.'

He paused, waiting for my response. I had no idea what to say.

'It is a great work, Lord.'

He considered me. 'I have heard interesting things about you. You have new ideas. You can trace the clues of a mystery to their hidden source. You persuade criminals to confess without torture. You enjoy the dark and dead ends of the crooked labyrinth of the human heart.'

'I am interested in how things happen, and why. So I try to look at what is in front of me. To pay attention.'

'To pay attention. I like that. Are you paying attention now?'

'Yes, Lord.'

He gestured for me to approach closer, concerned not to be overheard. 'Then listen. There is a mystery. An alarming mystery. The Queen, my Nefertiti, the Perfect One, has vanished.'

This was the worst possible news for me. A confirmation of a nagging concern that had been growing since Ahmose first approached me. I felt oddly calm for a man who suddenly found himself poised precariously on a high precipice.

He waited for me to speak.

'Permit me a question: when did this happen?'

He paused, considering his reply. 'Five days ago.'

I did not quite know whether to believe him.

'I have tried to keep this a secret,' he continued, 'but in this city of whispers and echoes it is not possible. Her absence is already the cause of considerable speculation, mostly in quarters who seek to profit from it.'

'This is motive,' I said.

He looked annoyed suddenly. 'What do you mean?'

'I mean, it may be that she has been . . . sequestered by such persons.'

'Of course. There are forces of ignorance working against us, against the enlightenment. Her vanishing will seem an opportunity to question

52

all that we have made and open the way to a return to the darkness of superstition. Their timing would be perfect. It is too convenient.'

I must have looked a little blank then.

'Have those who recommended you committed a gross error?'

'Forgive me, Lord. I was told nothing of the mystery or its circumstances. I was informed only that you wished to speak to me yourself.'

He gathered his thoughts, quickly and effectively. 'In ten days the capital's inauguration Festival will take place. I have commanded the presence and tributes of all the kings, governors and tribe leaders, together with their ambassadors and retinues from around the Empire. It is the revelation of the new world. It is what she and I have worked towards for these many years, and it cannot fail just as we are about to achieve our glory. I must have her back. I must know who has taken her, and I must have her back!'

He was suddenly shaking with rage – more, it seemed to me, with those who had taken her than with the loss of the woman herself. He whacked his staff across a table in fury. Then he shook his head, stood up shakily, turned away, calmed down, and pointed his gold staff at my face.

'Do you understand the trust I place in you by speaking in this way? By revealing such considerations?'

I nodded.

He stood up and walked to the fountain where he observed the water pulsing. Then he turned back to me.

'Find her. If she is alive, save her and bring her to me, together with those associated with the act. If she is dead, bring me her body so that I can give her to eternity. You have ten days. Call upon what resources you require. But trust no-one in this city. You are a stranger here. Keep it that way.'

'May I speak?'

'Yes.'

'I will need to question everyone who had access to the Queen. Everyone who knows her, who works for her, who cares for or does not care for her. That may include your own family, Lord.'

He looked at me, taking his time. His face darkened again. 'Are you implying that maybe your *motivations* exist within my own family?'

'I must consider every possibility, no matter how unacceptable or unthinkable.'

He was not pleased. 'Do what you must, with my authority. I will give you permissions. However, remember that this authority brings responsibility. If you betray it in any way I will have you executed. And if within ten days you have not succeeded, know this: I will also kill your family.'

My heart turned to a stone. The worst of my fears was confirmed. And he knew it. I could see it in his face.

'And as for that little journal you keep your thoughts in, if I were you I would burn each scroll as you write it. "Somewhere between a mule and a mother-in-law"? I was not flattered. Remember your own advice. Take care.'

He poked his staff at me, stared hard, and then I was dismissed from his presence.

9

As I came through the doors, Khety was waiting for me. He could tell I was shaken. He waited for me to speak.

'Where's Tjenry?'

'He had to go. Mahu sent for him. He'll meet us tomorrow.'

I nodded. 'I need a drink. Where does a thirsty man go in this dry town?'

Khety took me to a pavilion by the water, separated from the dust of the roadway by a wooden fence and a fancy gateway which was connected with nothing at all on either side. We could have stepped around it easily, but since someone had bothered to design and construct it, we complied and passed through. Inside, a large wooden platform extended a little way out over the water, and tables and chairs were arranged casually around it. A crowd of groups and couples were sitting there, their drinks and faces lit by lamps, and by the lanterns that hung over their heads. Most of the faces looked up to observe me. I noticed again how they came from all parts of the Empire. Perhaps they were already gathering for the Festival.

I chose a table to the side, near the water, and we sat. The wine list was interesting, and I ordered a jar of young Hatti: light enough for the time of day and for consuming with a snack. The servant returned with a plate of figs and – incredible rarity! – almonds, some bread, and the jar, inscribed with its date, origin, variety and maker. I tried it. Excellent. Clear as a bell.

'You do not order Egyptian wine?'

'No, Khety. I respect the wine from Kharga, and the Kynopolis stuff can be excellent. But for a foot soldier like me a Hatti white is a rare opportunity. Try it.'

'I know little of wine. I drink Egyptian beer.'

'Very healthy, but not much fun for the palate.'

'Actually the wine is fine. Light and clear. I appreciate it.'

'Try actually enjoying it.'

'Yes, sir.'

He took another sip. 'It is enjoyable.'

'Have an almond. They're delicious.'

'Oh, no, thank you.'

How would I get this man to open up? He looked at me like a wary and not particularly bright dog. I wished Tjenry were here instead. He seemed to have more of an appetite for life.

'Khety, we face an impossible task. Has your charming boss explained to you the nature of the mystery?'

'No, sir.'

'Well, I am going to tell you. And in doing so it will make us equal in one crucial respect, and one respect only. We are both under the same fate: if we fail to solve the mystery, we will suffer the same consequences. Do you understand?'

He nodded.

'Good. This is the mystery.' I paused for dramatic effect. 'The Queen has disappeared and my task is to find her and restore her to Akhenaten in time for the opening of the Festival.'

His eyes widened and his mouth stayed open. 'Disappeared? Do you mean . . .?'

It was the worst acting I had seen in some time. He knew. Everybody knew, apparently, except me.

'For heaven's sake, stop pretending. Apparently her absence is the talk of the town.'

His face cast about for a way out of his dilemma, but he quickly realized he was discovered. He put up his hands and shrugged with a frank little smile.

'Good. Now, perhaps we can start again.'

He looked at me, interested now.

'What's been going on in this city?'

'What do you need to know?'

'The politics.'

He shrugged. 'Dirty.'

'So, nothing new in the portal to the eternal, then.'

'What?'

'Just something Akhenaten said to me.'

I sipped my fine wine and pushed the rare almonds towards him. He took one, reluctantly.

'I'm just a middle-ranking Medjay officer,' Khety said, 'so what do I know? But if you're asking me, here's what I think.' He moved closer. 'Everyone who's come to the city is on the make. Most people are here because they're investing in the future – their own, their family's. They realize they can rise within the new administrations and authorities. It's a chance to rise above their stations. And there's so much wealth here. It's being siphoned off from the rest of the country, and for all I know from the whole Empire. A friend told me the garrisons in the north-east are hardly manned now, even though there is serious trouble brewing up there. Everyone here is from somewhere else, somewhere where they couldn't even scrape a living any longer. The preparations for the Festival have put enormous pressure on everyone; the craftsmen are charging five times as much for their work because of the conditions and the hurry, and their bosses are taking a cut.

They've drafted in thousands of immigrant workers but I'm sure the budget isn't all being spent on food and wages. The wealth's disappearing, the Treasury can't keep up with the overspending, the cutbacks are hurting the rest of the country . . . I think it's a disaster already happening.'

The sun had now disappeared over the river, over the Red Land.

'So what has all this to do with her vanishing?'

Khety went quiet.

'Don't be enigmatic, it's annoying.'

'Sometimes it's dangerous to speak.'

I waited.

'Two reasons. One, timing. The Festival is pointless without her. Two, she's far more loved and admired than him. I sometimes think the only reason everyone goes along with the new religion is because they believe in her far more than they believe in the worship of the Aten. Even people who have nothing but negative things to say about everything that's happening have to admit that she's an astonishing person. There's never been anyone like her. But that in itself is a problem. Some people see her as a threat.'

I took a sip of wine. 'Who?'

'People who have something to lose by her power, and something to gain by her death.'

'*Disappearance.* Why did you say death?'

He looked disconcerted. 'Sorry, disappearance. Everyone thinks she's been murdered.'

'Rule one: assume nothing. Just look at what is and isn't there. Deduce accordingly. Who would profit from such a situation, from the uncertainty?'

'There's not just one candidate, there are many. In the new military, in the old Priesthoods of Karnak and Heliopolis, in the Harem, within the new bureaucracy, even' – he moved closer – 'in the royal family itself. Apparently the inner circles of the court are rife with people saying even the Queen Mother has resented her beauty and her influence – things she herself lost a long time ago.'

58

We paused and looked at the suddenly darkening sky. He had spoken well, and everything he said had confirmed my worst fear: that indeed I was now caught up at the centre of a mystery as delicately complex as a spider's web that could destroy not only my life, but the life of the country. I suddenly felt a dark nest of serpents stir inside my stomach, and a voice in my head told me it was impossible, that I would never find her, that I could perish here and never see Tanefert and the children again. I tried to breathe myself calmly back to the task in hand. *Concentrate. Concentrate. Use what you know. Do the job. Think. Think it through.*

'Remember, Khety, there is no body. A murderer wishes only to hurt, punish and kill. A death is a death. It is an accomplished fact. This situation is different. A disappearance is far more complex. Its achievement is instability. Whoever has done this has introduced tremendous uncertainty and turbulence into a settled equation. And there is nothing worse for those in authority. They find themselves fighting illusions. And illusions are very powerful.'

Khety looked impressed. 'So how do we proceed?'

'There is a pattern to all this; we just have to learn to read its signs, to connect the clues. Her disappearance is our starting point. It is what we know we know. We do not know why, or how. We do not know where she is, or whether she lives. We must find out. And how do you think we should do that?'

'Umm . . .'

'For heaven's sake, have they given me a monkey as an assistant?'

He flushed with embarrassment, but his eyes glittered with anger. Good. A reaction.

'If you have lost something, what is the first question you ask your-self?'

'Where was the last place I had it?'

'So . . .'

'So we must discover the last place, the last time, the last person. And trace her backwards and forwards from there. So you want me to—'

'Exactly.'

'A name will be on your desk first thing in the morning.'

After a while I smiled. 'Khety, you are becoming a wiser man with every passing drop of this fine wine.'

His anger dissipated a little. I refilled his cup.

'No-one ever just disappears,' I continued, 'as if they had stepped out of their sandals and up into thin air. There are always clues. Human beings cannot help but leave traces. We will find and read these traces. We will track her footsteps in the dust of this world, and discover her and bring her safely home. We have no choice.'

We bade farewell at the crossroads where the Royal Road met the way back to my office. Khety saluted, then stepped towards the Medjay headquarters, no doubt to report everything to Mahu with the confident fluency of the inexperienced drinker. But perhaps I was too harsh. He had been candid with me, more than was strictly required. I could not trust him, nevertheless I liked him well enough. And he would be a useful guide to this strange world.

10

I woke early like a condemned man to the naivety of birdsong. I could not believe I was still here, and that I had committed myself and my family to this madness. I wanted Tanefert lying next to me. I wanted to hear the girls talking to each other next door, in their room. But the room was an empty box. Would that I could turn back the river that carried me here.

Khety and Tjenry arrived together. Tjenry carried breakfast, a jug of beer and a basket of bread rolls which he put down in front of me. Khety looked pleased with himself. He carefully placed a papyrus document on my desk. On it was written a girl's name: Senet.

'Who's this?'

'Nefertiti's maid. The last person to see her, as far as I can discover. She reported her disappearance.'

'Good. Let's go.'

'But we don't have an appointment.'

'Why do we need an appointment to speak to the Queen's maid?'

'Because it's how things are done, it's etiquette. She's not just any-one. Her family—'

'Look, Khety, in Thebes, I just turn up. I decide who I want to talk to, when, where and how. I go out into the streets, I talk to people who work, who have lives one can understand more or less at a glance; they talk before they've had a chance to work out their story properly. I know the way of things. I know how to find the people I need to find. I ask them questions. I get the answers.'

He looked worried. 'May I speak?'

'Only very quickly.'

Tjenry grinned. Khety ignored him.

'The capital is a very formal kind of place. There is always hierarchy to respect; etiquette, procedure, propriety. Even the simplest request for an audience or a meeting can take days to administrate and negotiate. People are very ... *sensitive*, and demand to have their status respected and acknowledged. It's all very finely balanced, and if you get it wrong and upset people, it makes things very ... difficult.'

I couldn't believe this. 'Khety, do you remember what we talked about last night? Do you realize how little time we have? We have ten – no, nine, as of now – days. At most. If we wait at these invisible doors, knocking politely and saying, "Please may we come in, please grant us a moment of your precious time, please may we acknowledge your high status, please may my assistant Khety kiss your honourable arse," we're never going to survive. And besides, we have authorities. From Akhenaten.'

I unrolled the papyrus, with its royal symbols – his two names written within the cartouches – and showed him.

Tjenry was impressed.

We walked out into the early morning and Khety showed me a ramshackle chariot that he had procured for the purpose of driving me from place to place.

'Sorry, sir, this is all that's available.'

'So much for honour and status,' I said.

We drove off, Tjenry following in another chariot that was in an even worse condition. There were still fine traces of night coolness in the air and in the freshness of the light. The twittering of thousands of birds, the already dazzling brightness of the buildings, the way the first light awoke among little things – in the blades of the grasses, in the leaves, in the running waters – helped restore my heart to the belief that perhaps after all I could solve this mystery and return to my family.

Khety drove us at speed away from the central city, along the wide Royal Road and then off on a spur which soon turned into a sinuous and beautiful pathway beside the river, beneath an avenue of mature palm trees.

'Were these trees already here when the city was built?' I asked.

'No, sir. They came by barge, and were planted to the design.'

I shook my head in wonder at the strangeness of things in our time: fully grown trees planted in the desert.

'And Senet – tell me about her.'

'She is the Queen's maid.'

'More, please.'

'She has the Queen's trust.'

'Is that rare?'

'I do not know. I expect so.'

'And this is the Queen's private residence?'

'Yes. She likes a less formal environment than the House of the King. She raises the children here. It is quite unusual.'

We drove on past vegetable gardens with their sparkling irrigation channels, and recently established orchards. The sun had now risen above the eastern cliffs and was immediately hot on our faces. The long shadows were banished. Thousands of nameless workers toiled at the black earth to produce food for the city, directing with their adzes the flow of water through the channels that ran alongside the fields. Thousands more builders and artisans laboured on the new constructions, their skin and hair permanently blanched with dust, the beat of the work drum as constant in their ears as a heartbeat.

Finally we arrived at the gate of the Queen's Palace. To my surprise it was a house set behind a high mud-brick enclosure, though of unusual, extensive proportions; not a palace in the sense of colonnades and high walls decorated with hieroglyphs and statues, but a place of elegant, human scale and design. Long, low roofs were arranged at different levels, with open spaces between to allow for the circulation of air, the high entry of light and the continually evolving presence of shade.

I told Tjenry to wait outside. He was not pleased, so I explained: 'I don't want to overwhelm the girl with Medjay officers. She'll be too frightened to speak.' He shrugged, nodded, and found a place to lounge in the shade.

The entrance was guarded, but when Khety and I approached flourishing the authority they unbarred the way and we passed through into a courtyard floored with alabaster, and with narrow, shallow runnels of water spreading outwards from a central fountain where a pure nub of water pulsed endlessly. The way the light played off the water encouraged sensations of pleasure. For the first time since I arrived in the city I felt almost relaxed. I instantly responded by tensing up again: a seeker's reflex. Nothing is more dangerous than relaxation.

We were led into the house by a girl dressed in white linen, like all the girls who appeared and then vanished as we made our way through a series of rooms and courtyards. Each room flowed into the next in a way that allowed for variety, juxtaposition, the interplay of inner and outer spaces, of brick and wood, light and shade, giving the highly unusual sense that the two worlds of the house and nature were happily co-existing. The long roofs were cantilevered to provide canopies above terraces, and I could not tell how such constructions were kept apparently floating in space. I noticed children's toys, papyri and drawing materials scattered around, collections of beautiful objects on tables, and varieties of plants gathered together in shady corners.

We were bidden to wait in a room with two long benches. Then a young woman entered and introduced herself. I expect such girls to be no more than suitably average in their beauty, the better to offset whatever claims their mistresses have to such a thing themselves. But this girl was slim, elegant and sophisticated. She wore her hair under a headscarf. I liked her at once. She had a warmth and sincerity that I found I did not wish to mistrust. And her affection for her mistress was obvious. As was her nervousness during the interview.

I took out this journal as a way to make her understand that I wished to make a permanent record of her words. I find this action often has a usefully intimidating effect during interviews. She sat with her hands, in fine yellow gloves, folded in her lap, and waited.

'You know why we are here?'

'I do. And I wish to be helpful.'

'Then you must tell me all the things that might seem important, but also all the things that might not.'

'I will do my best.'

'So, let us start. You reported the Queen missing?'

She nodded. 'She was gone from her room when I went to dress her. The bed had not been slept in.'

'Tell me about your relationship with the Queen.'

'I am her maid-servant. My name is Senet. She chose me as a young girl to live with her. To help with her clothes, her dressing. To look after the children. To bring her the things she needed. To listen to her.'

'So she talked to you? Of private matters?'

'Sometimes. But my memory is poor.'

She glanced quickly at Khety, and I understood her. It would be wrong and dangerous for her to break the Queen's confidence in his presence.

'Let us think back to the days before her disappearance. Can you do that? Tell me everything.'

'My Lady is always happy. Every day. But I believe I noticed recently that she was worried about something. Her mind was busy.'

'She is the Queen. Of course her mind is busy.'

Khety's interjection was unexpected by both of us. In fact, even he seemed surprised that he had spoken.

'It is more efficient if I conduct this interview without interruption,' I said to him.

'Yes, sir.'

But I could sense the ripple of tension in his body, as if his ears were laid back now like a dog.

'Do you have any idea why she was worried?' I continued, turning my attention back to Senet.

'Setepenra, the youngest princess, is teething, and not sleeping well. I know it is unusual, but you see she nurses the children herself.'

Senet looked at me in a way I could not quite interpret. Did she really think the Queen could have no other concerns? Or was she simply unwilling even to begin to refer to what they might be?

'She loves the children?'

'Very much. They are her life.'

'So she would not leave them alone much?'

'No, no. She hated to leave them. They cannot understand what is happening . . .'

For the first time, her eyes betrayed a depth of emotion, the beginning of tears.

'And now, please, would you think back to the last time you saw the Queen.'

'It was seven nights ago. The children were put to bed. Then she went and sat out on the terrace that overlooks the river and the setting sun. She often does this. I saw her, sitting, thinking.'

'How do you know she was thinking?'

'I brought her out a shawl. She had nothing in her hands, not a text, nor a papyrus and brush. She was just staring out across the water. The sun had gone down. There was little to see. It was getting dark. When I offered her the shawl and some lit lamps, she jumped as if she was afraid. Then she held my hand for a moment. I noticed her face. It was tense, strained. I asked if there was anything I could do for her. She just looked at me, slowly shook her head, and turned away. I asked her to come inside, for it seemed wrong to stay alone out there. She did so, holding a lamp, and made her way to her bedroom. That was the last time I saw her, walking down the passage to her room in a circle of lamplight.'

We all sat still for a moment.

'So you did not accompany her to her room?'

'No. She did not wish it.'

'She spoke to you?'

'No. I simply understood her.'

'Can you be sure she returned to her room?'

'No, I cannot.'

She was becoming more anxious now.

'And who else was in the house at this time?'

'The children, their nurse, and I suppose the other staff: the cooks, the maids, the night guards.'

'At what time do the guards change duty?'

'At sunset and sunrise.'

I took a moment to think through what to do next.

'We need to retrace her last steps. Can you take us to the terrace, and then along the route to her bedroom?'

'Is that allowed?'

'It is.'

She led us to a wide stone terrace with steps leading down to the water's edge, protected from the sun and from the possibility of scrutiny by a marvellous vine. A chair was placed under this sunshade, facing out to the waters and the opposite shore. No real construction had taken place there: just extensive fields, a few hamlets, and beyond that the Red Land shimmering in the distance. In the haze on the border, I could see just one significant building, a low tower or fort lonely in the heat, like a mirage. The water lapped, grey and green, against the salty glitter of the as yet unworn stone.

In the silence I calmed myself in order to absorb everything. Then I took a risk and sat down directly in the chair. *Her* chair. Khety looked nervous at this breaking of taboo, and the girl seemed genuinely upset. I felt around the edges of the cushion with my fingers. Nothing. I wanted to feel the shape of this vanished woman in the contours of the chair, as if a message, a clue, or some form of connection between us might be discovered in this way. What happened was I felt too big, too clumsy. I could not conform my body to the natural flowing shape of the chair. I sat still a moment longer, my fingers on the arms where her own fingers would have lain. I touched wood carved into the likeness of the paws, unclawed, of a lion. The grain was soft beneath my finger-tips. The fresh paint was smooth. I imagined her staring out across the river, into the inscrutable light. And thinking, thinking, her mind as clear as cool water.

I opened my eyes again and noticed what I had missed before. The fort, if it was a fort, on the opposite shore lay precisely in line with the view from the chair. She had sat here, gazing across the water at the land of the west and a fort. What was going on in her mind?

'And the way to the bedroom, please.'

The girl led the way, the corridor turning left, then right, then left again. We came to a pair of simple wooden doors. No heraldic symbols above them, no Aten disc, no symbols of royalty. Senet looked at me for permission. I nodded, and she opened it.

The room was a delightful surprise. Unlike the elegance of the rest of the house, here was the private world of a public woman, a living disorder that came as a relief after so much careful taste and refinement. Many chests lined one wall, their lids and compartments open, a vast number of robes and costumes collected there, arranged against each other like choices yet to be made. Chest after chest of sandals, the compartments specially made to accommodate the collection. A large polished bronze mirror sat on a cosmetic chest whose lid was strewn with little alabaster pots and containers of gold and glass: cosmetics, perfumes, eye-paints, ointments and creams. Open drawers revealed slate palettes for mixing, one still bearing the dried traces of ochre and black paste, and teardrop-shaped applicators, enough for a hundred pairs of eyes – enough to satisfy a theatre. Little statues and figurines of gods and goddesses, of animals and beasts. A necklace of flying fish and tiny sea shells in gold on chains of red, green and black beads. And some glorious antique pieces, less garish and elaborate than the work of our time: a winged scarab inlaid with cornelian and lapis; gold finger rings with frogs and cornelian cats on the bezels; bracelets of reclining cats in gold; and a scarab set in gold as a finger ring.

Here was no crime scene. The disorder was natural and likeable, betraying no evidence of struggle or haste. There was nothing inappropriate about it. She had not been taken from here.

'Is anything missing?' I asked the girl.

'I would not dare to look, or to know.'

'Then please, at my request, make as thorough an inventory as you can. Simply note anything that is not where it should be.'

She turned her attention to the chests, running her eyes and her fingers along the rich and colourful fabrics, her lips moving as if speaking the names of the dresses.

'One set of clothes is missing,' Senet announced after a short while. 'A long gold tunic, gold sandals, linen undershirt. But I remember that was what she was wearing on the last evening.'

So I knew what she was wearing when she disappeared.

'Now the cosmetic chest, please.'

Her eyes scanned everything on and in it. Her memory must, after all, be exceptional. She seemed to stop for a moment, as if mentally rechecking one of the compartments, her eyes ranging more widely as if looking for something significant; but then she closed it carefully.

'Everything I remember is here, except what she was wearing on the last night I saw her.'

'Which was?'

'A gold necklace.'

'Anything else?'

'No.'

I was about to question her further when there was a sudden knocking on the door. Khety opened it. It was Tjenry, alarm on his smooth young face. We made our way out into a courtyard to the side of the house, where I hoped no-one could overhear our conversation.

'A body,' said Tjenry. 'A body has been found.'

11

She lay cradled in a low dune, some way into the Red Land behind the northern edges of the city, among the desert altars to the east. A fine second skin of grey sand had been brushed over her and into the folds of her magnificent clothes – long gold tunic, fine gold necklace, gold slippers, linen undershirt – by the light attention of the wind. She was turned on her side, her legs drawn up, her arms holding each other like a sleeping girl; and facing the west, the setting sun, I noticed, as in a traditional burial. It was all wrong. Her stillness. The empty muffled sound of the desert, like a shuttered room with nothing living in it. The heat of near midday, which shimmered over us all. The offending sweet stink of recently killed flesh. And above all, the furious tormented excitement of flies. I knew this sound too well.

Her face was turned considerably to the sands. Holding a cloth to my mouth and nose, with Mahu, his slavering and overheated dog, and Khety standing at a distance, I gently touched her shoulder. She unrolled awkwardly towards me, the reluctant movement telling me at

71

once that death was likely to have taken place in the small hours of the night. Then I confess I jumped back. Where her face should have been was a seething mask of flies that, conjured instantly by my disturbance, shimmered up into the air around my own head, and then reformed again, a barbarian hive thick with the buzz of intense devotion, upon the bloody remains of lips, teeth, nose and eyes. I heard Tjenry puking. Mahu remained still, casting a large and very sharp shadow over me as I crouched again by the corpse of the Queen whose glorious and famous face had been so brutally destroyed. I understood at once the extent and significance of the mutilation: this spectacular barbarity meant that the gods could not recognize her and she would never be able to speak her name when her shadow arrived in the Otherworld. She had been murdered in this life *and* in the next – a royal outcast of eternity. But something was not right. Why here? Why now?

'I think you are out of a job.'

I looked up. Mahu's face was hidden in deep shadow. There was no tone of victory in his voice, but he was right. The Queen was dead. I was too late. Her own death surely signalled mine. My thoughts reeled. Was this the end of everything already? I had hardly begun.

The peasant who had found her stood at a distance, trying not to look, trying not to exist. Mahu signalled for him to approach. Trembling, he did so. Without expression, as if he were an animal, without even the basest preliminaries of execution, Mahu's curved sword whispered in an invisible arc through the thin air and the man's thin neck. His severed head fell to the sand like a ball dropped out of its orbit, and his body sank instantly to its knees and collapsed. Blood pumped from his neck. The unholy priesthood of flies renewed their disgusting celebrations. The dog moved forward to sniff at the head. Mahu uttered a sharp command and it returned obediently, still panting, to its master's feet.

Mahu looked at Khety, Tjenry and me, daring us to speak. My mind was racing like a crazed dog, driven on by fear. Suddenly a new thought flashed into my head.

'This may not be the Queen,' I said.

Mahu stared at me. 'Explain that.' He sounded nasty.

'The body seems to be that of the Queen, but the face is destroyed. Our faces are our identities. Without one, how do we know for certain who is who?'

'She is wearing royal clothes. That is her hair, that is her figure.'

There was tension in Mahu's voice. Did he prefer her dead? Or did he just not want to be proved wrong by me?

'Certainly those are her clothes. Yes, it seems to be her. Nevertheless, I need to examine the body and conduct a full investigation in order to confirm the identification.'

Mahu considered me, his gold eyes transfixed on mine. 'You are struggling, Rahotep, like a fly in honey. Well, you had better get to work, quickly. If you are right, which seems impossible, then there is more to this than meets the eye. If you are wrong, which seems certain, and Akhenaten, his family and the whole world mourn the loss of the Queen, you know exactly what to expect.'

We took her body, covered with a cloth, on a cart to a private chamber of purification, in conditions of absolute secrecy. It was the coldest room that could be found. Its limestone walls were built into the earth and gave off a ghostly chill. The candle flames shivered silently in the sconces, giving light without heat. I found linen bandages stored in a cupboard; jars of dry natron, cedar oil and palm wine stood on shelves; iron hooks for removing brains, incision knives and small hatchets hung beneath. Along another wall were ranged canopic jars for organs, their lids decorated with images of the Sons of Horus. Along a third wall, propped up in a line like an identity parade, was a variety of rich men's coffins decorated in gold and lapis, and above them shelves of mummy masks. And when I opened boxes I found, unusually, rank upon rank of glass eyes staring up at me, awaiting the sockets of the newly dead to allow them a vision of the gods.

There was a sudden commotion at the door: the Overseer of the Mysteries was demanding admittance to his office. When he saw

Mahu he shut up instantly, and after a word from Tjenry he backed out, apologizing as he went. Mahu then turned to us. 'There are guards outside. I want you to report to me within one hour.' And he went, taking some of the room's darkness and chill with him.

I turned to the body of the woman on the wooden embalmer's table. The flies had moved on to other, richer feasts, and the ruins of her face – black and crimson and ochre, the eyes gone, the brow and nose shattered, the lips and mouth smashed – remained clear. In a few spots the brain itself was exposed. I examined the features of the injuries. Her jaw and forehead still bore the rough imprints and indentations of something like a large stone, but there seemed to be no other mortal injuries. So that was how she died. She would have seen her own death coming. A brutal and not especially quick ending.

I quickly poured a sufficient quantity of natron powder mixed with acid over the face, in order to eat away the ruined flesh and congealed blood and expose the bone structure and any remaining skin. While the natron did its work, I turned to Tjenry, who was staring at the corpse with a young person's fascination.

'What would we do without this powder? It is found on the shores of ancient lakes, and the wadis at Natrun and Elbak are the finest sources. It cleanses our skins and brightens our teeth and breath, yet it also makes glass possible. Is it not interesting how something may look like nothing but may have many powers?'

Tjenry was still looking uncertain about all these obviously new experiences. He did not seem interested in a discussion of the virtues of natron.

'What a mess. Do you really think it's not her?'

'That remains to be seen. Indeed it seems to be, but there are many possibilities.'

'But how will you know?'

'By looking at what is there.'

We began at her feet. Her sandals were leather and gold. The soles of her feet were not cracked, and the skin was soft and clean. A woman of leisure. The bones of the ankles were neatly turned. Her toenails were painted red, but scuffed and scratched. There were dry smears of something on the sides of her feet.

'Look.'

Tjenry moved his face closer to the foot.

'What do you see?'

'The nails are carefully manicured.'

'But?'

'But they are scuffed. The varnish here is marked. And I see here, on the outside of the little toes, scratches, and traces of blood and dust.'

'Better. And from this we deduce what?'

'A struggle.'

'Yes, a struggle. This woman was dragged along against her will. But this we could anticipate. See among the toes? What do we find?'

I scraped between the big toe and its neighbour, and into my hand fell not only traces of sand but also a tiny deposit of darker dust: dried river mud. I moved to her hands. They too bore the marks of conflict: bruises to the knuckles, damaged nails and grazed skin. I examined under the nails. More mud. Perhaps the killers had ferried her across or along the river, in which case the river mud might be accounted for as they forced her, still alive, from the boat. But there was something else. With tweezers I drew from between the fingers clenched in death a long auburn hair. Strange. This woman's hair was black. Whose hair was this? Was it a woman's or a man's? The length told me nothing. I held it up to the lamplight. It appeared to be undyed and from a living head, not a wig. I sniffed it, and believed I caught the faintest trace of a subtle perfume, rather than any beeswax setting lotion.

I moved up to the torso and was about to begin to examine the clothing when the door slammed open and to my alarm Akhenaten himself entered. Khety, Tjenry and I dropped to the floor, faces down, by the table. I heard him move across the room and approach the body. This was a disaster. I still had none of the clues, those tiny shards of hope I needed in order to prove my instinct true. I desperately needed to examine the body and confirm my findings before informing Akhenaten. Now it must look as if I was working behind his back, to cover up the murder and the body of the Queen, and my own incompetence and failure. I swore at myself, wishing I had never come, never left Thebes. But here I was, trapped by my own ambition and curiosity.

I quickly glanced up. He was standing beside the body, his hands slowly moving across it, his eyes wide in rapt concentration, breathing with deep, uneven gasps as if in pain, as if trying to sense the spirit still hovering, as if he would try to raise her from the dead. He seemed mesmerized by the catastrophe of her face, as if he had never thought beauty were skin deep, as if he could not believe his Queen was mortal. It seemed to me in that moment that he loved her.

I thought: how ironic we should meet our fates in an embalmers' workshop. All we needed to do was step quietly into a coffin, close the lid, and wait for death.

Finally he seemed able to speak. 'Who did this?'

I had to say it. 'Lord, I do not know.'

He nodded sympathetically, as if I were a child in school who had failed to answer a simple question. He continued with a quietness that was more menacing than any shout. 'Did you hope to keep this secret from me until you had worked out a story to defend your failure to answer this simple question?'

'No, Lord.'

'Do not disagree with me.'

'It is the question I am trying to answer, Lord. It is not a simple question. And forgive me for saying so at this time, but there is another question.'

His glare was intense with contempt. 'What other question could there be now? She is dead!'

'The question is whether this is indeed the Queen.'

There followed a nasty silence. Akhenaten's voice, when he spoke, was a marvel of restrained sarcasm. 'These are her clothes. Her hair. Her jewellery. Her scent is still on the body.'

It was time to grasp the slender reed of chance.

'But appearances, Lord, may be deceptive.'

He turned to look at me, his face suddenly hungry with hope. 'That is the first interesting thing you have said. Speak.'

'We are all infinitely varied in terms of bodily shapes and colours and manners, but we are sometimes wrong when we think we know someone. How often does one glimpse a figure across a busy street and cry out to the school friend we have not seen for many years, only to find it is not he but someone in whom his features have been rearranged? Or the sudden flash of the eyes of a girl we once loved in the passing face of a stranger?'

'What are you saying?'

'I am saying this is a woman who looks like the Queen, who has her height and her hair, the tones of her skin, her clothing. But without the face, the mirror where we read our knowledge of each other, only one who knew her deeply – intimately – can confirm this.'

'I see.'

I looked down, careful not to risk damaging this delicate moment.

'With permission, there is a way, Lord, to confirm the identification of this body as the Queen's. But it requires personal knowledge. Private knowledge.'

He considered what I was implying. 'If you are wrong, I will do to you what was done to her. I will strip you naked, I will cut out your tongue so you cannot call for death, I will peel off your skin, strip by strip, I will hammer your face to a pulp, and then I will have you staked out in the desert where I will watch your slow agony as the flies and the sun put you to your death.'

What could I say? I looked him in the eye, then bowed my head in acquiescence.

'Turn away. Face the wall.'

We did so. He was opening her clothing, laying her bare. I heard the faintest shower of grains of sand cascading to the floor. Then silence. Then the sound of a jar shattering against a wall. Khety jumped. The scent of palm wine spread out quickly across the room. The next moment would decide the path of my destiny.

'This is a great deception.'

Hope leaped up in my heart.

'Your task is not yet done. It is hardly begun. And there is little time. Call upon what you need. Find her.' There was a look of exultation on his face, not just relief. 'This body is rubbish. Dispose of it.' And with that he swept from the room.

Khety, Tjenry and I looked at each other and stood up. Tjenry put his hand to his damp brow. 'This is too much excitement.' He laughed a little, embarrassed by his fear.

'How did you know that?' said Khety, gazing at the body.

I shrugged. I did not say how little I had had to go on in gambling our lives. The body before us was beautiful, perfect even. What detail had redeemed us and proved my strange hunch right? Then I saw a little white scar like a star in daylight on the belly, where a mole, perhaps, had been removed. That was all it had taken to save us for another day. But then the questions crowded into my head. Why had someone murdered a woman who looked exactly like the Queen? Why set such a sophisticated false lead? And where was Nefertiti herself?

Out of habit, I checked through the folds of the robes. Inside, near the heart, my fingers closed on a small object. I drew it out and found in my hand an ancient amulet, worked in gold and decorated in lapis. It was a scarab. The dung beetle, symbol of regeneration, whose offspring appeared as if from nowhere in the mud. The scarab that every day pushes the sun back into the light from its night in the Otherworld. Unusually the underside was inscribed not with the name of the owner, but with three signs: Ra, the sun, a circle with a dot at its centre, then 't', and then the hieroglyph of a sitting woman beside it. If I read it correctly it said: Raet. The female Ra.

I slipped the amulet into my pocket. It felt like a clue, or a sign – indeed the only one I had, apart from this faceless girl whose appalling death had in the end saved my own life. If only I could understand what was in front of me. I turned to look again at the body on the table.

'Right, here are the key questions. Who is she? Why does she look so like the Queen? Why is she wearing the Queen's clothing? And why has she been mutilated in such a desperate way?'

Khety and Tjenry nodded, sagely.

'Who makes all the images of the Queen? All those strange statues?'

'Thutmosis,' said Khety. 'His workshops are in the south suburb.'

'Good. I want to interview him.'

'Also, there is a reception this evening to honour the first of the arriving dignitaries for the Festival.'

'Then we should attend. I hate parties, but it might be important.'

I ordered Tjenry to remain with the body and organize security. 'Khety will relieve you later tonight.' He gave me a jaunty salute.

Khety and I made our way out to the embarrassing, cranky chariot. Over the jarring argument of metal and stone I said, 'Tell me more about this artist.'

'He is famous. Not like the other image-makers. Everyone knows him. And he's *very* rich.' He gave me a significant look.

'And how do you find his work?'

Khety paused. 'I think it's very . . . modern.'

'It sounds like you think that's a bad thing.'

'Oh no, it's very impressive. It's just . . . he shows everything. People as they are, not how they ought to be.'

'Isn't that better? Truer?'

'I suppose so.'

He didn't sound convinced.

12

The south suburb was residential. Here were substantial estates hidden behind high walls, houses with large floor areas surrounded by what seemed to be walled gardens, granaries, stables and workshops. There was space between the dwellings for privacy, although most of it was spilling over with building materials and sometimes rubbish. Over these walls one glimpsed interesting plants thriving by virtue of the wells and water channels: tamarisk, willows, miniature date palms, persea trees, fashionable pomegranate bushes with their red crowned fruits and impossibly messy honeycomb of sour pips. And flowers: sky-blue cornflowers, poppies, daisies. The buildings too spoke of great affluence: stone lintels, most inscribed with the names and titles of the owners; extensive timber pergolas with vines; large courtyards and grounds.

'Mahu has a house in this part of the city,' offered Khety. 'Also the Vizier Ramose.'

'It is where the members of the elite live?'

'Yes.'

'And is it always this quiet? It's practically religious.'

'Noise is disliked.'

The absence of human life was disconcerting, and the hush felt haunted, as if the place were a town of rich ghosts.

Khety knocked on the door of what seemed a house as substantial and silent as most of the others in the street. Eventually we heard footsteps, and an immaculate servant admitted us. Once inside, however, a hidden world of activity revealed itself. Across the court-yard, with its trees and benches surrounding a circular water-pool, came the faint chink-chink-chink of many chisels tapping away on stone. There were suggestions of activity in other rooms too: calls for help or of appreciation; someone whistling. The servant disappeared to announce us.

Eventually, a bulky figure appeared in the passageway and walked towards us. He was a big man in every direction, his round, curious face like a dish set with blue eyes and a thinning cloud of red-brown hair. He yawned as he showed us through the main house and into a secondary courtyard. Down the length of the south side was a row of little studios and workshops, all busy with figures at work, tapping, chipping and painting.

'You keep quite a large staff, I see.'

'It's hard to find enough good craftsmen to fulfil the demand. I had to bring most of them down from Thebes, *and* their bloody families. The rest I was able to recruit locally or from the delta towns. Sometimes I feel like I'm single-handedly supporting the economy of a small country.'

In the north-east corner of the plot stood another building which turned out to be his workshop, containing a large open space with rooms and passages leading off it. Light entered directly from the clerestory windows below the raised roof. He bellowed at his students and apprentices to leave and they hurried out obediently. On large tables and stands several works were in progress, recog-nizable body parts – fingers, hands, cheeks, arms, torsos – appearing

81

from the hewn stones criss-crossed with rough black marks. But I was truly amazed to see, ranged along a shelf that ran the full length of the walls, countless white/grey plaster casts of heads – young, middle-aged and old, various classes – so detailed, so truly lifelike: the bristles of the chin, the delicate eyelashes of a girl, the warts and spots of an old woman; the wrinkles of time, the lines of character – all perfectly reproduced. Each head had its eyes closed, as if dreaming together of another world, a far-world beyond time.

'I see you take an interest in my heads.'

'They are so lifelike, one wonders when they will open their eyes and begin to speak.'

He smiled. 'They might have interesting things to say to us.'

We sat together on a gilded bench in the corner of the room. Drinks were brought to us. Thutmosis sipped slowly and carefully from his cup, and I sipped from mine. A rich, deep red. Khety replaced his on the tray. I savoured mine, even though it was still early in the day for wine.

'From the Dakhla Oasis?'

Thutmosis turned the jar towards him and read the marks. 'Very good. Do you mind if I sketch you while we talk? My hands are only happy when they are working.'

He began to draw, his eyes roving over my face, his brush apparently working quite independently, for he never checked the marks he was making. First I asked him about his relationship with the Queen.

'Can I call it a relationship? She is my patron, and, sometimes, muse.'

'What does that mean?'

'She is my inspiration. I cannot put it better than that. I am the maker of her images, which is to say, with her consent I have the honour to embody her living spirit in the materials of stone and wood and plaster.'

'I think I understand.'

'Do you? It is a perpetual mystery to me.'

'Perhaps you could explain, in layman's terms, how it all works. The creative process.'

Thutmosis sighed, and continued to sketch. 'The Queen believes it matters to work from life. In the past, makers have been limited to embodying the virtues and perfections of the dead. Why? All those works are simply respectful copies, only remotely connected to their inspiration in life. All those enormous statues, so epic, so political, and so very uninspiring – unless you consider awe the only emotional response of value in art. And no doubt they were fat and crass and silly as people, but lo, here they are, with the physiques of gods, all muscle and wealth and contempt! Let's be honest, it's limited. Don't you think?'

He put aside his sketch and, shifting his position, began another. I was becoming an artist's model. I was starting to feel uncomfortable under his scrutiny. Yet I was curious to see how he had portrayed me.

'But you don't work that way?'

'No, I cannot. It turns the image-maker into nothing more than a social servant. The artist is completely anonymous. The work is formulaic, generic. Nefertiti is right: these are the dead forms of the past. You see, my ambition is not to *describe* a living form, but to *create* it. And I believe that in the unimaginable future, those who still worship at these images will know that this was *him*, this was *her*, and no other. At the very end of time, human beings, whoever they are, will still look upon Akhenaten and Nefertiti and know them for who they were. Now *that's* eternal life.'

He looked at me expectantly, hoping I would join him in his enthusiasm. I sipped my wine.

'May I ask how you proceed to create an image of the Queen? Where do you start?'

'We would have private sittings over many hours, many weeks. She would sit here and I would work directly from life. A life study.'

'And you would talk?'

'Not always. I would not assume her wish to converse, and also

I cannot chat when I am working. The concentration is intense. It sounds pretentious to say so, but one is barely in the world. Time passes swiftly. Suddenly the light will be fading, there will be more grey hairs on my head, the Queen will be smiling at me, and there under my hands – a likeness. An image. A form.'

Which was all a clever way of not answering my question.

'And the Queen, how does she pass this time?'

'She thinks, she dreams. I love that. To recreate her in the act of thinking, the mystery of the mind in motion . . .'

'So you do not recall what you talked about? Or how she seemed at the last sitting?'

'She was very quiet.'

'Unusually so?'

He looked directly at me. 'Yes, I would say so.'

'And what were you working on?'

'A superb bust. My finest work, I think.'

'May I see it?'

He put down his sketching and considered my request carefully. 'Do you have the proper permissions?'

'I do,' I said. 'I can show them to you if you wish.'

'No-one has seen this work in progress except the Queen herself. She would not wish it to be made public. It is a private piece. It is so newly finished that she had not yet had time to send for it, before . . .'

'Yes?'

'What do you think has happened to her? I fear the worst. Everyone is saying she has been murdered.'

'I do not know. But everything you tell me might help. Anything.'

I watched him carefully. There was a sudden, intense look of pain on his face.

'I sensed she felt she was in some kind of danger.'

'What do you mean?'

He paused, and looked at his restless hands as if they were two highly trained animals. 'A woman of her intelligence, her power, her beauty, her position . . . her popularity.'

'Is popularity a problem?'

'It is when you become more popular than your husband.'

Dangerous words. He looked at me, acknowledging the trust he was placing in me.

'It was Akhenaten himself who sent for me to investigate the Queen's vanishing.'

He gave me a quick look but said nothing more.

'It would help me greatly if I could see this latest work.'

'Would it? I see it might. Yes, if it helps. I'll do anything I can.'

We moved deeper into the heart of the house. Here it was cooler. Permanent shadows lay upon the walls and floors. At the un-distinguished door of what seemed a simple storeroom he stopped, broke the seal and untied the cord from the bolts. He pulled open the door, which was heavily built within a stone frame. He lit a lamp and we entered.

Inside, the room was lined with wooden or stone shelves, its walls constructed of stone blocks. The air was dry, dusty. Beyond the little penumbra of the lamp the room disappeared into pitch black. He lit sconces, and gradually, one by one, in the flickering light, dim shapes – cowled under sheets, some on shelves, others as big as human beings, children or adults – crowded the room. I felt I was in the Otherworld itself. Thutmosis set the lamp on a shelf and brought down one of the shapes. Reverently he set it upon a small circular table. Then deftly he slid the sheet off the form and revealed to us – a wonder. He revolved the table, showing us the figure from all angles, enjoying our astonishment.

I knew her at once. The hair was worn bold, under a dark blue crown. It gave her an exceptional authority. The poise was intelligent, powerful, self- possessed, with a remarkable equilibrium and purity. The skin had a bloom of life as if capable of changing expression, with the pale clarity of someone who lives always within the affluent protection of shade. High cheekbones, and a face of grace and sensibility. The lips red, strong, intense. And one eye: wide, complex, searching, proud, touched with a sense of humour so subtle as to appear and disappear as one looked into it, while the other remained as yet unpainted. And something else, too: hints of pain flecked through the power of the gaze. A secret of sadness, perhaps even suffering, it seemed to me, held in their depths. Did I imagine it? Could plaster and paint and stone reveal so much?

'Does that help?' Thutmosis asked.

'Yes. I'd know her anywhere.'

I could see he was pleased by the intensity of my reaction.

'And did she see it complete?'

'No, the eyes were missing. She was due to sit for the eyes. I always leave the eyes until last.'

The eye. It stared at me, into me, through me. That haunting smile. As if she was already living in eternity. I hoped not. I would not be able to bring her back from there.

The sculptor spoke again: 'There are other works here. Perhaps you would like to see them?'

I nodded, and he went about the room slowly drawing off the sheets to reveal image after image of the Queen. A life story figured in stone: a younger woman, her face less complete, less composed, but alive with the beautiful hesitant power of youth; the young mother sitting with her first child in her arms; Nefertiti on her inauguration day, coming into her power, into this new version of herself; a companion piece to a statue of her husband, her natural beauty a strange contrast to the weird, elongated proportions of his face and limbs. I moved among the images, seeing her from every angle, the lamp in my hand revealing the changing aspects of her many faces in the shadowy world in which they were kept. Khety remained by the door, as if afraid to walk among the living dead.

'What materials do you use to create these marvels?' I asked.

'Limestone, mostly. Plaster. Alabaster and obsidian for the eyes.'

'And the colours? How do you achieve them? They're so vivid, so alive.'

He stood behind the image, pointing with his finger, almost

but not quite touching the surfaces. 'Her skin is a fine limestone powder mixed with even finer red ochre, an oxide of some metal. The yellows are sulphide of arsenic, beautiful but poisonous. The green is a glass powder with copper and iron added. The black is charcoal or soot.'

'And from these powders and metals you create the illusion of reality.'

'You could put it like that. But then it sounds like make-up. This is its own reality. She will outlast us all.' He looked at his work with reverence.

'And have you produced similar images of Akhenaten?'

He shrugged. 'Only recently. In the early years he worked with another sculptor.'

'I've seen those statues. People found them very strange.'

'He knows we live in the Age of Images. He demanded to be seen differently to all the kings who came before. So the artists changed the ancient proportions. They made him taller than a man, tall as a god, and they recreated him as both man and woman, and more than either. Images are very powerful. Akhenaten understands this better than anyone. He knows images are a part of politics. He is the incarnation of the Aten, and the images have made him so, no matter how his mortal body appears. Art is not only about beauty. It is not only about truth. It is also about power.'

Then he slipped the dustsheet over the new piece, covering her eyes and those silent lips, and blew out the lamp.

He resealed the room and we walked back up the corridor in silence. Then I happened to notice something gleaming through an open doorway. Thutmosis saw my interest.

'Ah, my prize possession, the golden fruit of earthly success.'

It was a most magnificent private chariot. Built for ostentatious pleasure, it was exceptionally lightweight – one could easily pick it up with both hands – and of the most perfect design. Its shape – the wide, semi-circular, open-backed bent-wood frame, gilded with gold-leaf – was conventional, but the quality of workmanship and the materials of the fittings were superb. I walked around the vehicle, delighting in its perfections. I touched it gently, and the delicate construction responded immediately to my touch with a light, humming bounce.

'Can I offer you a lift back?'

There was only room for two. Khety in any case had to drive our own ramshackle contraption back, so he followed us, trying to keep up. The chariot was drawn by two magnificent little black horses – a rare pair – and Thutmosis drove at high speed. The leather mesh floor gave a marvellously smooth sensation to the ride, despite the ruts and stones of the way. The poised and elegant wheels whispered beneath us. For once I could hear the birds singing as we travelled through the light of the late afternoon.

He said, 'You feel you could almost reach the sky, eh?'

I nodded.

'I wish you luck in your great task.'

'I need it. I feel I am investigating images and illusions. The real thing eludes me at every step. I reach out to grasp her, and find that what seemed substantial is nothing but air.'

He grinned. 'It's a metaphysical mystery! I suppose a disappearance is just that. The questions are harder: why, not how.'

'There are reasons for everything, I believe. I just can't quite get to them. I have bits and pieces but I can't make out the connections yet. And this city doesn't help. It's intricate and strange, and everyone's playing a role so it's all charged up, but there's something about it I just don't like.'

He laughed. 'You have to go behind the appearances. It looks impressive, but believe me, behind these magnificent façades it's the same old story: men who would sell their own children for power, and women who have the hearts of rats.'

We rattled across a temporary bridge of planks laid across a spreading stream.

'What can you tell me about Mahu?'

Thutmosis glanced at me. 'He has great influence in the city

88

and much trust within the royal family. He is called The Dog. His loyalty is famous. And so is his wrath against those who fail it in any way.'

'So I believe.'

He looked at me carefully. 'I stick to my art. Politics and the like . . . a dirty business.'

'Isn't it the air you have to breathe here?'

'True. But I try not to breathe too deeply. Or I cover my nose.'

We rode in silence for a while, splashing through shallow streams that crossed the way, and entered the central city, all so neat in its arrangement, its ordered patterning. He dropped me at the crossroads. I had one more question for him.

'Would it be possible for a woman who looked very much like the Queen to have a place in the royal household, or in the city? Where would such a girl come from?'

'I've never heard of such a thing, but the only place such a woman could be kept in secret, if she were part of the city, would be the Harem. Perhaps you should look into it.'

'I'll do that.'

'Why do you ask?'

'Can't say, I'm afraid.'

He was about to move off, but a last thought stopped him. 'This city, this splendid and enlightened new world, this glorious future. It all looks glorious, but it's built on sand. Everyone's either determined or forced to believe in it to make it possible. But without her, without Nefertiti, it's not believable. It's not real. It won't work. It'll all fall down. She's like the Great River: she's what makes the city live. Without her we're back in the desert. Whoever took her knows this.' Then, with a practised flick of the reins, he rode off, his chariot flashing in the golden light.

I stood at the crossroads, the city like a strange sundial of bold light and powerful darkness as the buildings set their perfect angled shadows to Ra's ordered hours. The afternoon was changing into evening. The image of Nefertiti's face was strong now in my imagination. I held the scarab in my palm and looked at it again. The female Ra. I squinted at it, dazzling in the light, and offered a prayer of my own to the strange god of the sun whose swift journeys in his chariot were measuring out the little time I had left.

13

The reception was held by Ramose, Vizier to Akhenaten. Those considered influential and important enough to be invited from across the Empire had travelled for many weeks, by land and water, to make sure of their place and accommodations in the new city. Most had not made the mistake of leaving it too late to set out on their long journeys, fraught, even in our times, with danger and uncertainty. I could well imagine the preparations of the previous months: the slow exchange of letters and invitations, the negotiations about retinues and accommodations, the exquisite problems of hierarchy and status.

No-one who was anyone – and in this city being 'someone' seemed to be all that mattered – arrived on foot at the reception. And this, Khety told me, included ourselves, so we arrived in the ramshackle chariot. Its poor quality and condition was even more marked by the shameful contrast with the magnificent vehicles that thronged the packed thoroughfares and crowded ways, all of which made our progress excruciatingly slow; and as we neared the house we became trapped in a foul-mannered and angry logjam of chariots, sedan chairs and travelling thrones. Very important people, officials, servants and slaves shouted insults, commands and demands; everyone shoved for superiority. The noise, the heat, the sheer fury of it all was astonishing. The porters, verbally abused by their passengers, wrestled to free the poles of their carriages from those of competing chairs while also desperately trying not to risk a scratch on the immaculately buffed surfaces of their expensive vehicles. Horses whinnied as they struggled in their ebony traps; under their elaborate trappings they sweated, and their eyes swivelled, alarmed. Several wore the white-feathered plumes of high office, and some of the big men they were carrying stared malevolently out from their elevated chairs over the crowd. I had no idea who was who, and in the crazy jostling of the travelling lamps, faces and profiles appeared and vanished again before I could get a good look. It was like being at sea in an angry storm of fashion and vanity.

It seemed the other half of the city had also turned out to gaze at the silly, extravagant spectacle: men, women and children gawked like fools across the Royal Road from where they stood packed tightly in a great swelling crowd held back behind a single security rope, calling out prayers and requests, pointing out important figures, eating sugar cakes and swigging from beer jugs as if this was a show – which, clearly, it was. The elite in all their fashions, parading for their audience.

Finally our chariot drew up at, or rather was shoved up to, the raised platform. Khety shrugged. 'Shall we?' So we stepped out onto the carpeted reception area, lit by great hammered bowls of flaming oil. I was glad I had brought with me a spare pair of smart sandals and at least one decent change of clothes, but even the general level of refinery was extraordinary.

'I feel conspicuously unfashionable, Khety.'

'You look fine, sir.'

'I want to meet the key players. Make sure you introduce me. Especially Ramose.'

A worried look passed over his face. 'I can't introduce you to him. It wouldn't be appropriate.'

I would walk up to him myself then.

We passed through the stampede of the guard gate, our names having been checked, and emerged into a great colonnaded reception hall, open to the moon and the stars, crowded not only with thousands of people but also with great statues of Akhenaten and Nefertiti making offerings. Their icons looked down seemingly benevolently upon this society gathered in their honour. The noise was incredible. Musicians were mangling some sophisticated setting and competing with the roar of people trying to make themselves heard. Servants passed with sly hostility through the tangled thickets of elbows and shoulders and faces, offering complicated drinks and tiny refined dishes on trays. Khety snapped his fingers, but none of the servants took much notice, pretending not to have heard. Then a servant girl lilted past, her dress as insubstantial as smoke, and I grabbed two drinks in exchange for a brief smile. I handed one to Khety.

We were sipping these much too fast when an impressively rotund, competent-looking person with a large curious head, like a parrot pretending to be an eagle, emerged from the sea of figures, approached and offered a formal greeting. Khety stood back deferentially.

'I am Parennefer.' He smiled.

I smiled back. 'Rahotep.'

'Welcome to the Great City of Akhetaten. I know who you are. I am Overseer of all the Works in the House of Akhenaten. And I am delighted to meet you. I was informed of your presence here tonight, and I want to offer my assistance.'

'I didn't realize anyone knew I was here.'

'Everyone knows,' he said casually.

I introduced Khety as my Medjay associate and assistant. Parennefer nodded briefly, and Khety bowed his head.

'Let us find a quieter spot to talk,' he suggested with a little gesture.

'How about as far away from the musicians as possible?'

'You do not like music?'

'I like *music* very much.'

Parennefer admired my little joke with the superficial enthusiasm of a host at a party. We settled on leather benches. More drinks and little dishes were brought instantly and set down with flowers on a serving table. I reminded myself to drink slowly.

'So, what impression has our city made upon you so far?' he asked.

This called for diplomacy. If he was Overseer of the Works then he was responsible for the design of the buildings and the plan of the city. I did my best.

'It's quite a place. The architecture seems to me to respond beautifully to the possibilities of the light, and the space.'

He was carefully delighted. He clapped his many-ringed hands. 'God of the sun, a Medjay officer who appreciates buildings. You flatter me. It is the first time *ever*, I believe, that an architect has had the honour to design on such a scale, with a blank papyrus and a full treasury to draw upon. We have had to work quickly, of course. Akhenaten has a vision, and we toil to realize it.'

'Time is running short, I suppose, to have everything ready for the Festival?'

Suddenly his feathers looked ruffled. 'Not at all. Everything will be perfect.' And then he smiled deliberately, as if smiling would make it so.

I did not say: it seems to me you need another year to finish building the vision.

'I was at the Queen's Palace this morning. It seems she also has a vision. The construction seemed very unusual. I've never seen a house like it. Did you work on the design?'

'Yes! Oh, it was a marvellous commission, although the truth is she knows exactly what she wants, so it's a case of working out how to make possible the ideas she has. She's very radical, you know. She wanted it all to flow, and the roofs to float. She said to me, "Parennefer, we shall defy the laws of nature." Those were her words . . . very characteristic.'

The woman, it seemed, was perfect indeed.

'I have heard many fine speeches in praise of her qualities.'

94

'Everything you have heard is true. She is as beautiful as a poem. No, a song, for it has more expression and moves me more easily to tears. Her intelligence flows in every direction like bright water. She is not political in the way we tend to mean it these days. She understands power, but she is not in love with it. Although it is certainly in love with her. She rides her own chariot, you know. She's a very contemporary kind of person.'

My expression must have betrayed my reservations, for a cloud passed over his face. 'This is not sentimental praise. She really is remarkable.'

He watched my face. I tried to keep it still. We both waited. But it was my turn to speak.

'You understand why I am here?'

Parennefer tilted his head slightly. 'I think unfortunately everyone knows why you are here. There are few secrets within the city. Nefertiti has not appeared in public for several days. Occasions of worship, receptions for foreign dignitaries, the preparations and gatherings for the Festival – she has appeared at none of these. Her absence tonight is a cause for concern. These' – he gestured towards the crowd in the hall – 'are clever people. They pick up on everything. They notice even the slightest variations in ritual and etiquette; they can read the signs. They have little else to talk about, for this is a world unto itself. It is easy to believe that nothing and nowhere else exists. There is an enchantment to it, as if we live inside a beautiful mirror, gazing in at ourselves. But sometimes reality intrudes, doesn't it?'

'Does it?' I asked. 'It seems to have been kept at a helpful distance so far.'

'We cannot afford instability at this time, just as we are about to confirm the new order of things. The Festival must be perfect.' He opened his hands with a shrug, a kind of 'innocent' gesture that also managed somehow to be ironic.

'Can you introduce me to a couple of people? I need to meet the men around the Queen. Ramose in particular.'

He nodded.

We followed Parennefer into the roar of the crowd. He approached a tall, elegant, impeccably dressed man who was holding forth at the centre of a circle of male acolytes and female admirers. As we stood awaiting his attention, their curious, cool gazes passed over me, and they fell silent. Jewellery and ornaments glittered in the light of the lamps. These people were wearing enough treasure to finance a small kingdom; the cost of each outfit would have fed a working family for a year.

His proud, angular face stood in odd juxtaposition to the soft and subtle art of his clothes. So here was the man closest to Akhenaten. Here was the man who controlled everything in his royal names: foreign affairs, agriculture, justice, tax collection, building projects, the Priesthood, the army . . . Ramose was at the centre of all aspects of the management and policy of the Great Estate. Therefore he too must be deeply implicated in the Great Changes. He acknowledged me with the slightest inclination of his vain head, then casually named the people standing in the circle: his senior ministers, chief lawyers and accountants and their careful, artificial career wives with their tight wigs and caged smiles. Then he took me to one side and began a little inquisition.

'So, you are the seeker of mysteries?'

'I have that honour.'

'The Queen must be found and returned. Alive.'

'I have just arrived. It is early in my investigation.'

'Maybe so, but I imagine you know you don't have much time. We hear there is already a body?'

'It is not her.'

'So I hear. That is excellent news. Nevertheless, you are presented with an enigma. And she still has not been found. I mean, still you have not found her.'

He looked at me coldly. What could I say?

'You are reporting to our admirable chief of police?'

'I am reporting to Akhenaten himself.'

'Well, I am sure he is keeping a close eye on your progress, if that is not too positive a word.'

I could not resist. 'Of course, if the royal security had been good enough she would never have been taken. The Queen's Palace is hardly protected at night. Two guards and a couple of maids?'

He was angry now. 'The royal security is second to none. You have no right to question it. Just do your job and return her in time for the Festival.' And with that he turned away and rejoined his group of cronies.

Parennefer gathered up my elbow and steered me away. 'How did that go?'

'A charming man.'

'He's extremely important, and what's more, he is of the right view of things.'

'In what way?'

'He is deeply concerned for the stability of the new order, both domestically and in our foreign territories. He has much at stake in his public commitment to the Great Changes.'

'Then he must not be able to sleep at night.'

Parennefer was interrupted by an elegant man with an intelligent, open face who tapped him lightly on the shoulder.

'Ah, the noble Nakht. Meet our seeker of mysteries, Rahotep.'

We nodded respectfully to each other.

'Nakht has a wonderful garden here. It contains nineteen varieties of trees and shrubs.'

'Well, I have made a start,' the man said modestly. 'Green leaves, shade, a little pool of water, some vines, a few caged birds – and then I feel the world is not after all such a disaster. For a few moments, at least.'

I liked his tone as much as his face.

'I agree with you about the state of the world,' I said. 'But most people would say we are living in the best of times.'

'Then they're simply not thinking for themselves. In my opinion the great garden of this country is under threat from forces that are not being taken seriously, especially at the highest levels. There are powers within the court who are very focused on the making of this city and therefore the making of their own personal fortunes, and not at all concerned with the array of problems that face us in our time: a disaffected and confused population, an antagonized and disinherited ex-Priesthood, and then the little matter of the serious foreign troubles we are building up for ourselves along our borders to the north, and in our satellites and allied kingdoms. We have serious responsibilities there, and we neglect them at our peril. I've seen desperate letters from loyal vassals and garrison commanders describing assassinations of local leaders and vicious raids, and the crumbling of our authority. These leaders send us calls for urgent aid, support and renewed forces, but are they answered? No. We leave them to rot. Not only are innocent people suffering, not only is trade threatened, but the dominance of the King in these regions is being questioned and even tested. Our policy is one of non-intervention. But it is my belief that these little wars and skirmishes will not go away of their own accord. And a Festival is fine, if you want to hold a party, but it won't mean much in a year's time when the royal granaries are empty, the workers are unpaid and hungry, and the barbarians are knocking on the garden gate.'

We paused to absorb his words.

'Barbarians at the garden gate indeed.'

I recognized the cold sarcastic voice at once. Mahu joined us.

Nakht acknowledged him with the barest nod. 'Where's your dog, Mahu? At home, waiting up for you?'

'He doesn't like parties. He's happier in his own company.'

They were like mutually adversarial species: the elegant leopard of the noble intelligentsia and the lion of the lower ranks sharing the same habitat only by virtue of an agreement that could be terminated at any moment.

Parennefer, anxious to avoid confrontation, took the opportunity to announce his departure, effectively abandoning me to the charms of a man he must have known was not favourably disposed towards me. I would remember that.

'I expect we will meet again,' he said. 'It's a small world.'

'But I wouldn't want to have to paint it,' I said.

That was something my ex-partner Pentu used to say. I don't know why it came into my mind at that moment. Nakht laughed, but Parennefer just looked puzzled, shrugged, and then sailed off into the sea of conversation.

'It is encouraging to know we have a smart man on our side in these strange times,' Nakht said, turning to me. 'I hope we will meet again. Call on me for anything you need. Your assistant knows where to find me.' And then he too left us.

I was sorry to see him go. I felt I could trust him. And he could be a good friend on the inside.

Mahu stared balefully after Nakht's figure, then turned to me. 'You have a little fan.'

I shrugged. 'He seems a good man.'

'He is a noble. It is easy for them to be good. There is no effort in it. They inherit it, along with the power and the fortune.'

Neither of us spoke for a moment.

'You didn't come to see me with your news,' he said.

Of course I had not. This was deliberate. Nevertheless, I had flouted protocol and annoyed him. Again.

'I assumed Khety or Tjenry would report to you.'

'Who's the dead girl?'

'I don't know yet.'

I said nothing more, hoping he would go. But he just stared out at the people as if they were a herd of animals and he the hunter depressed by his lack of appetite.

'What do you make of all this?' he said, jutting his head at them.

'They're all trying to get by. We all have to swim in the same water.'

He gave me a brief, cynical look. 'Most of them don't know they're born. They think the worst that can happen is a slave stealing a handful of jewellery. While the rest of us are spending our lives keeping the deserts off their streets.'

'That's the job. Always more desert.'

99

'I want to know whose side you are on, Rahotep. I want to know what you think.'

'I'm not on anyone's side.'

'Then let me tell you something. That is the most dangerous position in this city. Sooner or later you will have to make a choice. At the moment, it seems to me you don't even know what the sides are.'

'That's what I'm here to find out.'

He laughed darkly. 'You'd better find out fast how things work, and who pulls what strings. Even your own. Good luck untangling them. And by the way, I've gathered a few friends together for a hunt on the river. Tomorrow afternoon. Do you hunt, Rahotep?'

I had to confess I did.

'Then I insist you join us. It will give me a chance to assess your progress.'

He patted me patronizingly on the back, and moved off with his predator's lope through the crowd.

I turned to look at Khety, who all this time had stood behind me ignored by everyone, and was surprised to see a flash of anger in his eyes.

'Take no notice, Khety. He's an old-fashioned bully. Don't let him get to you. Above all, don't be afraid of him.'

'Aren't you afraid of him? Just a bit?'

'I'm trespassing on his territory. He's a big old lion and he doesn't like that.' I changed the subject. 'Won't Akhenaten appear tonight?'

'I don't think so. I've heard he rarely appears at events after dark. And the invitations were issued in Ramose's name. But even so I'd have thought he needs to show himself to confirm there's not a problem.'

'Yet if he appears without the Queen that will only confirm the suspicions.'

I suddenly realized why the hall was so animated and noisy. It was as if the rules of the day – the worship for and respect of the new religion – were relaxing. And I felt like this too. Another girl was passing, and I intercepted her and took more drinks. I suddenly very much needed another drink. I drank it gratefully.

Khety gave me a look.

'What?'

'Nothing.'

Just then the orchestra concluded its excruciating labours and the dancers melted away. Trumpet blasts stopped the barrage of conversation, officials moved into formation, and all heads turned towards the raised platform at the centre of the hall. A herald announced him, and Ramose walked up onto the platform. The hall immediately fell silent. He stared about him for several moments before speaking.

'We stand together, tonight, in the new City of the Two Lands. A new city for a new world. Here we celebrate the Works and the Wonders of Aten. And over the coming days we shall welcome the arrival of kings, chieftains, heads of state, loyal vassals, officials and leaders. They are travelling here from across the Empire to pay rightful homage to the Great Estate of Akhenaten, through whom all things exist and in whom all recognize Truth. To those honoured guests who are already among us, I offer you welcome. To those of you granted the good fortune to reside here, in service of the Great Estate, I say: join me in that welcome. And to the world, which hears these words, I say, for Akhenaten and the royal family: worship the Aten, here in Akhetaten, the City of Light.'

There was a strange and uncomfortable silence at the end of the speech, as if more needed to be said, or indeed as if something else needed to happen, such as the appearance of Akhenaten and the family in the Window of Appearances. But there was nothing. I noticed people exchanging uneasy little glances with each other, communicating in the most careful way their responses to this dogma and to the discomforting tone, the odd flatness, of Ramose's delivery. Everyone knew someone was missing. Ramose descended from the platform to receive the offered congratulations of his officials. Slowly the level of noise restored itself, but this time with a different tone, one that spoke of speculation.

I had had enough for one evening. I needed to return to the office, to think, to sleep. I looked up at Nefertiti's statues again. *Where are you? Why have you gone just now? Have you been taken, and if so by whom? Or have you vanished – and if so, why? Who are you?*

Outside the hall, along the Royal Road, a number of citizens remained, still keen for a sighting of someone important. No-one took much notice of Khety and me, luckily, so we drove slowly away.

Now, as I lie here, I am considering the various strands of the evening. At my head stands the strange little icon of Akhenaten. I remember Parennefer's words: the city is a beautiful enchantment. But it does not seem so simple now. For all the language of light and enlightenment the same dark shades of human ambition, avarice and cruelty seem to reside here too, awaiting opportunities. It seems to me, suddenly, that Akhenaten is standing under the sun for fear of those night shadows creeping closer to him with every passing day. I too am now subject to the encroachment of these shadows. Mahu was right. I cannot yet disentangle truth from speculation, fact from fiction, honesty from lies.

I go to the window and look out at the bleak little courtyard. At least the heat has lifted a little. The desert makes this city tolerable by night; breezes cooled by the face of the moon move through doors and passages across our sleeping faces and into our restless dreams. Tomorrow I must pursue the identity of the dead girl. It strikes me I am investigating versions of possibility. I am pursuing copies in the hope of tracing their lost original. But at least I have my next move. The scarab and this journal I will place beneath my pillow on my headrest for safe-keeping. May the gods bless my children and my wife, and bring me to the new light of the dawn. Suddenly my love for them is singing in my breastbone like a stitch of pain.

14

I woke to an urgent knocking on the door. It was Khety. Something was wrong. It was still dark. We drove fast through the deserted ways, in silence.

I opened the door to the chamber of purification. It was very dark and very cold. I entered the room carefully, anxious to disturb nothing. I raised my lamp. The girl's shadowy body remained in the same position. The chilly air was tainted with decay. All the candles in their sconces had burned down. I walked slowly around the room, trying to observe everything, as is my method, breaking up the surfaces and spaces into squares, noting everything and moving on to the next. It was as I remembered it: the chests were closed, the implements in their places, the canopic jars on their shelves. The Sons of Horus stared down at me. I walked along the wall of empty, decorated coffins, holding up the lamp. Suddenly I leaped back: one was wide open. It contained a body, propped up like a bad scary joke.

Tjenry was upright in the coffin, his eyes open, a slight smile stuck on his bloodless handsome face. I waved the lamp over him and caught a strange glitter in his wide-open eyes. I looked carefully into them. Glass. I lowered the lamp. Something else was set on the floor at his feet. One canopic jar.

Khety and I lifted him out, with infinite care and sorrow, and set him gently down on a table. We could not look at each other. A few hours ago this thing of muscle and bone had been a young man of charm and prospects. In the glow of the newly lit lamps I examined every inch of the body. Apart from a loincloth he was naked, washed, clean. There were brutal red and blue gouges in the yellow and grey flesh of his wrists and ankles, and around his waist and chest. Over his forehead was a deep band of purple bruising. He had been bound down tightly. He had struggled greatly for life. There were also marks and little tears on his nostrils. I dreaded what I would find. I opened his mouth, stiff now like a trap, and pulled sticky red wadding from the cavity. What was left of the tongue was a chewed piece of meat, unrecognizable as the instrument of speech. I kept going, although my deepest wish was to walk from this room and keep walking, rather than go forward to the discovery I knew lay ahead. He had clearly been alive when all this was done to him. Everything pointed to an experience of slow, excruciating and terrifying agony. I looked up and saw the grim instruments of mummification hanging in the shadows on their hooks. I steeled myself and looked inside the canopic jar. His brain, mangled, torn and already tinged blue with decay, the organ usually thrown away, lay within, topped by his eyes on their bloody, torn strings.

I could barely believe it. Someone had bound him down, and while he was alive had removed his brain through his nostrils, as if he were already dead and ready for burial, using the iron hooks hanging innocently on the wall. It had been done meticulously, expertly. It had been done during the time we were at the reception, eating and drinking and talking. It had been done in this room.

I struggled to keep control of my feelings. I had seen bad things in my time. I'd smelled the sweet stench of human bone burning, and the steam from just-dead viscera rising from a gutted belly. But I had never seen anything like this inhuman enactment with its barbaric precision.

There was nothing now I could do for him. No prayers from the Book of the Dead would guard against the horror of this. I remembered that I had ordered him to remain behind. And now he was dead. I closed his delicate, cold eyelids over his strange, bright glass eyes. Khety and I left the room, with its appalling chill, and stood outside. The dawn was breaking. Birds were singing.

15

I commanded Khety to return to the Medjay headquarters to report the murder, while I waited. I needed time alone, before the shouting and the noise. I needed to think, even though my mind was emptier and more haunted than the Red Land. The images of what had been done to this promising young man stopped every thought in its tracks.

I watched the street wake up. An old man shuffled out of his dark doorway carrying a jug of water, which he poured tenderly around the roots of a sapling that had taken root in the earth. He seemed to have all the time in the world to accomplish his task. Then he picked up some of the broken rubbish from around the tree and threw it further into the street, and shuffled back into the darkness of his accommodation. Then the sun came up, and more people appeared, leaving their homes and going about their daily business.

Rage swept through me then – at myself for having let this young man die, at the waste of life, at the disgusting futility of this city, at the refined cruelty that had committed this crime. I knew, of course, that this act was aimed at me. It was as purposeful as the arrow on the boat. Whoever committed the crime wanted me to know they knew everything I was doing. They wanted me to know I was being watched closely. Also, they wanted me to know they could inflict worse things upon me if they so chose. There was something mocking in it, taunting. They were slowly and meticulously destroying the ground of authority under my feet. Soon I would be marooned on a tiny island of complete uncertainty. I had come to the city to investigate a missing person. Now I was investigating murders as well.

Mahu arrived, of course. He barely acknowledged me as he entered the chamber. When he came out, he inflicted the best of his fury on me. It was shaming, of course, in front of the other men, but I felt strangely immune. The facts of Tjenry's death made his noise and anger irrelevant and futile. Then he was gone again, with dire warnings and threats. He would inform Akhenaten. I hardly cared. I wanted to track down and trap this man, or woman. I had my own private revenge to drive me now. I needed to know what kind of human being could do such a thing to another. Was this person a monster, or did he or she have a heart and soul, blood and emotions, like the rest of us?

When everyone had gone, Khety and I sat together for a little while, not speaking.

'This is the worst thing I've seen in my life,' said Khety eventually.

'We've had two barbaric murders in the space of a few days. There's no reason to suppose they will stop here. There's every reason to suppose they are directly connected to our investigation. We're being followed.'

He nodded. 'And they're leaving no clues.'

'That's not exactly right. The manner of the deaths is telling a story. We have to work out what it is. And the next step is to trace the dead girl. I have an idea. We should ask in the artisans' village.'

'Why do you say that?'

'Because if she was a person of importance, her disappearance would have been noticed, maybe reported, by now. Someone in the city might have connected her to the murder victim. And we need to stop off on the way. I need to see the maid, Senet.'

The house was quiet when we arrived. The guards admitted us and we waited for Senet to appear. She bowed low to me.

'Can we go somewhere private?'

She showed us into an antechamber. As before, she was immaculately dressed, her hair covered, her hands in the little yellow gloves.

'I want to show you something. Please don't say anything. Just nod if you recognize it. Yes?'

She nodded. I opened my hand and showed her the scarab. Horror, rather than sorrow, descended on her face. Her hands trembled with shock.

'It is not quite what you think.' Her big eyes lifted, suddenly hopeful.

'Why did you not tell me the truth?'

'About what?' she asked breathlessly.

'That this scarab was missing from the Queen's jewellery?'

She tried to think quickly. 'Forgive me, but I did not know who you were. I mean, who you truly were.'

'You mean you did not know whether I could be trusted? As a Medjay?'

She nodded, grateful that I had said what she could not.

'I need to know if you have anything to say about this scarab.'

She looked at it. 'Please tell me, how did you come by it?'

'Someone else was wearing it. Another woman.'

She looked astonished. 'How could that possibly be?' she said, turning it over in her hands.

'I don't know. But I will tell you this. The woman who was wearing this once looked very like the Queen.'

She struggled to take in what I was saying. 'Once?'

'She is dead. I cannot identify her. Do you have anything you wish to tell me now?'

She suddenly looked away. 'This place is full of darkness.' She spoke the words with a new passion.

'Meaning?'

'People are animals, don't you think? The Queen says most people have good hearts. But I see their faces when they smile, when they say clever things, when they laugh at others' misfortune. I think the tongue is the monster in us all.'

'Why would you think that?'

'Because words have more power to wound and kill than knives.'

I left the thought to rest between us.

'Tell me more about this scarab.'

She held the thing in her delicate palm, tilting it this way and that. 'I see the possibility of new life. Proclaimed in eternal gold. The scarab beetle, least of all life forms, constantly renewing itself. Resurrection from the basest things of this world. I see the sun, from whom comes all creation, pushed back into new life in the claws of the beetle. I see the mystery of Ra's power contained in the dot at its centre. Like a child in the womb. I see a woman, the complete equal of the sun god in all things. I see this worn as a sign of hope. I feel it lying on warm skin, over a good heart.'

Suddenly she buckled, as if from a bolt of dreadful grief, and sobbed, her body racked with overwhelming emotion. Khety and I looked at each other, surprised. Then her agony passed, and she calmed herself. The little lapping sounds of the river meeting the terrace stones filled in the gap of silence between us. She waited for me to respond, her head bowed.

'You have spoken well,' I said. 'Nothing will be forgotten.'

I turned to leave but her hand reached out before I passed through the doorway.

'What about the children? I am sure they are miserable without their mother.'

'Where are they?'

'They've been taken to their grandmother.'

Her look of anxiety told me all I needed to know about what she thought of that arrangement.

'I will need to talk to them all. Do you want me to carry a message when I see them?'

'Please tell them I am here waiting at home for them.'

16

The artisans' village lay to the east of the central city. We drove as far as we could along the track. Ra, in all his glory – far too much glory for me – beat down mercilessly from his zenith. There was no relief anywhere. All shadows had retreated into their objects. Khety raised the parasol to protect our heads, and we drove on sharing the minimal relief of the shaky little circle of shade.

Various other tracks crossed our paths, radiating out into the eastern desert, some leading to the desert altars, others to the rock tombs and the security stations. Fatigued young men stood like shadow sticks at crossing points, and I could see, from time to time, tiny figures standing sentry at the border points of the city's shimmering territory – as much, it seemed, to keep the people in as to prevent incursions from the superstitious spirits and barbarians of the Red Land.

I pointed them out to Khety.

'The worst job of all,' he said. 'They're out there through the day with nothing more than a thin reed hut for shade. They're also guarding the tombs being cut into the higher levels of the hills.' He pointed up at the distant cliffs, white and red and grey, and I shaded my eyes in an attempt to see. They seemed uninhabited to me. 'They're working some way into the rock now. It's actually hotter the deeper you go.'

'How many tombs are being built?'

'I don't know. Many, I think. People who can afford it are putting a lot of their wealth into the projects.'

'So they must think it's worth the investment? They must think they're going to stay here and be buried here?'

'Yes, but also they need to be seen to think that.'

Such are the worries of wealth. This obsession with the dream of the afterlife sometimes strikes me as ridiculous. We will all vanish in the great light of the sun like flood water from a field, leaving nothing of ourselves but our children. And they in turn will vanish from life. I know how cynical I seem to others when I am like this. Tjenry's death had put me in this dark frame of mind. I remembered a verse of an old poem:

> *What of their places now?*
> *The walls have crumbled*
> *Their places are no more*
> *As if they had never been.*

It was not yet the hour of rest, and we had a little time to kill before the workers returned for their midday meal. The tension of Tjenry's death was still deep in my bones, and I knew action was the only remedy, so I decided to look at the boundary stones along the city's eastern edge.

Khety was reluctant. 'Don't you think it's too hot to go clambering up there?'

I ignored him, took the reins, and we drove on, Khety holding the parasol over my head. After maybe fifteen minutes following the now rough track, we abandoned the chariot and walked on across the dreary land until finally we clambered up some rocks and found ourselves at the foot of a huge new boundary stone carved from the living rock, and flanked by figures of Akhenaten and Nefertiti gazing out over their new land. I was sweating heavily; the linen was drenched on my back. We each took a draught of cool water from the flask Khety had thoughtfully brought with him. Then I began to examine the inscription, and slowly read it out:

Akhetaten in its entirety belongs to my father the Aten
given life perpetually and eternally –
of the hills, uplands, marshes, new lands, basins, fresh lands, fields,
  waters, towns, banks, people, herds, groves
and everything that the Aten my father causes to pass into existence
  perpetually and eternally

'That just about covers everything,' Khety said, staring out from our new vantage point.

We sat down together under our little shade and looked back across the wide and shallow plain. In the far distance we could just make out the river glittering through the trees and the city baked white and dry along its lush green banks. It looked unreal, a mirage. The temple banners hung down utterly lifeless in the midday stillness. The new fields – barley, wheat, vegetables – were a mosaic of greens and yellows inlaid into the dusty black of the fertile land. On the far side of the river, beyond the cultivations of the western shore, the dazzling delusions of the Red Land shimmered. I shaded my eyes, but there was nothing to make out there.

I asked Khety, 'Do you like it here?'

He gazed out over the landscape. 'I'm lucky. I've a good position. We're secure enough. We look after each other. And we've bought some land.'

'Do you have a big family?'

'I have a wife. We live with my father and my grandparents.'

'But no children yet?'

'We're trying. But so far . . .' He trailed off. 'I need a son. If I can't father a son, we can't continue our family's relationship with Mahu and the Medjay. It's the only way we can survive. My wife believes in charms and spells. She goes to some unqualified doctor who makes her believe that a concoction of flower-distillation and bat-shit, a full moon and a few offerings is going to bring us a boy. She even says the root of the problem is me.' He scowled and shook his head. 'Mahu offered to recommend us to the Doctor of the Palace. Someone who really knows about these things. But we feared the indebtedness.'

I decided to meet him as an equal in this new frankness. 'I have three girls. Tanefert, my wife, went crazy before Sekhmet was born. We were so nervous, worrying over every sign. She's not especially superstitious, but one night I found her pissing into two containers, one with wheat, one with barley. I said, "What are you doing?" and she said, "I'm going to see which one will grow, and then we'll know whether we're having a boy or a girl." Neither of them really grew, although she swore the barley was taller, so we expected a boy. Then Sekhmet arrived, yelling and beautiful and entirely herself.'

I heard a shout. Two young guards were looking up at us from below the rocks. We clambered carefully down. Both were young, maybe seventeen, both obviously bored out of their minds with nothing to do all day, every day, but throw stones, dream about sex and wait for the end of their endless shifts.

'What are you doing up there?'

I showed them my authorizations. They squinted at them. Illiterate.

'We're Medjay,' said Khety.

They backed off immediately. We walked back with them along the track to their tiny hut where they sat or slept on a reed mat. It seemed an inadequate thing next to the mighty claims of the boundary stone. They propped their weapons – two crude spears – against the door. There was a barrel of water, a jar of oil, a pile of onions and a torn but fresh barley loaf on a shelf.

114

They asked where I was from. When I told them I was from Thebes, one of them said, 'One day I'm going to go there. Take my chances. I've heard it's great. Things happening. Parties. Festivals. Plenty of work. Nightlife . . .' The other shifted on his feet, unsure, unwilling to meet our eyes.

'It's a great place,' I said. 'But it's hard. Watch yourself when you get there.'

'We're going anyway. Anything to get away from this miserable hole.' The quieter one looked alarmed by his friend's candour. His friend, emboldened, continued. 'We're going to join the new army.'

This was news to me. What new army?

'There's only one army,' I said carefully. 'The King's army.'

'There's a new man rising up the ranks. He sees things differently. He's going to make things happen.'

'And what is this new man's name?'

'Horemheb,' he said, with respect and even a touch of awe.

Then a faint call came from the next border post; the boys raised their hands in salute and yelled back. We left them there, with a brief farewell, and drove back towards the village.

'Have you heard of this Horemheb?' I asked Khety.

He shrugged. 'The Great Changes have opened up many new routes to power for men from the non-elite families. I've heard his name; he married the sister of the Queen.'

This was new information. A new army man who had married ambitiously into the royal family.

'So he will be attending the Festival?'

'He would be obliged to.'

I thought about all this as we rattled our way over the broken stones.

'And where is the Queen's sister?'

'No idea. They say she's a bit strange.'

'What do you mean?'

'I heard that once she cried for a year. And she rarely speaks.'

'But he married her anyway.'

Khety shrugged again. It seemed to be his habitual response to the way of the world.

In contrast to the sophistication and enormous scope of the central city, the artisans' accommodation was stark, functional and hurriedly constructed. There were several crude altars and little chapels built around the outside of the thick mud enclosure walls, among pig sties, stables and outhouses; domestic life carried on regardless in these chapels, with animals feeding in them and women cooking bread in ovens.

Khety and I entered through the gate. The houses seemed more or less identical: a small forecourt ran along the front of each dwelling, full of animals and storage jars, and beyond that was a higher, airy central room, with smaller rooms at the back. The architects of these repetitive shacks had failed to add stairs to the roof, so the occupants had built their own crazy zigzags using bits of old cast-off timber wherever they could find access. As in Thebes, the roofs were a vital part of the house. They were covered with trellises and vines, and fruits and vegetables were laid out in the sun to dry.

The houses ran in parallels, creating narrow lanes made narrower by piles of goods and materials and junk. Pigs, dogs, cats and children ran about under our feet, women yelled across at each other, a few sellers called their wares. Itinerants in stinking rags, cripples with rotten limbs and the hopelessly workless sat on their haunches in the shadows. We struggled to make our way between pack-mules and herds of men. The contrast with the classy green suburbs was overpowering, and I confess I felt at home for the first time in days. It was good to be back among the business, chaos and mess of normal life, and away from those highly considered and artificial precincts of power.

A few well-directed questions from Khety led us to the door of the Overseer. I knocked on the lintel and peered into the dark of the interior. A rough-looking giant, his tough face bristling with harsh stubble, glanced up from his table.

'Can't I even eat my lunch in peace? What the hell do you want?'

I stepped into the low, hot room and introduced myself. He grunted, and reluctantly invited me to sit down on the low bench.

'Don't stand watching while I'm eating. It's rude.'

Khety remained outside the doorway.

I sat down and looked him over. He was a typical builder made good: paunch resting on a powerful frame, gold collar around a thick neck, big hands that had worked hard all their life, broken, blocky nails packed into strong, stubby fingers, adorned with more cheap gold, that tore into the bread with need not pleasure. He ate continuously, mechanically, using all five fingers, feeding himself like an animal. Behind him, a woman's and a girl's face peered from behind a curtain that separated the room from the kitchen yard. When I glanced in their direction they looked intently at me, like stray cats, then vanished.

I showed him my authority. He could read it, as could many of these artisans, for they had to understand plans and building instructions, and carve hieroglyphics. He touched the royal seal and grunted, suspicious and, although he disguised it, alarmed.

'What does a person with written authority from the King want in a dump like this?'

'I'm sorry to interrupt your rest but I need your help.'

'I'm just a builder. What kind of help could I give a man like you? Or any of those performing monkeys that pass for our Lords and Masters?'

I liked his courage and his contempt. Something relaxed a little between us.

'I'm looking for someone. A girl. A missing girl.'

He carried on eating voraciously as he spoke. 'So why look here? No-one cares about missing girls, they're glad to be rid of them. Shouldn't you be down in the city?'

'I've a hunch her family might be living here.'

He pushed the bread towards me. 'Hungry?'

I took a piece and ate it slowly. I'd forgotten we'd had no food today.

117

'Tell me about this missing girl,' he said.

'She would be a young woman. Beautiful. She would have been raised to a position in the city.'

He wiped his hands and face. 'Not much to go on, is it?'

'Someone would miss a girl like her.'

'What colour are her eyes? What kind of face has she got?'

'Her face is missing. Someone beat it off her.'

He looked at me, whistled and shook his head slowly, as if this information just proved his theory of the way of the world. Then he stood up abruptly and gestured to the door. 'Come.'

The crowds parted swiftly along the narrow lanes to let us pass; this man was respected and feared. He was the Overseer, with the power to give and take away privileges, work and justice. He was as powerful as Akhenaten himself in this, his own domain. We came to the village's only open area, covered by colourfully decorated linen shades that threw patterns on the hard dirt floor and the benches that ran the length of the space. Hundreds of workers from all over the Empire, from Nubia to Arzawa, from Hatti to Mittani, sat talking, yelling and even singing in their own languages. All were eating quickly, helping themselves from large bowls placed along the benches. The sentry boys at the boundary stone were missing out on all this. Women moved up and down serving thick barley beer in bowls. The noise and heat were incredible.

The Overseer stood at the head of the central bench. He knocked his staff of office on the wood three times and the place was immediately silent. All heads turned in his direction, attentive but keen to get back to the business of eating.

'We have an important visitor,' he announced, 'and he wants to know if anyone's missing a girl.'

There was a brief ripple of laughter, but it died fast when the Overseer slammed his staff down hard again. Everyone looked at me to see who was asking this question, and why. I knew I needed to speak.

'My name's Rahotep, Thebes Medjay. I'm investigating a mystery.

No-one here's done anything wrong, but it's important to me to find the family of a girl who's missing. I believe she worked in the city but that she came from among you. All I'm asking is, does anyone know of a family who might be concerned about their daughter or sister?' The men stared at me. 'Anything anyone wants to tell me will be confidential.'

There was a total, hostile silence. No-one moved. Then a young man at the back slowly stood up. I led him to a space on a bench away from the crowd. The Overseer left us to talk, saying, 'I want him back at work in no time.'

We sat down opposite each other. His name was Paser. He had the hard, precise, honed physique of a skilled labourer, his hair locks white with dust, his hands already callused by the harshness of the stone that will be the most familiar thing – more than his wife's body, more than his own children – he touches all his life. But he looked back at me with eyes that seemed intelligent; perhaps not clever, exactly, but thoughtful and independent.

'Tell me about yourself, please.'

He looked suspicious. 'What do you want to know? Why are you here asking questions?'

'Why did you respond to my question?'

He looked down, his thick fingers crossed into each other. 'I have a sister. Her name is Seshat. We grew up in Sais, in the western delta, but the town was falling apart; nothing to do all day but sit around waiting for work that was never going to come again. So we all travelled here praying we could find employment. We were lucky. When we got here father and I found construction work because my father's a cousin of the Overseer, and Seshat went to the Harem Palace.'

Khety and I exchanged a glance. At last, an interesting connection.

'When did you last see her?'

'I'd rather not say.'

'Why?'

He hesitated.

'Nothing you say will go beyond these walls.'

'You are Medjay. Why should I trust you?'

'Because you must.'

He had little choice, and eventually he spoke. 'I've been working on new offices within the Harem Palace. Sometimes we were able to speak to each other. We'd find a quiet corner for a few minutes . . .' He paused. 'We used to see each other several times a week. We made an arrangement. But the last time she didn't appear. I thought she might just be busy. She always sends my parents something every week. But this week . . .' He shook his head. 'Where is she?'

He took me to his parents' house. They shuffled about, uncertain of the seating or standing protocol, awkward in my presence. In the back room, the grandparents worked. They nodded politely, and returned to their tasks. I was glad to notice the old gods were still displayed in the family shrine: amulets of Bes and Taweret, and statuettes of Hathor – the old protecting deities of the family, fertility and festival. The new religious iconoclasm had not yet conquered this little home.

The father, a middle-aged man, began talking about his daughter, his treasure: how well she was doing, the way her beauty and grace had given her a new opening in life in the Harem Palace. His pride. His joy. Their bright future. And all the time, although I could not yet be sure, I sensed in my bones that this man's daughter was lying dead, brutalized, destroyed for eternity, on a slab. I saw the mother at the curtain, her face confused with worry at my presence, and at these questions. But I had no proof, and that was what I was here for. I could not be swayed by arguments of emotion, not now.

'And you haven't heard from her for some little time now?'

'No, but she's busy, you see. We can't expect it. No doubt working too hard! They do work them hard, I know.' The father smiled uncertainly.

'I have to ask you a personal question. Does she bear any birth marks? Any marks on her body?'

The father looked puzzled. 'Birth marks? I don't know. Why are you here, asking all these questions? Why is a Medjay officer sitting in my home asking questions about my daughter?' He now looked frightened.

'I hope to find her.'

'If you want her, why don't you go to the Harem Palace and ask for her there?'

'Because I am afraid she is not there.'

The truth was beginning to dawn on them. The mother stood, struck silent and still as a statue, at the entrance to the room. Slowly she pointed to her belly.

'She has a scar, like a little star. Here.'

I left that house in a silence from which I knew it would never recover. The father's gentle face had broken open as surely as if I had smashed it with a rock, wondering why I should have come into his home to ruin the contentment of his old age. The mother's refusal to believe any of this was real. The son's bitterness would refine itself, over time, into a pure hatred of the gods that had permitted the vicious destruction of an innocent life. I told them only that she had been murdered; I failed to find the courage to tell them the rest. But I promised to have the body returned to them for proper burial. All I could leave them with, besides this agony, was the scarab. I could only hope it would cover the costs of a good burial and all the necessary rituals. And after all, as far as I was concerned it belonged to the girl. The least I could do was help to make sure she would not be left to rot in some desert grave, not after what she and her kin had suffered already.

We drove away from the now silent village. Eventually I broke the silence.

'At least we have an answer, Khety. Something we know we know.'

'The dead girl's connection with the Harem Palace.'

'Exactly. Take me there right now. I'll need to interview everyone.'

'We have our authorities, but we'll have to inform the Office of the Harem first.'

I sighed. Was nothing simple?

'There's no time to waste. Come on, let's go.'

Khety squirmed like a child caught lying.

'What?'

'Perhaps you've forgotten? The invitation?'

And then it struck me. From Mahu. To a hunt. This afternoon. I cursed my stupidity in accepting.

'Here I am, with the first decent lead we've had in days, and you think I am going to waste time on a hunt? With Mahu, of all people?'

Khety shrugged.

'Stop shrugging! We're going directly to the Harem Palace.'

Khety looked uncomfortable, but did as I ordered and drove back into the city.

We were just entering the outer precincts when suddenly from a side street, out of nowhere, Mahu appeared driving his own chariot. His ugly dog, as obvious a symbol of a man's soul as ever I saw, stood with its paws up on the sill beside him.

I turned to Khety, furious. 'Did you tell him where we were going?'

'No! I don't tell him anything.'

'Well, you work for him, and here he is, just as we're on the trail of something at last. It seems like a strange sort of coincidence, doesn't it?'

Khety was about to bite back when Mahu yelled over at me, 'Just in time for the hunt. I'm sure you hadn't forgotten.' He jerked his reins viciously, and charged ahead.

17

The hunting party gathered at the main jetty of the river – a long, narrow construction of newly laid timber boards on supporting piles of stone and wood built out perhaps fifty cubits from the land, and perhaps five hundred cubits in length. A few cargo barges carrying stone blocks were being unloaded, and a squat, crowded ferry was setting sail across the river with its cargo of men, children, animals and coffins, between the east and west banks. But otherwise at this hour of the afternoon there were just pleasure-boats – one particularly elegant, with a double-storey cabin, which I had not seen before – with their masts down and resting on their stands. Among these drifted a number of skiffs with small linen sails dyed vivid blues and reds. The chimes and peals of cultivated conversation and laughter tinkled and lilted on the travelling waters.

The sounds coming from the hunting group were different. The voices were assertive, masculine, testing themselves against a kind of underlying silence, a palpable tension. A typical group of young men from elite families, together with a handful of Medjay officers. All swagger and machismo, all standing on their hind legs, the mood hyped up and belligerent.

Khety tried to insist again that he had had nothing to do with Mahu's intervention. I could not credit it. 'I had begun to trust you,' I said, and walked off towards the group of men. My feet felt as heavy as river mud. I was trapped by protocol, just when I needed to follow the new lead.

Mahu introduced me. 'Glad you could join us,' he added, with heavy sarcasm. Here was a man who made everything he said sound like a threat.

'Thank you for the invitation,' I said with as little enthusiasm as possible.

He ignored me. 'I hear you've been scratching around in the workers' village. You've a missing woman and a dead officer on your hands. Time is ticking.'

I wasn't going to give him anything. 'It's surprising how things apparently unrelated to each other are in fact deeply connected.'

'Is it? Perhaps you can deeply connect your aim with a flying duck, if nothing else.'

A condescending ripple of amusement rang out from the other men. I looked around their gathered faces. They all wore imitations, more or less successful, of Mahu's lion grin. All dressed up in pristine hunting outfits, they looked like they were going to a fancy dress party. Their muscles had the appearance of vanity, not work. Hunting for them was a pastime, an amusement. Necessity, that simple and true god, had never visited them. The angle of the sun exaggerated the shadows of their haughty faces. Here were heads of offices, scions of Great Families, all members of the power elite.

Although I have made clear my hostile opinions about the Great Changes, even I must admit that one of the consequences is the way they have opened up new possibilities of advancement to a wider social spectrum. People such as myself. I am from a so-called 'ordinary' family. Yet how inadequate that word seems to the truth it contains:

people caring for each other, improvising ways to get by, to enjoy their pleasures, to live well. These elite families, son after father, father after grandfather, have held on to the offices of earthly power and the locked stores of riches of our land for as long as time has trickled through the water clock. They have held on to it as if it could protect them from everything. And in truth it does – from poverty, from most kinds of fear, from want, from the diminished or destroyed horizons of a life's possibilities; from powerlessness, from humiliation, from hunger. Yet not from the suffering and vulnerability to misfortune that affect us all as a necessary part of being human.

Mahu interrupted my thoughts, as if reading them. 'Well, time flies. Let us take to the boats. Good hunting.'

We walked over to a group of papyrus-reed boats. Servants stood ready to attend us on the hunt, their own skiffs already prepared. I had grown up sailing these lovely craft – so simple and so elegant. We partnered up. Khety appeared at my side looking anxious, but just as he was about to step onto the boat beside me, one of the men from the group stopped him with a rudeness that amazed us both. But I had no wish, in any case, to waste the next hour with Khety whining in my ear. The stranger introduced himself as Hor. He had with him his cat on a leather lead. It leaped at once to the front of the boat, and sat down, washing its front right paw, glancing at me expectantly, critically.

Hor, who seemed uninterested in conversation, produced a superb bow from a linen carrying cloth. He tested the tension of the bowstring with the thumb-ring. The fine threads – probably around sixty for a weapon of this quality – were neatly joined at each end to loops of tightly twisted sinew – a marvellous way to avoid fraying. I found, in a wooden box, a carved throwing stick I could use myself, as of course I possessed none to bring with me. There was also a weighted net and a spear in the box, in case we caught anything bigger. All pretty basic, and nowhere near as powerful as the costly sophistication of the bow.

As Mahu gave the signal and we moved in silence out onto the wide river, as smooth and rippling as a banner in a light breeze, towards a reed marsh further north along the river from the city, I was already desperate for the hunt to be over. The cat remained poised and keen on the prow, mesmerized by the far songs and hidden calls of the marsh. Soon the city disappeared behind the wide, tree-lined curve of the river. The eastern cliffs, where the tombs were being built, rose up on our right-hand side to form a high natural barrier to the river's course, but to the west the river widened and flattened into water marshes and thick, dark papyrus forests. Birds pitched their warnings as they drifted, circling in the high light.

The skiffs silently, one by one, entered the tall stands of the motionless green and silver reed marsh, and disappeared. As I punted along, I tried to keep track of the others; it was hard to keep one's gaze steady among the flickering verticals of the reeds. The hunting cat was up on all fours, pacing about its little territory in the bow, its head rising up to scent the air. Hor stood up, preparing his bow and glancing alertly through the reeds, as if looking for something. I looked back and saw, briefly, Khety some considerable distance behind me. He was trying to track my progress. I slowed my pace. He raised a hand, trying to signal, but then he disappeared again behind the dense forest of the reeds. Hor said gruffly, 'Don't lose the pace. We don't want to miss the fun.' I looked down to make sure the nets and throwing stick were near to hand.

Suddenly we came into a clearing among the reeds, and there were all the other skiffs balanced on their own reflections which stretched and wavered then came to rest. I saw Mahu, standing in his boat, observing the reeds and the sky. All was silent. Everyone listened.

Then he beat a pair of clappers together, shouted the hunting call, and the evening air filled with the sound of thousands of birds taking to the skies. Everyone hurled their sticks at once, tens of them whirring into the pandemonium of the suddenly risen flock, and those who possessed bows let their arrows hiss into the chaos. I took some kind of aim and threw my stick. The cat went crazy, dancing like a mad thing. There were shouts and cries, the skiffs separated to follow the hunt,

126

and then the great air was filled with the flutter and thud of bodies tumbling down to splash into the water. The cat appeared from among the reeds with its catch, a bloodied duck, in its mouth. The iridescent colours of the feathers were marked with blood under the wings, but otherwise it seemed perfect in its moment of death.

I ducked down to grasp a spear. We had entered another forest of reeds. Suddenly I could see nothing of the other boats.

I looked up and found myself face to face with Hor. His bow was pointing directly at me. It was drawn back, and an arrow tipped with silver, and bearing the hieroglyphs of the Cobra and Seth, I now noticed, was poised in its tense embrace.

'You missed me last time,' I said.

'I meant to.'

'That's what they all say.'

He was not amused, and tightened the bow's tension. He could not miss me now, and he smiled. I held my breath. I thought: you idiot, to walk into this trap. This would appear a sorry accident, as if I had been cut down by an unlucky hunting arrow as it fell back to earth.

Then, suddenly, he fell sideways – from nowhere a throwing stick knocked him down. His arrow flew off with an almost comic twang into the reeds. I struggled to keep my balance, and almost fell into the water. Khety came into view, gesturing in fear. Hor stirred in the bottom of the boat, groaning and clutching his head. There was blood on the reed floor. I threw the weighted net over him, and as he tried to rise I pushed him over the edge and into the water where he thrashed and struggled, enmeshing himself ever deeper in the fine labyrinth of the net. I had no choice. I cast the spear deep into his chest, pushing him down under the surface. The spear met the tension of solid muscle, the resistance of bone. I stabbed and thrust again, and this time the blade passed right through into his body and out the other side. I drew it back and got ready to strike again, but it was not necessary. Even under the water he looked amazed, then dis-appointed. The water blurred, clouded red, then he slowly swung over onto his front.

I turned the skiff around and began to sail for my life. I glanced back. The body bobbed just beneath the water. The reeds slapped into the prow and my face. Luckily I was lighter by one man so my pace was faster now. I saw Khety again, also alone on his boat, ahead of me. I gestured for him to keep going. Behind me I saw Mahu turn to look in my direction; then came shouts and calls. I disappeared again into the hissing reeds. The cat worried and danced away at the dead bird, guiltily snatching little mouthfuls of feathers. I was gaining distance, drawing closer to Khety. He gestured to me to be silent as from the river came the sound of more boats, and the louder sound of men calling. I had to assume that accomplices in this new assassination attempt were among these men, and indeed that Mahu himself had sanctioned it. No wonder he had been so insistent on my presence.

We moved deeper into the marsh. I motioned to Khety to slow down. Among a thicket of reeds we came to a stop and waited, barely daring to breathe, listening. I could hear the boats coming towards each other, and then the calls of warning and recognition as they appeared through the reeds. Moments of discussion followed. They decided to split up and fan out to search the marsh. I glanced around me. It was growing dark and becoming impossible to be sure which way lay the shore, and whether we could save ourselves upon it.

I wrestled the dead bird from the cat's reluctant mouth, its damned claws scratching my wrists, and broke open the bird's neck. Quickly I smeared the blood along the floor and the side of the skiff, and threw the body away. The cat glared at me with spite and anger at the waste, and began howling and sniffing the blood to see what could be saved. Then I motioned Khety towards me and climbed over onto his boat. As quietly as I could I pushed my skiff away into the reeds with my foot. It slowly disappeared into the rising mist, the cat on the prow staring balefully back at me.

We poled the skiff as silently and as deeply as we could into the dark reed forest and sat waiting.

'Good throw,' I whispered.

'Thanks.'

'Where did you learn that kind of accuracy?'

'I've hunted all my life.'

'Luckily for me.'

Then we heard it: the reeds parting stiffly to allow a skiff to pass. It was no more than twenty cubits from us. We could see nothing. I tested the bow, prepared an arrow. The bow's pure energy sang beneath my fingers. We waited, our breath held absolutely silent. Then came an urgent exchange: they had found the bloodied boat. We crouched down and waited for fate to take its course. Would they take the bait? We could hear them talking, as if they were in the next room. Then their voices gradually faded as they moved away, taking the other boat with them.

We sat there for a long time, still as crocodiles. Gradually the voices and the night lamps of the boats faded into the darkness, and we were left alone with the noisy evening life of the marsh, the newly appearing stars and, luckily, an early-risen half-moon: there was enough light in the sky to help us home, and the lengthening shadows would be our disguise.

'Thanks for saving my life,' I said.

I could tell Khety was smiling, pleased, in the dark.

'It seems that someone dislikes me here, Khety.'

'I didn't tell Mahu anything. Believe me.'

This time I decided I did.

'But why would he take such an obvious risk? Surely if he wanted me out of the way he would have found a subtler way to do it than inviting me on a hunt.'

'He's not that bright,' Khety said, with some kind of pleasure.

'Let's head back.'

'And then what?'

'Pick up the trail. The Harem. A night visit.'

18

The city came into view, its pale new buildings gleaming in the moon-light, the desert around it dark but for the cliffs and boulders lit by the same light, as if giving back what the sun had granted by day.

We jumped ashore into the shadows near the harbour. Khety led the way, keeping to the moonless side of the passages and thorough-fares. 'There are three royal palaces,' he said, 'the Great, the North, and the Riverside. The Great contains the main women's quarters.'

'And where does Akhenaten sleep at night?'

'No-one knows. He moves between the palaces, according to the Duties of the Day. He shows himself to the people as he progresses between temple worship, official business and receptions. I suppose he has sleeping quarters in each palace.'

'It's a hard life.'

Khety grinned at me.

We crossed the Royal Road and came to the Great Palace. It was enormous, a long structure that ran along the western side of the road.

At the main gate stood two guards. 'We're in luck,' said Khety quietly. 'I know them.'

'This is a bit late for you,' said the younger one, clapping Khety on the shoulder. 'Still working? And who's this?'

'We've business on the authority of Akhenaten.'

There was a moment of uncertainty between the guards.

'Your permissions?' said the older one.

I took them from my case without speaking.

He glanced over the papyrus, and shook his head slowly as he puzzled over them. Eventually he nodded. 'Go on then.' He looked me over, noting the bow. 'You must leave that here. No unauthorized weapons in the palace.'

I had no choice but to hand it over.

'Take care of it. You realize its value, I hope?'

'I'm sure it was very expensive, sir.'

And with that we passed into the palace's main court, contained by high mud-brick walls. The court itself reminded me of the columned halls of Thebes, except that this was open, with small groves of trees planted within. Khety knew where he was going, and we moved ahead through the shadows cast by the moonlight, trying to be as silent as the proverbial thieves.

'This place is enormous!' I whispered.

'I know. In the centre are the Halls of the Festivals and the private shrines. The north side consists of offices, residences and storerooms. In truth, everyone complains about the accommodations. They say everything's too small and it's all falling apart already. The plaster's cracking and crumbling, and the insects are everywhere. They say the wood is cheap, painted to look expensive, and it's already a feast for the beetles.'

Through hall after columned hall, we made our way onwards. Everything seemed deserted, silent. Sometimes we heard faint voices, and once we hid ourselves behind a stone column while a trio of men passed by, deep in earnest discussion. Many other rooms gave off the central halls, but all seemed uninhabited.

'Where is everyone?'

Khety shrugged. 'The city is built for a great population. Not everyone is here yet. Many have yet to be born who will inhabit these halls and offices. And don't forget, they're anticipating a huge influx of people for the Festival.'

We came to the edge of a lovely courtyard garden, rich with cool night scents. I looked down and saw that the floor had been painted with a matching scene depicting a pool surrounded by blue and silver marsh flowers and plants.

'Here we are again, walking on the water.'

Khety looked down. 'Oh yes,' he said, surprised.

'What is it with these people and their river scenes?' I asked.

'Aten's creation. They need to see it everywhere.'

We walked across it anyway, and came to a great door. It was beautifully panelled, and within it was a smaller door, and within that a smaller shutter the size of a little window. The mural beneath our feet showed nothing but still water. Khety knocked quietly on the shutter. We waited, and again I experienced the prickling sensation that we were being watched. I looked around. There was nothing to be seen. Then the shutter was opened from within.

'Show your faces,' said an odd, strange-pitched voice.

Khety gestured for me to approach the shutter, and as I did so a strong light shone directly into my eyes. Then the little door swung open on silent hinges and a patch of light fell onto the floor. I stepped into it, and through the portal.

Inside, the light continued to dazzle me. I held my hands up to shield my eyes. I seemed to see now a multiplication of little lights, a repetition of small moons, all shifting about. Suddenly I realized they were decorated papyrus lanterns bobbing and turning on slender reed stems. And holding these lanterns were girls. Pretty young girls. The lantern directly in front of me was lowered and I saw a face, large-boned but elegant, with painted lashes and mouth, and skin whitened thickly with powders. And a body dressed in the most elaborate costume yet belonging, in stature, to a prize-fighter or a cart-driver.

'It's rude to stare,' she said. The voice matched the body, not the face.

'Forgive me.'

'I appreciate your *interest*.' She slurred the last word as if she were licking it off a plate.

'Good evening. We're with the city Medjay. We need to interview the women of the Harem.'

'At this hour?'

'It doesn't matter what time it is.'

She looked annoyed. 'Which women do you mean? We have all kinds of women here: seamstresses, dressers, women of the right hand, dancers, musicians, right through to the foreign parties. I don't think any of them would want to see you at this hour.'

'Oh? Let's see. I know one of them is missing. Vanished. A very special girl. A kind of mirror. Her sisters will know what I mean. They must be worried. Frightened, probably. It's worse not to know what's happened, don't you think?'

She looked at me intently, her big face furrowing. And then she let us in.

'She's a eunuch!' whispered Khety.

'I know,' I whispered back. I've seen everything Theban nightlife has to offer, all the lower depths of the clubs and dens, and the other places men go to realize and enact their most secret desires. Boys as women, women as men, men with men, women with women.

She walked ahead of Khety and me and the girls followed, giggling and whispering, their lanterns jiggling and bouncing as they skipped along. What with the strangeness of the surroundings and the constantly dancing lights and shadows, I soon lost my sense of direction as the passage turned left, right, right, left . . . We walked ever deeper into this dark labyrinth, passing empty reception rooms full of unoccupied couches and heaped cushions, low workrooms where little figures sat hunched, stitching by close lamplight and ruining their eyesight, silent laundry courts where washing bowls were stacked and white linen dried on endless racks, shut offices, and dark sleeping quarters where tired women came and went in different states of dress, their hair down. The eunuch stepped lightly, elegantly, ahead of us, occasionally glancing back slyly to make sure we were still following.

At last we came to another door. The girls gathered around us, their lanterns and chatter finally resolving into stillness and quiet.

'We can go no further. We are not permitted.'

The eunuch knocked at the door, whispered urgently, then ushered me in. Khety was not allowed to follow. The last I saw of him he was standing in a pool of light with a sad entourage of pretty girls smiling up at him. Then a thick curtain was drawn across the portal, and he was gone.

'Good evening.' Her voice was light, amused, intelligent. 'Forgive the girls, they're silly and over-excited. We don't usually see visitors at this hour, but I've been expecting someone.'

She was dressed in a pleated outfit, the whole garment seeming to shape itself to her body, giving prominence to her naked right breast, which was beautifully displayed. Golden sandals on her immaculate feet, her shining and perfumed hair hanging loose. She looked not unlike the woman I had seen carved and painted everywhere in the city.

Her name was Anath. We were in a comfortable entertaining room, with elaborately wrought high-backed wooden chairs inlaid and gilded, and finished with lions' feet. On a stand between us lay a board set out for a game of *senet*, the board itself a beauty, its thirty squares decorated with ivory.

'Do you play?' she asked.

'At home. With my wife and my daughters. My oldest is smarter than me. She beats me often now. She remembers all the moves, she thinks through every permutation, and she almost always throws exactly what she needs.'

'Girls are more intelligent than boys. They have to think for themselves from the day they are born.'

We sat down, and I told her everything. As I spoke, a few other women gradually drifted out of the shadows and into the room, one by one taking up positions in chairs and on heaped cushions to listen to me. I tried to focus, to attend to the face of the woman before me. She was listening intently.

There was a shocked silence, then a murmur of sorrow, and little gasps of grief from around the room. I looked up now at the other women, six in all. Suddenly I too felt as if the world had lost its balance. As I looked from face to face, gathered now in the flickering light of the lamps, it seemed I had wandered by mistake into a room of living mirrors. For these women, though different from each other in slight details, looked more or less identical. In their poise and their profiles, they could all pass for the same person. The Queen.

Eventually Anath spoke. 'We are raised here, sometimes from girlhood, in this harem within the Harem, because we were all born with one gift. There are other offices in the Harem Palace serving different purposes, but here, the spirit of the Queen's perfection is reflected, however dimly, in each one of us, and we labour and struggle to bring those elements of ourselves – our eyes or our noses, the length of our legs or the sound of our laughter – that are not quite like her into a closer harmony. This is a great purpose, wouldn't you agree?'

I did not know what to say. 'But why?'

'To protect her. To pass for her when she needs us.'

I looked at them all, unbelieving. 'Is she here among you now? Is the Queen one of you? If she is hiding here, please come forward. I will bring you safely home. I swear.'

I looked around the silent faces in the still light of the candles. I was desperate, in truth, to recognize her, for her to step forward and say, 'You have found the Queen. Your search is over.' But no-one moved. I realized they were all terrified. They looked anxiously at Anath, who looked confused.

'Why would she be among us?' she said.

'Because she has vanished. I have been sent for to find her and return her to safety.'

The silence in the room became more concentrated.

'Please, tell me: what happened the night Seshat disappeared?'

'Three nights ago,' Anath began, 'a sealed message came from the Queen. There were detailed instructions. It was imperative that no-one, including ourselves, should know of their contents.'

A second woman spoke: 'We thought nothing of it. It was not unusual to receive such a command from the Queen.'

'The instructions were particularly for Seshat,' Anath continued.

'And who brought the message?'

They looked at each other, and Anath shrugged. 'We do not know. From the moment we walk through the door, all is secret. Of course we can describe everything to each other afterwards, when we return. But not this time. For Seshat never returned.'

When I described the scarab amulet, they knew nothing of it. It did not seem to have belonged to Seshat. I was still glad I had given it to her grieving family.

'What sort of men would destroy our sister with such terrible brutality?' asked one of the women.

Another voice spoke up angrily from the back: 'What sort of men would want our Queen herself murdered?'

'That is what I am trying to discover.'

'Some sort of monster,' said one.

'No,' said another, 'there are no monsters. Only men.'

I bade farewell to the hall of strange women. Anath took me by the arm and led me out along a dark avenue of sycamore figs to the furthest edge of a garden lit by the moon, and by many lamps. At the head of a pool was a statue of Nefertiti. She stared, all-seeing, all-knowing, across the dark water at her feet. We sat down for a moment on a bench, listening to a solitary night bird.

'Where I live, within the Harem, we have little contact with the outside world,' Anath said after a short while. 'I know people think the Harem is a place of desire and mystery, and perhaps for some it is. Perhaps they imagine the things they would like to find in the secret world of women. But it is not like that for those of us who live here. We have our dedications, our daily rituals, our tasks. Sometimes I have felt like a bowl of silence, untouched, undisturbed by the outside world. But your news has destroyed my tranquillity. That bowl is cracked now. What an illusion it all was, that this world is kind and good.'

What could I say to her? There was no purpose in telling her that in my experience violence was buried deep within each one of us, a potential written into our very bones, something we shared even with the gods.

'I don't know what will become of us if the Queen too is dead,' she continued. 'If someone would murder the Queen herself, then what will they do to us? What good would we be to anyone? Who would want us? We would be nothing more than pale reflections of the dead. We will be spirits trapped in life.'

'I do not think the Queen is dead,' I said. 'I believe she lives.'

'May the gods prove you right.' She sounded relieved to hear my words. She turned my hand over in hers so that the palm faced upwards. 'I think I see something here.'

I felt myself seizing up inside. I cannot abide the nonsense of fortune-telling and horoscopes, all that silly business of spells and potions and mumbo-jumbo. Seeing patterns and meanings where none exist. It goes against my training and my instincts.

She must have sensed this at once, for she smiled and said, 'Don't worry, I am not going to tell your fortune like a market-place prophetess. All I want is to say what I feel. That you are a good man. That you want to get home.'

I felt like a piece of faience that has suddenly been caught by sunlight. Ridiculous. The white statue of Nefertiti, still meditating on the black pool at her feet, ignored us. 'May she protect you on your journey,' she said, quietly, as if she knew already that I would have to travel into much darker places before I could finally, if ever, reach that longed-for place that seemed to recede with every step and every day.

'I won't forget you,' I said.

She smiled ruefully, then opened the doorway back into the main Harem building. I stepped through it. The ghost of her scent stayed with me for a moment, then disappeared.

19

Khety was waiting for me on the other side. I asked him to take me to the house of Nakht, the noble. We arrived there without being seen. The street, in the south suburb, was shadowy and silent, the dark villas and estates secure and hidden behind their high walls. The air was thick with heat. Nothing stirred. I knocked quietly on the door. Quickly, it was unlocked, and Nakht's kind face, not the porter's, appeared. He looked tremendously relieved.

'It's the middle of the night and you open your own door,' I said.

He gestured for us to enter, and we passed through into the sanctuary of his house without speaking.

We sat in his garden, around a single lamp. The scents of strange flowers hung richly in the warm night air.

'Can anyone observe us?' I asked.

'No. I built this place for privacy.'

The walls were high, and the frogs around the pool talked louder than we did. He poured some wine.

'I'm honoured to offer you some sanctuary.'

'It will just be for one night.'

He inclined his head. 'So you survived Mahu's hunt. Apparently you were the intended duck.'

'Is my demise the talk of the town?'

'It is indeed. It has contributed to the feeling that no-one is in control any more. First Nefertiti. Then the young Medjay officer. Now you. Everyone is convinced she has been murdered. And the city is obviously still unprepared for this ill-conceived Festival. The entourages are arriving to find unfinished accommodations, in-adequate supplies and a King without a Queen. It all seems to be escalating into chaos.'

'Someone is in control of this, but it is not Akhenaten,' I said.

'Nor is it Mahu, if that is what you are thinking. Whatever else he is, he's famous for his loyalty, and he's not so stupid as to have you killed at his own party.'

'So who, then?'

Nakht shook his head. 'I don't know. But you must be getting warm to earn this kind of attention.'

'I feel I'm getting nowhere at all, and time is dripping away fast. Before long the basin will be empty and dry.'

'We know the dead girl's identity, and we know some of what happened that night,' said Khety, encouragingly.

'Who would want Nefertiti dead?' I asked Nakht. 'Who would want to destabilize everything? Ramose?'

'I cannot see that. Ramose stands at the heart of the new order. He admires the Queen, and it seems to me he prefers dealing with her than with the King because she has a more pragmatic understanding of the affairs of the Great Estate than he does. He's obsessed with his grand design, and his new religion.'

I gazed into the fast-dwindling shallows of my wine. 'What about within the old Priesthood? The Amun faction? What kind of power could they have here?'

140

'The whole point of the city was to create a capital apart from them and their power-bases in Thebes and Memphis,' Nakht said, refilling my goblet.

'But surely they still have their powers? Akhenaten can ban them, but he can't destroy whole families, whole generations. They won't give it all up without a struggle.'

Nakht nodded and looked off into the dark foliage of his garden. 'I was one of them myself. Yet now I'm here. There were many of us who chose the pragmatic way of conversion to the Aten. But it was more than pragmatism. The Amun Priesthood was not of course just a Priesthood, although they venerated the god, kept the rituals and managed the festivals. As you know, they controlled vast commercial interests too. They owned a great deal of the land and its riches. Their commercial and political interests clashed repeatedly with those of the royal household. It was inevitable that at some point one or the other would have to make a bold move for absolute supremacy. Now, I have my private doubts about the Great House and their melodramas, but' – he smiled quietly – 'in the end I thought how much more interesting it would be to see what would happen when Akhenaten committed us to his enlightenment. Perhaps, after all, it will be to the greater benefit of many people. It has opened many doors previously shut in the faces of talented but non-elite men. It has brought the business of worship out of the carefully preserved secrecy of the temples and into the light of day for all to see. And there is something about it, in its finest forms, which tells people not to be afraid to live. Let's not forget, the Amun families are generally repulsive. They take their supremacy for granted. It was a special pleasure to see the shock and amazement on their arrogant faces as Akhenaten and Nefertiti stripped away their powers and riches. Welcome to the human race!'

He looked unembarrassed by this confession.

'But of course in converting to the Aten you also managed to preserve your own fortune,' I said.

He smiled. 'I can't see the purpose of destroying my life and the work of my ancestors just to prove a point, especially since it was a point I disagreed with. It was a way of converting their efforts into something new, something more generous. I wanted to explore the new possibilities. Do you think I was wrong?'

'No, I think you did the necessary thing.'

'Not the *right* thing, then.'

'I am wary of the words "right" and "wrong". We use them far too easily to judge things which we have no competence to judge. And I could not say that the things I have seen here in Akhetaten are *right*. People are people: avaricious, ambitious, strutting, careless. That doesn't change.'

He nodded. 'Certainly. The way is difficult. Things get messy and complicated as soon as they descend from the realm of the ideal into the chaos of the human. There are many people here who harbour serious doubts about what has happened lately. They see idealism changing into fanaticism. There are the same old self-serving struggles for personal power. But to return to the Amun question, it is quite likely they are here too, under the guise of conversion, perhaps waiting for their instructions, waiting for the opportunity to bring down the new regime.'

I drank some more wine. And then a name popped into my head. 'And Horemheb?'

Nakht sat up. 'Now that's a name to reckon with.'

'We met some young guards who seemed to be completely infatuated with him.'

'I'm not surprised. He seems to have come from nowhere, built himself a brilliant career, married the Queen's mad sister, and is now clearing a path for himself up the military tree by galvanizing the whole force.'

'Who is this mad sister?'

'Mutnodjmet. She has a palace role as lady-in-waiting, but she has always been kept away from the court. Something happened when she was a child, they say, and she has suffered from black depressions, hysterias.'

'And he married her?'

Nakht nodded. 'He must be very hungry for something. I can't imagine it was a match made from the necessities of the heart.'

'And he will be coming here?'

'I believe in the next day or so. And also Ay.'

'Who is Ay?'

'He is a courtier who rarely appears in public. As far as I know, his titles do not extend beyond Master of the Horse. But he is the King's uncle, and it seems the King listens to him.'

'So, the jackals are gathering.'

20

The early sunlight under the still curtain, and the sound of people stirring and talking beyond it, did little to contradict a feeling of deep unease as I woke, as if after a bad dream. I needed to move, to challenge it with activity, so I dressed hurriedly, splashing my face and hands with water to bring the reality of the new day a little closer. I smoothed my hair into some appearance of order. My mouth was as sour as tainted milk. I rinsed it out. I was hungry. And I needed to piss.

'Did you sleep well?' asked Nakht, who was waiting for me along with Khety.

'Fine. Apart from some strange dreams.'

'What dream isn't strange? That's the point of them. Should we consult a Compendium of Shadows and interpret them?'

I shook my head. He smiled.

'What are your plans now?' he asked.

'Given the level of my unpopularity in the city at this point, the likelihood that the story of my apparent death will only protect me for a short while longer, and the cruel fact that the days are passing fast, I've decided to request an audience with Akhenaten. I think it's time to bring him up to date. Besides, I can't do my job if I have to run around the city in disguise.'

Nakht shook his head, thinking. 'There is to be a public ceremony honouring Meryra today. He is to be named High Priest of the Aten. Akhenaten may be too busy to see you.'

'High Priest? I thought Akhenaten was the High and indeed the only Priest of the Aten? I thought that was the whole point?'

'Yes, it's interesting he has felt it necessary just now to elect a deputy. Meryra is totally obedient. And totally ruthless. Plus, he is the chief opponent of Ramose, who has been encouraging a more conservative approach to the government of the Great Estate for some time now. Meryra will support Akhenaten against Ramose. All religion now is about politics.'

Khety had been listening with a look of profound anxiety. 'But even if you get in, what are you going to say to Akhenaten? We're no closer to solving the mystery.'

'I'm going to tell him the truth.'

'Yes, but you can't just go in there and say, "Oh, and by the way, your loyal chief of police Mahu, who wields almost as much power as you do, wants my skin for a donkey's nosebag." Besides, if Mahu finds out you've made accusations he'll be after me. He'd kill me.'

'Well, he tried that already.'

'No, sir, he tried to kill *you*. He'd kill me, and then he'd kill my family. And we don't even know for sure it was him.'

He had a point. 'Khety, I'm not so stupid as to turn up in Akhenaten's court with no evidence making wild accusations with no ascertainable connection to the mystery, which will only alert the very people we want to keep out of this. What we need to do is give him some kind of progress report to make him feel like we're getting somewhere, even if we aren't. Then, having bought some time and some renewal of my authority, we need his permission to interview the Queen Mother and the princesses.'

'Tiy? What do you want to see her for?'

'Because I need to get to the heart of this strange family. I want to find out what she knows.'

'She's said to be vile. They say she has gold teeth and her breath rots fruit.'

'Nevertheless, she is the mother-in-law to the missing woman, and as such she has a, let's say, particular point of view on all this. And we can hold our breath for as long as required.'

Nakht grinned. 'Your friend is right, she's an evil bitch. Give her my fondest regards.'

The ways were busy with officials going to work. Carts and kiosks sold honey-cakes, bread in a variety of shapes, and beer. Most people ate and drank as they walked, already too busy, like us now, to spare the time for a proper breakfast. Khety bought some honey-bread with figs, which was wonderful, and beer, and we consumed it all like hungry dogs round the back of a building, along a side street where only labourers passed. No-one took any notice of us, preoccupied as they were with the appalling prospect of another long day of hard labour under the all-powerful sun.

Food always cheers me. It is a weakness. I wish I were the kind of man who can survive for days and nights without a single mouthful, thinking of nothing but truth and beauty. But I am not. I like to eat, as well and as often as possible. Even after a funeral, I look forward to the feast. Tanefert's cooking is adequate, but mine, I have to say, is superior. I go about it like a mystery, tracking down unusual condiments and assessing the mysterious complexities of flavour for the constituent, and sometimes surprising, elements. I take pride in knowing where in the market and among the maze of shops to buy the richest meats, the freshest herbs, the best honey. My favourite dish is leg of gazelle marinaded in red wine, with figs. I wish I could prepare it now. My old life, in which I cook gazelle while the girls prepare the beans, Tanefert talks to my mother over wine, and my father dozes or plays with the girls, seems like a lost world.

As we ate, the pain of absence flashed through my bones. To take my mind off it, I asked Khety how and where we could find Akhenaten.

'It depends,' he replied. 'Some mornings he undertakes a progress with the sun from the North Palace along the Royal Road, before the people. He worships at the Aten Temple, usually the Small. Then he receives officials and makes decisions of policy, and conducts audiences and hears petitions—'

'With what sort of people?'

'All kinds. Civil servants, provincial governors, representatives from the councils of judges, army commanders . . . everyone, right up to the northern and southern viziers.'

'And then?'

'And then he might distribute Collars of Honour at the Window of Appearances. In fact not many people know this, but there are two windows: the main one on the bridge, which he uses for the bigger audiences, and a smaller, less well-known one within the Great Palace, where he meets dignitaries, foreign ambassadors and envoys.'

'Extraordinary. And if he doesn't undertake the progress?'

'Well, he usually does, but if he doesn't then no-one knows where he stays. There are palaces and residences throughout the city, and as far as anyone knows he moves among them for security. But probably the North Palace by the river; it's surrounded by the highest walls, and almost no-one from the administration ever goes there. They say it has a great artificial lake for fish and birds, and a sanctuary park for all the animals of the kingdom. They say he spends his free time there, among the living creatures, at the centre of the world.'

Khety cast me a quick glance to see what I thought of that.

'The things people say,' I said, and smiled in a general kind of way. We still could not trust each other with regard to heresy.

We hurried through the crowds to a point where a side passage opened out on to the Royal Road, and chose a good vantage spot to observe whatever happened next.

'At what hour does he usually proceed?'

147

'Always the same time, unless it's a Festival day. He chooses to greet the sun in private, and then proceeds when it has risen to the height of the ninth hour. So the light is exactly right. And after his audiences, at the twelfth hour, Ra will be directly overhead, and he proceeds to the court of the Great House. The ceremony for Meryra will probably take place between those hours.'

'So if we wait here, and he feels like it, he will pass?'

Khety nodded. 'Of course, it will be unusual for the Queen to be absent. She drives her own chariot. Sometimes the princesses accompany them in their own small chariots. People seem to love it. The family. Perhaps today he will not come.'

So we waited. Ra rose in his blinding chariot at his own speed, far too slow for me, higher into the ever-blue sky. I passed the frustrating time observing the people going about their apparently vital business, and dreaming casually about food. Then, finally, up along the Royal Road, we heard a rumbling, a commotion of activity. Anyone walking on the road was quickly pushed aside as an advance guard, blasting loudly on their trumpets, cleared a path – although in fact almost no-one was standing anywhere near. Rather, as if by a conjuring hand, crowds of people appeared from the side streets, jostling and pushing to take up positions as close as possible, calling, crying out enthusiastically, extending their hands imploringly towards the chariot which now came into view, protected before and after by running footsoldiers. As Akhenaten himself passed in pure white, crowned, on the high dais of his carriage, motionless and unresponsive among the roar and music of the occasion, the cries rose to a pitch of frenzy and the reaching hands became more urgent. He did indeed look like the King of the World. Yet I remembered the man I had met in private, wincing with pain.

The level of security prominently displayed by this parade of power was high. Nubian, Syrian and Libyan archers held longbows, their arrows pointed at the rooflines or down into the adoring crowds. Bare-chested soldiers wore military kilts and carried ox-hide shields and axes, all polished and dazzling. At the turn into the Great Palace, phalanxes of guards created an impenetrable fence between Akhenaten and the people. The retinue turned quickly under the pylons and vanished into the court, and the armed guards fell in swiftly to protect the entrance. It was an impressive, carefully drilled, perfectly executed display of might – no motley, casual recruits here. And as soon as the King had passed, the gates were shut tight, and silence returned. But what Khety had said was true: people noticed the Queen's absence. Meaningful glances, comments whispered into companions' ears, responded to with questioning looks or nods of agreement.

At least we had found him. I made my way through the throng, and Khety followed, trying to keep up. We walked along the perimeter wall of the palace. There seemed to be no other entrances, but finally, around the back, we found one: a small doorway, a trade and staff entry and exit, with a little window set into the wall beside it. A porter was barely contained within, as in a box outgrown by its bulging contents.

'Let us pass.'

The porter slowly turned his head, as solid, battered and implacable as a rock, to consider me.

'It's important. Here are my authorities.'

I pressed the papyri to the bars on the window. He motioned me to pass them through, which I did, and he read them slowly, breathing heavily, his finger leading his frustratingly slow progress.

'You have full authorities. And yet you want to enter the palace through my door.'

'Yes.'

He considered me. 'No.'

Khety pushed his way to the window. 'He's chief detective with the Medjay. I'm assistant to Mahu, chief of police. Stop asking stupid questions and let us in.'

The porter slowly lowered his massive eyebrows again and, breathing more heavily now, pushed the authorities back through the grate. I pulled the papers from his sweaty grasp and hurried through the door he had opened.

We walked up some wide steps and found ourselves in a large kitchen yard. Ducks huddled in the dust, and mounds of vegetables lay in corners. We moved through the kitchen offices, past men chopping fast at tables or watching over great pans boiling on open fires, into a servery, and then a high-ceilinged and silent state dining room set with tables and stands. Carrying on with a confidence we had to show but did not feel, we passed through double doors and found ourselves in a vast, high, central-pillared hall. Massive slabs of burnished sunlight lay across the highly polished floors. Doors gave off this hall to many smaller rooms. The silence seemed rich with power. From ducks in a yard to the polished halls of authority in a few moments: such was the strange adjacency of things in this place.

Then through a closed door I heard Akhenaten's voice raised in anger, and a second voice, powerful but quiet, as if calming a child, but with an undertow of menace. I knew the voice, but could not place it. We edged closer to try to overhear the conversation. Akhenaten's voice came again, insistent, demanding, uncompromising; the other sounded like he was asking for something impossible, or something, at least, that Akhenaten could or would not assent to. I just about made out 'challenging my authority . . . public humiliation', then a word I could not catch – 'weakness' perhaps? Then 'intelligence reports indicate . . . opportunity we need to shut down now,' and then a tense silence, as if the conversation was now being whispered. Finally, a door slammed shut.

Khety looked at me. He had heard these fragments too. After a moment or so of total silence the door slammed open again and the magisterial figure of Ramose in fine, impressive clothes swept out. He walked away fast, obviously furious.

Suddenly we were surrounded. Guards appeared from between the columns and threw us down on the ground with excessive force, shouting for us not to move. I heard the footsteps stop, turn and approach me. Ramose's feet halted at my face, which was pressed to the cold stone of the floor. His long feet were blue-veined and gnarled in their gold and leather sandals.

150

'What are you doing here? How did you get past security? Let him stand.'

The guards backed off at once. I stood and brushed myself down.

'It wasn't difficult. I mentioned before that the security here seems inadequate.'

His expression turned thunderous. Something about this man made me want to rile him, even though I knew it was a foolish impulse.

'That is fine advice from a man who disappeared on a *duck shoot*.'

Then another voice spoke. Light and clear. 'Please look into the ease with which he managed to find his way in here. What are things coming to in this land? Come,' Akhenaten said to me, dismissing all others, including Ramose, who still looked furious, with a light wave.

We walked into a private room, and the doors closed softly behind us. But he quickly turned on me.

'Such was the silence and lack of progress I assumed you were indeed dead. Which you might as well be. Speak.'

'It does seem someone else here would prefer me to be dead.'

He stared at me. Then he beckoned me to follow him quickly out through an archway into a walled garden. We walked a little way down the path until we were some distance from the building.

'The palace was built to guard me, but it is also a listening device. One notices the slightest thread of cool air from time to time, seeming to come from nowhere – and that tells me there is a tiny gap in the wall so slight as to be invisible yet so powerful that words and information pour away into the world. Words are very powerful, but also very dangerous.'

We sat opposite each other on two wooden chairs, our knees almost touching. The heat was shocking. Sweat burst out of me. He looked as comfortable as a lizard.

I informed him of the identity of the dead girl. I pointed out that this identification was a major discovery with several important implications, not least that it suggested the Queen was not dead. To this he gave little reaction other than a quick sideways nod of the head.

I described the horror of Tjenry's murder, then the hunt and the attempt on my life, but held back from naming Mahu directly. I left him to deduce that information. But I made it clear there were forces within his city that were hunting me down. He was suddenly, mercurially, annoyed.

'The days are passing like water through your hands, and you sit here telling me nothing. All you have achieved so far is to make enemies. And you have told me nothing certain about the whereabouts or fate of the Queen, or who has taken her.'

I let him simmer for a moment, then I said, 'I am closer to solving the mystery than before. But I need further permissions and, with them, certain protections.'

'Such as?' he snapped.

'I would like to interview the Queen Mother. And your daughters.'

'Why? Do you think my own mother has kidnapped my wife?'

I pushed my argument. It was all I could do. 'I need to speak to everyone who may know something, or may have noticed something which they did not think to be important. I am trying to trace the tracks of our mystery in the dust of the past. All clues are vital.'

He pondered this for a moment, then made up his mind decisively. 'I will grant this. But remember my promise to you. Fail, and you and your family will suffer accordingly. For the last time I say to you: your time is running out.'

I was saved from having to reply by a light *tap-tap-tap*, the sound of someone approaching with a stick. Up the path came a young boy. He was the striking image of Akhenaten, from the charismatic, angled face and thin body to the exquisite crutch tucked under his arm. His gaze passed slowly over me. I experienced a slight shiver. He looked like an old soul in a child's twisted body.

Akhenaten nodded coolly at the boy, who gazed at us both then swung himself away with a practised confidence and elegance that implied a small lifetime of infirmity. I could hear the crutch counting out his steps as he moved away into the echoey chamber beyond. Akhenaten made no comment on this strange appearance.

'I will give you your permissions,' he reiterated. 'You may meet the Queen Mother and my girls this evening. And I will make one suggestion.' I waited. 'I have created many alliances and many friendships, but inevitably I also have many enemies. You can imagine who they are. Disaffected Priests from the redundant cults. The old Karnak families. Theban nobles whose corrupt fortunes are diverted now towards this city's meaningful vision. And if I have these enemies, imagine how much more they must hate the Queen. A powerful man in command of the world is one thing; a powerful woman is quite another. And now I must move on. I would like you to attend the presentation of Meryra in the Great Temple. To see how far we have come in the direction of truth. He is a most trusted servant and the only Priest besides ourselves who is granted the honour of interceding between the world and the god. All will see him honoured.'

My heart sank. I accompanied him back inside, and there waiting for us was Parennefer. Charming, chatty, powerful Parennefer. He bowed low to Akhenaten, who instructed him to accompany me to the presentation and left without uttering a farewell. We remained with our heads bowed respectfully for several moments.

'Well,' said Parennefer laconically, 'I hear you've been a busy man.'

21

Parennefer took Khety and me back to the main open courtyard, where we waited for the royal procession to gather and organize itself. The last servants and late officials hurried into their places, the guards took their positions, and then, with a beating of the drums and a skirl of reed pipes, the whole group made its way back across the courtyard and up the stairs to the Window of Appearances between the palace and the Great Temple. In the road below, a great crowd was waiting and chanting in the sun. Akhenaten, dressed now in a glorious sash embroidered with cobra-heads and fringed in a multitude of colours, passed down gifts of collars and dishes rings to the lesser members and dignitaries of the gathered population. There was a young girl with him, dressed in similar clothes. 'That is Meretaten, the oldest princess. She takes her mother's place today.' Parennefer nodded meaningfully.

From beyond the Window, Akhenaten's appearance must have seemed strong, bold, secure. From my vantage, I could see how hard it was, physically, for him to maintain that impression. In fact, while he appeared from below to be standing, he was supported on a kind of palanquin, invisible to the crowd. Around him were gathered, in the fortunate shade of the bridge, a frieze of faces – the Empire illustrated – all intent on the enactments of the ceremony but also glancing at one another continually as if testing and judging everything, and their place within it. Those on the outer edges peered carefully over the shoulders of those closer to the heart of things, as if looking into a glorious light, touches of envy and anticipation illuminating their faces. And what faces they were: not just Theban and Memphis men, but also the handsome, powerfully composed faces of Nubian royalty, Arzawis and Hittites, Assyrian princes and Babylonian diplomats.

Parennefer nudged me and whispered again into my ear. 'So you see how complex the world is in our time. Everything is connected to everything else. Our cities are growing at a tremendous rate. And with the new building programmes and the influx of foreign workers, the kingdom has become a hungry monster with a vast appetite that must be fed on more and more of the world. Hence – well, everything.'

I nodded as if I agreed. Which was a mistake, because he just carried on.

'We have the Great River, but without it what are we but sand in the wind? We cannot dine on sand. No, if we want our fine linens, and our incense, and our rare timbers for our floors and our festivals, and our trinkets from Punt, and our gold from those remote Nubian mines, we must make pacts and terms around the world. Look, even here, those men – a delegation of Alashiyan traders and dealers, I believe. Their little island is vital for copper and timber. And of course they all send their girls as brides, and their sons as hostages of loyalty to be educated here. Well, they should be so lucky! Yes, they are separated from their own worlds when they're young, but look how they gain a new and infinitely greater one. There is a nursery in the palace. Such a confusion of languages, but when they're that young they very swiftly learn our speech and soon they are yelling at each other quite fluently. My own son's best friend is a Kushite. Imagine.'

His great monologue ceased for a moment, and before it could

155

find a new course I couldn't stop myself asking, 'And what is it that we give these people in return for the tribute of the riches of their lands?'

He looked at me incredulously. 'Well, that's obvious, isn't it? Status and security. Of course they need gold to shore up their own power, and troops and the threat of our intervention to support it when challenged. But what they need most is to shine to their own people and to each other with some of our reflected glory. It behoves them to serve us well. They will not bite the hand that feeds. For instance, when there is trouble between the city lords in, say, Palestine, Megiddo, Taanach, Gath, and so on, and they start getting up on their hind legs and playing stupid games, that creates a problem with the routes of trade. We have an economic problem. So how do we deal with it?'

I shrugged, annoyed by his smugness.

'By letting the locals do the heavy lifting! We tell them they need to put their houses in order, and get together to deal with the problem. Or else! So they do, because they know if they don't – no more gold! No more friendly international relations! No more invitations to the Great House! Sometimes they complain, or make pleas for help – recently quite desperate – but often it is their little local problem and we cannot and should not interfere. Now I know there are exceptions, and these people we call our enemies! And of course we do not spare them. No. We turn our other harsher face to them, and kill them in large quantities.' He laughed, pleased with his bleak joke.

There was a call of praise from the crowd, and the retinue rose. Akhenaten was assisted from the Window by hands that everyone pretended were invisible, and the procession moved on, across the bridge and down into the Great Temple. 'Come,' said Parennefer, 'time for the show.'

And what a show it was. As we reached the end of the enclosed bridge, wide steps descended into the main courtyard of the temple, affording us a panoramic view. There were thousands and thousands of people waiting in attendance, who called out the formulas of praise to the King; national and international parties and delegations all waiting to join the procession, everyone shuffling and pushing surreptitiously to maintain or improve their positions while simultaneously sustaining their dignity. For all this power gathered in one place, it was not an edifying sight. I was suddenly overcome with a wish to walk away, fast.

The open area was vast, at least twenty times the size of the Karnak Temple courts. First went an advance group who were greeted by the temple guards. Then came standard bearers from all around the Empire: a Nubian with feathers in his hair, a bearded Hittite carrying a spear, a Libyan with the traditional short hair and long side-locks, and others carrying insignia: square tablets held high on papyrus staffs, and a model sacred barque, its ribbons and plumes fluttering as they moved through the overheated air. At the heart of it all was Akhenaten, high up on a palanquin, with runners, grooms and attendants beside him. I have seen smaller ceremonies in Thebes, where the ancient mutual antagonism between Priesthood and royal authority was very clear. Not so here. Akhenaten seemed to have it all under his control. After all, he had proclaimed himself the incarnation of the god. Now he was going to have to prove it.

We passed through one great court, under the burning eye of the sun, through the deep darkness of another pylon, and out again between its banners into another court of even more enormous dimensions, like a jubilee field, with a large altar and feast offerings laid out on tables at its centre. Here waited hundreds more people in carefully rehearsed rows; and at the centre of the first row was Meryra, surrounded by members of his court, family and friends. He was wearing a long white gown with a decorated sash, its end held by a kneeling manservant. Behind him was his private retinue. Rows of officials held scrolls and reed pens – scribes to record the announcements and speeches. Medjay officers stood behind them carrying batons. And for each person there was a servant holding a sunshade against the harshness of the sun.

'I hear it's not all love between Meryra and Ramose,' I said to Parennefer.

'Well, you'll have noticed that Ramose is not here. It is a public blow for him. People are saying that Meryra has been promoted precisely to balance Ramose's extensive influence. There are key areas of disagreement.'

'About what?'

'Financial control. Foreign policy. And hidden within that is another struggle about the whole direction of the Great Estate.'

'Tell me more.'

'Not now. Later. Watch.'

Akhenaten's palanquin had come to a halt and was placed on supports beside the altar. An absolute silence fell. Even the swallows seemed to settle down. Akhenaten and Meretaten stepped up to the high altar. He raised his hands to the sun, holding up on high a bowl of something – of light, it seemed, for the beaten metal shone as if he were holding up the dish of creation to the Aten for it to sip at. And every single person followed him. Thousands and thousands of hands reaching out to receive the gift of the light. Lightland, our world of light. 'Light, light, light!' they cried out.

I loathed the cries, the stupid conformity; but it struck me forcibly how clever Akhenaten had been. He had brought the god out of darkness and mystery into the light of day. This was not some secret figure hidden in a dark shrine, accessible only by the intercession of the Priests, but an overwhelming god of heat and light, the first fire without which there could be no life, no world, no songs, no crops, nothing. I raised my hands like everyone else, reluctantly and without, I hope, the moronic expression of devotion I observed with contempt on those around me. Yet I must confess I almost felt the quiver of belief. Here was something I could see and feel rather than something I was called upon to believe in on the authority of tradition. I felt for a moment as if I too could be drawn into this great story, this boundless wonder of the god and the word, the divine being who grants us life.

But I pulled myself together. After all, this great being, source of light and life, needed no worship from me. And I have seen this god's darker works, the ones that do not belong in songs and chants and prayers and poems. And, if I might risk heresy, he did not need it either from all these men, their hands raised in worship not because they believed in the religion, but because they believed they must be seen to do this in order to survive. No. The person who needed such worship was the strange man at the heart of all this ceremony, the one I had seen wincing with pain.

We stood for some time like madmen in the blazing light of midday. Eventually Akhenaten lowered the bowl, and suddenly there was action. Fan bearers and sunshade bearers came forward, and Priests led on an ox, its horns decorated with a blaze of coloured plumes, a woven garland around his neck. The Priests offered up the prayer, then one of them came forward with a knife. The calm beast understood nothing of what was about to happen to it. The blade was raised high, flashing, and then it swung down quickly, slicing through the beast's strong white neck, showing the butcher's world beneath. A shower of crimson blood spattered onto the hot stones and splashed into the offering bowl. The animal's expression seemed troubled rather than devastated. Then, with a bellow and a sigh of complaint, it slipped and skittered in its own blood and the fallen petals, and collapsed. Quickly, other Priests got to work. What had been a living being just moments before was jointed and hacked into body parts carried forward to be offered on the tables. Blood and flowers – the gods' delights. I thought of Tjenry, and his mutilated remains.

Music and dance followed swiftly. The dancers moved back and forth dressed in their veils and linen robes, shaking their sistra and their breasts, while a troupe of blind singers and a harpist, their faces turned considerately away from the Lord, beat their palms on the ground to keep time. Old and bald, with folds of fat hanging from their comfortable bellies, their sightless faces entranced by the power of the music. Alas, to my ears these venerable gentlemen sounded more like a pack of sincere but tone-deaf dogs.

Then Meryra came forward, attended by three subordinates and three Priests, and slowly ascended the steps to kneel down, his arms still lifted in salutation, his collars glistening in the sun, at the feet of Akhenaten, who leaned down towards him and placed another collar around his neck, this one finer and larger than the others. Meryra remained where he was as Akhenaten spoke.

'I, Lord of the Two Lands, let the Commander of the Treasury, the High Priest of the Aten in the Temple of Akhetaten, receive gold on his neck and his feet for his obedience to the House of the King. I, who live by the Truth, Lord of the Two Lands, say: I make you, Meryra, High Priest of the Aten in the Temple of the Aten in Akhetaten. And I say: my servant who hears the Teaching, my heart is satisfied with you, and you shall enjoy the Gifts of the King in the Temple of the Aten.'

More silence. Then Meryra made his answer. 'Life, prosperity, health to the Great Son of the Aten. Grant that He endure for ever and ever. Abundant are the gifts which the Aten knows to give, pleasing his heart, the Living and the Great Aten, Lord of the Orbit, Lord of Heaven, Lord of Earth, within the Temple of the Aten in Akhetaten.'

And then there were other, lesser speeches from other, lesser figures. Eventually even Parennefer looked bored and hot, even though he seemed to love this kind of thing. As if reading my mind he leaned over and whispered, 'Ceremonies are the glory of any civilization, but will this *never* end?'

Eventually it was over. The heat was disastrous, and the older men in particular were suffering. I looked along the rows; most were surreptitiously trying to mop their brows, or inch a little deeper into whatever shade they could find. Several were swaying dangerously, others were being propped up by their servants. And then I felt the hair bristle on the back of my neck. A pair of topaz eyes glittered out of the shade opposite me. That compact, cropped grey hair. The fine, shining gold draped around his shoulders. Mahu. On seeing me his expression did not alter in the slightest.

Parennefer, clever Parennefer, picked up on my reaction. He immediately saw the cause. He pretended to be making some pious comment to me, but he whispered, 'What is going on between you two?'

'Well, he would much prefer my absence to my presence, by whatever means necessary.'

'He is a rather powerful man, you know. It would be better not to annoy him.'

'It seems I annoy him just by being here.'

Parennefer, clever Parennefer, had no reply to that.

The ceremony concluded, and Akhenaten and Meretaten processed back out of the temple courtyard, back under the pylons, back across the bridge. Everyone followed. It took ages. Mahu was ahead of me, taking his due place right behind Akhenaten. I kept my eyes on his metallic hair, his powerful shoulders and back. I knew he was alert to everything that was happening, his gaze roving ceaselessly across the crowd and the high walls, in the habit of surveillance. And I'm sure I could feel him staring at me through the back of his skull.

We slowed down and let the vast crowd move ahead of us. Sweepers were already attempting to clean up after the sacrifice, and to lay the troubled dust of the courtyard to rest again with their deftly sprinkled handfuls of water, so that it would not unduly besmirch the dignitaries left behind.

'What are you doing next?' Parennefer asked.

'I have interviews, before sunset, with the Queen Mother and the royal children.'

'Oh, do you?' He went oddly quiet.

'What can you not say?'

'Nothing. Oh – just be very careful with her.' He leaned closer, turning his back to the crowd, and whispered like an actor in a comedy: 'She's absolutely ghastly.' He smiled, pleased with his courage in transgressing the rules of politeness. I saw Khety nod, as if to say: I told you so. 'But of course later you must attend the party,' Parennefer added.

I looked blank.

'The celebration at Meryra's villa, of course. By invitation only. I thought you would like to attend.'

It seemed important to meet this new figure of authority, but first I

161

needed to wash and prepare myself for the coming interview. Parennefer offered us his own house nearby, and I accepted, glad to stay within the protective penumbra of his influence. Mahu had disappeared, but I felt as if he could see through walls. I had no wish to return to my bare little office.

The bathroom alone was worth the visit. A large square room, with grilles for light and beautiful geometric multi-coloured patterns painted on the lower portions of the walls, with marsh and river scenes and semi-naked girls above. The stone floor contained channels and a drainage hole and we stood in basins while servants poured cool, scented water over us.

'Well, I never in my wildest dreams thought I'd have a shower in a palace like this!' said Khety.

I didn't feel like talking. I peered into the mosaic of reflective glass on the wall above the basin, and shaved using a bronze blade whose handle was shaped like a naked, curvaceous woman. All sorts of unguents and potions were set out in little pots together with tiny spoons for their application. Khety experimented, trying out the whole range, until I told him he stank like a girl.

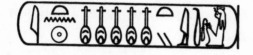

22

Someone's shadow was standing over me. I jumped up, shaking my head to sort my senses into some order. Lamps had been lit along the walls. I had slept like a village idiot. For a moment I could not remember where I was.

'It is time.' Khety looked amused.

Some dates and figs lay in a bowl and I wolfed down a handful hungrily. Sweetness in the late afternoon gives me at least the appearance of energy.

We were prepared as well as possible in our dress. Parennefer drove me slowly and nervously to the royal palace in his own chariot, while Khety followed behind. Parennefer was one of those drivers who seemed to look no further than the horses' noses. Certainly he did not look up ahead to see what was happening on the crowded way.

He gave me one of his solicitous, tilted looks. 'Have they told you much about Tiy?' he said.

'I hear she's not in the finest form of beauty these days.'

'I could not say. But she is here only to attend the Festival. Although the King has constructed for her a palace and a temple, she has not until now wished to visit the new city. I've heard she thinks it has all gone too far, this move to the new city, the Great Changes and so on. But she feels compelled to support it, now that everything has happened. Everyone knows, I think, that her words are still powerful with Akhenaten.'

'Well, that's how it tends to be between mothers and sons,' I said, thinking of my own mother and her clever ways.

'Of course, but not only that!' he cried, as if I had not learned my lesson well. 'Firstly she is herself of royal status as the beloved wife of Amenhotep, Akhenaten's father, the Magnificent, Builder of the Monuments. But also, and not least, because her own family is the most trusted in the service of the royal family. Indeed, her father, Yuya, who began his career as Officer in the Royal Charioteers, rose to become Amenhotep's most trusted adviser. And her brother, Ay, today holds his father's offices, and is an extremely close adviser to Akhenaten.'

'I have heard of this Ay. What do you know about him?'

'He is known only to a closed circle; apparently he prefers to remain publicly anonymous. His family has grown around the royal family like ivy, until through marriage they have eventually become almost indistinguishable from it. It is a powerful alliance.'

These genealogies were mind-numbingly complicated. Who knew how, in future days, such chains of birthright and power-bargaining would be untangled? How such and such a girl would come to be sold to another foreign power for the price of a little peace or the cost of a small war? Whose names would survive, whose stories would turn to dust and blow away? But I had to get this clear in my mind or I knew I would make some stupid error in front of the woman I was soon to interview.

'So, Tiy is Queen Mother. Her father was an up-and-coming young man from a well-placed family who became very powerful. Her brother, Ay, is in the inner circle.'

'Yes,' said Parennefer. 'His father, who was a good as well as a

164

powerful man, ensured his son's position at the heart of things from a young age. I think in fact he was the youngest ever Master of the Horse.'

'And what is the nature of this man's relationship with Nefertiti, the Great Royal Wife?' I asked.

'I do not know.' And with that he clammed up, his face no more revealing than a sealed tomb.

I thought it through as we continued to drive through the now chaotic streets in the evening light. Here was a man at the heart of the royal family. Everything had been done by his own family to ensure the succession and improvement of that alliance. And it seemed to have succeeded astonishingly well. Yet I did not know anything of this man or his power.

'Is he here in the city?' I asked Parennefer.

He looked as if he was surprised I should still be thinking about Ay. 'Not at this precise moment, I believe. I understand he travels constantly between Thebes, Memphis and here. He has his own ship of state. But few know of his movements. Certainly not me.'

We arrived at the royal palace. Parennefer hurried us through the gateway, waving his hands loftily at the guards, who made themselves invisible. He led us down more long corridors, deeper into the complex. We were turning a corner when suddenly he held me back in the shadows.

'Be careful what you say in your meeting with the Royal Mother,' he said. 'She feasts on fear. She has the tongue of a crocodile. She can turn your life to dust. She will be meeting you with the princesses. Apparently she insists on being present during their interview.'

'That's the last thing I want,' I said, cursing my stupidity in not foreseeing this.

We came to a door, he knocked, and we were admitted. I heard the familiar sound of girls shouting and arguing, punctuated by the apparently pointless instructions of a woman's voice. Nurses and servants ran about looking tense and tired.

'It must be bedtime for the princesses,' said Parennefer. He looked more worried now than before. 'Marvellous. I must be going. I will leave you in the capable hands of the governess. Ah, here she comes now.' Then he looked at me again and said quietly, 'We are early. I thought it best to arrive early.'

I understood him. He hoped to give us a little time alone with the princesses before Tiy arrived. I gripped his hand, communicating my thanks.

A middle-aged woman moved anxiously towards us, alarmed to see us there so soon. She was unprepared. She had just opened her mouth to greet us when she was interrupted by a sharp scream; a small ball of blue and red leather flew through an open door with all the furious inaccuracy of a child in a tantrum, and shattered a plant pot. Soil went flying across the floor. The door slammed shut.

The woman blushed. 'Come, clear this up, quickly.'

Servants hurried across to sweep away the mess.

'The princesses have such a wonderful appetite for life that the idea of bedtime is distressing to them,' she continued, addressing me. 'They grow tired, and then cannot account for themselves in the way I am sure they would truly wish.'

I interpreted her meaning. I tried to help her out. 'My girls are the same. Although the promise of a story can quiet them for a little.'

She nodded. 'But then one must be careful, for the Royal Grandmother believes literature is an unnecessary stimulation and may keep them awake all night.'

'Could I meet them now, before they sleep?'

'I was strictly instructed only to begin the interview when the Queen Mother arrived.'

'Well, I am here now. And they seem ready for bed. Could I perhaps meet them immediately?'

She was shaking her head fearfully when a girl appeared at the doorway. Meretaten. I remembered her from the ceremony.

'Bring him in now,' she ordered imperiously, and turned back into the room with a confidence that somehow was unattractive.

We entered the nursery. It was a long, high room with windows and doors to the terrace now covered with bright curtains. In the centre was a long, low wooden table. Alcoves contained beds. Toys of remarkable invention and beauty of construction overflowed from trunks. Papyrus collections of stories were packed onto shelves. Little statuettes and votive figurines were lined up along a shelf. The walls around each bed were hung with drawings, stories and poems on beautifully illustrated papyri. Servants were apprehensively attempting to restore some kind of order to the room's colourful and lively chaos.

At the table sat three girls on low stools; Meretaten stood at the head. As we entered they all looked at me expectantly. Their mother was in all of them. Their faces were fine and haughty, their hair black and glossy, their skin pure, their postures elegant and perfect. They sat as if posing, straight-backed and self-conscious, not with the indolent pleasure of my girls. Their governess introduced me to them: Meretaten, then Meketaten, Ankhesenpaaten and Nefernefruaten.

'I don't know if I can remember those names straight away,' I said.

Meretaten stared down her nose at me. 'Then you must be a fool.'

There was a little silence while the other girls waited to see how I would react. I asked her how old she was.

'Fourteen.' She gazed at me.

'And you other girls?'

'Twelve.'

'Ten.'

'Seven – and I'm not the youngest. Nefernefrure and Setepenra are already asleep.'

I sat down with them, at their level, on a low stool. The silence continued. The girls looked uncertain. I realized there were a number of women in attendance, waiting and watching. I whispered to the governess to ask if I could be left alone with the princesses.

'It is forbidden for men to remain alone in the nursery,' she replied.

'Then could you perhaps dismiss the attendants, and stay yourself as the chaperone?'

She considered it, but it was Meretaten who nodded her agreement and clapped her hands. The attendants filed out of the room and closed the door behind them. As soon as they were gone, Meretaten relaxed slightly. Meketaten got up from the table and went to sit, cross-legged, on her bed, her sleek sidelock falling over her ear as she repeatedly combed it through.

'Do you mind if I talk to you all a little?' I said.

'That's why you're here, isn't it?' said Meretaten. She looked at me curiously now.

'Are you a seeker of mysteries?' asked Ankhesenpaaten.

'I am a detective in the Thebes Medjay, and your father has ordered me here. Perhaps you are aware of the reason why?'

'Because the Queen has disappeared,' said Meretaten. Those were her words, spoken with a strange kind of bitterness. No mention of the fact that it was her own mother who had vanished. She must have seen the look of surprise on my face, for she covered her tracks quickly. 'That's what people are whispering.'

'And what do you think?' I asked.

'I think you're here to find her. Which means she's been kidnapped, or stolen. Or she's dead.'

I was shocked by her casual tone.

'I must be honest with you and admit I don't yet know what has happened to her, but I believe she is alive, and I am determined to find her and bring her back to you. She must miss you as much as you miss her.'

I heard behind me a little snuffle. Nefernefrure had appeared, silent tears trickling down her face.

'Now look what you've done,' said Meretaten.

The governess took the child in her arms and comforted her. The tears subsided, and the tiny girl glared suspiciously at me.

'I know how difficult it is to talk,' I said, 'but I wanted to meet you all because I need your help. I need you to tell me anything you remember about your mother in the days before she disappeared. Or anything about your mother you think I should know. Can you do that?'

The girls all looked at Meretaten, as if they were silently discussing an agreement. Then Meretaten took up and set spinning on the table a faience top. It whirled on its single point of balance, the bright colours blurring together so that the image of a smiling face appeared where, in stillness, there had been nothing more than lines. It was a rare and surprising object.

'That's a beautiful spinning top. Who gave it to you?'

'Our mother,' said Meketaten, pointedly.

We all watched the top in silence. The princesses were mesmerized. Gradually it lost its poise, wobbled, subsided, and then fell over. Meretaten seemed to read its behaviour as a tool of prophecy, or at least decision-making, for she considered it for a little while before eventually nodding. They drew a little closer to me.

'She was behaving strangely. Her face was dark, sad. Full of shadows and worries.' The lamplight flickered in Meretaten's eyes as she spoke.

'Do you know why?'

Meketaten, lying on her divan, called out, 'She and father had a fight.'

'No they didn't,' said her older sister.

'Yes they did. I heard them. Then she came in to say goodnight, and you were all asleep. She was crying but she was trying not to show it. I said, "Why are you crying?" And she said, "No reason, my darling, no reason." And she said it was our secret, and not to tell. Then she kissed me and hugged me like I was a doll or something, and then she told me to go to sleep and not to worry because she'd make every-thing all right.'

'And when did this happen?' I asked.

'I don't remember the day. But not long ago.'

'And did she talk to any of you other princesses in the same way?'

They looked at each other and shook their heads. Meretaten was angry and silent now. 'I thought you said it was a secret. You've said it out loud now.' She glared at her sister, who glanced back at her, but wilted under Meretaten's angry look.

She turned back to me. 'They have fights. Everyone does. It doesn't mean anything.'

'Have they had lots of fights?' I asked.

Meretaten refused to reply.

Ankhesenpaaten, along the table, was playing with a mechanical toy of a wooden man and a big dog worked by strings and pulleys. As she turned the peg the wooden man raised his arms to defend himself as the dog leaped at him to attack. Over and over, the dog biting the man. The white fangs and the wide red eyes and the raised hair along his back. The little girl laughed and pointed at me. 'Look,' she said. 'It's you!'

I was disconcerted. Then I thought of something.

'I should also pass on a message to you all,' I said. 'It's from Senet. She wanted me to tell you she misses you all.'

Meretaten's face hardened. 'Tell her—'

Then the door opened behind me. The girls stood up and hurried to their beds. The governess trembled.

'Who permitted this *man* to enter the nursery and address the princesses without my presence?'

Her voice was like nails scraping on a board. There was a horrible silence. We all stood like statues, looking at the floor. I felt like I was back at school. I had to speak.

'Highness, I am to blame.'

By the shuffling noise they made I knew her feet were weak and old; her breath came short with anger. For all the finest perfumes of the land, she stank. It was the sickly-sweet stench of decaying flesh. Then she reached out and grabbed my face. I was shocked by the contact, and jumped. She gripped me with bony, resilient strength, and I had to make myself stand still while she drew her fingers, with their long, nasty nails, down across my face.

'So you are the fool who believes he will find her. Look at me.'

I did so. Time had withered her beauty into a wizened mask of rage. But for the crazy opulence of her dress – veils and robes draped around her bones – and the dyed lengths of her own hair, she would seem a madwoman, a wild nomad from the desert. Her mouth was like an old leather purse, her eyes milky, the colour of the moon. They drifted in their sockets as she spoke. Her laugh was accompanied by a gust of stagnant marsh gas. She grinned as if she could see my reaction, revealing an array of false gold teeth among rotting black stumps.

She shuffled around the girls like an ancient animal or a seer in her fantastic rags. The princesses instinctively backed away from her. Meketaten held her nose and made a face behind the back of the Queen Mother. Suddenly, with shocking accuracy, she slapped the child hard across the face. The girl forced down the tears that sprang to her eyes.

'Now that I have made the effort to come here, what do you wish to ask these girls? Hurry. It is late.'

I racked my brains.

'You waste my time. Speak.'

'Highness, I have no further questions. We have already talked.'

She scowled at me. Then she turned to the girls. 'Sleep! Now. Any child who speaks will be punished.'

Nefernefrure began to sob again, great waves of unhappiness welling up inside her. The old monster shuffled over to the little girl and shouted into her distraught face. 'Stop blubbing! Tears are futile. They have no effect upon me whatsoever.' None of the other girls had the courage to defend their little sister.

She turned back to me. 'And you and your idiot slave, follow me. Governess, the room is a disaster. See that it is ordered.' And she shuffled out.

Khety blew out his cheeks, as if to say: I told you so. And he was right. Time was taking a slow and terrible revenge upon her, bone by bone. She was like a living corpse, except somewhere in that mind, probably over-complicated with the fears and terrible imaginings of a lifetime in power, was a keen intelligence and a refusal to submit to mortality without a struggle. But that did not account for her cruelty and viciousness. It was as if all human emotion had long since rotted down into a bile which ran black and vicious in her heart. Perhaps it was all that kept her in the land of the living.

We followed at a respectful distance. As she passed, everyone stepped back, lowering their heads respectfully, and then looked up frankly at Khety and me, with little more curiosity than if we were dinner for the crocodiles in the Sacred Pool. She seemed to know her way without help, and no-one offered to guide her. When she came to steps she showed no sign of hesitation but with quick, practised touches of her slippers quickly found her way onwards.

Eventually we came to a private chamber. Guards were set on either side of the door. As she passed, she flourished her hand and the doors were closed silently behind us. The room was devoid of personal touches: nothing more than a meeting room furnished with a throne on a raised dais which she ascended. She did not sit down in it but remained standing above us.

'I will grant you a few moments of my time, which is short in every sense. But only because the King, my son, requests it. I have no wish, whatsoever, to discuss affairs of state with some ambitious and unimaginative little Medjay meddler. Speak.'

Here was a woman who had seen and engaged in the operations of power for decades. A woman who had presided over the most powerful reign of the dynasty and still influenced the present King. She waited, her blurred eyes open. It was a strange and disconcerting sensation to address them directly.

'Highness, kindly describe your relationship with the Queen Nefertiti.'

'She's the wife of my son and the mother of six of my grandchildren. My female grandchildren.'

'You have others?'

'Of course. There is a harem; there are other wives.'

'And other grandchildren?'

'Yes.'

Stones speak more candidly than this. But the stoniness perhaps defended information that was delicate. Other children. Other claims to power.

As I hesitated, uncertain how to proceed, her blind eyes glittered with a kind of bitter amusement. But I would not let myself be distracted. I tried a different approach.

'Your Majesty has ruled at the heart of the kingdom for many years, by the grace of Ra.'

'Your point?'

'Your Highness knows better than any the . . . *challenges* which Queens must transcend. Men are born with advantages; women must create their own. It is, as in your own example, if I may say so, a noble achievement.'

'Don't you dare to praise me. Who do you think you are?' Once more she was breathless with anger. 'I was born into a family of great power. My gender was *always* to my advantage. I made it so. It gave me a useful cover for my intelligence. And it has enabled me to do all the things I have achieved. Most men fear powerful women. But there are a few who enjoy them. My husband was one. Without me, this city and its god would not exist.'

Khety and I exchanged glances. Even though she was blind I still felt she could see everything.

'And the Queen?' I asked.

'What about her?'

She stared at me, hard. There would be no yielding here.

'Would this city not exist without her?'

'It seems to be surviving so far.'

Silence.

'You are lost already,' she continued, decisively. 'You know nothing. You have nothing to ask me because you have discovered nothing and understood nothing.'

It was somewhat true, and all the more infuriating for being so.

I said, 'I find a young woman, to all purposes identical to the Queen, murdered, her face removed. I find no evidence that the Queen's disappearance was either violent or against her will. I do, however, find reasons why she might have decided to disappear of her own accord.'

She grinned, baring her gold teeth, in reply. And then she was caught out by a racking cough. She spat out a little phlegm, careless of where it landed. Khety and I just stared at it.

'Can you hold dreams in your hand?' she continued. 'Can you say why people need gods, and why power's legs must needs be crooked on the straight road? Can you say why men cannot be honest? Can you say why time is more powerful than love? Can you say why hate is more powerful than time? There are many questions your method cannot accommodate.'

I could not say why any of these things should be so. I played my last card: 'She is not dead.'

Her face did not change. 'I'm delighted to hear your optimism in the face of so much evidence to the contrary.'

'Why do you think she disappeared?'

'Why do you think she *has* disappeared?'

'I think she had to make a choice. Between fight and flight. She chose flight. Perhaps it was the only way for her to survive.'

Her face puckered with rage. 'If that is the case, then she is a despicable little coward,' she spat. 'Did she think it would be so easy, to just disappear when things got difficult? Pack up her tender feelings, abandon her children and her husband and disappear, crying her futile tears? Damn her for her selfishness, for her vanity, for her weakness.'

Her anger echoed around the cold room. Then, suddenly, she staggered a little. Her hand flew up to her face while the other searched about for the arm of the throne, but in her panic she missed, her legs lost all power, and she slipped down to the stone platform. She made no sound. Her veils had fallen from her shoulders and lay about her like white and gold linen snakes. For a moment she was quite still. I moved to her aid, and as I did so her breath began to rattle and shake as she struggled, tangled as she was in the folds of her robes. As she moved the clothing came away from her chest. Its brown skin hung in shrivelled folds from the bones. She seemed more a shadow doll, all sticks and string, than a living thing. Then I saw, with horror, black and blue cankers, open sores, blossoming where her breast should have been.

Without thinking, I touched her shoulder. And she screamed. The noise seemed to pierce the stone of the walls. I heard feet running towards us outside in the corridors. Then she grasped my head and pulled it down towards her rotting face. Her grip was supernatural, and she whispered urgently, wetly, into my ear: 'Time himself is feasting on me. He is dining with care. He is powerful. But my hatred will survive me. Remember that, when you see beauty, for this is the end of beauty and power. That is my final answer to all your questions.' Her sightless, moony eyes were fixed with strange concentration in that doll's skull. Then she let me go, and all strength departed from her body.

I reached out to cover the horrible sight again, but she cried out a second time, and I realized that every touch caused her agony. It could not be long now. And there would be little work left for the embalmer to finish.

23

We drove to Meryra's villa. By now the population was clearly changing and growing, as people arrived for the Festival. The atmosphere was changing too: it carried a new tension, partly from the fact of there being too many people cramped together in one place that was not yet ready to receive them. But there was something else, an undercurrent of fear that had not been there before. I noticed more armed Medjay on the streets, and not in pairs but in units, as if preparing for the great event. It seemed, suddenly, that these new buildings, temples and office complexes could shiver, quake and collapse into the dust of their making for no reason. The world no longer felt solid; it felt conditional. There were tremors of uncertainty under our feet.

We arrived at the villa just as Meryra's celebration procession was making its way along the street. The man himself was carried on a high throne, together with his wife in a long wig and a pleated linen gown. They both looked highly satisfied with themselves and their elevation above all others. He seemed the man of the moment. The late light shone on his gold collars. The parade passed into the main house with shouts and cries, and Meryra was lifted down and, to calls of praise and congratulation, and the casting of flowers, accompanied inside his house, presumably to change his robes.

Suddenly Parennefer was at my side.

'How did it go?'

'Everything you said about her was true.'

He gazed about the crowd, taking note of who was and who was not there. 'No sign of Ramose of course. Apparently he was invited but sent a message of apology saying he had urgent affairs of state to resolve. But of course no-one's buying *that*.' He paused meaningfully.

'Let me guess,' I said, as we pushed past the guards and into the open courtyard of the villa. It was paved with alabaster, and lined with trees. A long pool glimmered by candlelight. 'He's jealous of Meryra's promotion.'

Parennefer clicked his tongue and flicked out his hands. 'Of course that. But not only that. It creates a dilemma. Meryra's politics are opposed to Ramose's. And now, since he's been publicly favoured by Akhenaten, he has the power to influence events and decision-making.'

'And what are his politics?' I asked.

'He's dedicated to domestic issues. He doesn't care about much else other than flattering the King. Ramose thinks the Great Estate is threatened by the barbarians that surround us. He thinks we're all ignoring the instabilities in our foreign territories. He thinks we need to turn our attention to solving them through military campaigns. Meryra thinks we can solve them and our domestic issues simul- taneously by inviting the various parties to the Festival. Bring them all here, give them a talking-to, show them a good time, demonstrate who's in charge, and so on. Ramose thinks that's like inviting a gang of tomb robbers to dinner, giving them your knives and offering them your wife.'

'I think Ramose has a point,' I said.

Parennefer sighed. 'I know. But Meryra has the ear of Akhenaten.

We must have Nefertiti restored. What would happen if, during the Festival, she's still not here, or, worse still, is revealed as having been murdered? It would hugely damage the prestige of the event in front of everyone. It would open up all sorts of flaws in the appearance of power, just at the moment when we most need to assert our supremacy.'

I decided not to mention the argument between Akhenaten and Ramose, and the few fragmentary words I had overheard, which now seemed to take their place, like shards of evidence, in a possible version of that conversation which ran along the lines: do you not see the danger to which you are committing us by bringing together these conflicting and mutually adversarial foreign powers at the worst possible time? But Akhenaten's dilemma was acute: preparations and negotiations had taken many months, if not years; all the visiting parties had to travel for several weeks at least to attend; most were on their way, arriving within a few days. If he abandoned the Festival now, the consequences could be catastrophic for his authority and his power-base. His enemies would say he was significantly weakened either way. No, cancellation was not an option. I wondered how he slept at night.

Suddenly I heard a scream. I looked up and saw a small sun of intense, crackling white fire, with arms and legs struggling below it, emerge from the main door of the house and run as if dancing crazily in small, agonized zig-zags, emitting high shrieks. Everyone hurried back, crying out in horror, as the burning figure ran blindly among the crowd.

I ran forward and cast a jug of water over the figure: but this only enraged the fire. So I pulled a decorated covering from a bench, and threw it over the man, pulling him to the ground to suffocate the flames that seemed to burn ever more fiercely. The heat was more intense than ordinary fire, and gave off a strongly noxious smell; quickly it was burning through the covering. Khety swiftly found a heavier cloth, and we finally extinguished the flames. We stood back, brushing the last burning tatters from our own clothes and hands.

178

The body itself twitched and trilled rapidly in its mortal agony, and then fell still. The stench of burned flesh and hair was disgusting. The courtyard was absolutely silent. I pulled away the burned and scorched materials from the upper gown, which was expensive and magnificent, and saw gold collars.

It was Meryra.

Then his wife emerged from the house. She stepped towards the body as if in a trance. When she saw all that remained of her husband, she let out a high, ululating scream, and then collapsed into the arms of her attendants. Instantly there was pandemonium among the guests, who fled in panic like a herd of desert antelope, the women kicking off their sandals the better to run.

Among the chaos, and surrounded by Priests in white linen gowns, I examined the corpse. I carefully peeled back the textiles that were now fused to the head's remains. Not much was left. The flesh was charred, and as I gently separated the burned material patches of white bone were exposed. It looked indeed as if the flesh had been eaten away, as well as burned. The eyes were milk-white, like a cooked fish. I noticed around the scalp, however, patches of something black and viscous like tar, still steaming. Bitumen. This would account in part for the noxious scent I had noticed. Adhering to this sticky pitch were tufts of burned, matted fibre. Hairs. The remains of a wig. It must have been painted with bitumen on the inside, and then suffused with some intensely distilled, highly volatile substance that, once alight, burned with a terrible incandescence. And in turn the greater the heat, the more liquid and flammable the bitumen would have become. The burning wig would very quickly have become fused to the victim's head. I tried again to understand the scent, but although I caught something – strange, pungent, acidic, almost with a hint of garlic in it perhaps – it was confused by the stench of the burned flesh.

Parennefer stood to one side in shock, his face glistening with perspiration, his eyes blinking. 'How could this happen?' he said, over and over. I felt like slapping him. It seemed very clear to me: this was another accurate blow aimed at the vulnerable heart of the Great

Estate. The High Priest of the Aten had been burned to death on the night of his glory by a fire of judgement.

Suddenly, the courtyard was stormed. Armed Medjay on chariots thundered through the gate, leaped down and surrounded us and the body. Others were swiftly directed to fan out and search and occupy the villa and its outbuildings. From the dark heart of this noisy operation appeared a tall, solid figure. Mahu. He stood over the body, ignoring my presence. He looked carefully at everything. Then, still without looking at me, he said, 'Take him away.'

I was tied up, trussed like a pig and thrown onto a wagon, which was driven away at speed through the city. The shadows of the buildings ran over me. I looked up at the roofs of houses and the high, still stars above them. I knew where we were going.

24

I was dragged fast down the dark corridors, my feet scrambling under me, until we arrived once again at the over-official, over-impressive doors, with the emblem of the Aten and its many hands bearing their ankhs above the lintel.

The mind is a strange thing; at moments of disaster it obsesses itself with nonsense. I remembered my old partner, Pentu. We were from the same city, the same streets. We had studied together, and come up through the lower ranks. We'd been called to a robbery, a jewellery shop in the lower quarter, near the main square. We were just making our way through the mess of the shop, shattered wood and broken vases and knick-knacks crunching under our feet. Pentu gestured to me that he would check the back room, and he went carefully in. For a moment there was silence, then he looked back around the door. 'Empty,' he said, and shrugged his broad shoulders. And then the point of a dagger appeared in his chest. Blood spread across his shirt. He looked shocked, then very disappointed. He sank to his knees. Behind him stood a young man, no more than sixteen or seventeen years old, a look of vicious fear on his face. Without thinking I threw my dagger. It whirred through the air, struck him hard in the heart, and he collapsed without a sound.

I ran to my friend and turned his face up to me. He was still alive. The blood was pulsing out of him. Too much blood. 'Shit,' he murmured. 'Shit,' I said. I couldn't think of anything better. We sat like that for a little while, the sounds of the afternoon coming to us remotely from the street. Everything seemed very far away. Then he whispered, 'D'you remember that old story?' I shook my head. 'The bit where the King says, "I want to drink a vat of Egyptian wine." And then he does. And the whole country goes, "The King has a terrible hangover," and he says, "I won't speak to anyone today. I can't do any work."' He smiled and then he died. Just like that. His last words. Nonsense. We almost all die with the same thought: *but I have not yet finished!*

I stood waiting with these useless thoughts, and I record them not because I believe them to be insights but because there was nothing else. My mind should have been racing with panic to find a solution to my dilemma. Instead, nonsense commanded my attention. Is this our mind's way of helping us survive these moments of disaster? Do we enter the Otherworld to meet the gods with our minds in such disorder? Or is it just me – a fool, in the final reckoning?

The doors opened and I was untied and thrown through them and onto the floor. Mahu was already sitting at his desk. He remained turned from me, attending to something far more important. These games again. Finally he looked up, and those lion eyes gazed at me. Neither of us spoke. I was certainly not willing to start this conversation.

'Do you remember the last time we met in this office? I told you I was here to help. I may not approve of you, I may not like you, but let me offer my hand in professional respect,' he said.

I stayed silent.

'Yet you have chosen to ignore my generosity when it could have been such a support to you.'

'I don't count assassination with a bow and arrow as support.'

He got up, came round the desk, as annoyingly tidy as ever, and then, out of the blue, he whacked me hard across the face. I blinked back the humiliation and anger. But beyond this, I was pleased. I had made him furious. This was good. He was breathing heavily.

'If it were not for Akhenaten's incomprehensible but of course indisputable trust in you, for such an accusation I would already have had you sent away in fetters to the gold mines in that barbaric land of Kush where you could perish slowly from the heat and the labour, and think a scorpion sting a gift from the gods.'

My silence after that outburst seemed to irk him even more. I wiped a drop of blood from the corner of my mouth.

'If I wanted you dead, Rahotep, do you not think I could have arranged a more convenient, more effective, less confusing end for you and a less embarrassing one for me? You could have asked me, "Who was that fine gentleman who tried to shoot me?" And I could have told you something about him. But no. You could have made me a friend. Instead you have made me an enemy.'

He stepped away. He had, I must admit, the beginnings of a point, though I was sure he was bluffing about knowing the identity of my would-be assassin. I was unable to silence myself now.

'You have wanted me out of here from the start. Why? Is professional jealousy motivation enough? I doubt it. Perhaps you have something to hide.'

Swiftly he swung towards me, his face close up to mine. I saw the lines around his eyes, the sparks of fury in his cold eyes, heard the hissing tension in his voice. His breath was unpleasant. I smelled the tang and taint of loathing on it.

'Only the protection of Akhenaten – and we both know how weak that is becoming – prevents me from killing you now.'

The slavering dog barked. 'Silence!' he yelled, whether at me or the dog neither of us could be sure. The dog retired, whimpering. I smiled. His hand flew up again to strike me, but he controlled himself in time.

'Oh Rahotep,' he said, shaking his head, 'you believe you live a charmed life. But listen to me now. Since you arrived here nothing has been as it should. I respected the wishes and commands of the King. I let you make your moves. And look where it has got us. Dead girls. Dead Medjay officers. Dead Priests. I feel chaos coming upon us, and I think you are to blame. So now I have to set things right again before it is too late.'

'There's nothing you can do,' I said. 'If you were capable of finding the Queen, or of solving these assassinations, you would have done so by now.'

His voice went very quiet. 'Do not make the mistake of underestimating me. I can silence you. I can make you talk. I can make you sing like a girl, if I want. I'm going to present you now with a very simple choice. Leave this city, tonight. I will provide an armed escort. You can go back to Thebes, take your family away, and disappear. I will protect you from Akhenaten's anger. Or stay. But you will make me your worst enemy. Whatever you choose, remember your family. Your lovely Tanefert. Your lovely little girls. Sekhmet. Thuyu. Nedjmet. Who think life is music and dancing and sweet dreams. And remember: I know everything about them.'

The way he spoke those names, sacred to my heart, filled me with dark fury. But I would not let him see this. I would not let him win. Suddenly an idea came to me, and before I could even begin to consider its ramifications the words were out of my mouth.

'You have your threats, and I have mine.'

'Such as?' he said, uninterested.

'I am not only working under the protection of Akhenaten. Let me mention another name. Ay.'

I let this hang in the air. It was a huge risk. I knew nothing of their relationship. He gave nothing away, but for the swift passage of some thought, some consideration, some idea, in his mind's eye, as if for the first time I had played an interesting move in a game he commanded. I am sure I saw it.

'I'm glad we've had this little talk,' he said after a short while. 'The

184

next time we meet, if we meet again, will be interesting for both of us. Good luck with your big decision.'

He opened the door with ostentatious politeness, allowed me to pass through it, then slammed it shut behind me. It did not slam particularly effectively, because, as I noticed earlier, the door had warped slightly in its frame. So much for his grand gesture.

I was escorted out of the headquarters, past the rows of new desks where new recruits with no experience waited for someone to tell them what to do, then out onto the Royal Road. It was late, and the ways were empty but for the light of the moon. In any other city at any other time the streets would still be busy: little stalls and kiosks lit by lamplight still selling food and necessities; drunks parading up and down performing their turns of comedy or tragedy, or standing up to each other on staggering hind legs, yelling their magnificent soliloquies of injustice and ill fortune. But tonight, in this city of façades and appearances, people were afraid. They were inside, hiding in safety. On the streets there was nothing but silence and shadows as we passed by the monolithic buildings of this mud-brick nightmare of power. I longed to hear a dog bark, and another reply from across the city. But this was the kind of place where they slaughtered dogs to avoid the sound of barking in the night.

The guards accompanied me to my room and made it clear they would be staying outside the door throughout the night. Not as a comfort to me, of course. I entered the room I had left two days ago. The guards had given me a lamp, and I stood looking to see what had changed. The jug stood by the bed. I sniffed the water – stale, with a slight film of dust. The bed and its sheet – untouched. The statuette of Akhenaten – unmoved. I passed the lamp back and forth over the floor, trying to see whether there were prints of any kind. I could see nothing. I set it down on the desk, took out this journal, and wrote down all I recalled of the last two days.

The one thing I returned to was the look that passed, like a brief complication, no more than a shadow, across the face of Mahu when I mentioned the name of Ay. Who was this man? Could I gamble on the unknown power of that name, at least for a few days? Perhaps. But it felt like risking my life, and those of my family, on a wild guess.

I sat looking out into the courtyard lit by the full moon. Companion of my night work through my life. How many nights had I spent under his light, seeing things in the dark? The night life of our world, when the god travels on his barque through the perils of the Otherworld, and I in my way travel through mine (on foot of course). When I could have been sleeping close and quiet with Tanefert, I had spent too many nights stumbling among the dark detritus of mortal crimes and unredeemable tragedies. Regret comes to us always when it is far too late to change that which we have done.

As I unrolled the scroll to start another sheet, and at the moment when I had run out of all thoughts and possibilities, I found written, but not in my hand, these signs:

A shiver ran through me. I scanned the room again, as if someone might now be standing in the shadows, waiting with a knife. But there was no-one. This writing must have been done – could have been done – at any moment in the last few days. And I could not but believe that someone had written this here knowing I would find it about now, this very evening, perhaps; they needed to tell me something they could not, or did not, wish to communicate in any other way. But who, and how, and why?

186

I read the hieroglyphs. This was my interpretation:

Do you go to the necropolis. Do you go down into the Otherworld
As it is said in the Chapters of Coming Forth by Day
Do you find there stability
When you reach what you seek it is a woman
Her sign is Life

Enigmatic instructions! It seemed like nonsense. I read them again. I had seen the site of the necropolis near the artisans' village. There were also of course the noble and royal rock tombs under construction in the cliffs to the north. But how could anyone go down into the Otherworld, following the instructions and prayers of the Book of the Dead, unless they were themselves dead? And then came two signs of hope: the hieroglyph for stability, the pillar of power raised upright before the Gods to restore order to the world. The hieroglyph was also worn as an amulet to accompany the dead. And then those final hieroglyphs: *Her sign is Life*. The symbol of life was the Ankh, which I had seen everywhere in the city being passed down to creation by the Aten.

Her sign. Was 'She' the source of this strange message? If so, was this proof she was still alive, and instructing me to find her? Possibly. But why in this mad way? And then came another idea: was Mahu playing with me, luring me by means of this puzzle to my doom? I had no choice. I could not ignore this message. I had to act while I still had the advantages of darkness and surprise.

There were guards posted at my door, but were they guarding the unfinished terrace beyond the window? I looked out for a minute, and no-one passed by. I listened at the door, and I heard the two guards speaking quietly to each other as they paced up and down. I went back to the window, and the moonlight showed me the way I needed to go: across the terrace and over the wall.

I write these words not knowing whether I shall ever write more. Will there be more to tell? Or will this journal be found and returned to you, Tanefert, my beloved? What else can I write on this scroll, perhaps the last, but a message to you and the girls. *I love you*. Is that enough? I do not know. I leave the empty scrolls that follow in the deepest hope that they will soon be covered with more writing. Not, please Ra, left blank after my death.

25

There are wise men and seers who claim to have visited the Otherworld in visions. They starve themselves, or sing in the language of the birds, and all we mortals can do is believe, or disbelieve and say, 'These men are mad. Lock them away, in prisons of stone and silence, so that their visions and their impossible tales cannot frighten us.' I am now one of those men. And now I must seek the words to explain the mystery.

I could hear the guards outside the door, playing a game of *senet*, casting their astragals and moving their pieces accordingly through the long, snaking journey of chance, the propitious and the unlucky squares. I was lucky, for the game preoccupied them. Boredom is the fugitive's greatest gift from the god of chance. Carrying only my leather satchel, I hopped over the lintel of the window and landed silently outside. I crouched there for a moment in a sliver of shadow, for the moon was still full, and the silver light, creating vacant silhouettes of trees and buildings, made everything seem like a vast and perfect simulacrum of the absent world by night.

It was as well I waited, for just then a guard ambled past me, a body's length away. He was looking up at the stars. I saw how his hair needed cutting, how his sandals were in poor condition, how his callused feet were dusted silver in this light. He stopped, looked up for a moment, took a slow breath, thinking about something – his destiny, or his debts perhaps – then carried on. I could have taken him, and with a swift jerk of the head despatched him in silence, but it was not necessary. I thought too of the family, somewhere, who would grieve his loss. To me he was a passing figure, to them a unique, irreplaceable life. Why add to the woe of the world? And besides, his body or his absence would have alerted the others. Better to slip away unnoticed. Better not to leave traces of change. People notice change more quickly than anything.

So he passed and I moved forward, making less than no noise. There were gods in my feet that night; my body seemed suddenly to be possessed by a different energy, a kind of lightness. I scaled the wall, its height perhaps ten cubits, as if it were nothing, as if the laws of the world were already slipping and changing, becoming fluid with possibility.

I dropped softly on the far side and found myself in the garden of a house. I crouched down behind a small shrine. I looked carefully around the side, and saw that there was a dinner in progress. Lamps lit up the white napkins on small tables set beside a pool that rippled with luxurious light. Another world, suddenly: the tinkle and murmur of people eating and talking casually. A little drama of talk and food, in a small halo of light under the vast panorama of stars obscured for them by the glow of a few lamps.

I skirted the garden's borders, keeping to the shadows, hoping no dogs kept guard. I sensed that the wall continued all the way around the property. I had little choice but to try to reach the front of the house. As I moved I kept my eyes on the dinner party.

A woman stood up, making some comment whose astuteness and wit precipitated a round of laughter. She moved out of the light and into the house. I used this moment to move quickly along the far border of the garden. A long dark passage to the side of the house lay ahead of me, except where an open doorway's patch of light fell across my path. I hesitated, listened. I could hear the woman moving about in the interior, humming, as if assembling the next course of the meal, and issuing instructions to the servants. I heard footsteps passing away from me, up a tiled corridor. The woman's humming continued. It was close. I held still. Suddenly she appeared in the light. She looked up and saw me. Quickly I put my hand over her mouth and at the same time a metal dish slipped from her hand. Despite my attempts to catch it, it hit the ground and clanged noisily.

We froze. A man called, 'Is everything all right?' Her eyes were wild with fear, and her body struggled. But as her gaze took me in, she went still. She realized she knew me before I made the connection. It was the woman from the boat. The intelligent, handsome woman. I slowly took my hand away from her mouth, begging for her silence with a simple gesture. She nodded. She called back to the man, 'Yes, I just dropped something.'

Suddenly I realized how close, how tight, I was still holding her. She didn't resist, but looked wryly up at me.

'What are you up to?' she whispered. 'Are you some kind of classy thief?'

'Can't say, I'm afraid.'

'Oh, the mystery man.'

'Must be on my way now, though.'

She regarded me. 'Join us. Have some wine.'

I smiled. 'Another time.'

She sighed. 'I hope we'll meet again. I'd like to hear more of your stories, when there is time to tell and listen. The street is that way.'

I confess to you now, she then kissed me slowly on the lips before letting me go. I slipped away, smiling, into the dark.

I found a lane that led me in the direction of the necropolis. My eyes were now accustomed to this night walking, and my other senses had become more acute too. I knew this sensation, this strange way of experiencing the world; it was as if I had begun to live the animal in me. I sensed things without knowing them exactly: the presence of a low branch invisible in the darkness before I walked into it; changes in the height of the path; loose stones in my way; guard dogs behind high walls. I zigzagged my way through the suburb, believing rather than knowing where I was going.

Even at this hour there was a risk of passers-by, of night guards. But what did I have to fear? Few in the city knew me by sight. And even if I did happen to cross the path of someone who recognized me, I could improvise a story, just as I had done in the garden. No, the real feeling was this: with no reason but with total conviction, I knew I must not be seen by anyone else on this journey. I needed to disappear without a trace.

I took a turning along a wider road. The moon whitened one wall, the opposite remained dark. I heard arguing voices from a room, and passed by quickly. Somewhere a child cried. In the shadow of the wall a couple were kissing, the man's body up hard against the woman, her hands alive with rings and polished nails, moving on his neck and back. Not even my passage through the near air disturbed their intimacies. Her whispered encouragements as he moved inside her sounded as close as if she were in my own arms. I felt as if I could be anyone, a visiting spirit passing through the bodies and the feelings of anyone I chose. A kind of delight seized me, an old relish for this dark freedom. Then I moved fast across open ground like a jackal.

The necropolis was no more than a big open space, surrounded by a mud-brick wall. Most of the cemeteries in the cities I knew were built to the west of the river, closer to the setting of the sun. Perhaps this was a temporary ground, or perhaps the location of this new city, so far from civilization, its border more vulnerable to attack, predisposed the planners to bury the dead nearer the suburbs of the living, rather than risk interring their worldly goods and bones in a place where they could not be defended from tomb robbers.

Not enough people had died in the new city yet for the necropolis to be well populated, but even so there were markers and little shrines, and perhaps twenty larger private chapels in various stages of construction. None of these would be for people of noble rank – their tombs were already being carved into the rocks of the hills that surrounded the eastern edge of the city and its hinterlands, closer to the gods. This was a burial place for anyone who was neither a labourer – they had their own burial grounds close to their village – nor a Priest. Here would lie everyone in between: the foreign bureaucrats who died far from their lands; the middle classes; professional, family people who committed their lives to the quieter slavery of offices and desks, seeking to inter their own kind with some sense of reverence and permanence in this new place without a history – at least a human one.

What now? I had no more clues, but something must be here. I wandered among the chapels, trying to move in silence, trying to stay out of the moonlight that cast its blueness upon the black and grey ground. When we were first married and I was working the night patrols, Tanefert insisted I wore an amulet for protection against the spirits. And though I would not confess it to anyone, I was glad to feel it now against my chest.

I had begun to hate the woman I was seeking. Her vanishing seemed more than ever a case of selfish flight. I had so far discovered nothing in the circumstances of her life that seemed so terrible, so awful, as to justify the abandonment of her children and the abdication of her responsibilities. Now here I was, a man she had never even thought of but whose life and fate were bound up with hers. Her beauty seemed cursed – a Queen of disaster.

As I thought these futile thoughts, I began to notice the silent presence of cats in the shadows, having been alerted by a brief squabble among their dark population. Every necropolis has its population of starving cats, and we worship these animals in our temples, adorning them with *wedjat* amulets and gold rings through their noses, and painting them on the walls of our tombs in the role of Ra himself slaying Apophis, the serpent-headed god; finally they are buried, mummified with a look of surprise on their faces, in careful shrouds of cotton and papyrus cloth. One of these cats was staring at me from the top of a large tomb. She did not, I have to admit, bear the attitude of superiority common to her kind. Instead, she jumped down and ran over to me with a friendly greeting and a tinkling of the bell under her collar. Her thick black coat, lustrous in the moonlight, caused her to vanish completely whenever she passed into shadow, but for her eyes, white as new moons, which kept their regard for me. She wound herself around my legs, attempting to converse in her idea of my language, and despite myself I reached down and stroked her full length, allowing her tail, curved into a question mark, to pass through my hand.

What was I doing, in the middle of all this, in the middle of the night, attending to a cat? I was losing my mind. I straightened up and continued my attempts to investigate the necropolis in a consistent and professional way for some kind of answer to the clues that so mystified and irritated me. The cat would not leave me, however. 'I have no food for you,' I whispered to her, thinking all the time what a fool I was being. She continued to purr quietly to herself. I moved off, but when I looked back she was sitting in the moonlight in her ritual pose, scenting the air of my departure, her tail swishing with the power of her thoughts. So I turned around. And this pleased her, for she moved off, her tail up high, curved now like a crook, and pattered off a little way before turning to check that I was following her. Given that I had no idea myself as to where to turn, the random nature of her invitation appealed to me as part of the gamble, the belief in luck, that was pulling me on. I confess here that I, Rahotep, chief detective of the Thebes Medjay division, investigator of the great mystery, gave up all my training to follow the enigmatic instructions of a black cat through a moonlit graveyard. I can hear the hysterical laughter that would greet such a confession back in the office.

The cat nimbly skipped her way through the stones and monuments. Sometimes I lost her in the shadows, but then she would reappear, an elegant black figure against the silver-blue ground. I tried to keep my eyes open for anything along the way that would remind me of the enigma whose power had brought me to this point. But there was nothing.

Then she came to one of the private chapels. With a backward glance, she entered the forecourt and disappeared. It was recently constructed, and one of the bigger ones. Panels of moonlight illuminated the interior. I moved carefully through the outer hall, and into the inner hall. The cat was crouching at the sanctuary niche, eating carefully from the offering bowls. Someone had freshly filled them. She looked like a hieroglyph of herself against the carved stone stele and the symbols of the *hetep* offering table: the reed mats and many-shaped loaves of bread, the cups and vessels, the trussed ducks whose cold images stood for the reality of provisions for the dead.

I stood watching, not wishing to disturb her feast by stroking her. I had no offering to make to the owner of the chapel. In the light of the moon I found I could make out the hieroglyphs of the offering formula. It began at the top in the usual way with *hetep-di-nesw*,. 'a gift which the King gives to Osiris', followed by the standard list of food. And as my eyes moved down the sides of the panel I saw, yes, the figure of a man seated before the offering table. My eyes continued down the stele to the title and name of the deceased. It read: 'Seeker of Mysteries' and then: 'Rahotep.'

The cat stopped eating and looked up at me calmly, as if to say: what else did you expect? You are here. This is the moment of your reckoning. It licked its lips, then quickly slipped behind the stele and vanished.

I had walked into an obvious trap, led on by need and gullibility. How could I have been so stupid? Mahu had fooled me with the kind of tale that appeals to women, children and Priests. I had to get out of there. My tongue was thick and dry. Panic surged through me, its concoction of bile and fear embittering my mouth. Images of my girls swept through my mind, and then a feeling of terrible waste and loss, and something like that snow falling, cold and eternal and silent.

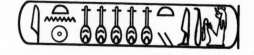

26

I ran back through the halls and out into the desert, gasping to restore my breath and slow my heart. But then I stopped. If the cat had found a way forward, then perhaps I was meant to follow. If I fled this dark place now, I would never know. I hit the wall of the chapel with my fists, forcing myself back to reality, these actions helping me to achieve a state that felt enough like clarity to enable me to make a decision. It was as if I heard Tanefert in my head urging me, 'Don't let your fear conquer you. Use your fear. Think.'

I gathered up all my courage – some Medjay officer, some detective, who was suddenly afraid of the dark! – and re-entered the chapel sanctuary. I felt around the back of the stele. Nothing but builders' dust. So much for the materials of eternity. I felt along the edges of the wall. I licked my finger and held it just slightly off the wall. Was I imagining it? A cooling, the remotest possibility of a current of air where there should be none?

I slipped with difficulty into the narrow space behind the stele and found a gap, barely wide enough for me to pass through to a dark and dusty space, lit, strangely, by a single oil lamp. What little light this gave revealed the cat sitting in the dark, waiting. It turned, its tail curled as elegantly as a temple dancer's finger, and slipped down some stone steps and disappeared. I picked up the lamp. It had an exquisite beauty that reminded me of other sophisticated and elegant things I had seen in the city. I put the thought to one side and raised the lamp, revealing more of the way. By its wavering light I took my first steps down into the deep shadows.

At the bottom, perhaps twenty steps down, I found the cat waiting for me. I greeted her, but she darted away down a tunnel that vanished into a yet deeper darkness. The little tinkle of the charm around her neck was quickly lost. I held up the lamp. Its flame struggled against little gusts of hot air charged with the scents of sand and humid blackness that rose up to me from the region of spirits. I was afraid. But what choice did I have now? 'Do you go down into the Otherworld, as it is said in the Chapters of Coming Forth by Day.' So I began to walk.

It was not a straight path, but a winding serpent, sometimes sinuous, sometimes zig-zagged, and soon my orientation was baffled. The Otherworld is said to be populated by monstrous-headed beings who haunt its terrible caverns and treacherous passing points. The Book of the Dead has efficacious prayers and spells to be spoken to those monstrous guardians who will yield only to their secret names. But could I recall any of those prayers now? Not one. I shivered, hoping no monster would rise up invisibly in this darkness to block my path and demand the fatal passwords.

I had walked now for a long time in my circle of light. The lamp was growing fainter and weaker. I could not estimate, even from a rough count of my paces, where I was. Then the wick guttered, flared for a moment in its last struggle for life, and died. I was plunged into a far deeper blindness than I had ever encountered; always, no matter how obscure the last corner of the alleyway or the deepest room in a deserted house, some light from the world had suggested itself somewhere, but not here. My eyes swam with half-ghosts, the strange, jumbled imaginings of my mind. I dropped the useless thing, and as it hit the stone it jarred horribly. Echoes noisy enough to wake the dead ran like banshees up and down the passageway.

I put out my hands either side of me, but they were invisible, as if numb in the dark. Then I touched the wall of the tunnel, and like a blind man who feels the world only through the point of his stick, and not through the hand that holds it, I began to edge my way onwards into the chaos of the dark. I tried to keep count of my paces as I had no other way of gauging my progress in time or space. But soon the numbers blurred, and I felt disorientated by the slow count.

I walked on like a dead man without his spirit, grazing and bruising myself on unseen corners, banging into the twists and turns of the walls. What few crumbs of comfort I had had – the lit lamp, the presence of the now-vanished cat, the enigmatic message – now lost all meaning and all hope.

Then, as I peered ahead into the endless blackness, it seemed to me I could see a star low in the dark. I walked on, concentrating on it, my lost hands still struggling to guide me between the walls. The more I wanted to believe it was brightening, the more it did. But could my imagination be tricking me with shadows? Or was this the approach of the moment of death, the bright light shining described by those who claim to have approached the threshold of the Otherworld and returned? The star then became a shape, a threshold of light framing a figure – waiting, it seemed in my madness, for me. I began to panic, afraid the opening would slam shut before I could reach it. I struggled on, my knuckles grazing sharply against the walls. I licked the blood and its saltiness shocked me back to a sense of life.

And then I was running, running, my breath rasping, my heart thudding, through the darkness towards the changing, expanding star, reaching out to the figure of a waiting woman. Tanefert? I heard myself shouting her name: 'Tanefert! Tanefert!'

And then I collapsed through a doorway into light.

27

Everything went dark. Words went round and round in my head like a little dream of nonsense: 'O my heart which I had from my mother. O my heart of my different ages . . .' Then I came back to myself, opened my eyes, and slowly sat up. The cat was sniffing my hand delicately.

I struggled to my feet and looked around me. I was in a long stone chamber illuminated by lamps, hundreds of them. The walls and ceilings were decorated with hieroglyph panels and the Aten and the many little hands reaching down with the Gift of the Ankh to the divine and royal worshippers. In niches all along the walls were set solitary figurines and statuettes in crowns and masks, and I knew them: the forty-two gods holding their symbols of judgement. And I knew too that all of this, the old religion, was banned at Akhetaten.

In the centre was a large set of scales, bigger than a man, made of gold and ebony, surmounted by a carving of a seated woman – the goddess Maat, the regulator of the seasons and the stars, of earthly and divine justice. How often had I seen her image on the gold chains worn by all-too-human judges, below their gaunt and jowly faces, compromised and corrupted by luxury, brutality and time? The scales hung at this moment in equilibrium. The atmosphere was perfectly still around them. Then there was a motion. The cat looked up, her eyes green and clear, then ran off into the dark.

Next to the scales appeared a tall, black-skinned figure in a gold girdle, with the large black and silver head-mask of a jackal. Anubis. The figure stared at me, waiting. He said nothing, so I spoke.

'Where am I?'

'This is the Hall of the Two Truths.'

The voice came not from the mask but from the deeper shadows of the chamber. It was a woman's voice, confident, direct, beautiful. I knew at once I had found her.

I said, 'I thought the thing about truth was there is only one truth.'

'There are many truths. Even here. There is your truth, there is my truth.'

'And then there is the Truth.'

It was as if I could see her smile, though she remained invisible in the shadows.

'How wise you are,' she said. 'You and all the others who speak of such things as the Truth. I wonder what you have been writing about me in your little journal. Which truths have you recorded there?'

She knew everything already. I tried to keep up with her.

'Not truths, necessarily. Stories.'

'Ah, stories. And how do they help us?'

'They are versions of things. Possibilities. Of you.'

'How many sides are there to that story? I would say many. I would say perhaps an infinite number.'

Was she right?

'Perhaps.'

'So every story has an infinite number of sides. A circle, perhaps. Is every story a circle?'

'Every true story, perhaps.'

'Perhaps we arrive at the end only to find it is a beginning, but now we know this truly for the first time.'

Neither of us spoke for a moment. I was a little enchanted by our cleverness. There was a quickness to it all, an intimacy, as if already we were thinking and completing each other's thoughts. Suddenly I needed to see this long-lost, troubling, enigmatic woman.

'Will you show yourself?'

She was silent for a moment, then made a sound somewhere between a sigh and a light laugh. 'Perhaps. But you must answer some questions first. You must be judged. Your truth must be judged. Your sins must be judged. Your heart. I hope it is a good one. A true one.'

The jackal-headed god gestured for me to approach. 'Your heart must not lie in the presence of the god,' he said. His voice was sonorous, firm, and with an accent I knew came not from the Two Lands but from beyond the cataracts. Nubia.

I nodded. This was a game, a play of masks and scenes. I understood. At the same time, it was deadly serious. We were enacting the prayers and spells in the Book of the Dead. Everything we were doing was proscribed now. My answers, I knew, would determine my fate, regardless of anything.

'I will not lie,' I said.

'We will commence the Negative Confession.' He began to recite. 'You Gods of the Soul's House who judge the Earth and the Sky . . . Worship Ra in the Ship of the Sun . . .' More incantations about the fire serpent and the Children of Impotence, and seeing the sun disc and the moon disc unceasingly: 'May my Soul go forth and travel to every place which it desires, may my name be called out, may a place be made for me in the Ship of the Sun when the God sails the Sky of Day; and may I be welcomed into the presence of Osiris in the Land of Truth.'

As he mentioned the Great Name of Osiris, a fear burned in me that my whole life was suspended on the thread of this moment, gathering like a single drop of water into fullness, only shortly to fall. On one side of the scales was the matter of my life: my childhood, my wife, my girls, my love for our precious little world, all the things, good, bad and indifferent, I had thought and felt and done and been. On the other was the future, as intangible and unknowable as that strange snow in a box.

The jackal-headed figure bade me approach a spot to one side of the scales. I looked about me. The further reaches of the chamber disappeared into shadows, but now I saw the two statues on either side of me: Meskhenet and Renenutet, goddesses of fate and destiny, who would speak for the dead. And on the other side, a crouching beast like a lion with the long jaws, ferociously armoured, of a crocodile – the Devourer, ready to consume me and my little lies. He looked as if he was made of stone, but I could not be sure.

The Perfect One spoke: 'What is your name?'

'Rahotep.'

'Why are you here?'

'I am seeking the answer to a mystery.'

'What is the nature of this mystery?'

'I seek one who has disappeared.'

Silence. Then the Jackal came forward and bade me speak my words of reply into one of the gold dishes of the scales. His questions came fast, insistent, not pausing for me to think, and out of my mouth came a litany of responses: 'No, I have not lied; No, I have not committed adultery; Yes, I have killed; No, I have not stolen' and so on, until I found myself pouring out the words of my good and bad deeds as if into a cursing bowl. Then the Jackal dropped a white ostrich feather which zigzagged through the air into the other dish of the scales. The device seemed calibrated to the weight of nothing for it shivered slightly as the feather touched down; as if it might dip under the grave doubts of such lightness, and indicate my doom. But it gradually returned to absolute stillness. The air around me had held its breath. Now it began to breathe again.

Then she spoke again: 'You are a Truth Speaker. Welcome. Close your eyes. Come forward.'

I shut my eyes and stepped like a blind man into more shadow. Her hand took mine, led me forward, and suggested I sit. I sensed her moving around me.

'All that remains is to return you to yourself. For if you were truly dead, your soul would be a bird, fluttering between the worlds. Is your soul fluttering?'

I could not answer.

'The Truth Speaker is lost for words?'

'Not everything can be expressed in words.'

'True. But now it is time for me to restore your five senses. I cannot speak for the others, the senses of humour, honour and so on.'

She led me to a bench and I sat down.

'According to the directions of the rite, you should really be lying in a coffin, but I think that would be melodramatic. Do you recognize this?'

I nodded, feeling the object she was holding, recognizing the fish-tail flint blade. 'It is a *peseh-kef* knife.'

'It is said that the Priest will point the right leg of a freshly slaughtered ox at you to try to transfer some of its strong spirit into your resurrected body. I will not be using the right leg of an ox.'

She placed the knife at my mouth. I felt the cold kiss of the blade against my lips. I smelled the warm scent of her body. I felt suddenly filled with warmth, with the possibility of life. I began to believe again that I could accomplish the task set for me, and return home to my life. She held the blade there for a little while as these feelings opened up inside me, then slowly she lifted it away and placed it over my eyes, right, then left, and the same for my ears. Again the cool touch of the metal. I felt myself blush like a lover.

'You may now speak, and eat, see and hear. You are alive again.'

So I opened my eyes.

28

The shadows were drawn aside like a curtain, and I saw her.

I was sitting in an antechamber. It seemed the walls and floor were made of silver; but perhaps this was just the cumulative effect of the multitude of lamps, and besides, by this point I would have believed anything, such was the state of confused enchantment in my mind. There was nothing in the chamber but steps disappearing up into further shadows, a low bench, a small table set out with food and drink, and two chairs. She was sitting in one of them. She was wearing the blue crown, revealing the pure shapes and contours of her neck and shoulders, and accentuating the open beauty of her face.

She sat with her hands in her lap, watching me quizzically, observing and enjoying, I believe, the play of thoughts and feelings that passed no doubt plainly across my face. I would have told her anything. And it seemed she knew this, for as the thought occurred to me she smiled quickly. The brief smile passed through me like a wave of delight, of warmth, of . . . where are the words for moments like these when we feel ourselves most alive, most alert to another living presence, to its mysterious spirit, tingling to the very borders of our physical being and beyond so that we feel we are not after all limited by skin and bone but have become a part of everything? I am nothing more than a Medjay officer, a detective, just one passing character in the world's charade; yet for a moment, in the glory of her attention, I felt like a small god liberated from time and the world. Then her smile passed. I knew I wanted it to come back, knew indeed that I would do anything to return it to that remarkable, dignified, open face.

'What time is it?' I finally asked, and immediately felt like a fool for asking such a simple and irrelevant question.

'It is the hour of Akhet.' Her voice was calm and clear.

'Remind me what that means, please.' I felt crude next to her.

'It means the hour before dawn. It is also what the Books call the time of becoming effective. Another way of thinking of it might be this: the *akh* is the name we give to the reunion of the person with his soul after death. Some think this reunion endures for eternity.'

'That's a long time.'

She returned my nervous irony with a careful look. It reminded me I did not need to play the Medjay man here. The challenge was harder: to be myself.

'And another way of thinking about it is this: in the sacred language the sign *akh* is the sacred ibis, bird of wisdom. Think of it as the dawn chorus of your new life.'

We looked at each other for a moment. What was happening to me?

'Is this my new life?' I asked. 'Did I die? Am I reborn?'

'Perhaps, if you look at it in the right way. The true way.' She tilted her head to consider me.

'I am honoured to meet you,' I said.

'Oh, please don't be honoured. I am tired of honours. I'm sorry to have made things so difficult for you. So dramatic. All these tasks and

206

tests. You must have felt like a man in a fable. But I had to know whether I could trust you. Whether you were the true man. Are you hungry? Thirsty?'

She gestured to the table and poured me a goblet of water. I drank it down, not realizing how parched and dull my mouth was, how warm the room had become. Perhaps that was why I was talking such rubbish. She refilled the jug from a small fountain set into the wall, and placed it before me. Every gesture and movement was perfect. A woman in complete possession of herself. Even the water pouring into the jug had seemed to command her full attention and pleasure. She was alive to everything.

'You have sweet water here?'

'Yes, there's a spring beneath the building. That is partly why I chose this site.'

'For what?'

'For my sanctuary.'

'Sanctuary from what?'

She paused. 'I must not forget you are the man who finds the answers to the great mysteries by asking simple questions.' She poured me more water, then walked slowly away, up the chamber. 'Is that how you found me? By asking questions?' Her eyes glittered. Amusement. Curiosity. Interest. 'How do you know what you know?'

At this moment I had no answer. I felt as if my life's work, my actions and thoughts, my dreams and ideals, had dissolved into a handful of dust being cast by her hand, glittering in the lamplight as it fell. And I liked that feeling.

'Our Lord—'

'Call him by his name. Names are powerful. Call him Akhenaten.'

The way she spoke his name was as complex as a phrase of music. There was some melody of affection in it, but also dissonances and sharper conflicting emotions. She moved further into the darkness of the chamber.

'Akhenaten called for me, rather than for the chiefs of the city Medjay, to try to find you.'

'He did not call for you. I did. And I have been watching you since you arrived.'

I felt as if a door had opened where no door had been. She turned back to me, her magnificent face revealed again by the light. She waited calmly for my reaction, her cool eyes appraising mine. For a moment I floundered, trying to incorporate her words into the information I had collected so far – trying, in truth, to see the whole mystery anew from the perspective demanded by those few simple words. I suddenly felt a terrible vertigo. Seshat, the dead girl? What about Tjenry, and Meryra? And why this magnificent and horrible charade?

The cat sidled up to me, rubbing her long flank against my leg, sending a silvery cascade through both of us. I stroked her. Nefertiti smiled, and this time the smile was more open.

'She likes you.'

'I like her.'

'But you are a man who does not like cats.'

'Things change. How could you know she would find me, and lead me to you?'

The cat moved over to her mistress, jumped onto her lap and looked back at me, bowing her head a little, her tail curled neatly beneath her.

'I didn't know. I believed.'

I felt lost again in uncharted territory where things are not what they seem. Where truth is many things. Where belief can make things happen. Where I did not know what I knew.

'I knew she would come back to me. And I believed you might follow.'

I said, 'I have the strangest feeling that I'm a character and you're writing my destiny.'

'We are in a story that includes us all. I had to call you to me because I do not know the ending. You have set the birds to flight. But now we are in the difficult middle of it, and can only find the end by living through what is to come. I know what I wish for my ending, but it is not sure. It cannot be, until it is enacted, accomplished, made real. The Book of the Living, if you like. And for that I need your help.'

Her cleverness was exciting; I relished the nuances of her expression as she talked – the ebb and flow of emotions, of intelligence, of wit. The thought occurred to me, fleetingly, that I was watching a great actress, deeply involved with every word yet superbly in control of herself. I also began to perceive something else: an absolute dark well of need in her. She was desperate to reveal herself, her story, her reasons and perhaps even her fears. She needed someone to talk to. I suddenly realized she was alone, in a small boat, adrift on a sea of troubles. And she was asking for my help.

I am a sceptic where words are concerned. I have learned to mistrust them for often they lead us astray or tell us apparently simple things that disguise or deny darker, less appealing paradoxes and truths. There is a slipperiness, an unreliability, in words. But there is also something in their power that sometimes has its own inevitable beauty. And is it not true that part of the story of words is that they metamorphose into other things – into stories we tell about the world or ourselves or each other, or into dreams we half recall, or into the silence beyond words? I had to hear her story. After all, I was a part of it now.

'Tell me what you need me to do,' I said. 'And please tell me why.'
She sat down again, opposite me. 'It's a long story.'
'Am I in it?'
'You are.'

29

'I have to go back to the beginning,' Nefertiti said. 'Most stories start with birth, and childhood, don't they? I was born in such and such a place, and at this time and this season; these were the propitious or the unlucky stars that witnessed the moment of my birth and held the secret of my destiny. But such things are far away now, so far I do not know them. I was lucky, I suppose, to be raised in a family that possessed power and influence and wealth and pride. So much abundance! We forgot the fragility of all fortune.'

I listened. She was seeking the thread of her tale.

'Apart from fragments which might as well be dreams – running through a green garden between the sunlight and the shadow; the sounds of the Great River on a boat in the evening; travelling home one night in a carrying chair, my head on my mother's lap as I gazed up at the stars – my first real memory is of being taken by my father during the Opet Festival to walk the new processional colonnade at Luxor. I held his hand for I was frightened by the avenue of sphinxes:

they seemed like monsters with sunny faces. I couldn't understand why there were so many of them! As we walked my father told me fables: of Thutmosis, who answered a dream and removed the encroaching desert sands from the Great Sphinx in return for the throne of the Great Estate; and of the dashing Amenhotep, who loved horses above all things, who distributed and displayed the corpses of his conquered enemies on the walls of the city, and who was buried with his favourite longbow; and of his grandson, Amenhotep our King, the Handsome, now grieving the sudden death of his first son. I remember he told me the dead prince was buried with his favourite cat, whom he called Puss. Puss went with him into the Otherworld. I liked the thought of Puss sitting in the prow of the Great Barque of the Sun, his green eyes looking upon the mysteries of the Otherworld, and on the green face of Osiris himself.

'When I asked my father, as children do who are delighted by stories of men and women of greatness and power, what happened next, he said, "You will see." And one day, I did. One day my father called for me and said, "I want you to be very brave. Will you do that for me?" His face was always so serious. I looked at him and said, "Can I grow my hair now?" And he smiled, and said, "Now would be a good time." I clapped my hands. I thought: *now* I am about to become a woman! So he sent me to the women of the family, and I was initiated into their secrets: their bowls and spoons and combs, their little laughs and lies and gossip. But I also remember my mother looking at me, as if from further away, something unspoken passing between us. As if she wanted to tell me something but could not find the way to say it.'

She poured the cat from her lap, rose, and walked a little way along the room, remembering and pacing, the two things working together.

'The next morning, the women returned together, with many robes and jewellery. They were silent. Something was happening. They dressed me in layers of gold and white clothing. I was wrapped up like a gift. A High Priest came with my father, the women left the room, and he gave me instructions. What to say, what not to say, when to speak and when to remain silent. I looked at my father, who said, "This is a great day for you, and for all our family. I am very proud." Then he picked me up, my mother kissed me goodbye, and he carried me out of my home.

'I remember the sun and the noise along the crowded ways. All the litters and chairs had been cleared so there was just me and my father on the avenue, riding in a chariot. I could hear the birds singing in the air above the noise of the crowds, who all seemed to be paying their respects to me. To me! I held my father's hand tightly. We were driven to the palace. But the further we left my home behind, the more I began to feel like a piece of furniture on a cart and less like a princess in a fable.

'We arrived at the palace and I was carried through court after court, chamber after chamber, all crowded with dignitaries and officials who bowed as we passed. My world retreated and disappeared behind me. I remember I was set down beside a curtain. My father said to me, "Here you stand on the threshold of a great future. I am passing you forward, now, to your new life." I think I tried to wrap my arms around his neck, to cling on to him, but he prised my fingers gently away, held my hands and said, "Remember your promise. Be brave. And never forget I love you." I believe there were tears on his face. I had never seen my father weep.'

Nefertiti stopped speaking for a moment. The memory seemed to overwhelm her.

'I would have cried out then, but I saw something strange: passing along the corridor, as over-burdened with clothing as I was, the slight figure of a young man. He raised his head and looked at me. His eyes were thoughtful. What happened in that moment? Understanding, recognition, complicity? I knew we knew each other and that our lives were entwined in some profound way. Then a ribbon was tied over my eyes, and the world vanished.

'The noise in the chamber on the far side of the curtain suddenly hushed. I heard a chime and chant of words, the rattle of sistra, an announcement, then my father's hands gently pushing me forward through the curtains and into the chamber. I looked beneath the ribbon at the ground and saw lotus flowers and fish, and I walked across this painted water. Hands received me at the end of this long walk, and they turned me around. My head was raised, the ribbon untied, and I saw a blur of people, hundreds of them all staring at me, their eyes moving over every detail of my being. I was so heavily clothed I could not have raised my own hand to my eyes, yet I felt naked, stripped down to my last skin. I dared to look quickly to my side. The boy's face, a long, serious face, glanced quickly at me, a partner in all this strangeness. I felt a small gladdening in my heart, which was tight with fear. Some of my spirit returned to me.'

She stopped her pacing. Her sad smile was charged with all the loss and strangeness which that girl, alive now inside this woman as she spoke, had suffered. I wanted to make it all right. I wanted to console her.

'Don't feel sorry for me,' she said suddenly. 'I don't require your pity or your sorrow.'

She continued to pace again, as if each careful step returned her to the story.

'I remember little else. I suppose the ceremony was concluded satisfactorily; I suppose the audience dispersed to their dinners and their gossip and their criticisms. I followed my new husband down a different hallway, not the one through which I had been brought in but into a different part of the palace. I remember looking at him a few steps ahead of me, hobbling on his crutch. I liked it – the way he had turned the difficulty and effort into a kind of grace. I imagined I could see him smiling, secretly, for my benefit. I remember I thought of him, kindly, as weak; as the one sheep the hunting lion would pick out from the flock and kill. So you see, I was the more deceived.'

I did not press her on that point. Not yet.

'Ahead of him his father, the Great Amenhotep, led the procession. I had imagined him as a great hero, the builder of monuments, and a close friend of the gods. But who was this old man huffing and sighing under the troublesome burden of his heavy body, and complaining of the terrible pain in his teeth, and cursing the heat of the day?

'We arrived in a private chamber, and I found myself surrounded by my new family. Amenhotep turned to me, took me by the chin and turned my face to examine it like a vase. "Do you know, child, how much talk and contest and disagreement have preceded your arrival among us?" I kept my gaze on him. In my mind all these impressions and thoughts blew about me as in a storm. I felt I was a leaf dragged into the course of a mighty river, the river of history. "You will soon understand how things are. Did you hear the poets calling out your praises?" Again I shook my head. "Be worthy of those praises." He was stern; his breath was bad. I remember even now his sad face, his bald head, the ruins of his teeth. But I liked him. His wife, Tiy, my new mother, said nothing. Her face was like a stone.'

She came and sat down again, and drank a little from the goblet of water I offered her. Then she continued her story.

'Once the sun was low on the horizon on that changing day, I was led into a chapel of a kind I had never seen before. Unlike the dark temples, this was a sun court illuminated by the rich light of the setting sun. At a certain moment a gold disc set into the wall caught the exact angle of the late light, and blazed. Led by Amenhotep, we all raised our hands to this sudden fire until, as the moments passed, it diminished and died, and the sky turned dark red, dark blue, then black. The old man said to me: "Now you too have received the great gift of the one god." And he hobbled away. To me it was the last of the many incomprehensible revelations that came to me on that one day.

'That night, I was taken to my husband's chamber. I did not know what to expect and I think neither did he. We both looked at each other, uncertain and afraid, and for a time after the last adviser and diplomat and lady of the chamber had left, neither of us spoke. Then I noticed a papyrus scroll upon a table, he noticed my interest, and we fell to a discussion. The first night of my new life we talked. And my new husband told me another story. Different from any I had ever heard before. He told me the story of the Amun Priests and their great

214

possessions, their gardens and fields, their huge estates employing thousands of officers, armies of serfs, legions of servants. I imagined a great green fable of a pleasant land, but he said I was wrong. That the land might be rich, thanks to the gods, but that men and Priests, despite their fine words of praise and worship, were interested always and only in power and treasure. And in stealing it. He said, "My father has not allowed this to happen. He told me it was our sacred duty to preserve the order of the Great Estate from this dangerous unbalancing by the power of the Priests of Amun."'

She smiled. 'I was very young. I thought everything was a question of right and wrong. Now, of course, I have little choice but to think of the world as a game of checks and balances, between the Priesthoods and the people, the army and the Treasury, of negotiations and compromises backed up with the threat of force and death. But then, I thought it was simply a question of right and wrong.'

I allowed myself to speak. 'I remember. Amenhotep forced the reconciliation of the two greatly opposed Priesthoods under a new agreement. It was an astute manoeuvre. And with that new balance of power achieved he began to build the great new works of Thebes. This was our childhood.'

'Yes. Our childhood.'

'So why did things change? Why the Great Changes?'

She looked at me. 'Why do you think?'

'I know what I heard. That the Amun Priests grew richer still, that their granaries held more grain than those of the King. That the poor harvests and the arrival of new immigration were starting to create problems.'

'And something else. Something was missing. And the thought, when it came, leaped far beyond this previous reconciliation to something even bolder, even more radical. What is the one thing all peoples, no matter where in the Empire they are born, have in common? The supreme experience present every day to the eyes of all living beings?'

The Aten. Light. In whose blaze all other gods had now been

overshadowed. This was a turning point for us both. I waited to hear what she would have to say.

'You are wondering: how is it we arrived here? Why did we choose to build the city here, away from Thebes and from Memphis? Why did we choose to make ourselves gods? Why did we risk everything in the world to bring forth these changes?'

I nodded. 'I am.'

Nefertiti said nothing for a little while, and I realized that a faint light had crept into the chamber, countering the many lamps that were now guttering down to extinction.

'We are back with the question of stories,' she said. 'Which one shall I tell you? Shall I tell you about the dream of a better and truer world? Shall I tell you about the day we first commanded the companions, the great ones of the palaces, the commanders of the guards, the officers of the works, the officials, the minor officials, their sons, to come before us and kneel in the dust and worship us as we worshipped the light? Shall I tell you about the looks on their faces? Shall I tell you about the happy births of our daughters, and the general sorrow at the lack of a son? Shall I tell you about the enemies among friends moving against us, men of the past to whom we opposed the loyal younger men? And shall I tell you what it was like to *feel*, to *relish* our new freedom from old constraints, old lies, old gods? To know the beautiful force of the present moment, the glorious possibilities of the future? We built this dream out of mud, stone, wood and labour, but we also built it out of our minds, our imaginations, like a Book of Light, not a Book of Shadows, to be read, if you have the knowledge, like a map of a new eternity.'

I stared at her.

'Do you think me mad?'

She asked the question intently, seriously. I could answer honestly.

'No, not mad,' I said.

'Most did, secretly. We knew what was passing for conversation in the streets, at tables in people's homes, in the offices. But our ambition was nothing less than *ankhemmaat*. Living in Truth. Remember the poem?

> *You create the infinite possibilities out of yourself:*
> *Cities, towns, fields, the journey of the great river;*
> *Every eye sees you in relation to all things*
> *For you are Aten of the light over the world,*
> *And when you depart none exist . . .'*

I remembered my intuitions on seeing the Great Temple for the first time. All those loyal and conforming citizens raising their hands and their babies to the light of the sun; those old men, sweating in their dignity during the ceremony for Meryra; and the poor dead girl whose face had been beaten off. What did all that have to do with living in truth?

She turned away from me and walked along the edge of the last shadows that still lay across the floor.

'But I now know that to exalt human nature, especially one's own, beyond reasonable limits is a terrible mistake,' she continued. 'Passionate commitment to the idea of a better world can disguise passionate hatreds. Beliefs that claim to transform men end up debasing, degrading and enslaving them. So I think. I pray it is not too late.'

She hugged her arms about herself. The spell of the lamps had given way to blue dawn light descending the stairs. In that light she seemed less magnificent, less exceptional, more ordinary, more human. There were lines of tension and tiredness etched into her face. She wound a fine shawl around her shoulders for warmth and came and sat down close to me.

'I see now the horror we have unleashed. It is a monster of destruction. The streets are filling with soldiers, homes are being broken open, fear is occupying the cities like an invading army. I heard that a band of Medjay set fire to a village, mutilated the temple icons, killed, cooked and dined upon the sacred animals in the sanctuaries, and then forced the men out naked into the wilderness. Is this the future of which I dreamed? No. This is barbarism and darkness, not justice and enlightenment. Even the little things, even jars of unguent and incense, are to be made illegal if they carry the symbols of the old gods. It is madness.'

I said nothing. I agreed with everything she said. But I was really waiting for what came next.

'But Akhenaten does not think so. My husband, the Lord of the Two Lands, is blind to what is happening. He is obsessed with his vision. And by deluding himself that all is well he plays into the hands of his many enemies. He demands greater responses, stronger enforcements, an ever harsher light shining into every part of people's lives. And of course the people start to hate him. He has persecuted the Amun Priests beyond what was necessary and tolerable, and he has ordered the names and images of their gods to be hacked from temple walls and local shrines, even tombs. He has cast them out upon the streets where they cry havoc and revenge. And he ignores the growing turbulence elsewhere in the Empire; he ignores the pleas for help from his northern allies. The territories become unstable, caravans are attacked, and the work of generations to extend and confirm our power over the vassal states is lost in a year. The local wars become more severe, the populations lose the security they need to produce goods, supply routes become too dangerous, fields lie derelict and produce only weeds, taxation is not collected, and those loyal to us lose their towns and their lives to bandits whose only interest is immediate profit and whose only kindness is slaughter. Above all, he ignores the fact that there are men of great power who wish to manipulate this nightmare, this chaos, to their own ends. Monsters at our borders and nightmares at our gates work well for them. Do you begin, now, to understand why I had to leave?'

She looked at me with a desperate plea for understanding in her eyes. Again I had the sensation of vertigo, of finding myself on the precipice of a terrible abyss, and no bridge but words to cross it.

'This is the talk of the city,' I said. 'I have heard it whispered wherever I have gone. But it has not entirely come to pass yet.'

'No, not yet. And *that* is the story we must enact. Everything is at stake. Not just my life, or the lives of my daughters and the continuance of our family, or of you and your own children. Not just the fate of this city, and its Great Truth. But the future of the Two Lands. Everything that Time has created out of nothing, all this gold and green glory, will be lost to chaos and suffering, returned to the wilderness of the Red Land, if someone does not stop it now.'

I built the only bridge I could to her. 'I will do anything you ask of me. Not only for these reasons, but also because I want my old life back. My home and my family. I cannot return to them unless I go forward.'

She touched my hand gently. 'You are living in great fear for their well-being. I am sorry to have brought you to this. But perhaps now you understand why.'

We sat there, quietly, as the light evolved through deepest indigo into long, low streaks of red and then to a pale gold that brightened the room, the signs and symbols in the stones, and her face, the new day like a scarab of power and promise.

'There are many forces working against me,' she said eventually. 'Too many threats. Some within the family, some in the Medjay, some in the military, and of course the Priesthood, who would overthrow the new god and return the Two Lands immediately to the old and more profitable ways. Many of the new men in power would have opposed me without a second thought, for their lives and fortunes are dedicated to the new regime. Do you know what it is like to trust no-one, not even your own children? That is why I had to choose flight over fight. Why I had to leave behind my life and myself, why I had to cover my tracks and find a way to save us all. And I could not bear to be seen to condone the Great Changes now, by appearing beside my husband at the Festival.'

'And the girl? Seshat?'

'I heard the news.'

219

'Her face was beaten off.'

She turned away in a gesture of sorrow. 'I know.'

I stared at her. When she looked back at me her eyes were lit with pain and anger.

'You think I ordered her death to cover my disappearance?'

'The thought had occurred to me.'

'You think I would kill an innocent girl? To save myself?'

She walked away, the anger suddenly seething inside her. I had to admit that the possibility of such guilt no longer fitted the woman I had found. I almost wished I had not spoken. I had hurt her. Still, I could not help but add, 'And you know about the deaths also of the young Medjay officer Tjenry, and of Meryra the High Priest?'

She nodded, returned to the couch and sat down, shaking her head. Neither of us spoke, but I could see she was thinking, like me: who could have committed such brutal atrocities, and why?

'Why me?' I said, suddenly.

'What do you mean?'

'I mean, of all the people you could have called upon, why me?'

She shook her head, smiled sadly, then looked me straight in the eye. 'I had heard a lot about you. You are a rather well-known young man. I read the classified papers on your accomplishments. I was intrigued by your new methods, which seemed clever and, in some strange way, beautiful. I knew there were men of the old order within the Medjay who did not like you. And as I read more, I felt that you would not care. That you might be afraid but you would not act out of fear. There was something in all this that I trusted. Why do we trust anyone?'

The question hovered between us, unanswerable. But I had something else I needed to say now.

'Sometimes telling people that we trust them confers on them the responsibility to live up to that expectation.'

Her expression of amusement acknowledged the burden she was placing on me.

'Yes. Of course. And will you?'

'What choice do I have?'

She looked disappointed by my answer; her face suddenly lost its animation and its curiosity. It was as if I had dropped a level of play in a complex game of *senet*.

'You always have a choice,' she countered. 'But that is not what I am asking. You know that.'

Now it was my turn to tell a little story. I set everything out so that there could be no misunderstanding.

'Akhenaten has threatened to execute my family, including my three girls, if I do not find you in time for the Festival. There have already been several attempts on my life. Mahu, the head of the Medjay, has told me he will have me tortured and garrotted, after he personally destroys my family, if I trouble him or this delightful and disastrous city of yours. I have been made to stand in the sun in the middle of the day. I have been led by a black cat through a crazy tunnel, and made to believe I had scared myself to death in order to test my loyalty to a woman whose disappearance has brought all this about. Is it surprising that the thought of catching the next boat up the river and going home is perhaps a little appealing? It has been a busy five days, and I have to say, my Lady, I still think there is something you're not telling me.'

For a moment she looked amazed to be addressed in this way. And then she laughed, deeply and happily, and as she did so her face seemed to release itself from its tensions. I must admit, I had to work hard to keep the smile from my own face. Gradually her amusement subsided.

'I have waited a long time for someone to talk to me like that,' she said. 'Now I know you are the man I believe you to be.'

I sensed now a welcome sparkle of candour between us.

'Perhaps there are a few things I have not told you,' she continued. 'I will tell you everything I can.' Her face hardened. Suddenly she was made of stone. 'I have a plan. It requires your assistance. I can promise you only that I will return in time to save your family from the sentence of death.'

'When?' I asked.

'By the time of the Festival.'

I nodded. Suddenly we were agreeing a deal. The politician in her was now paramount.

'I need to know now whether you will accept. If not, of course, you are free to do as you wish – to go home to your family. But I will say this: if you do, the future will turn out only one way, and I promise you it will be a time of darkness. If you decide to stay, you can help me save us all, and take part in a great story. You will have something exceptional and true to write in that little journal of yours. What is your choice?'

I was taken aback by her sudden coldness. I tried to calculate the options in my head. I still had the best part of a week's grace before Akhenaten's sentence of death on my family could be confirmed, but Mahu could still move against me while I was missing. Perhaps I could get a message home to warn Tanefert; perhaps he would not make so open a move before he had proof of my failure. And what of Ay, whose name I had invoked so recklessly? It seemed clear to me that the only way truly to protect the lives of my family would be to see this through to the end. Otherwise we would always be walking in fear, every shadow seeming dangerous.

'What do you want me to do?' I asked.

She looked truly relieved, as if I could have answered differently.

'I need you to protect me when I return,' she said. 'In order to do that I need you to find out who is plotting against my life.'

'Can I ask you some questions?'

She sighed. 'Always questions.'

'Let's start with Mahu.'

'I do not think it wise to prejudice you with my own opinions about individuals.'

'Tell me anyway.'

'He is as loyal as his dog. He has served us well. I would trust him with my life.'

I couldn't believe my ears. Surely she was wrong.

'He tried to kill me. He loathes me. He wants me dead.'

'That is because his pride, which is great, has been insulted by your presence. But that does not mean he does not want me found for the right reasons.'

'I don't trust him.'

She said nothing.

'Who else?' I asked. 'Ramose? Parennefer?'

'These are key players. They all have their motivations. Ramose is a wise counsellor. I have never seen him act out of meanness, revenge or personal ambition. This is rare. He seems like a castle – strong, harsh, defended. But he loves beauty and appearance. You have noticed how well he dresses? He was once Master of the Wardrobe.' She smiled at my look of surprise.

'And Parennefer?'

'Parennefer likes order. He has a horror of messiness. His desire for precision goes very deep in his personality, and is very powerful.'

I tried my trump card. 'And Ay?'

She could not dissimulate the fear that flitted across her face like a hunted animal. What had I touched upon? A name to conjure with. The name I had used against Mahu.

'Can you tell me about him?'

'He is the uncle of my husband.'

'And?'

'He will attend the Festival.'

She looked cornered.

'Are you afraid of him?'

'Your simple questions, again.' She shook her head anxiously, then continued. 'He will be arriving in the city shortly. Along with all the players in this drama, and with the heads of the army; and with them all the tribal chiefs from north and south, all the city dignitaries from across the lands, all those who pay tribute, whose children are retained in the royal nurseries, whose daughters are married into the Harem. In short, every man and woman of power and family will arrive in the city in the next few days. I have to act decisively against my enemies, and with my friends, in the certain knowledge of who they are, and what they plan against and for me.'

'And when and how will you return?'

'I will tell you when the time is nearer.'

This made me angry. How dare she keep me in the dark like this?

'I have spent the last few days trying to track you in the words of the people in power,' I said. 'Now you wish me to return, openly, risking everything, and walk further into this nest of snakes? And you will not tell me what you plan?'

She did not flinch from my anger. '*Think*. What if you are caught? Akhenaten would do anything to have me back. I am all that stands between him and disaster. What if Mahu tortures you, or hurts your family? Could you hold back from saving them? I doubt it. What you do not know you cannot tell.'

'They would torture me and my family anyway.'

She took this in. 'I know. What else can I do? Trust me in this. I can give you guidance and information. I can offer you the assistance of one or two loyal supporters. And a promise that I will tell you every-thing, when I can.'

Here I was again, having to choose between the only attractive decision – walking out of there – and the inevitable one – following this through to the end.

'The only loyal supporter I have been granted so far is a man who cannot tell the difference between a fine wine and well water. And even his loyalty is not beyond question.'

'I see.'

She went to a door, which I had not even noticed before, and knocked quietly. It opened, and into the chamber stepped a familiar figure, on his face an expression of profound amusement struggling to masquerade as respect.

'Morning, sir.'

'Khety!'

He bowed to the Queen.

'Khety has been under my command since you arrived. I would

trust him with my life. I trusted him with yours, although you did not know it. He will escort you to a safe house in the city and inform you of the things you need to know. '

I didn't know whether I wanted to punch him or hug him. He had certainly sustained the illusion of a young fool very convincingly. I turned to the Queen and bowed.

'We will talk further,' she said, 'but now you must rest, before we move forward together.'

We followed the dawning light up the staircase and emerged into an enclosed courtyard, full of plants. At the centre, water pulsed into a stone basin. Birds experimented with short calls and trills.

We separated to rest.

So I sit and write this down, in sunlight, in the warmth of the new day. I know what I have to do, and why. I know Nefertiti is alive, and why she has cast me in a role whose purpose is greater than I had imagined. My feeling of foolishness is dissolving slowly, leaving me with a new sense of purpose, and, I must confess, a wish above almost all other things to earn again the smile that had graced her face. Would it be possible to accomplish the task? She, Khety and I are almost alone against the great forces at work against us, with all their advantages of knowledge, security, wealth and power. But we have one advantage: we are invisible. No-one knows where we are, whether in the next world or in the shadows of this one.

30

Khety continued to look unnecessarily pleased with himself. 'Oh, the great seeker of mysteries . . .' He kept nudging me and winking like a stage fool, as if there was now between us a complicity of trust, and not only that, but an equality of accomplishment. So when he said 'Did you really not work it out?' for the third time, I had to reply.

'Khety, your impression of an idiot was so good that it never occurred to me you had a sand grain's worth of sense in your whole character. Perhaps the reason is that you were not altogether acting a role. Perhaps there was some truth in it.'

He looked hurt for a moment. 'Well, I told you several things about myself that were completely true. And by the way, I do like wine and I love almonds.'

Perhaps I was merely trying to repress my own sense of foolishness. I detest being caught out. We both sulked like children for a few minutes.

We were sitting in the shade of the courtyard protected from the sun by overhanging eaves and lengths of linen shades.

'You understand the seriousness of the situation in which we find ourselves?'

Khety nodded. Once again, he knew everything.

'You know the Instruction of Ptahhotep: "Do not take control of a matter whose ending you will not be able to control"? Well, that is exactly what we have no choice but to do. I'll need you to enlighten me on all the background matter. I still can't understand why you didn't tell me before when you knew how much was at stake.' He tried to interrupt but I put up my hand to silence him. 'Yes, no doubt you were sworn to utmost secrecy. No doubt there were other, greater issues at stake. Now, I need to know about a safe house, and about the security measures for the Festival. Above all I need to deal with Mahu.'

'How can I help?'

'I want to pay a visit to the Medjay information archives. Can you help with that?'

'Yes, but why?'

'They hold information on everyone. On you, on me, on Ay, even on Mahu himself. We need to get deeper into the underworld of what's happening here, so we have to know more about the plotters and conspirators and their secret histories.'

Khety thought it through. 'I have a contact, a scribe. He could get us in and help us find the relevant documents.'

'Can he be trusted?'

He grimaced. 'He's my brother.'

'In these days no-one, not even one's brother, can be trusted.'

'He's my younger brother.'

'That makes it worse then: younger brothers often betray and murder their elders. Sibling rivalry.'

Khety just laughed. 'He likes music and reading; he's not interested in politics. He'd rather spend his time in the library. Trust me.'

Nefertiti entered the room. I confess I could not take my eyes from her. There was something incandescent about her presence.

'This will not serve as a useful safe place for you both in the next days,' she said. 'However, Khety knows a house in the workers' suburb – a secret location. I'm afraid it is not particularly comfortable. But I imagine no-one will think to seek you there. And I'm sure you can find a way to disguise yourselves among the arriving populations.'

It was a sensible suggestion. The poor are invisible to the rich.

'We will be, as the saying goes, poor men in the house of the rich,' I said.

There were no doors or windows to the outside world in the walls of this building. The only way out was down into the labyrinth again. So we bade a swift farewell and descended a set of winding stone stairs. This time plentiful lamps and rush torches illuminated the way. I noticed wonderful images on the walls – birds, animals and gardens lit up by an underworld sun and moon.

'Khety, where are we?'

'You remember when we went to the Queen's House? And you sat in her chair and looked out across the river?'

The low fort on the far shore. He had known all along.

'If you are smiling that smug little smile of yours again, Khety, I'm going to push you down these stairs.'

His laugh echoed away down several passageways that disappeared off into shadow. The last of the daylight slanted down to where we stood.

'Well, as the adventurer said, "all paths lead somewhere",' he replied.

'Very wise. But as I recall in that story the adventurer never returned home. Which of these takes us where we need to go?'

'The passages are designed to trap intruders for ever. Fortunately, I know them like the back of my hand.'

He nodded towards one of them. We each took a torch in our hands and set off in silence among the strange company of our footfalls and shadows. Soon we came to a junction. Khety hesitated.

'What?'

'Just trying to remember the way.'

He set off with purpose in one direction, then suddenly stopped. I walked into him.

'What now?'

'Sorry, wrong way.'

'And you're the man who's going to help me save the world.'

I knew we were under the river. Little gusts of hot wind, ghostly underworld breezes, tugged at the flames of our torches but could not extinguish them. I caught glimpses of more painted scenes on the walls, the spirits of the dead enjoying the delights of the Otherworld. We tell ourselves stories of happiness and liberty beyond the grave, but we build our temples and tombs in darkness, and frighten ourselves with fables of monsters and secret names. In the confident light of the torches and in Khety's bright company, however, the passageways that had so alarmed me the previous night lost their power to conjure fear in my mind.

After some time walking in silence we came to a long set of stairs ascending towards a dark trap door. Slivers of light cut through the wooden planks like long knife blades. We listened carefully, but could hear only a kind of shuffling and a snuffling; something like slow, clumsy dancers. With infinite caution, Khety lifted the trap door. The light dazzled us after our time in the darkness. He looked out carefully, then pushed back the door, and we pulled ourselves up into the daylight.

The first thing that assailed me was the smell. Pigs. The rotting stink of old mud, old vegetables and pig-shit. They looked like a gathering of corrupt dignitaries, their undiscerning wobbly jaws not ceasing to chew as they observed us with only one question in mind: were we consumable? The sty was low, so we had to crouch as we hurried through it, holding our noses, trying without success to keep our feet out of the mess. We emerged into a fetid, narrow lane, detritus and human and animal shit gathering in the foul gullies to either side. Labourers were passing in crowds where the narrow passageway opened, some way along, on to a wider thoroughfare, and the noise of daily humanity from a better world washed over us. There was a doorway covered with a rotting tapestry directly opposite the sty, and we passed quickly across. We found ourselves in a hot, dusty storeroom piled high with rubbish, old jugs, jars, broken bits and pieces of everything. There was a further door that led into another room with two simple straw mattresses, a supply of water in a stone jar, and a box containing basic rations. A rickety old ladder with rungs missing led up to a door that gave on to the roof. Khety locked the front door from the inside.

'Home sweet home,' he said.

Inside another box we found workers' clothes, simple bolts of rough cloth and cheap rope sandals, together with more middle-class but undistinguished clothing, from which we could fashion our appearances as required. But first I wanted to go up onto the roof to get my bearings. I quickly pulled a relatively clean cloth around my head and shoulders, and ascended the ladder. I pushed open the roof door and carefully looked out. It was a view of the city unlike any I had noticed before. A chaos of adjoining roofs made up, in their crazy, improvised pattern, a kind of small shanty town. It was no doubt home to many of the invisible poor who kept the city clean and working. The heat shimmered in the air, and nothing stirred. The whole place had the abandoned feel of mid-afternoon, but it seemed lifeless too, lacking the intense colours of drying fruit and vegetables, the chickens scratching in their enclosures, and the daily washing hung from lines which characterized the rooftops of Thebes. No leaping children here, just a few old women moving about desultorily, their heads bowed to their perpetual labour, rearranging tatty clothing as it dried on boards or on lines in the bleaching glare of the afternoon sun. No-one took any notice of me.

The best view was to the river, and in particular down to the long dock from which I had sailed with the hunting party only a few days ago. Now, however, instead of pleasure boats and singing young women, the whole dock was crowded with river traffic, and on the open water packs of boats jostled one another, waiting to land their various cargoes. It was like watching a slow, untidy battle from the curious and remote vantage of a fly.

Some of the ships were carrying timber, stone, fruits and corn. From one, amid a fury of calls, cries and trills that made up an anxious music, appeared howling monkeys on strings, gibbering and shrieking with confused excitement, cages of coloured crying birds, trained hawks on gauntlets, and in a strong box a large baboon, staring out at this crude, noisy world with dignified contempt. Gazelles, antelope and zebra slipped and shivered on their neat hooves as they were roughly manhandled down the gangplanks. From another ship came a troupe of pygmies from Punt executing quick movements, walking on their hands, tossing one another through the air for the delight of the crowds.

All of this for the Festival. The gifts, tributes and supplies of food and drink and entertainment from the Empire and beyond were starting to arrive in the city to support and satisfy the appetites of a unique congregation of the rich and powerful. It was an event none would relish but to which all would have been deeply offended not to be invited. To be seen here, in state, participating among the great powers was a signifier of high status. And each king would bring his family, his retinues, his ambassadors and civil servants, their officials, their secretaries, their assistants, their assistants' assistants, and then ranks of servants, in their own hierarchies. The city still did not seem ready for such a vast swelling of its population, and I imagined the crowds becoming so great that people would have to sleep in the desert, in the tombs above the city, or in the fields, like a plague of locusts.

There was a noise behind me, and Khety's head appeared through the trap door. He joined me on the parapet.

'Crazy, isn't it, a jubilee festival now?' he said. 'I mean, it hasn't been thirty years since the beginning of the reign.'

'Akhenaten desperately needs to assert his status and confirm the new capital,' I responded. 'And he knows that in a crisis one must celebrate a festival or start a war. Even if he refuses to accept it, his chief advisers know things are in danger of falling apart in the country, and outside it. He has domestic and foreign problems, and the harvest last year was poor again. People are not being paid regularly. They're worried, and if he's not careful they'll get angry. He needs to demand homage in public from everyone, not least his internal enemies and foreign allies, and to reassert his territorial claims and rights over the kingdoms of the Empire. But this whole spectacle will be undermined unless the Queen is restored. No wonder he's so desperate.'

The prospect of a major celebration brought back memories for me. 'I was a young child during the last jubilee, under Amenhotep. People said it was unlike any other witnessed before. He ordered the Birket Habu lake to be created near the palace where he and the gods and the royal family could process on barges. Can you imagine, Khety, an artificial lake of that size? All the years of labour, all the lives sacrificed for one day of festivities. My father held me up on his shoulders so I could see above the crowds. It was all happening a long way away, but I remember a giant crocodile cutting through the water, its tail moving slowly from side to side, its eyes moving to and fro, glittering as if packed with broken glass, and its jaws, with great white teeth, opening and closing. Of course it had been constructed out of wood and ivory and some kind of clever mechanics, and built on the bed of a boat. But to my eyes it was Sobek-Ra, the crocodile god. I was terrified! And then came Amenhotep, on a huge gold barge rowed by many slaves, seated on a high throne, wearing the two crowns. And the gods, hidden in cabins, travelling on their golden boats from the east to the west. I could hardly breathe. Strange, the things that compel us. Now I would look at the same spectacle and see illusion, make-believe, a show. I'd see nothing but the crude mechanisms, the wealth and the engines of labour that work the scenes of the spectacle. Am I better off now, or was it better when I believed?'

There was no useful answer to this question, and besides we had other thoughts to preoccupy our minds. We looked out at the panorama of activity below us. Among the ships just docking I noticed one remarkably fine specimen, distinguished by its elegant shape, the glossy perfection of its costly woods and inlays, and the glorious richness of its sails – a military ship of the highest class. Clearly this was transporting a VIP. Dockers caught the ropes cast out by its sailors, and deftly manoeuvred the ship into its place. Among the figures of the working sailors in their uniforms appeared another of stature, surrounded by officials. I was too far away to see him well, but he was accorded the utmost respect: there was a military reception and an official guard awaiting his arrival, no doubt sweltering under their umbrellas as they waited for the tedious business of docking to be accomplished. The sound of a fanfare came quietly but clearly across the hot, thick air as the mystery man stepped down into the throng.

Khety shaded his eyes. 'Horemheb.'

I gazed at this figure who had suddenly assumed a great importance in my mind. As I watched, there was a moment of ceremony between the reception committee, the brisk, no-nonsense man, and the retainers who followed him at a respectful distance down the gangplank. Then he moved off through the crowds, his armed escort beating back with sticks and batons any careless person who did not instantly bow his head and make way.

Khety, who could pass unnoticed in a crowd more freely than I could, departed to speak to his brother and find a means of access to the archives. After he left, I stayed watching on the roof as the cavalcade of materials and people continued to flow into the unfinished, soon to be overwhelmed city. And above us all the birds, circling; and beyond that the infinite opposition of the desert. I thought of my girls, and Tanefert. What were they all doing now? Were my girls asking about their father? Was their mother making up some story with her rich invention? Or were they just running around, or reading, or executing new acrobatic movements over and over and over until something was knocked flying?

As I sat there pondering the imponderables of my life, a frail figure emerged onto one of the nearby roofs. She shaded her eyes and looked around, and when she noticed me she made a polite, deferential bow. I nodded back. It would do no harm, I thought, to discover more about this quarter of the city, not least because secrets and information are not the preserve of palaces alone, but are found equally in the most dismal of shanties. So I stepped over the parapet, making my way cautiously over the crumbling roofs – in places the dry reeds, bundled and plaited together, which served as roofing material had already broken or given way – and joined her on the opposite parapet. Her skin was darker than mine, her features nomadic, her dress clean but poor, adorned with a few trinkets of traditional style. She might have been no more than twenty years old, but hard labour had aged her well beyond that: as always the hands, with their callused skin as tough as hide, gnarled knuckles and broken nails, told the story. Still, there was life and humanity in her smile. We greeted each other.

'I am from Mut,' she said, by way of introduction.

I knew of it – a desert settlement to the south-west, near the Dakhla Oasis.

'I've never been there, but I enjoy the wine,' I said.

She nodded without comment.

'Why did you come to the city?' I asked her.

'Ah. The city.' She shaded her eyes and shook her head slowly. 'My husband overheard a wonderful story someone was telling in the market, of the new capital, about the need for workers. He came home and told me, "We can escape, make something of ourselves." I was afraid to leave everything I knew and cared for to set out on such a dangerous journey. We'd heard other tales of gangs of convicts and even the soldiers of the Amun Priests robbing travellers by night. But he wanted to go, and there was nothing for us where we were. So we surrendered all we possessed to a guide, who guaranteed safe passage. He told us about a green city of towers, gardens and ample work for all. Even I was beguiled by his words. We left, with our two young children. Parents, grandparents, brothers and sisters – we left them all behind knowing we were unlikely ever to see them again. We were five families who set out together that evening.'

She paused for a moment, her eyes swimming with the memory of departure.

'We travelled for days beyond telling. Then one evening we were surprised and surrounded by a band of Medjay guards. We were forced to march, and eventually they rounded up other straggling groups of desperate people from all over the Red Land. We were nothing but cattle. *Cattle.*'

She held out her ruined hands in a gesture of helplessness.

'Finally we arrived at the Great River. But all the sweet waters that flowed before my eyes could not have satisfied my thirst to return home again, and know my own hearth. We were shipped down the river to the city and set to work. We were not slaves, but we were not free men either. Men and women had to wait together every morning for the Overseer and his assistants to make their selections: who would work and eat, and who would not work and starve. Always the fittest and strongest worked, and while these lucky ones tried to bring supplies back in secret for the others, gradually those not chosen died away in the filthy hovels where they were left to fend for themselves. I worked as a labourer. My children are now mixing the mud for the sun-dried bricks that, one by one, are building the city. My husband is now the foreman of a work gang. But it has soured his soul. He drinks. We fight. And now . . .'

She gestured to her foot. I saw that it was bandaged.

'It is broken?'

She slowly unwound the stained linen and showed me the damage: it had been crushed by a stone building-block. The flesh was mottled blue and crimson and rotten yolk-yellow, the shape distorted, the toes curled into themselves. It looked to me as if the bones were smashed, the flesh rotting. She would have to lose the foot.

'I am as useless now as a dancer with one leg.'

It was tempting to read a parable of suffering and wisdom in her dignified face. But what I saw there was simply hopelessness.

'I wish we had not come,' she continued. 'But what choice did we have? All we had left to sell was ourselves. And this is a world in which if you have nothing to sell, you die.'

What could I do for this woman? Our green and gold world, our life of houses and linens and fine wines, is built on the invisible, inescapable labour of the multitudes. Not a new thought, of course. There had been many occasions in my life when I had been exposed to these unpleasant realities. My work had shown me day after day the effects of this poverty: in the crimes committed out of the despair of drink, in particular; the delirious exuberance, the indifference to cares, the sorrowful songs of misfortune soon giving way to irredeemable acts of rage and violence.

We sat for a little while, listening to the birds' free music. It seemed like a beautiful joke at her expense, a sweetness she could never possess; but she closed her eyes and drank it in like wine. I pressed upon her the only thing I could offer: a draught of water from the jar. She drank a few sips, grateful more for the offer than the thing itself. And then we made our farewells, and she hobbled away across the rooftops in the burning afternoon.

Not long after that Khety returned with the news that we could attempt to enter the archive that evening. He was full of problems and concerns: how would we pass through security, how would we find the necessary information among so much papyrus, what would happen to his brother and his family if we were caught? But in such situations I find myself becoming less, rather than more, concerned.

'Don't waste my time with your worries,' I said. 'Concentrate on solutions, not problems.'

He didn't like that.

'Listen, Khety, there are two things in our line of work. One is knowledge, under the heading of which I include planning. The other is improvisation, under the heading of which I include errors, mistakes, cock-ups and the general chaos to which all things inevitably, especially in our business, tend – and that goes for planning too. So let's make a plan, and then, when it goes wrong, we'll improvise our way out of trouble.'

31

It was in the personae of a court scribe and his assistant that we left the safe house. I had my story prepared. We were researching an official history of the reign of Akhenaten to be presented to him by the Office of Culture on the occasion of his jubilee. It was to be a surprise, and must be kept secret. We carried with us documents of permission from the Akhetaten Medjay office which Khety had forged, having stamped them with some kind of blurred approval-seal in his office. I also had with me the original papers of authorization, but they would not help us now that we were in hiding.

'Did you see Mahu?' I asked Khety.

'He was out. I timed my visit carefully. He's been asking for me.'

'I imagine he has. What does he think you are doing now, since we were arrested after Meryra's murder?'

'He's been too busy to care. The murder has badly damaged his prestige, and he's on the rampage to fit someone to the crime. I guess he's furious that you've disappeared again. I'm sure that's why he wants to see me.'

I gave myself a moment to relish the satisfaction Khety's words brought me. With the Festival coming, and the escalating security tensions after Meryra's murder, Mahu was almost certainly too pre-occupied with his immediate problems to make good on his threat against my family.

It was a strange experience to walk once more through the streets of the city. The absolute single-minded purpose that characterized the attitude of the citizens during my first days here had changed now; among the new crowds there was a sense of uncertainty, touching on anxiety, as if everyone was apprehensive about the coming events and the arrival of so many strangers. But that was all to our advantage, as it enabled us to move far less conspicuously up and down the roads. Nevertheless, we covered our heads in the vague imitation of some kind of religious modesty. No-one paid us any attention.

We walked away from the slums and up the Royal Road heading north, where Thutmosis the sculptor had driven me in his chariot. We continued towards the central city among the evening crowds, past the Small Aten Temple, which was besieged with worshippers clamouring to enter through the first pylon. I caught a quick glimpse of the open sun court packed with people, their hands raised to the many statues of the King and Queen, and to the rays of the late sun. We followed to the right along the long northern wall of the temple, struggling against the current of the crowds, until we passed the House of Life and came to the complex of the Records Office. Now we were in more danger. We were more likely to be recognized here, not least because Mahu's office in the Medjay barracks was only a few blocks away to the east.

Khety confidently made his way down a narrower avenue between high walls, past offices where all kinds of bureaucratic activity seemed to be taking place. We turned through a formal portal decorated with the insignia of the Aten sun disc, and found ourselves in a small courtyard. Here we encountered our first set of security guards. Khety wafted the permission briefly before their eyes, and I tried to look haughty. They glanced at us suspiciously, but nodded. We were about to move on through the courtyard when a commanding voice called us to halt. Khety looked at me. Another guard approached us.

'This office is not open for public attendance.' He scanned our permission. 'Who authorized this?'

I was about to start speaking, to try to improvise a way past this danger, when a high, clear voice cried out, 'I did.' The thin young man who had spoken had the serious, pale face of those who avoid the sun. He stood at the threshold to one of the offices. 'They have a meeting arranged with me. I've been assigned to offer them assistance. It is a great honour. Don't you know this is one of the finest writers of our time?' He nodded respectfully in my direction. I bowed almost imperceptibly to acknowledge the compliment, in a way I copied from a public reading I had once attended, on Tanefert's insistence, given by a writer much admired for his supposed wit and brilliance. I had spent the endless time marvelling at his pomposity, his bad but costly dress, and his affected speech. The young man gestured respectfully for me to lead the way, and as we passed beyond the jurisdiction of the guards he whispered to me, with a quaver of fear in his voice, 'Fortunately none of them can read.' And with that we passed through the immediate danger and into the building.

Khety's younger brother was as unlike him as was possible, as if he had only been able to define himself in opposition to his sibling's character.

'You might as well know I'd rather be reading about this kind of thing in a cheap story than actually *smuggling* you in through security. Have you no idea of the danger you place us all in? At a time like this?' He addressed this last comment to his brother.

Khety raised his eyes at me. 'Sorry, sir. He's led a sheltered life.'

A group of Medjay officers passed us in the corridor, and we all fell silent. I felt sure I recognized one of them from the hunting party. His eyes met my glance curiously. I looked away, and kept walking. I dared not look back. Their footfalls paused for a moment – would he call

239

after me? – but then continued until they died away behind us. We walked on.

Khety's brother introduced himself as Intef – 'it is a name I share with the Great Herald of the City, although unlike me he is also known as "Great in Love", "Lord of the Entire Oasis Region" and "Count of Thinis", which, as I'm sure you will know, is Abydos' – as he pushed open a door with a flourish. We followed him into a large chamber lined with high wooden shelves and furnished with many desks at which men studied scrolls and papyrus documents in the last of the light from the clerestory windows. Few looked up from their scrutinizing; some were now packing away their materials, notes and documents to leave. I saw that many corridors and passageways led off from this central reading room. Fortunately there were no guards here.

'This is the main library,' Intef said. 'Here we keep all the documents and publications relating to the current works of the city. We have separate sections for Foreign Affairs and Correspondence, Domestic Internal Information, Criminal Acts and Judgements, Cultural Documentation including poetry and fables, Sacred Texts heretical and orthodox, Historical Records public and not, and so on. Sometimes it's quite difficult to know under which heading some kinds of information fall.'

'So what do you do then?' I asked.

'We send it to be classified. And if that fails it is passed on again to a room in the library which privately we call Miscellaneous, Mysterious and Missing. Sometimes we know we ought to have a certain document, certain kinds of evidence in writing, but for whatever reason it is not in the library. So we may also make a record of its absence, so to speak, and again we send this to the Missing Room. In some cases we may make notes towards the definition of what is missing in terms of secret information – what we know we don't know, in a way.' He smiled.

'I think I follow you. Those must be quite extensive records. Do you include missing persons in this Missing Room?'

He looked at me suspiciously, then at his brother. 'What exactly are you looking for?'

'Not what, who. I do not think the information we are seeking lies in this room.'

Intef glanced at the men preparing to leave the main room. He nodded quickly and anxiously, and we followed him out. He hurried down one of the passageways, and we entered into a great labyrinth of papyrus. The corridors were lined, floor to ceiling, with shelves on which were piled a dusty infinity of documents and writings: unbound papyrus sheets, bound collections, some cased in leather, others in scrolls, wooden boxes containing millions of clay tablets in many scripts.

'What language is this?' I asked, picking up one covered in a series of complex slanted marks.

'It is Babylonian, the language of international diplomacy,' Intef said, taking it off me quickly with a click of his tongue and fastidiously replacing it.

'No wonder everything's so confused. How many people can read it?'

'Those that need to,' he replied piously.

Then, with a quick glance up and down the corridor, he pulled us aside into a small, barely lit antechamber lined with shelves. Like a bad actor playing a conspirator he addressed me too loudly: 'It is indeed a great honour to help you in your project. What can I do for you?' As he did this he gestured with his thumb at the walls and winked over and over.

I played along. 'We are researching the glorious acts of our Lord . . .'

He made a kind of *more* gesture.

'And we ask you to honour us with access to the archives on the subject of his early life.'

At the same time, Khety handed him a tiny scroll of papyrus on which he had written the names of those we really wished to research. Intef secreted the scroll in his robe.

'Please follow me,' he said, almost comically bellowing now. 'I am sure we have many treasures pertaining to our Lord's Great Works.'

We walked faster now through the passageways. Intef whispered more urgently and silently this time: 'I cannot afford to get into any kind of trouble. I'm only doing this because my brother insisted. I should have known . . .'

'I asked Khety to ask you. Why don't you read the list of names?'

He did so, and I watched as his complexion achieved an even weaker shade of pallor. He held the papyrus like a poisoned thing.

'Do you have the slightest idea of the danger in which you are placing me, yourselves, our . . . lives?' he hissed.

'Yes,' I said.

He was speechless. He made the old gesture of blessing over himself and led us on to another chamber, long, dark and narrow, deeper inside the building. He checked carefully for guards, then crept up a staircase into a vast, dusty and low chamber, like a tomb, barely lit, which, he explained in another low whisper, contained the classified stacks of the collection.

'Guards patrol at all hours of the day and night,' he warned.

The many stacks of shelves, each marked at its entrance with a different hieroglyph, disappeared into shadows. So many words and signs, information and stories were gathered here. A torch brushing casually against a shelf, a forgotten taper falling over on a pile of papyrus, a mistaken spark ascending, caught by a draught and delivered like a firefly onto the yellow corner of an ancient tome, and this hidden library of secrets would be ablaze in moments. It was tempting.

First we searched for Mahu's file. The information was stored with bureaucratic precision. There were already thousands of documents on citizens whose names began with M. I flicked through some of them: Maanakhtef, the Officer of Agriculture under Akhenaten's grandfather; Maaty, Treasury official; Madja, 'Mistress of the House'. I glanced down her paper and read 'informer of the artisan community . . . sex worker'. There were countless other individuals whose names

242

and secrets passed in a blur. Then, there it was: a single slip of papyrus contained within a neat leather binding. How like his office and his manner in its minimalism. But the content was disappointing. The papyrus held only the most elementary information: date and place of birth (Memphis), family antecedents (ordinary), long lists of accolades, successful entrapments of fugitives, statistics of success rates, bringing armed robbers to trial, numbers executed . . . and then the words: PAPERS X CLASSIFIED. He must have written it himself. In a way I had expected nothing more. What sort of a police chief would leave his best-kept secrets written down in his own archive?

Meryra was next. I flipped through, casting a quick eye over Merer, gardener; Merery, Priest, senior, of Hathor at the Dendera Temple in the Sixth Nome, also Keeper of the Cattle; then Meryra. Parents: father Nebpehitre, First Priest of Min of Koptos; mother Hunay, Chief Nurse of the Lord of the Two Lands. Interesting to find the same few families continuously maintaining their proximity to, and influence on, the royal family. Koptos was a rich place, for its gold mines, its quarries and its prime location on the trade route to the eastern seas – a tremendous source of income for the father. Min, I knew, was a god associated with Amun and the Theban cults, as well as Protector of the Eastern Desert. His main role had been to assist in the ceremonies of coronation and festival; he was the god of potency who ensured the power of the King. So the family had moved its allegiance as required, and very successfully, negotiating coinciding positions within both the Amun hierarchy and the Great House. But it seemed Meryra had been given the opportunity – or was it perhaps a threat? – to pledge total allegiance to Akhenaten and the Aten cult.

I ran my eye down his biography, which contained nothing exceptional. Educated in the usual schools and admitted to various hereditary and additional offices; then he seemed to have allied himself unequivocally to Akhenaten soon after the death of Amenhotep. He had been one of the first to arrive in the new city. He had become chief adviser to Akhenaten on domestic policy. In this way he would have been able to protect and advance the family assets within the

243

land, I supposed. Well, no more. He was dead now. But what was there here to help explain why he had been targeted? Obviously the assassination of the newly appointed High Priest of the Aten was an astonishingly powerful and well-aimed blow at the façade of Akhenaten's power. And the timing was immaculate. Who were the benefactors? I assumed his possessions would largely devolve to the Treasury. Similarly, Ramose had motive: at a stroke he would have wiped out his chief opposition. But the way Meryra was murdered did not fit that idea: Ramose would have been subtler and quieter, and he would have made certain the death did not reflect back so obviously on himself. Also, Nefertiti had said he never acted out of revenge. No, what had happened had been designed to continue and extend the destabilizing of the regime in the most effective, most public way possible.

Intef was getting more and more anxious, listening to the circling footfalls of the guards. I ignored him and began to look for Horemheb. Harmose, musician, minstrel of Senenmut, minister, PS buried with lute; Hat, Officer, Cavalry – informer. I hurried on past Hednakht, Hekanefer, Henhenet, past scribes, royal consorts, chamberlains, singers, trumpeters, priests, tax collectors, incense-grinders and bureaucrats, a great parade of titles and conditions, low and high, of works and betrayals, until I found him.

The biographical details were in themselves interesting. Born of a distinguished Delta family. Also known by another name, Paatenemheb – an Aten name. It was interesting that he maintained the two, and therefore the two alliances to past and present, while also letting himself become known by his non-Aten name. Trained at Memphis military school. Distinction. Top of year. A canter through the middle levels of the military, company commander and so on, to reach chief deputy of the Northern Corps at the age of twenty-five. Campaigns in Nubia, Mittani, Assyria. Married Mutnodjmet, Nefertiti's sister. This highly effective political liaison brought him right to the centre of power. His latest promotion had just taken place: Commander of the Army of the Two Lands. This was a very significant position. He would now be reporting directly to Ramose, and perhaps to Akhenaten himself. I turned to the next sheet, but it was blank, as if the archivist already knew there would be a long future to record.

I moved on to Ay. I found him next to Auta, sculptor, homosexual . . . commissioned, carved representation of Princess Baketaten. Ay's document was interesting, for it consisted of the facts of his birth – son of two of the most influential people in the court of Amenhotep III, and brother to Tiy – his own marriage to Ty, 'wet nurse to the Queen Nefertiti', interestingly, and then only these words, spaced on a fine sheet of papyrus:

Fan Bearer on the King's Right Hand
Superintendent of the Royal Horses
God's Father
Doer of Right

The first two were significant but not really exceptionally powerful positions. They were marks of status. But what did the third and fourth mean?

I was puzzling over these enigmatic titles and ignoring Intef's increasing agitation when the sheaf of documents suddenly slipped from my grasp. I rushed to grab them, but they fell and scattered noisily across the floor. We froze. The footsteps ceased their perpetual round. Khety gestured in alarm from the end of the stack. It was then that I noticed it: a single feather that had been slipped into the binding of Ay's documentation. It was worked very finely in gold. It was large and regal – perhaps an eagle's or a hawk's? I picked it up and twirled it in the light of the lamp.

Then the guards' footsteps began to move quickly in our general direction. I placed the gold feather in my robe pocket. We hastily gathered up all the fallen papyri and moved deeper into the dark stacks, extinguishing the tiny light of our lamp; but in truth there was nowhere to hide: the stacks came to an end against a wall. We held ourselves very still. Two guards appeared at the entrance, holding up their lamps to peer into the dark where we crouched. The light just failed to reach us. Luckily, the architects of the library had left a good deal of empty space for the future accumulation of information. We slid as deep as possible into these long, horizontal empty spaces as if we were lengthy manuscripts.

Then I saw, with alarm, through the gaps between the shelves that one sheet of papyrus remained on the floor, just outside the pool of their light. My skin prickled. If they saw it, they would know someone was here. I heard their footsteps approaching, the light of their lamp growing brighter. The sheet was clearly visible now. I wondered for a moment whose life was written there, and then a foot stepped on the sheet. There was a moment of pure silence. I could not breathe. Just then a shout, in the distance. One guard gestured to the other, who raised his lamp suspiciously. The end of the wall was now fully illuminated. If he came two steps forward he would surely see us. But they turned and walked away. Their footsteps receded, and then there was silence.

Intef looked sick. He was shivering. 'They're changing the watch,' he whispered. 'We've got no more than a moment to get out of here.'

I picked up the sheet from the floor and re-filed it (in the wrong position, for my own satisfaction). We made our way cautiously to the edge of the stack. No sign of any guards. Then it occurred to me: I wanted to check my own file. I beckoned Khety to follow me.

'Come on, we've got what we came for,' he said urgently.

But I ignored him, and found the passageway beginning with my hieroglyph. Rameses, military officer, see under Horemheb; Rahotep, royal scribe; Raia, musician; Ramose, Vizier, Chief Minister, born Athribis, mother Ipuia . . . Where was my file? I checked back along the documents. It was missing. Why? I suddenly felt like a non-person. Who would remove my file, and why? Nefertiti said she had read it. Perhaps she still had it, or perhaps it was lying somewhere in Mahu's office. There must be a simple explanation . . .

Khety dragged me away, holding his finger to his lips. We moved silently back down the staircase, then heard more footsteps marching towards us, up the corridor we had taken earlier. Intef panicked, hurried us into a small storage room and shut the door. Khety and I looked at each other intently, trying not to breathe. Intef's eyes were shut tight. Once the new detachment of guards had passed, we slipped out and hurried through the building, back through the now empty and silent library, until we finally reached the courtyard. Bowing to Intef, who looked emotionally devastated by the adventure, Khety and I pulled our linens over our heads and walked past the guards, out into the noise and chaos of the street.

'So what did we get from that?' asked Khety.

I carefully showed him the gold feather. 'I found it in Ay's file. It was hidden there. I don't know what it means.'

I twirled the beautiful, strange thing in the late light.

32

After dark, the streets were transformed by the sudden influx of the visiting population. Suddenly I liked the city better for it. Impromptu performances of magic or dance or music or juggling were taking place in the ways; temporary restaurants and canteens had been set up in any spare space under cheap, bright bolts of cloth illuminated by torches and lamps; here was a night market, with sellers offering monkeys and birds, tailoring and jewellery, fruits and spices heaped like the perfect hills of a multicoloured land. The atmosphere was lively, noisy, men and women from all over the Empire jostling for service or pushing through the crowds at the performances. Dignitaries and senior families progressed to dinners, receptions and meetings in their finery, staring straight ahead, demonstrating their pride and superiority.

Sudden parks of tents had sprung up in the empty spaces around the central city, and they spread down to the water's edge. The dark river was busy with boats. I felt drawn down there, under cover of the night, by the busyness of the crowds and the delicious cool of the northern night breeze. Khety and I watched as hundreds of small barques, most rented from an enterprising man on the dock, bobbed about on the black water, their paper lanterns creating shifting archipelagos of illumination for the lovers who occupied them. Under them ran the ever-flowing river, the transient brightness of the present visiting the darkness of the gods. Behind us the palaces and the temples, the offices and the libraries, stood mostly sinister as prisons. I wondered what, of all that had been built here in so short a time, would survive. Or would it all pass away and be lost under the encroaching desert?

We returned to the safe house, keeping to the shadowy edges of the ways, past arguments and calls for drink and the last banging dinner pots being washed by old women at the public wells. Groping quietly for our straw pallets, we settled down for the night. Khety wanted to talk through what little we had found, but I was unwilling. The information was frustratingly enigmatic and inconclusive. And time was ever shortening. I twirled the gold feather in front of my eyes and tried to think everything through. Akhenaten and his problems. Mahu, his loathing of me, and the Queen's doubts. The assassination of Meryra. Ay, of whom she was afraid. And Horemheb, this strange and ambitious young officer, married directly into the heart of the family, to a girl who wept for a year. I prayed that the night would permit my dreaming mind to discover some pattern that eluded my waking brain.

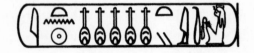

33

I woke up with the name Horemheb going through my mind. I looked up at the dust drifting through the blades of strong light already piercing the broken strips in the reed roof. Khety's pallet was empty. I heard someone moving through the outer room, and reached for my dagger. The door scraped open, and in he came, carrying a basket. How had I slept through him leaving? I must be losing my touch.

'Breakfast.'

We ate fruit and sugar-bread, and shared between us a jug of beer and a handful of olives.

'I want to pay a visit to Horemheb,' I said. 'But how?' I was, after all, supposed not to exist.

We munched on our olives, thinking.

'What if he doesn't know you've disappeared?' Khety said after a short while. 'Why should he? Who would think to tell him? What if you just request an audience, say who you are, and that Akhenaten has commissioned you to investigate a very important mystery and you need to speak to him?'

It had the merit of simplicity. Akhenaten's name would get me through the door. I could be who I really was and, during the interview, feel my way carefully to see whether I could sense or test the direction of his loyalties. I could inform him of the disappearance of Nefertiti, and observe his reaction. I could assess his relationship with Mahu perhaps, without compromising further the safety of my family. On the other hand, he could have me arrested. But it was worth the risk.

Khety discovered where Horemheb was being accommodated, in the northern suburbs – not, as I would have expected given his status, in the southern. Perhaps this was because he was therefore closer to the northern palaces, which were the more domestic and private of the royal residences. We decided to avoid the streets, despite the cover of the crowds, and since we could not make our way along the banks of the river – for the royal gardens ran down to the water's edge – we hired instead a small barque. We skirted the docks, which even at this early hour were busy. Even more boats of all kinds had anchored overnight, nodding and bumping together like a floating shanty town.

We sailed slowly down the river. The first of the light as it rose above the eastern hills revealed the brilliant colours of the Red Land as well as the languorous, shining currents of the river, illuminated here and there by the shafts of light angling down through the eastern riverside trees. The hillsides, with their rock tombs and construction gangs, remained in grey-yellow and black shadow. Shadoufs, those clever new designs, worked ceaselessly under the trees, drawing water to supply the green force of the city. And on the west bank, workers and slaves, Egyptian and Nubian, bent to the green and yellow fields. No rest for them if they were to supply the endless, monstrous appetite of the city.

We steered the barque into a small pier and tied it to a post. Here were fewer people, although a cargo boat was unloading goods and foodstuffs, and several smaller vessels were ferrying field workers and crops to and fro across the river. We walked up to the Royal Road. To the south, in the distance, we could see the Great Aten Temple, which set the northern boundary of the central city, rising above all other buildings; its pennants drifted in the faint morning breeze. To the north, villas had been constructed on either side of the road within high mud-brick walls. A number of larger buildings in complexes stood out from the low-lying houses. Khety knew them; he told me the north city included the Riverside Palace, a square tower that lay next to the river, just under the northern hills where they curved to meet the river, while to the south of us stood another palace.

'Who resides there?'

'I don't know. It's empty. They say it's full of amazing paintings of animals and birds.'

To the east were the desert altars facing the rising sun. And above them, cut into the hillsides, Khety pointed out more great tombs.

'Whose are they?'

Khety shook his head and shrugged. 'The rich and powerful.'

The rest of the area seemed a more haphazard collection of low-level buildings. In the darkness of their workshops carpenters laboured, metalsmiths hammered; the pungent smells of wood shavings, hot fires and beaten metal drifted into the street. Rubbish of all kinds – food, building materials, broken pots, ruined sandals, bits of toys, scraps of linen – lay dumped in every vacant lot like temples of detritus for the scavenging cats and birds to worship at.

Like many of the other villas, Horemheb's lay inside a rectangle of long, high, crenellated mud-brick walls with just one main gateway and no other windows or doorways. The lintel over the gateway was not inscribed. No-one, it seemed, had yet claimed ownership of this house, although someone must have paid for its costly construction. The finish on the exterior was immaculate, almost shiny it was so new.

We gave my name and authorities to the guard at the entry. He was uniformed. I asked him which division he belonged to. He looked me up and down as if I was too fat and soft, and replied, with the tone of hostile politeness that afflicts so many of our military, 'Akhetaten division, sir.'

We were escorted up the entrance path, past a small domestic chapel where there were small statues of Akhenaten and Nefertiti. I paused, deliberately making some kind of fake, sanctimonious gesture of respect.

'Do you worship much?'

The guard was irritated. 'We worship as we are commanded to worship.' But there was a tone in his voice that said: and we don't much like it.

We turned right, walked on through the gardens where the heat of the day was now settling, and arrived at the welcome shade of a small courtyard with high walls. At this point the guard passed us over to another guard. He saluted as dismissively as possible, and turned away. The new guard led us up some stairs and into the main house.

A large, cool, airy loggia gave on to several other still more ample and airy pillared rooms around a central space lit by high windows. The air smelled of fresh paint and wood dust. The floor was unscratched and polished to a mirror shine. And the furniture looked as if it had been placed there that very morning. There was also a similar air of efficiency and purpose in the conduct of the uniformed men going about their business. These were career men, not conscripts or mercenaries. Quiet conversations were orchestrated with crisp nods, appreciative tilts of the head, wry smiles, evidently sensible remarks, and smart glances around the room. Several Nubians of high rank were gathered together in a serious conference in the loggia on the far side of the main room.

A secretary seated at a desk noticed us. Khety addressed him quietly. He shook his head. Khety remonstrated with him, and produced the authorities from Akhenaten. The secretary nodded, and walked off crisply along the corridor. We eased ourselves into two elegant chairs, their scrolled arms ending in gilded sphinx heads.

As we waited, I looked at these men, the commanding set of their young faces, the confident manner of their conduct, the precision and understated expense of their garments and uniforms, the inclusiveness of their racial and social backgrounds, and above all the vivid sense of the secret codes of their society in their measured gestures and responses. And I began to realize that here, after all, was the future, not in crazy worship of the sun or in new cities built in the desert, conjured by treasure and labour out of the dust and the light. No, the future was the military. These were the next generation of the King's sons, from the elite Egyptian families. Many of them had been taken from their foreign homelands and raised as child-ransom in the nurseries of the Great House – all now grown into ambitious, educated, clear-minded young men, seeing the opportunities for advancement opening quickly before them. Who knew what loyalties, grudges and ambitions they nursed? They looked like men who had a plan, who knew their entitlement and were waiting for their time to come. They looked like men who were not afraid.

The secretary approached us and murmured to me that I would be seen now. Leaving Khety to wait for me, I followed the man along more corridors and into a private chamber. He knocked on an ordinary-looking door, and I was admitted into an ordinary kind of room, transformed into a small office by a desk and two chairs. Absolutely nothing to show the status and ambition of the man, as if he had refused all superficial trappings of power.

The man at the desk was shockingly handsome. His frame was not remarkably sturdy or robust – he was no giant – and his head, on his small but powerful shoulders, was not exceptionally noble, but his body was pure worked muscle – not a *deben* weight of casual fat on him anywhere – and his face exhibited pure focus, not the carnivorous appetite of Mahu but something alert and entirely unsentimental. I judged he wouldn't kill for pleasure, but that he would kill for his own reasons all the same, and think nothing of it. I guessed his heart was nothing more to him than a well-disciplined muscle that pumped his cool blood.

He moved away from the desk, shook my hand with a brief firmness, and looked me directly in the eyes. There was not a trace of uncertainty in his look. Neither of us spoke for a moment. Then he gestured for me to sit and offered me refreshments, which I declined. He sat down in his chair – the same as mine, on the other side of the desk – his posture poised like a heron beside a fish-filled pond.

'What can I do for you?'

He meant: state your business. I outlined my office and my role in the investigation of a great mystery. He kept his eyes on me all the time, observing my face as much as listening to my tale. When I had finished he looked away, up at the small, high window. He stretched out his legs, put his hands behind his head. His handsomeness continued to puzzle me, as I could not locate it in any particular feature; it seemed to come from a collusion of parts that were in themselves not especially remarkable. I recalled another of Tanefert's writers who said that most people had enough material in them for several faces. Not here. This man had one face only.

He fixed his eyes on me. 'You have told me an interesting tale, full of great excitements and dangerous possibilities, but what I don't understand is this. Why you are here? Why do you wish to talk to me?' He sat up again, and leaned forward.

'Because you are related to the Queen, and the Queen has vanished.'

'You think I am involved in her disappearance?' His face was cold, challenging.

'I need to speak to everyone who knows the Queen as part of my investigation.'

'Why?'

'I am trying to build up a picture of the circumstances of her disappearance. Not just the forensic detail but the emotional and political background.'

'And from this you will deduce the guilty party.' It was not a question.

I nodded.

'Your method is flawed,' he said, lightly.

'Oh? Why?'

'Because it will not get you to the heart of the matter. Talking never does. It is overvalued in every way. Also, you have nearly run out of time. If the Queen is not recovered in time for the Festival, then you have failed.'

'There is still time.'

He paused, then said, 'You are Medjay. I am Army. Why should I talk to you?'

'Because I have authorizations from Akhenaten himself, and those transcend the hierarchical distinctions between us.'

'Ask me a question, then.'

'What is your relationship to the Queen?'

'She is my sister-in-law. You know this already.'

'I know the facts. I mean, are you close?'

He sat back and stared at me. 'No.'

'Do you support the Great Changes?'

'Yes.'

'Unequivocally?'

'Of course. You have no right to ask such a question. It has no bearing on the matter in hand.'

'With respect—'

'Your question is disrespectful. You imply treason.'

'Not at all, and the question is relevant. Whoever has taken the Queen has a political motivation.'

'I support unequivocally the suppression and destruction of corruption and incompetence.'

Which was not quite the same thing, and we both knew it. We had quickly reached an impasse.

'Are you or are you not accusing me of having a role in the disappearance of the Queen?' His eyes narrowed on me.

'I am not accusing you of anything. I am trying to understand the truth.'

'Then you are failing. This has not been an impressive display of your qualities as an investigator. I fear for the Queen. Her life is not in competent hands. I wish I could be of more assistance in her recovery,

but now I must continue with my work. There are preparations made before the Festival.'

'Such as?'

'None of your business.'

He stood up and opened his office door, dismissing me. I needed make a move. I produced the gold feather and placed it on the d between us. He suddenly looked very interested, and quietly clos the door.

'Where did you get that?'

'Can you tell me about it?'

He picked it up and twirled it between his fingers. 'It opens doors

'How can a feather open doors?'

'How literal you are. It opens doors to rooms that do not exist, and to words that are not spoken.'

Interestingly, Horemheb clearly did not possess such a feather. But I could tell from the way he handled it, moving it slowly in the light, that it held considerable attraction for him.

'Who would possess such a thing?'

He put it down with a reluctance that betrayed his desire to possess it for himself.

'I believe seven such feathers are in existence,' he said.

'Who possesses them?'

'At last. The right question.'

I waited.

'I am not going to do all your work for you,' he said.

'Let me talk something through, then. Let's say there are men of great power, disposed against the changes.'

'It is a revolution. Let us be precise in our language.'

'These are men who stand to lose a great deal of wealth and power, men who inherit the world through each generation.'

'Go on.'

'Families close to Akhenaten who will not, for one reason or another, benefit from the Great Changes.'

'Go on.'

'Led by one particular individual.'

He looked at me enigmatically. I decided to play my card.

'Ay.'

I let the name sit there, like the feather, on its own. He smiled, conspiratorially. I felt like I had won a round of *senet* against Thoth himself, the wise baboon. But the victory lasted only a moment.

'You speak carelessly,' he said softly, opening the door again. 'If he were to hear of such a thought, he would be displeased. He is as close as possible to the King himself. There is not a hair's breadth between them.'

I was about to rise, certain the interview was concluded, when he spoke again.

'Let me just offer you one clue before you leave. The Society of Ashes.'

His tone was full of a concentrated implication, and there was something malicious in it. He was feeding me words with the intention that I unwittingly fit in with his plans.

'The Society of Ashes? What is that?'

'A mystery.'

He picked up the feather, twirled it enigmatically in the light, and offered it back to me. I moved to the door and took it. He was smiling in the way men do who do not know what a smile is.

As I passed him, I asked suddenly, 'How is your wife?'

For the only time in the meeting he looked unguarded for a moment. In fact he looked disgusted. Perhaps also a flicker of pain, quickly disguised, passed over his face.

'My wife is none of your business.'

The door closed in my face.

34

As we walked away up the street, Khety asked me what had happened. I found it hard to give him a concise account, for the truth behind the conversation – the things we could not talk about – was elusive. I asked him about the Society of Ashes. He had never heard of it. 'It sounds like something aristocratic, one of those invitation-only, shake-hands-in-a-funny-way type of things.'

'It's connected somehow with the gold feather.'

'How do you know that?'

'Because I showed Horemheb the feather, and almost immediately he mentioned the society. I feel a tingle at the back of my head. I just can't quite . . . get to it.'

The heat was now tremendous, and no northern breeze lightened its burden. We walked slowly in the shadows of the buildings, thinking and thinking as we made our way back along the side of the Royal Road. Wagons and chariots struggled for right of way with calls and curses from the drivers. The constant traffic was a sign of the closeness of the Festival. There was a nervous tension in the air you could almost taste, a mix of metal and dust and something else – fear. I remembered the excitement I had felt on the first day of all this, the unforgivable thrill at the prospect of mystery in such high places. What a fool I was. I had understood nothing.

We walked out of the suburb. In the near distance stood the strange palace, square and squat and dark like a locked box. Curious, I made my way over towards it, Khety trailing uncertainly behind me. It looked abandoned. The great doors sagged slightly against each other. From inside came strange cries, like those of children, but wilder. Then came the questing, trilling call of a flute . . . and a repetition of the same cry.

I pushed the door cautiously, and it swung back heavily on its hinges. There was no sign of anyone. We moved up some marble steps into a large courtyard open to the sky. A dry fountain, stained with what looked like centuries of grey and white bird-shit, stood in the centre, and from it ran four low canals of stagnant green water. Over the open roof a web of netting had been strung, and here and there lengths of cloth, once boldly coloured, now faded, were laid out to provide shade. Under the arches of the courtyard hung many cages, some empty, some still containing little birds. Suddenly a parakeet, on brilliant wings, dashed across the empty space, squawking as it went. His activity seemed to spark off the others, and the air filled with a chaos of calls.

In the middle of all this a voice called out, 'Who's there?' An old man stood up slowly from his bench in the shadows and shuffled over towards us.

'We heard the cries . . . the door was open,' I said.

'So you just thought you would come in and satisfy your curiosity.'

'Who lives here?'

'No-one. Not for a year now. Someone has to look after the birds. No-one else cares about them.'

He called out, and the parakeet fluttered down from its perch. It landed, a storm of greens and golds, on his shoulder and nibbled appreciatively at his hairy ear. Then it looked up at us and let out a terrific aria, as if imitating some highly trained singer who might have performed here.

'Who used to live here?' I asked again.

'A queen. Well, she was almost a queen, for a time. I wonder if her name is still known now that she is no longer a favourite.'

'What is her name?'

'Kiya.'

The bird repeated it with the sing-song call of a disappointed lover. I had not heard of her.

'What happened to her?' I asked.

The old man shrugged. 'She fell from grace. Power is like fire. It consumes everything. And when it is gone, all that's left is ash.'

He spoke as if this could happen to any of us at any moment, and we too would turn into ash and shadows. I looked about at the faded, failed grandeur of the place. How quickly the present becomes the past.

We left him there, with his birds and their fading calls, returned to the barque and set off back up the river towards the central city, no northern breeze helpful in our single sail, the sun magnified by the water, burning our faces and heads. We shaded our eyes as best we could and kept close to the eastern bank whose overhanging trees afforded occasional shade. But as we approached the main dock, a line of papyrus skiffs manned by uniformed and armed soldiers prevented all traffic from getting closer. The water around the dock had been cleared of traffic and we could see occupying this bright clearing an exceptional ship of state.

It was enormous, at least a hundred cubits in length, with two deck-houses, and stalls for chariot horses at the deck level. Above those, reached by a staircase – stairs on a boat! – were elaborate accommodations and porticoes built out on slim columns. A floating palace. The hull curved in a vast, elegant shape up to gold lotus-buds, topped with an Aten disc. A large protective Horus eye was painted on the prow. Streamers ran from prow and stern. There were at least thirty rowers on either side, their sweating heads just protruding above the gunwales. The vast blue sail, decorated with a pattern of gold stars, hung from a mast that ran in height almost to the equivalent of the full length of the ship, and along two long yardarms. A golden falcon stood on the top of the mast. Priests holding wands and fans were lined up on deck. An orchestra must have been hidden out of sight, for the sounds of their music came to us across the water.

There were few such ships in the fleet. I had seen others before, in Thebes, and had once even toured *The Beloved of the Two Lands* while it was in dock. But this was something else. Only a very, very important person could travel in it. Ay. It had to be him.

The ship, with an attendant flotilla of lesser craft to guide it, slowly and perfectly negotiated its arrival at the dockside with hardly a bump. I was desperate to see what this man looked like, who carried such mystery and precipitated such fear. The boat deck was now crowded, not only with Priests and sailors, but also with dignitaries and officials who had ascended the gangplank as soon as the ship had docked. Among them I struggled to make out a figure to whom they all bowed. I could see nothing. It would be a long time until the jam of river boats was cleared.

I began to move our boat to the shore, trying not to attract the attention of the soldiers on the river, who, in any case, were also fascinated by the spectacle of such an arrival. The bank was no more than twenty cubits away, and I hoped it would seem we were just drifting away from the main body of onlookers. We managed to secure the barque to the trunk of a palm, and stepped into the warm, shallow waters.

'I hate getting my feet wet,' said Khety.

'Then you should have taken an office job.'

We made our way up a service path that ran beside a little watercourse. Here, among the foliage of the trees, all was suddenly quiet and still.

'Where are we?' I asked.

'We're just below the main gardens of the Great Palace.'

'Terrific. Guards everywhere. How do we get onto the road without being seen?'

'Like this.' And with a quick hop Khety leaped up and shimmied over a wall. I thought, not for the first time: the security in this place is shocking. I made the same movement, although I confess with less elegance.

I wish I hadn't, for as I dusted myself down I looked up to see two armed guards facing us. The alleyway in both directions was empty but for a child playing with a ball. Khety looked at me, I looked at him, and then, as if we had been operating in this way for many years, we launched ourselves simultaneously at the two men. The force of my first blow sent my opponent staggering back off-balance and off-guard against the wall opposite, where I swiftly followed up with a couple of hard punches to the gut and the face. He parried the second, and I felt a blow to the side of my head: he had clouted me with his wooden baton. But no pain came, and before I knew what I was doing I had picked up the baton from the dust where it had fallen and was beating the man's head and body. He curled into a tight ball, shivering and scrabbling to shield himself from the blows, and I heard the crack and snap of his finger bones as I beat down hard. Suddenly blood spattered brightly against the wall and the dust, and his little cries and moans ceased. I realized that Khety was holding back my arm, saying, 'Enough, enough, let's go.'

We abandoned the two inert bodies to the flies and the sun and ran to the top of the alleyway. I knew even then it was at least unwise to have left them there, but what could we do? The child with his ball had vanished.

The alley gave on to one of the thoroughfares leading to the Royal Road. Winding our linens around our heads again, we passed into the busy passage. Everyone seemed to be moving in the same direction, keen to witness the spectacle of the arrival of Ay. We emerged onto the Royal Road at a place between the Window of Appearances and the Great Aten Temple. The road itself was empty, in that odd way when everything is pushed aside to make a clearing for ceremony.

Crowds had gathered along its sides, though, and many more observers crowded onto balconies or huddled at windows and on roofs. There must have been thousands of people, but they were so quiet, so hushed, it was possible to hear the birds chattering.

Up to our right, the air suddenly seemed to charge itself, and a team of chariots appeared, the hooves of the horses clattering on the stones in time with each other. Trumpets blared like the announcement of battle, with the crowds on either side of the road like puzzled opponents. Khety and I pushed our way through for a closer view and saw, as the cavalcade slowed down, in the central chariot a tall, haughty man dressed in a white tunic and modest amounts of gold and jewellery.

His face was bony. Condescension seemed to seep from every pore. His manner suggested his utter contempt for the world in which he was being forced to make an appearance. The cavalcade came to a stop. Dust whirled in the hot air. Ay turned slowly to stare balefully at the Window of Appearances, which at this moment was significantly empty. With barely disguised reluctance, while stage-managing an expression of sombre respect across his tight face, he lazily raised his arms to the empty space and waited. We too continued to stand, observing the man at the centre of this.

Then Akhenaten himself appeared suddenly in the Window, accompanied by his girls, Meretaten taking the place her mother should have occupied. The crowd instantly noticed the absence of the Queen. A man next to me whispered to his wife, 'See? She is still not there. The child stands in her place.' The wife made a gesture for him to be silent, as if this too were a treasonable thought.

The two men looked at each other for a few moments, and it seemed as if an understanding of great complexity was taking place between them. Akhenaten made no gesture of recognition of the raised and respectful arms for at least a minute. 'Not a hair's breadth between them,' Horemheb had said. But it did not immediately seem so. Ay maintained his posture, his head now bowed, without wavering. The two men stood in their attitudes, and I thought how odd was the balance of power between the Great Akhenaten and the fastidious courtier, older in years. Then Akhenaten took a magnificent gold and lapis lazuli collar from a cushion and lowered it ostentatiously around the thin, waiting neck of Ay. This was a signal for a fanfare, and Ramose himself stepped forward to recite the liturgy.

It was during this recitation that I noticed there were spots of blood on my sandals. Then Khety surreptitiously nudged me and nodded. Coming through the silent gathering, at some distance yet, a set of guards. And with them, riding on the shoulders of another man, presumably his father, the small boy with the ball. The boy was looking through the crowd. As I turned my head he saw me, and pointed.

At this moment the liturgy finished, and the cavalcade moved on towards the Great Aten Temple with a noise of trumpets and hooves and obedient cries of celebration from the crowd who had raised their arms, as one, to the sun disc. Through this forest of conforming arms, which had the added advantage of screening us, we pushed our way out. I glanced back and the boy's mouth was open, shouting, but drowned out by the general noise. We moved faster, trying not to make ourselves too obvious, but it was clear from people's surprised faces that we were behaving strangely. No-one stopped us, though, and we reached a passageway and hurried down it.

'Where shall we go?'

'The safe house?'

I turned and looked again, just as the boy and the guards reached the top of the passage. He pointed, and his yell came loudly down the narrow walls. We ran. Khety knew his way through the back streets, but we were disadvantaged by the regularity of the city's layout: where were the crooked labyrinths of Thebes when I needed them? People turned to watch us run, and we had to double back when we saw soldiers moving up the road towards us. I have never before been on the wrong end of a chase. Always it is the Medjay in pursuit; now I was the pursued, running for my life.

We ran between the half-built shadows of the shanty town, and it seemed we had escaped our pursuers. The alleyway of the safe house was deserted. With a quick glance either way, we slipped behind the tatty curtain into the room, and bolted shut the heavy wooden door. We lay there, trying to suppress the jagged gasping in our aching chests; we were making too much noise in the listening silence.

'What do we do now?'

For the first time since I had met him, Khety looked honestly frightened.

'I don't know!'

We just looked at each other, praying to the old gods that some inspiration or luck would come to us. But there was nothing. We were on our own.

'We could go to my family.' Khety looked at me, frightened but brave. I was grateful to him for the honourable intention with which he made the offer. He meant his family would hide us. But the risk to them was far too great. Discovery would mean torture and execution for the men, mutilation and slavery for the women. I would not expose them to such a catastrophic fate, even though so much was already at stake.

Perhaps I saw a blur of a shadow of a movement, perhaps I imagine this only now, but suddenly a bronze axe-head shattered the middle panel of the door. It stuck there, and I could hear the curses of the man trying to free his weapon and the barked commands of his superior officer. We ran up the ladder just as another blow from the axe-head smashed into the door. As we reached the roof, I could hear the cries of alarm from along the street. I peered over the rooftop into the street and saw it was full of soldiers: the whole street was being ransacked by heavily armed guards. I recognized the woman with the smashed foot; she was arguing and gesticulating with the guards, pointing to the rooftop where we had conversed. I could not blame her. She had to survive. Then the axe flashed in the sun as it rose and fell again, and I heard the door come away with a groan and a slam.

We ran across the roofs, vaulting the dividing walls and pulling down lines of washing. A few old women watched us, but made no move. I followed Khety, who as usual had a better sense of direction. I looked back, and already there were many troops on the rooftops, running after us.

'Split up!' I yelled at Khety. He stopped running. 'Where will we meet up?'

'You know where!' He gestured across the river. 'After dark!' He pointed for me to run in one direction, grinned as if this were some wild adventure, and set off in another.

I ran. Almost immediately I jumped across a little crevasse between two shacks, missed my footing, clung to the far wall, and had to haul myself up, scraping my hands and knees. The troops had divided into two, and my section was closing on me. I had lost sight of Khety, which was good: he must have made it to ground level and perhaps evaded capture. I ran on, throwing behind me whatever I could grab – pots, crates, firewood – to trip them. I planned to get to the streets and mingle again with the crowds. But up ahead of me, on the next roof, armed Medjay swarmed up the steps, followed by a familiar figure with close-cropped metal-grey hair, standing taller than all the others. His lion's eyes focused on me, a little smile of anticipation flickering on his cold face.

I stood still, returning his gaze. If this was a game of *senet*, he was standing like Osiris on the last square; except Mahu represented my passage into the next world in the worst possible way. Would they capture me and bring me down, or would I be executed on the spot? But I still had options. I was standing on a roof near the edge of the shanty. I could take my life into my hands with a leap into the unknown. Certainly I had little enough knowledge to defend myself against Mahu. In his power again, I doubted I could survive.

Before I even finished the thought, I ran towards the edge of the roof and jumped.

35

I walked slowly up my street towards my house, my case in my hand, my journal in my case, my heart singing like a bird in my chest. I was returning home at last. I was older now. How many years had passed? I could not tell, and it no longer mattered. Time was a long, slow river. The early evening sun inscribed shadows on the clear air. People turned to look at me and waved as if I had been gone a long time.

I stepped through the gate and opened the door into the courtyard. The children's toys lay scattered about on the tiles. I entered and called out. *Tanefert? Sekhmet? Girls?* No answer came. I passed through the sitting room. In the kitchen, fruit rotted in the bowl, and the dishes served only the dust of many days. The children's room, where I had last held them and kissed them goodbye, was empty, the beds unmade. One of Sekhmet's stories – she had written hundreds – lay scattered across the floor. I bent to pick it up and saw with horror on the papyrus the imprint of a dirty leather boot. My hands started to shake.

I ran through the rooms, shouting their names, throwing aside chairs, opening doors, ransacking storage chests to see if they were hiding inside. But I knew now they were gone and I had lost them for ever. In that moment I heard a howling, like a grieving animal, from very far away, lost in a dark, dead wood.

I woke to that strange howl. It was my own bitter, unanswered cries. There were disgraceful wet tears on my face. I struggled to become myself again, out of the misery and confusion of the dream. I wanted to sleep so deeply I could know and feel nothing, but someone was telling me I must not. I must wake up. Suddenly I felt frightened of what would happen if I did sleep.

No light entered into whatever place this was. So much for the god of the sun; he had deserted me. I could see nothing. My body was far away. It occurred to me I must bring it back. I recalled I had muscles for use. I concentrated on the word 'hands' and something stirred, but coldly, remotely, heavily. I switched to 'fingers', and this time I could feel them moving more clearly. But what was this, rough and harsh? A crude shackle around my wrists, which were wet. I brought my hands slowly together and discovered they were linked to a rope. I struggled to bring everything towards my mouth, for taste was the only sense I could believe in. I licked something familiar and strangely comforting. A memory came in a flash: a knife blade held to my lips. Then it vanished again, and a feeling of implacable sorrow replaced it. I struggled against it. *No! Keep thinking!* The shackles had worn away the skin and flesh. I must have struggled, in my dream, to free myself from my bondage.

I let my fingers move across my face: eyes, nose, mouth. Chin. Neck. Shoulders. *Keep going.* Chest. Nipples. Arms, two – abrasions, places that hurt, suddenly, when I touched them. Bruises? Wounds? *More. Find yourself.* Belly, thighs – and another sudden flash: I saw boots kicking again and again into my groin, and the torn sensations of agony, rage and vomiting. Now my mouth recalled its own taste: stale, parched, disgusting. Suddenly I wanted to drink and drink. Water!

My fettered hands scurried, desperate as rats, across the invisible floor of this place. A jar. I raised it to my lips, the contents sloshing over me, stinging where the flesh was cut, and then I sent it flying into the dark. Cold piss. My wrists throbbed where the short ropes yanked against them. My gorge rose, but spewed nothing more than a dribble of some intense bile whose bitterness flooded my throat.

Then I remembered. Mahu. The rooftop. Before I jumped. This was his work. He was to blame. Then my fetters were tearing again at my flesh. I was raging, raging like a demented animal, kicking against my confinement.

There were commands, shouts. A door slammed open and a jar of cold water was thrown over me. The shock of the light, the freezing shock of the water and the fear of reprisal made me crawl back into a corner of the cell, its filth and stone walls partly revealed. There were strange markings gouged into these walls, the desperate signs of the condemned who had passed through here on their way to death and oblivion. Now I was one of them.

Two Medjay guards aggressively hustled me into a standing position. Fetters ached and weighed, cutting into my ankles as well as my wrists. My nakedness was exposed to the light. The guards ignored me, and no-one gave me clothing. I found I wished to speak, but what came from my mouth was the croak of a crow. They laughed, but one of them gave me a jug. I held it, trembling, and a little cool water entered my mouth. Tears filled my eyes at the same time. Then the guard roughly pulled the jug from my grasp.

I cannot tell how long we stood there like that. I was so tired, but they forced me to stay standing, prodding me with their batons as I wavered on the spot like a drunk who has lost his memory and his way.

Then a thick shadow appeared, moving slowly, purposefully, one step at a time, in no hurry at all, towards the door, as if descending into a tomb. It stooped to enter the cell. Mahu. He looked at me casually. The guards stiffened to attention. Suddenly I broke out towards him, punching, lashing out, desperate to beat his smug face with my bare fists, my feet, anything. But I was stopped by the ropes as short as a mad dog's, and I fell jerking and thrashing at his feet. At that moment I hated him and his thick panting hound. I would have torn his squat throat apart with my bare teeth, smashed open his ribs and feasted on his entrails and his fat heart.

He smiled. I said nothing, trying to control my ragged breath and the storm of hatred inside me. He shrugged, waited, patient as a torturer, then leaned down near me. I could smell his stale scent.

'No-one knows you're here,' he said.

I returned his gaze.

'I warned you, Rahotep. You only have yourself to blame. If you are suffering now, that is good. If your suffering has taught you hatred for me, that too is good. It is a fever that will infect, corrupt and rot your soul.'

'I will kill you.'

He let out a short laugh, a bark of contempt, rolled his head on his solid neck, and nodded. The guards held my arms, and he grasped the hair of the back of my head with his meaty hands, forcing me to look up. His breath was hot and foul on my face. His teeth needed cleaning. His nose, I noticed, carried tiny broken red lines under the greasy skin. His spittle, as he spoke, flecked my face.

'Hatred is like acid. I can see it now, penetrating and corroding your mind.' Then he methodically and casually worked two fingers into my eye sockets, and pushed until brief stars of agony exploded in the red sky of my head. I thought he would crush my head in his hands. I struggled in my bonds, spat at him, flailed uselessly. 'Before you lose your mind, I want answers. Where is the Queen?'

I refused to answer. He pressed harder. My head lit up with incandescent arcs of pain.

'Where is the Queen?'

I still refused to answer. Would he crush my eyes in my head? Suddenly the pressure vanished. I blinked but could make out nothing but a strange vision of whirling shapes and colours. I shook my head to try to clear my sight. His kick caught me in the face. The force of the blow travelled fast through my head. Acrid bile seeped into my mouth.

Sickly sweet blood dripped from my split lips. I could feel the outline of my teeth blooming and swelling on my bruised mouth.

Through the roaring in my head I heard him ask again, without changing the expression of his voice: 'Where is the Queen?'

'As it is said in the Chapters of Coming Forth by Day.'

'What?'

'As it is said in the Chapters of Coming Forth by Day.'

'I dislike riddles.'

'Her sign is Life.' And this time I smiled.

He punched it off my face. 'I will break every bone of your fingers if I have to. And then how will you write in that little journal? You won't be able to hold your own cock to piss.'

I waited a little while, then with all the strength I had I said, 'Do you go down into the Otherworld.'

His anger showed in his face. Good. Then, with a sigh, as to a recalcitrant child, he casually picked up my left hand and with a swift motion jerked back the little finger. The tiny crack echoed around the cell. I cried out.

He looked closely into my eyes, as if to enjoy at close range the spectacle of my suffering. I saw the black dots of his pupils, and my own distorted face reflected in his eyes. 'No-one is going to save you this time, Rahotep. It is too late. Akhenaten himself does not know you are here. You have disappeared into thin air. You are nobody. Nothing.'

The pain was still singing in my hand, and I feared I would vomit again.

'You have very little time left to find the Queen,' I croaked. 'And if you cannot, then the Festival is going to be a catastrophe for Akhenaten, and for you and for this city. I am your only lead. You cannot afford to kill me.'

'I don't need to kill you. Others will take care of that. But I find I do need to hurt you very badly. And we can go on for some time.'

'No matter what you do to me, know this: I will not tell you what I know. I would rather die.'

'It is not you who will die. Do you understand me?'

I looked into his eyes. I understood his threat. Hathor, Lady of the West, forgive me now. I did the only thing possible.

'As it is said in the Chapters of Coming Forth by Day.'

His eyes turned colder, as if all light had suddenly abandoned them. He reached for my hand again. I prepared myself, silently uttering a prayer. My whole body was shivering now. He waited, relishing my suffering, timing his move.

'Tell me where she is.'

I looked into his eyes with all the defiance left in me. 'No.'

He grasped another finger to snap the next little bone.

36

A quiet but entirely authoritative voice possessed the sudden silence of the cell: 'What is happening here?'

He had entered unnoticed. Perhaps both Mahu and I had been too engaged with the enactment of our mutual antagonism, the blood and sweat of what was happening; but it was as if he carried no shadow, made no noise, as if he had suddenly appeared from thin air. Ay. His very name was weightless. Thin air, indeed, seemed to describe his presence. But what force has thin air that it can cause a thug like Mahu to leap to his feet, alarmed, already stammering his excuses?

'Release this man from his bonds,' Ay whispered almost, to ensure we all listened carefully.

Mahu nodded, full of hatred and uncertainty, and the guards did as they were ordered. I cradled my damaged hand and bloody wrists.

'This man is naked,' Ay added, as if mildly puzzled. He looked enquiringly at Mahu, who gestured vaguely, at a loss to answer. Ay's face modulated into an expression that in others would have constituted a smile. His lips pulled back to reveal evenly spaced fine white teeth, the teeth of a man whose diet is so refined nothing ever rots or damages them. But his grey eyes smiled not at all. 'Perhaps you should offer him your own clothes,' he said softly.

Mahu looked so surprised I almost laughed. And his hands did indeed stray towards his own linens as if he would actually obey this absurd command. Then Ay, with a dismissive nod, made it clear that my clothing should be brought for me – which it was, instantly. I dressed as quickly as I could, despite the sickening pain of my broken finger, and immediately felt stronger, more equal. The three of us stood in silence. I wondered what could possibly happen now. Ay let Mahu suffer; he stood there wishing he were made of stone.

'Did this man not expressly state to you that he was under my protection?' Ay enquired of Mahu.

If it was possible, I was momentarily the more startled. Mahu glanced at me.

'Yet what do I find? The chief of police personally enacting his own little inquisition. I am very surprised.'

'I detained him in the course of my duties, and with the authority of Akhenaten himself,' Mahu countered.

'I see. So the King knows you have this man here for interrogation?'

Mahu could say nothing.

'I do not think he would approve of your treatment of a fellow officer whom the King himself decided, from the depth of his wisdom, to appoint.'

Then he turned to me and I looked for the first time properly into his frozen grey eyes – full, it suddenly struck me, of snow.

'Come with me.'

I would save my vengeance on Mahu for later, and relish it then. It took all my willpower not to punch him hard in the face with my good hand as I walked past him. He knew it, too. Instead I just stared at him, then carried on, as well as I was able, and followed the footsteps of

Ay up the stone stairs, towards the weak light of day staining these miserable walls.

We were soon in a wide brick-lined shaft, perhaps a hundred cubits deep, like an enormous well that had not yet struck water, and never would. Stairs wound up the sides, and at every level chambers like those in a catacomb disappeared quickly in different directions into inky shadows. The entrances to these were barred but I saw, as we passed, the still-living mortal remains of men in the darkness, little piles of skin and bone, some with their white eyes open, in tiny cages not fit for dogs. In another space I saw men buried up to their noses in large sand-filled clay vases, like the ibises and baboons we dedicate in sacred catacombs. Madness and despair showed in their eyes. These men had been abandoned here and could no longer speak to defend or betray themselves. There was almost no sound.

Ay acknowledged the existence of none of this horror; he just walked up the stairs methodically, step by step, as if it cost him no effort. I followed, my mind bewildered by events and these sights, until finally, out of breath, I stepped out of that pit of suffering and misery and into the ordinary light of day. Suddenly there was the world again: heat and brightness, and guards sitting bored in the shadows of a reed hut. They all rose instantly to respectful attention when they saw Ay.

Ay got into a carrying chair, already prepared with uniformed carriers, and motioned for me to sit beside him. Shading my eyes against the blaze of daylight, I suddenly recognized where we were: in the Red Land behind the city, south of the desert altars. It must be late morning, for the shadows had gone and all was hazy with heat and overwhelming light. I felt very weak and tired. Ay handed me a little water jar, and I drank slowly as the carriage moved away along one of the Medjay paths. Servants ran beside us holding shades against the light. I think he had a profound aversion to the sun. We sat in silence. I found myself unable to think, only to feel the strange adjacency of these two worlds, the one buried deep, the other open to

Ra and the light of day, and me passing between them, fortunately in the right direction.

'How long have I been imprisoned?' I asked Ay.

'Today is the eve of the Festival,' he replied calmly.

Two days. Because of Mahu, I now had only one day left. How could I solve the mystery in so little time? And how could I now save my family? My hatred for him intensified, like a pure flame.

'And what news of my assistant, Khety?'

'I know nothing of this man,' said Ay dismissively.

That was the one piece of good news. Perhaps he had escaped.

The carrying chair took us to the border of the city, and soon we were passing through the ways of the central city, where the people were going about their daily acts and affairs so absurdly unconscious of the atrocities being committed on their fellow humans nearby. For a city in so much sun, I saw dark shadows everywhere. Parennefer had described the place as an enchantment, but now it seemed a mockery, an appalling delusion. Ay looked out at the spectacle, occasionally glancing up at building work in progress, at the many teams of artisans and workmen moving about anxiously and hurriedly on the high walls, trying to make the place look as finished as possible in time for the Festival. He seemed sceptical. He noticed me glancing at him.

'Do you believe they will finish in time for the ceremonies?' I asked.

He replied in his quiet voice: 'This is a fools' paradise, made of mud and straw, and soon it will crumble and collapse back into the base matter from which it is constructed.'

We passed the Small Aten Temple and the Great Palace, and continued along the Royal Road until we arrived at the harbour. I had not stopped, at any point, to consider my position. Here I was in the company of this man of enormous power, having been saved from the loving attention of Mahu and his gang; but of what nature was this new company? What did Ay want from me? He had freed me from one trap, but was I entering another? No guards accompanied us; I could simply have stepped out of the carrying chair and walked away up the street. But then what? I felt that he would be able to locate me anywhere.

He gestured to me to board a reed boat. I saw anchored out on the water his magnificent ship. So, this was our destination: his floating palace, a movable estate of power. I boarded the reed boat, as he knew I would.

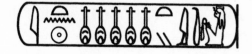

37

The ship seemed to hang in the water by its own immutable laws, a self-contained creation of stateliness. The streamers had been removed, the Priests and the orchestra had gone, and now, as I stood on the main deck, it gave above all a sense of power, clarity and grace. Ay moved swiftly into the shade of the portico, gesturing for me to follow. 'The physician will examine your injuries,' he said. 'Then we will dine.'

Instantly, serving men came forward to guide me to a room with a low bed, made up with fresh linen. They indicated that they wished me to undress so that they could wash me, but I refused. I wanted to wash my own wounds, even though my finger was throbbing horribly. I managed to get myself out of my old clothes and slowly cleaned the cuts, the sores on my wrists and ankles, and the sweat and dirt from my face and neck. Mahu and his guards had cut me up: bruises and knife lacerations criss-crossed on my inner thighs, and under my arms. Then, as I was drying myself, there was a knock at the door, and a man of middle age, wearing an understated but costly tunic, entered. He had a strange, empty face. His lips were thin. He reminded me of an abandoned house.

'I am the chief of physicians to God's Father,' he said in a voice that was almost colourless. 'I will need to examine you now.' I experienced a reluctance to allow him to touch me. He saw this. 'It is necessary.' I nodded.

He placed his hands upon me at different points; then his fingers quickly probed the cuts and wounds, squeezing at the broken skin to test for infection or vile fluids. When he lifted my hand to observe the broken finger, taking it between his own to test it by moving it about, the pain was horrible and I flinched. He did not seem to notice. He just nodded, as if this confirmed the obvious conclusion that the finger was truly broken.

He opened a small chest, which I noticed contained jars of minerals, herbs, honey, fat and bile. Next to them were vessels for the mixing and storage of essences and oils, and then an array of surgical instruments; sharp hooks, long probes, cupping vessels and vicious-looking forceps hanging from hooks. It was precise and highly ordered; a small working laboratory. How similar such instruments were, I realized, to those used in the processes of embalming and mummification. I remembered the Chamber of Purification. I remembered Tjenry and his glass eyes. I remembered the canopic jar and its appalling contents. I noticed a statue of Thoth, god of knowledge and writing, in his baboon form looking down at us both from a niche. Guardian of the deceased in the Otherworld.

'I see you are interested in alchemy,' I said.

He closed the chest and turned around. 'It is a way of knowledge,' he replied. 'Transmutation. The purification from base substance of eternal truth.'

'By what means?'

'By fire.' He looked at me with his desolate eyes. 'Turn to face the wall, please.' He handed me a dish.

'What is this for?' I asked.

He did not reply. I turned away. I felt him laying out my fingers on a board, the broken one tender and crooked to one side.

'I have heard of a substance, known only to the alchemists; a water that wets not and yet burns everything.'

Suddenly an intense pain exploded in my little finger, shooting up my arm. I vomited into the dish he had given me. When I came back to my senses he was already binding the finger in the splints. Now the pain was gone, replaced by a thrumming ache.

'Your finger is reset. It will take time to heal.'

He busied himself with returning his room to its state of meticulous order.

'As Chief of Physicians you must have access to the Books of Thoth?' I asked.

After a short silence he said: 'You could know nothing of such matters.'

'The Books are spoken of as compendiums of secrets and hidden powers.'

'Power is hidden in everything,' he replied. 'There is great power in this knowledge. And also great danger to those who are not correctly initiated into its secrets and responsibilities.'

We stared at each other. He waited to see whether I would try again. Then he nodded discreetly and departed, shutting the door silently behind him.

I was taken to the state room, with its gold chairs, long benches and Hittite wall hangings, and left alone to wait. Two trays on stands had been set – crisp linen, precious metal dishes, alabaster goblets almost pellucid in the polished light entering through the cabin windows. I was starving, and the prospect of a fine feast, however tense the occasion, set my stomach grumbling.

I was just pondering the glorious objects around me when I felt a drift of air, and there was Ay. We sat beside the trays, the two of us attended by a silent servant who was able to serve us perfectly and to maintain an air of not really being there. He brought us many dishes, including a fish cooked in a package of papyrus with the addition of white wine, herbs and nuts – a thing I would never have imagined.

'The fish is considered a poor man's meal,' Ay said, 'but correctly prepared it is delicate and makes meat seem crude. After all, it comes from the heart of the Great River, which gives us all life.'

'And carries away our rubbish and our dead dogs.'

'Do you see it that way?' He thought about it, then shook his head, dismissing my comment. 'The fish is an impressive creature. It lives in a different element. It remains silent and pure. It has its secrets but cannot speak of them.'

He delicately peeled the tail, spine and head away from his fish, and placed them on another dish. I followed suit, more messily. The two greasy heads lay on their sides as if listening intently to our conversation. Ay ate a few mouthfuls of the delicate flesh.

'I brought you here because I know you have found the Queen,' he said. 'Otherwise I would have left you to the tender care of Mahu, who hates you.'

I said nothing. Anyway, my mouth was full.

'In fact, I will express that thought another way. She is a clever woman, and would not have led you to her unless she wished to be found. True?'

Again, I did not reply. I needed to see where we were going. I remembered the look of animal fear upon that beautiful face when Ay's name was mentioned.

'Therefore she has a plan, which to some extent depends on your participation. And of course this plan must be to reveal herself again during the Festival. Why else would she sequester herself?'

It was not a question requiring an answer.

'I have not found her,' I said. 'I do not know where she is.'

He stopped eating. Those snow-filled eyes stared at me. 'I know you have found her. I know she is not dead. I know she will return. So the only question is, what happens next? She cannot know, so this is the area of interest to me.'

At a nod from Ay, the servant cleared the dishes and set new ones.

'And what have I got to do with all this?'

'You are her go-between. That being the case, I wish you to take her a message from me.'

'I'm not a messenger boy.'

'Sit down.'

'I'll stand.'

'The message is this: ask her to come to me, and I will restore order. There is no need for this melodrama. There are sensible solutions, correct choices to be made, for all of us. She does not have to fight us all to return stability to the Two Lands.'

I waited for more, but he said nothing.

'Is that it?'

'That is what I wish her to know.'

'It's not much of an offer.'

Suddenly he was angry. 'Do not presume to comment on what does not concern you. You are lucky to be alive.'

I watched him, the flash of intensity, the brief revelation of his power.

'Tell me one thing. What is the Society of Ashes?'

Ay gave me the long stare.

'And do golden feathers mean anything to you? And a water that wets not, and yet burns?'

His face gave even less away, but this time he got up and walked away without bidding me farewell.

So I sat down and finished my lunch. After everything I had gone through, a good meal was the least I deserved.

38

I was returned to shore, my belly full, wine in my head, my finger still throbbing. I turned back to look at the great ship. Ay seemed like a mirage: vividly there, but gone when looked at from the wrong angle. Was he a figure of infinite power, or some magician's trick of smoke and mirrors?

It was mid-afternoon now, and the sun, remorseless above the simmering cooking pot of the city's landscape, did nothing to clarify my state of mind. Nor did the crowds, overheated and overwhelmed, that now packed the harbour and the city's ways. Something was blurring the atmosphere of the place. After the hours on the ship, on the flowing water, and the lost time in jail, I felt heavy and weary, as if dry land was pulling me down. I felt like I wanted to wash and then sleep in the dark.

But I had to see Nefertiti. Not because I wanted to carry Ay's message – although I wanted to see its effect upon her – but because I needed to see if Khety had managed to reach the Queen's fort; and also because I had things to say. Things to tell her. Shards of story. I knew she could put them together better than I, if she chose.

I made my way to the necropolis. No sign of the cat. I approached the chapel for the second time, checking to make sure I was not observed, and entered its little precinct of stone and shadow. In the flat afternoon glare it seemed less mysterious, less convincing. In the sanctuary, the offering bowls had been kicked away. The hieroglyphs had been defaced. My name was scored out. So now someone knew about this place.

I examined the narrow gap through which on that night I had entered the Otherworld. But it was now sealed up. There was no way in. How, then, could I reach her? And why had this place been vandalized? It was obviously deliberate. Was she preventing me from reaching her again? I was furious. What did she want of me?

I went first to the pig sty, and rooted about like a fool for the trap door while the pigs sniffed at me. But the door refused to open. Suddenly I had the sense of being watched. I glanced up and down the alleyway – empty. It was oddly quiet, though. Someone could have trailed me, and stepped back into the shadow of a doorway. No other choice, then: I almost ran to the Great River, taking a zigzag route through the streets and ways, moving through crowds then slipping into a side passage, then doubling back. I kept glancing over my shoulder; I felt in my bones I was right, yet no-one seemed intent upon pursuing me. I scanned the crowds, but they all seemed occupied with other plans. Perhaps the unreality of the city was finally influencing my mind. Still, I could think of several people who would benefit from trailing me now and I could afford to take no risks, not with so much at stake.

I pretended to be moving in a northerly direction towards the Aten temples, and joined the throng on the Royal Road. Then I took a side turning to the east and, using the advantages of the grid pattern of construction, turned right and right again, doubling back upon myself, checking at each corner that no-one seemed to be following, then slipping through the crowds again on the Royal Road and heading west, through the warren of streets to the docks.

I chartered the worst kept and least noticeable skiff, kicking the old boatman out of his afternoon sleep. He rubbed his eyes, and began to row. I looked back across the crowded dock. Many people were observing the water. Many other boats were setting out. None seemed to be following me.

We crossed in silence. The man glanced at me curiously once, then pretended to concentrate on the river. The traffic was busy, and we passed in and out of the bigger ships, the slow ferries, the flotillas of pleasure-boats, and a small herd of water-buffalo struggling across, their heads held up above the waterline.

He left me on the far side. Suddenly the simple quietness of the world returned to me: a few birds, some children playing at the water's edge, the occasional calls of women working in the fields. No other boats were approaching or landing here. The sun, slowly descending towards the western cliffs, guided me towards the general area where the fort lay.

I set off between the fields of emmer and barley. How immaculate they were, tended to perfection over all time as if the fields themselves were worshipped gods. At one point a group of men riding donkeys appeared ahead of me, but we nodded and continued without attending much to one another. The track between the fields reached a wider path, and I followed it north, along the axis of the river's course, through a tiny settlement where the people still lived in the same low, dark mud shacks with their animals as they had done since time began. Everyone, including the babies and the old men reclining on their low benches, stopped to watch me pass. I felt as if I had stepped down from the sky. These were the working poor who had possibly, probably, never even crossed the Great River to the city. To them it was a kind of fable.

Then I was back again among the fields and date palms, and the sounds of early evening. Where was this place? Eventually, sweating and frustrated, I found myself standing at the boundary between the Black Land and the Red. Behind me the verdant yellows, viridians and spring greens of the cultivated world; one step in front of me began the stony dereliction that surrounds us. A flat, forsaken plain extended to a continuous wavering line of crumbly red cliffs. The Red Land continued beyond them, eternal, unseen, sacred, to the end of the world.

And there, up to my right, stood the building, its squat walls giving no sign of the life within. Of course there were no doors and no windows, but I had assumed I would be able to call, or find some means of access. I stood in the shadow of the east wall and, feeling like an angry fool, called out. No answer came. I called again. Just the mocking reply of a bird in the trees some distance behind me.

What else could I do? I circled the building but there was no way in. The mud-brick crumbled under my fingers when I tried to grip it and lift myself up. I kicked the futile stones at my feet. Damn her. Enough. It was time to take my chances, forget this charade, and go home. I would charter a boat and get out of the city as fast as possible. Enough.

I returned by the same route, but as I set foot upon the path I heard something up ahead. Even the birds in the trees seemed to have quietened. A brief wind rustled through the dry heads of the barley. The hair on the back of my neck prickled. I quickly dropped down and scurried into the barley field. Before long I could make out the sound of marching feet and wheels upon rough ground. A troop of soldiers appeared and passed close by me, followed by a chariot, bumping precariously on the track, carrying two Medjay officers. They were unmistakably heading for the square fort.

Keeping low in the barley, I scurried in the opposite direction, skirting around the village. The evening light had arrived now. The village seemed deserted. Everyone must be hiding inside. When I reached the edge of the river I spotted further along the strand a military ferry roped to the trees, a few guards set about it. Before me the Great River ran ever strongly. The city's buildings were gilded, and beyond them, in the distance, the eastern cliffs were lit bright red. How would I cross? And once I had crossed, where would I start to search for Nefertiti?

Then I noticed, paddling as if to stay still against the current, keeping almost hidden among the moving shadows near the water's edge, another skiff. The boatman seemed to be examining the shoreline. I crouched back into the trees. There was something familiar about the outline and the movements of the figure in the boat. I peered more closely, but the figure moved in and out of view. If he was an enemy, why would he be working so hard to stay unseen, and why would he be here?

I picked up a pebble and cast it carefully in the direction of the skiff. A moment of silence, during which it seemed to me the guards' voices lulled, and then a faint splash. I saw the figure in the boat turn quickly towards the source of the noise, and then peer into the dark fringe where I was hidden. He paddled closer, but not close enough. I threw another pebble. It landed nearer the shore. Immediately he followed the sound. Because we were on the western shore, the trees cast a long shadow across the edge of the water, even while the city was still lit up. But I believed now I recognized the shape of the figure's head.

I waited for the guards to resume their conversation. When I heard the murmur of their voices, I ran, crouching, across the narrow strand towards the skiff. I was right: it was Khety. I jumped in behind him as quietly as possible. He did not smile, just raised his finger to his lips and allowed the skiff to slide away with the current, away from the soldiers.

When we were at a safe enough distance, we turned to each other, our minds crowded with questions. The most pressing of which I voiced.

'Where is she?'

'I'll take you to her. But first I have to know what happened with Ay.'

'How do you know about that?'

'You were taken to the ship. You talked?'

Khety had never used this tone of urgency with me before.

'I'll tell her what happened.'

'You have to tell me first. Or I cannot take you to her.'

His expression was determined. This was not the unconfidently confident young man I had met just days before. He had assumed a new authority.

'She doesn't trust me now?'

He shook his head – direct and honest.

'You know I was captured? By Mahu?'

'Yes. And we thought that was the end. But then we learned you were freed. By Ay. This could only mean—'

'What? That I betrayed her? That I have been working for Ay all this time? Is that what you think? After all we have been through?' It is hard to be furious in a small boat on open water. 'Take me to her. Now.'

He looked at me, made his decision and nodded. He deftly turned the skiff and guided us across the strong currents of the river. The evening wind was ragged, blustery and hot – a different wind, not the cool of the northern breeze but something born of the south and its remote deserts. A nearly full moon had now risen above the city. Strange shadows of long, hazy clouds were being drawn like dirty veils across her face. The city's white façades stood out here and there above the darkness of the trees.

We made our crossing of the jittery dark waters leaving a confused wake, and sailed directly to a jetty of new stone where little tongues of black and blue water lapped agitatedly. The steps led to a place I already knew. A wide stone terrace under a marvellous vine that made it a secret place, quiet and free of the rising wind. And a beautiful chair, set near the water, so that the occupant could sit watching, thinking. I remembered the feel of the missing woman's figure in its shapes and contours. And there Nefertiti sat, real now, her fingers thoughtfully stroking the carved lion's paws at the end of the chair's arms, her mind seemingly as cool as a goblet of water.

I stepped out of the boat. The cat dropped casually down, stretched elegantly, walked over to me and wound herself around my legs.

'She still likes you.' Her voice carried a light trill of tension.

'She has faith. She believes in me.'

'It is in her nature.'

I said nothing. Khety, who had disappeared for a moment, brought another chair, then retired, perhaps to stand guard. I sat down opposite her, the cat purring in my lap.

'So, where do we start?' I said.

'With the truth?'

'You think I am here to lie to you?'

'Why not tell me your story? Then I will see whether or not I believe it.'

'More stories.'

She said nothing.

'I went looking for plots and conspiracies. I found men with reasons to want you to disappear for ever, and some of the same men with reasons to want you back. I found out about the golden feathers of the Society of Ashes. Does that mean anything to you?'

She shrugged. 'It's the kind of name men give to something they take too seriously.'

'Your brother-in-law told me the golden feather opens invisible doors. He seemed excited by it.'

'You see? Men love their riddles and codes and strange seals. It makes them feel clever and important.'

'That's more or less what your mother-in-law said. So did Ay.'

I watched her carefully. Something in her eyes flinched at the name – not for the first time. She changed the subject.

'Mahu got hold of you.'

It wasn't a question. I held up my finger in its splint. It looked silly.

'I didn't talk,' I said. 'Well, not much. I told him about the Otherworld and so on, but strangely he didn't seem to believe me.'

'He has no imagination.'

'He does seem to be quite a literal man.'

'But I am puzzled. How did you escape?' she asked, returning again to the same point, anxious as a cat trapped in the wrong room.

'Your friend Ay came and talked to him. Mahu seemed to be persuaded after all that he should brush me down and let me go. Then Ay invited me to lunch, and of course I had to accept. It was quite interesting.'

I wanted that to hang in the air. I wanted her to ask about it.

'I imagine Mahu tried to hurt you in your heart and soul. I imagine he threatened your family as well as your little finger.' Her face did not bother to make an expression of sympathy.

'He's threatened me with my family before. You know that. And anyway, while I was in the prison I had a bad dream. It was almost worse than anything he could do to me.'

'Dreams,' she said quietly. 'Tell me your dream.'

I looked away, across the river. Why should I tell her anything? But of course, I wanted to tell her everything.

'I dreamed I was home at last. It had been a long time. I was glad. But everyone was gone. I was too late.'

In the silence that followed I stroked the cat over and over, as if my distress could pass into her but cause no harm. She looked up at me with her calm green eyes. I found I could hardly bear to look up and meet the equally direct gaze of her mistress.

'It was a dream of fear,' she said.

'Yes. Just a dream.'

'Fear is a strong delusion.'

'It makes some of us human.'

I was suddenly angry. Who was this woman to tell me about fear? But she was angry too.

'And do you think I do not suffer fear? Do you think I am not human?'

'I see fear in your eyes when I mention Ay.'

'What did he say to you?' Again, she would not leave this alone, worrying at the question like a cat with a dead bird.

'He was very reasonable. He asked me to give you a message.'

That stopped her. Now she was on to something. I could sense her hunger, her need to know.

'Give me the message.' She said this too quietly.

'He said he knows you are alive. He knows you will return. His question is, what then? His message is: meet him. He will work with you to restore order.'

291

She shook her head in disbelief and, somehow, disappointment. The noise in her throat was something between a sob and a tiny lost laugh at something that was never very funny.

'And you thought it right to bring me this message?'

'I am no messenger boy. I'm telling you what he said. It sounded reasonable.'

'You are so naive.'

I killed the anger that leaped into my mouth. I tried another line of enquiry.

'What power has Ay got over you?'

'No-one has any power over me,' she said.

'I don't think that's true. Everyone has someone who frightens them. Their boss or their mother, their sworn enemy or the monster under the bed. I think you're afraid of him. But the strange thing is, I think he's afraid of you too.'

'You think too much,' she said, quickly.

'People don't think enough. That's the whole problem.'

She stayed silent. I knew I had hit upon some nerve, some thread of truth. Some secret bound them together, I was sure. But she changed the subject again, trying to turn the tide of my questions.

'So you have found out nothing for sure about the plots against me, and instead you have brought me a foolish message and led them, like a decoy, back to me. It's as well I anticipated the problems.'

I refused to change course. 'It's clear what is happening. Tomorrow is the Festival. Akhenaten is besieged by troubles at home and abroad. These troubles are focused now in the very event with which he hoped to resolve them. Why? Because your absence destroys the illusion he needs to perpetuate. Your return will precipitate enormous changes. This is anticipated by several men, including Ay and Horemheb, both of whom are waiting to see what happens when you do reappear. I imagine they wish to take full advantage of any change of authority. You, having sent me back into the lions' den, then assume me guilty of betrayal when I return to you with the little information I have been able to glean, at some personal cost to myself.

And the interesting thing is, Ay is right. I think you have no idea what happens next.'

I found myself, at the end of this outburst, pacing the terrace. At the door, Khety looked alarmed. The waters of the Great River seemed to be listening carefully for Nefertiti's reply. Eventually it came, very calmly, concealing everything.

'You are right,' she said. 'I have no idea what happens next. I will make my prayers for an outcome that restores peace and stability to all of us.' She looked out over the dark waters then, and added, 'I have one request.' Her eyes searched for mine. I confess my breath was tight in my chest. 'Will you accompany me tomorrow, when I make my return? Will you do that for me, despite everything?'

I did not even have to think about it. 'Yes,' I said. I wanted to be there.

I realized, as I said this simplest of words, that I wanted to face the uncertain future, with its fears and its dreams, with her, no matter where it would take us. I felt suddenly as if the wide, dark water was flowing under my feet; as if this terrace and all of this strange city, this little world of frail lights and hearts like flickering lanterns, were floating on the blackness, borne along on the currents, the fluent and the turbulent, of the river's long, deep dream.

39

Despite the deprivations of the last few days, for all the gold in the deserts of Nubia I could not sleep. The pain in my finger throbbed in time to my heartbeat, as if it intended to keep me awake – perhaps punishing the rest of my body for its apparent well-being. Perhaps also it was a reminder of my deepest fear. The fate of Tanefert and the girls tormented me, and I turned and turned again from side to side. The weather, too, was heavy, discontented. Irritable gusts of wind cast handfuls of sand and dust in frustration against the outer walls. I could hear a loose door banging in the wind, like a warning. Someone must then have gone out to close it, but somehow the silence after that was worse. Once this coming day was over, and its changes – whatever they were, however good or bad – were brought into being, I would take the first ship south, back home. I would row myself all the way back against the current in a little papyrus reed boat if I had to. The distance and the uncertainty had made me miserable, and I vowed never to leave my family like this again.

I was tossing and turning with these thoughts for company, when I heard footsteps outside my door. I had been given a side chamber to sleep in, and as we three had walked through the house some hours earlier, in a deliberate silence, hardly even bidding each other goodnight, the house had seemed deserted, the rooms shut up, the furniture covered. We were careful to light no lamps, nor give any evidence to the outside world of our presence. Nefertiti had assured us that no-one would think to seek us here, in her own palace. But now the quiet footsteps. They stopped outside my door. I lay very still, holding my breath. Then they continued, softly, and quickly faded away.

I dressed swiftly, and opened the door as quietly as I could. No sign of anyone. The passageway was dark, relieved only by a silvery light where it opened up ahead on to the terrace. All the rooms appeared silent and empty. I arrived at the end of the passage and looked out on to the terrace. The moonlight threw down a tangled labyrinth of black shadows from the vine onto the stones; and among the well-defined tendrils and leaves stood a familiar figure. She seemed part of the design, as if wound into the complicated filigree of light and dark.

I walked across to Nefertiti, now part of the dark design myself. We were silent for a moment, looking out across the moonlit river rather than at each other.

'Can't you sleep?' she asked eventually.

'No. I heard someone moving about.'

'Perhaps we could play a game of *senet*?'

'In the dark?'

'By moonlight.'

I knew she was smiling. Well, that was something.

We sat down at the board, facing each other across the thirty squares, three rows of ten, in a ℥ shape, the snake of life.

'Green or red?' she asked.

'Let's throw for it.'

She cast the four flat sticks, all of which landed face up on the black side – a propitious start. I threw them and got two white, two black. She chose green. 'I like the little pyramids,' she said. I took the red reel pawns and we placed our fourteen pieces in readiness.

She threw, and moved her first piece from the central square, the House of Rebirth, onto the first square. We played in silence for a little while, casting the sticks, moving our pieces forward, occasionally knocking each other's off the squares and returning them to their original position, where they waited in limbo for a lucky throw to begin again. Sometimes the hot wind interrupted our silence, insisting on something. I watched her thinking, considering her moves. She was beautiful, and unknowable, and I felt, with something not unlike amusement, that I was actually playing against a spirit in the Otherworld, and for the well-being of my immortal soul.

Soon we reached the last four squares of the game, the special squares. She threw, and landed on the House of Happiness. A rueful smile broke over her face. 'If I were superstitious, I could believe the gods have a sense of irony.'

I threw, and my first piece landed on the next square, the House of Water. 'If I were superstitious, I'd agree with you,' I said, pushing my piece off the board and back to the House of Rebirth again. 'Here we have strategy and chance, the two forces encountering each other. I feel like Chance; I think you're Strategy.'

She didn't smile. 'You have your strategies too.'

'I do. But I rarely feel I am in control of them. I apply them to the mess of the world, and sometimes the two things seem to correspond.'

She threw, and played.

'So you think the world is a mess?' she said, as if the question were another move in the game.

'Don't you?'

She thought for a while. 'I think it depends on how you look at the experience of being alive.'

She threw the three white faces required by the square of the House of the Three Truths to move her first pyramid off the board, and looked pleased to be winning. I wanted her to win.

'This is turning into the kind of conversation lovers have when they've just met at some drinking den late at night,' I said, before throwing and losing another piece.

'I've never been to such a place.'

I could see her there, though. The mysterious woman waiting for someone who isn't going to come, sipping her drink slowly like lonely people do, making it last.

'You haven't missed much,' I said.

'Yes I have.'

She threw again, and moved another piece off the board. She would beat me hands down.

The wind lulled then, and the quietness under the stars was strange and welcome. The moon had drifted further across the glittering sky.

'There are things I'd like to ask you,' I said. I could see her eyes in the darkness.

'Always asking questions. Why do you ask so many questions?'

'It's my job.'

'No. It's you. You ask questions because you fear not knowing. So you need answers.'

'What's wrong with answers?'

'You sound like a five-year-old boy sometimes, always asking why, why, why.'

She threw again, and moved another piece ahead to the House of Ra-Atum, the penultimate square. I threw. Four black sides; a six took my first piece on to the last square.

'Speaking of answers, what is there between you and Ay?'

She sat back and sighed. 'Why do you keep asking about him?'

'He's waiting for you.'

'I know that. Perhaps I am afraid of him. Consider what happened to Kiya.'

'I have heard that name,' I replied. 'She was a queen, yes?'

'She was a royal wife.' Nefertiti looked away.

'And she bore royal children?' I asked.

She nodded.

'What happened to her?'

She stared at me. 'Here is an interesting answer for you. She disappeared one day.'

'That sounds familiar.'

I thought about this. A royal wife and mother of royal children, and therefore a competitor to Nefertiti herself within the royal family. Why did she disappear? What kind of threat did she represent? Was she despatched on the orders of someone; Ay, perhaps? Could he have the power to organize and plan to the level of assassination? Or – almost unthinkably – was Nefertiti herself capable of such ruthlessness?

She watched me carefully.

'A story that turned out well for you,' I observed.

'Perhaps. But where has your question taken you? To the truth? To a greater understanding? No. It has taken you to more questions. You are in a labyrinth in your head with no escape. You have to go beyond the labyrinth.'

'But what is beyond the labyrinth?'

She gestured around us, as we sat together over the squares and pieces, the chances and the strategies, the secrets and the nonsense of the unfinished board game.

'Life, Rahotep, life,' she said.

She had never used my name before. I liked the way she said it. Her face was half in the light of the moon, half in the dark of the shadows. I would never really know her.

She rose quietly. 'Thank you for letting me win.'

'You won all by yourself,' I said.

We looked at each other for a long moment. *The eyes, the eyes.* Nothing more could be said.

We parted then, leaving the pieces of the game set out on the board as if we might return to them in the morning. At her door she wished me a good night – what was left of it. I knew she was afraid. She left her door ajar, but I could not cross this threshold. I drew up a stool and sat down to sit out the night like a playing piece on the last square of the great game of *senet*, on a board the size of this strange city, with its lucky and unlucky squares, its chances and its plots, waiting for the throw of fate.

40

I was woken by Khety, who found me slumped like a village idiot against the wall outside the Queen's chambers. He had that amused look on his face.

'You can wipe that grin off,' I said.

I felt weary and nervous at the same time, as if I had not slept at all. I stood up and knocked on the double door. For a moment there was no sound, and then it opened to reveal Nefertiti's maid Senet, her quietness, her honesty. She smiled, but she was not pleased to see me. She looked as immaculate as ever, but today she was not wearing gloves.

'Good morning,' she said. 'The Queen is ready.'

'I have a quick question for you.'

She glanced back into the chambers. 'We have no time. The Queen is ready.'

'It is a very simple question.'

She stepped out of the chamber and pulled the door gently closed behind her. Her face assumed an expectant look.

'It's probably nothing,' I said.

She nodded.

'You went to the Harem Palace to deliver instructions for one of the women, a specific woman, from the Queen.'

It was hard to gauge her reaction.

'Yes.'

'As you know, that woman died under violent circumstances the same night.'

'You told me.'

'Please tell me which woman was to follow the Queen's instructions.'

She looked uncertain. 'I did not read the instructions. They were sealed, in any case.'

'I see.'

We both waited for something.

'I may as well tell you the name of the woman who died,' I said.

'I do not need to know it.'

'It was a girl called Seshat.'

She stared at me, her mouth open. It was as if she were glass and I had shattered her. She made to go back into the chamber, but I held her arm.

'Did you know her?'

'I'm afraid I never knew this unfortunate woman,' she said evenly. But her eyes, brimming with tears, gave her away. Then she wrenched her arm free and swiftly slipped inside.

A short while later the doors opened and there stood a figure of gold. Nefertiti looked like a statue, like a *ka*-figure in a tomb. She was framed by the wide doorway; the light coming from the windows inside her chamber lent her outline a lambent glow. No-one spoke. Her sandals were pointed with precious stones; her linen gown was gold; the sash around her trim waist was the red of Kings; around her neck a gold ankh necklace; on her shoulders a strange and wonderful cape which wove together countless small Aten discs to form a shimmering constellation; under that, a shawl that looked like the gold feathers of Horus; and on her head the double crown with its high back and rearing cobra. Even her nails and lip paint were gold. Only the kohl, the colour of fertile earth and promise of rebirth, and the elongated black lines around her eyes contrasted with the golden glamour.

I thought of Tanefert, and how she would ask my opinion of her appearance before we set off in the evenings. Sometimes she would adjust a new outfit with a slightly discomfited air, as if she were unsure of her own beauty; the girls have exactly the same habit before a mirror. I always liked her best when she used least art in her appearance; she seemed most herself then. Some sign of casual disarray pleased me more than all the sophisticated artifices of our time. I'd rather see a loose-hanging curl that begged to be coiled back behind the ear than the untouchable strain and tension of perfection.

But the woman I had talked to last night in the small hours, and who had now transformed herself into something more than human, had become who she needed to be: a goddess; the Perfect One. There was a new distance between us all. I felt I should bow my head, or prostrate myself, but almost immediately dismissed them as foolish urges. There was still the lovely glitter of amusement in her eyes. But it was complicated now, by other things. Necessity. Power. And for all the uncertainty about the outcome, I could see excitement in her eyes.

The Festival would be commencing about now with worship and offerings at the Great Aten Temple. Akhenaten and his daughters would be riding at speed in their chariots, their red sashes trailing in the breeze, down the Royal Road, past the packed crowds seeking a glimpse of this moment of history; past the prostrate kings, viziers, lords, commanders, diplomats, tribal chiefs, governors of provinces, nomes and city states ... but the Queen would be absent, as they would all immediately see. I could imagine Akhenaten now, determined, resolute, furious not to have had restored to him what he most needed. And I could imagine, too, the quick understanding and intensive commentary among the gathering of the most powerful people in the world: she was missing, and Akhenaten was flawed. *She is dead. Who killed her? Why?*

'It is time,' she said, and from that moment I knew she would not speak again until all had been accomplished, or all had failed.

Ra, in his dazzling ship of day, had sailed higher in the blue sky. We, too, on our own shining ship of gold, a craft built for ancient ceremony with twenty attending women also dressed in gold and the tall, solitary Nubian who had played Anubis standing guard, sailed slowly upon the equally blue and glittering waters of the Great River. Nefertiti sat high and still on the deck of a small ceremonial divine barque of the Two Lands that was carried on a bier. She was holding the crook and flail crossed in her hands, and wearing now the false gold beard of kingship. The fierce illumination of the midday sun was amplified by the gold of the ship and her costume. It was almost impossible to look at her.

As we rowed slowly on, people gathered on the banks; at first just a few, but soon there was a multitude, shading their eyes, pointing, standing along the shoreline and in the trees. Most of them quickly prostrated themselves before the entirely unexpected Perfect One. From my position at the east side of the ship I could hear the constant slapping of the crested waves against the gold-leafed hull of the ship, and the high breeze, still from the south, shaking and rattling in the red and green sails, as we made our way against the current.

We must have made an astounding sight. Yet I could see the truth of the ship: how the ropes were a little frayed with age; how the blindfolded rowers sweated and exerted themselves to the beats of the two drummers, and the calls and instructions of the captain; how the immaculate gold-leaf of the outer shell gave way to unvarnished wood on the inside.

As we approached the harbour, the crowd massed and swelled, and the noise grew to a continuous turbulent roar – of awe or anger or approval it was impossible to say. The ship docked, and instantly a team of men dressed in gold emerged from the hold and lifted the ceremonial barque, with the Queen, high onto their broad shoulders. She briefly gripped the rails of her little ship – a moment of human nerves – as it sought to rediscover its balance.

We were no longer on the calm isolation of the river, but among the hot chaos of the land. A pathway opened up in the monstrous crowd and we processed carefully and in state up to the Royal Road, inexorably, step by step, towards the Great Aten Temple. More people shouting prayers and jubilations flooded into the swelling crowd, which was now jostling and rising like the waters of the inundation against the walls of the buildings, and overflowing from the tributary passageways. The twenty attending women processed ahead of us, throwing yellow and white flowers in the path of the Queen; still she appeared to see and hear nothing, remaining high and as still as a shrine statue above the chaos. I could see the temple ahead in the near distance, the freshly white-washed walls already dusty, the banners thrashing occasionally in response to the gusts of wind that carried with them the grit and sand of the Red Land. I was worried now as much by the strangeness of the weather as by the danger we all faced at this moment of exposure to the unknown forces ranged against us.

All along the way, the crowds prostrated themselves on their bellies in the dirt, but the Medjay troops kept their weapons poised. The air was thick with smells: baking bread and roasting meat, incense and flowers; and already many of the younger men in the crowd were drunk. A kind of collective frenzy was taking hold, an atmosphere of danger and excitement and instability, as if now anything could happen. The future was taking shape in these very moments, and we were a part of it.

As we approached the temple we slowed, paused to acknowledge the crowd, then turned into the gate. Momentarily the sentries seemed about to bar our path, arguing among themselves; but in awe of the living statue of the Queen they backed off, lowering their heads, and opened wide the gates of the first pylon.

The Queen's ship passed through the great blocks of shadow and entered the temple's vast interior space. Nefertiti stared directly ahead. From enormous bronze incense burners rose clouds of perfumed smoke, over-sweetening the already thick, shimmering air. The altars were piled high with every good thing of the earth: huge bouquets of lotus and lilies, safflowers and poppies; red pyramids of pomegranates; stacked yellow heads of corn; and vases of oil and unguent. And here were hundreds of delegations from across the world arranged in ranks, awaiting their turn to be presented to the most powerful man in the world. They had brought tribute to lay at Akhenaten's divine feet: shields and bows, animal skins and collections of gorgeous plumage, spices and perfumes, piles of gold rings and other nonsense made from gold – little trees, little animals, little gods – as well as living creatures: monkeys, terrified gazelles, snarling leopards, even an anxious and timid lion, his ears flat on his head.

Far away, over the prostrated figures and heads of the crowd, I could see Akhenaten and his daughters, little gold figures enthroned on top of the Ramp of Offerings under a great canopy decorated with a multitude of ribbons. The crowd was turned correctly towards them. But when the Queen entered it was as if the polarity of the whole world changed in a moment. Everyone turned their heads.

A hush fell then, punctuated by cries of wonder and amazement. Many people prostrated themselves immediately; others raised their arms; others looked from King to Queen and back again, utterly uncertain how to respond. Was this a statue made of the matter of this world, or a living being returned from the next? Then Akhenaten himself turned from the rituals to see what was happening. The two gold figures looked at each other across the empty space. No-one moved. I looked around the perimeter wall and saw troops of archers poised for Akhenaten's word.

And then an even more extraordinary thing came to pass. Nefertiti, taking command of the moment, came to life. There was a rolling gasp of astonishment as she suddenly raised her hands, holding the crook and flail to command the attention of the gods. And then she began to sing, her voice ringing out pure and strong, the long, clear notes filling the great hushed auditorium. As if suddenly recognizing the song, and their place in the music, the temple trumpeters joined in, their instruments raised brightly to the sun. And this encouraged the temple singers, who began clapping and singing. Then the other musicians joined in, lyres, lutes, drums and great double harps adding their different tones and powerful rhythms. Soon Nefertiti's voice was riding the swelling wave of an orchestra, and the music seemed to transform the people's faces as if its harmonious spirit brought a new order and power into existence.

As the music continued, the ceremonial barque was carried forward. It seemed as if Nefertiti, her arms raised to the Aten now, was sailing through a sea of people's faces, and they divided to let her pass. The light of the sun's rays was magnified by the gold of the boat and her dress, as if she were made not of flesh and bone but of some impossible immaterial incandescence. She who was dead was returning in glory as a living god, outwitting her clever husband and triumphing over her enemies – for who now would dare to challenge such a figure? Thousands of the most powerful people of the world stood in utter silence, witnesses to the miracle. But these were no fools. They knew this performance for what it was. And they waited to see what would happen next.

The music concluded, and complete silence fell again. Instead of joining the King on the ramp, Nefertiti approached the sacred stone in the centre of the temple precinct, its high, round-topped column on a raised dais. She slowly reached forward and touched it with one hand. And then something unfolded as if from inside the woman: a whirr of feathers and bones which became a heron, the crested bird of resurrection. It flapped its long, elegant grey wings as if rising from the stone, lifted itself high above the Queen's head, and flew off towards the eastern hills.

A pure, sacred bird. Gold feathers. Rebirth. The goddess returning from the Dead. Sign of the rising sun. It was perfect.

Nefertiti remained standing for a moment, surrounded by thousands of normally cynical, now awe-struck people, their mouths wide open like wondering children. I moved forward to the front of the bier. I saw familiar figures, now, among those closest to Akhenaten. Ay, his face inscrutable, not allowing the slightest flicker of surprise to register. Ramose, in magnificent costume, looking astonished by the appearance of the Queen and the bird. Calculating Horemheb, looking from the woman of light to Akhenaten and back again. Parennefer, in a secondary row, whose raised eyebrows said: you've done it now. And Nakht, the honest nobleman, who gave me a swift nod of acknowledgement. I expected to glimpse Mahu occupying some dark corner, but although I could feel him in a prickling sensation at the back of my neck, he was nowhere to be seen. The Society of Ashes. Who here held one of those seven gold feathers? And who here did not, yet greatly desired one?

I looked along the roofline of the temple and saw hundreds of archers still poised, bows tensed. All around the interior perimeter walls were armed Medjay guards. Had we walked into a huge and powerful trap? I would not put it beyond Akhenaten, with one nod – or would it be Ay, or Horemheb? – to bring down a rain of deadly arrows upon all our heads. The whole project seemed to be in the balance.

I looked back at Akhenaten and saw him staring directly at Nefertiti. They were on the same level now, above the crowd, but in every other way she had upstaged him. It seemed to me he trembled with conflicting rages and emotions while outwardly maintaining near-immaculate control. The princesses tried to stay still, but their eyes were filling up with tears, torn between duty to their father on this most important day and the urge to run to their lost mother.

Nefertiti, however, gave no sign of maternal affection. She held the crucial gaze of her husband. I thought of two snakes poised, swaying slightly, unblinking and cold. Then suddenly he offered her his hand. She gave a command, and the barque moved forward. The crowd made a sound like a wave sighing after it has arrived on the shore and collapsed, retreating through the stones. She stepped onto the Ramp of Offerings and slowly took her place by the side of Akhenaten on the throne. And behold a picture for the world to witness: the royal family reunited before the audience of the Empire. But with this one difference: here was a Queen returned, as none had ever done before, from the Otherworld. She raised her arms as if they were the gold wings of Horus, and the sun's light glittered off the many gold discs on her shawl and played across the walls of the temple and the roaring faces of the crowd. A triumph.

I watched those faces closely. What would they do now? Then, almost as one, led ostentatiously by Ay, the thousands gathered in the temple precinct sank to their knees and prostrated themselves seven times in loyalty. Nefertiti and her daughters turned and raised their hands to the offerings of the rays of the sun. The multitudes followed suit. The musicians took up the song again, and the trumpets blasted their fanfares.

I looked at her up there, the woman with whom I had talked, played *senet*, and argued, and she was now very far away, in a different world. She had restored *maat*, stability and order, to the world, while also assuming power. And I felt too that my task was complete, if accomplished in a way I could never have anticipated. I had, at the very least, returned the Queen to her family, and the Two Lands. I consoled myself that I could now turn away from this labyrinth of power, this city of shadows, and go home.

But then the wind, which had been subdued like a charmed and invisible monster at the feet of the Queen, stirred, tugging at the ceremonial gowns and the fine embroidered linens of the dignitaries, and wafting the incense smoke angrily. Women reached to readjust their hair and clothes, men shaded their eyes, and everyone turned to look up at the sky whose perpetual blue was challenged now by a thick grey-red cloud as if a thunderous army were approaching blown up by Seth, god of storms and desert lands. Countless tiny specks of grit began to sting our faces and eyes. A sudden strong gust blew through the precinct and a huge pile of pomegranates collapsed from an offering table with a thundering sound and scattered across the floor. People shielded their faces with their robes and began uncertainly to back away, huddling together for protection as the wind grew fiercer, more volatile, casting its handfuls of scouring sand and overwhelming dust against the walls of the temple and the high façades of the pylons. The temple banners streamed out now, lashing and kicking at the crazed air, as if to fend it off. And the Glory of the Aten, to whom this city and its whole enterprise was dedicated, suddenly dimmed and diminished to a faint white-edged red disc, its power failing on the very day of the great Festival of Light, at the very moment of triumph, before the shadowy might of Chaos.

I knew what was coming. I had seen sandstorms many times before and should have taken the early warning signs more seriously. We had little time if we were not to be overwhelmed. Nefertiti, the girls and Akhenaten were still standing on the ramp. He looked baffled, but her face was alert with anxiety. She understood the peril, grasped the girls' hands and hurried down to meet me. All around us the crowd was breaking apart, stampeding towards the only exit through the narrow pylon gates. The fallen pomegranates were squashed to a red pulp; people slipped and fell in the sticky mess.

But it was hopeless: the gates were far too narrow to allow such a vast crowd to pass, and quickly the terrible tide bunched up, everyone shoving and pushing, demented with panic and fear. Guards shouted and tried to hold back the crowd, but they failed to impose any kind of order, and soon they too were struggling over everyone else to escape. Cries and calls for help mixed in with the whipping sound of the wind, and I saw frailer people vanishing under trampling feet.

I looked around for another way out, or at least for protection. And then I saw Horemheb gesturing furiously to the soldiers stationed around the perimeter to advance towards the royal family – whether protectively or aggressively I could not tell. I did not want to stay to find out. I saw a look on his smooth face – the look of a man grasping an unexpected opportunity. I did not like it.

'Is there another way out?' I shouted to the Queen over the noise.

She nodded, and we set off against the current of the crowd. The sand was thicker in the air now, and we tried to shelter the girls with our own bodies. I looked back to check on Horemheb and his soldiers and saw them gathered around him while he gestured at our receding figures. And then, to make things worse, among the rushing people driven by the tremendous gusts of wind I noticed a single figure standing as still as a statue, as if immune to the chaos which churned

309

around him, observing us. Ay. Something like a smile played upon his face, as if to say: so this is what happens next. And then he disappeared from view.

I had no time to concern myself with him now. My immediate duty was to take the family to some kind of shelter, away from Horemheb, and then consider the next move. I glanced at Senet, who was carrying the baby Setepenra. Her face was stricken. She was looking in the direction where Ay had been standing. What was he to her? Then Khety appeared at my side and picked up Nefernefrure, I grabbed Ankhesenpaaten and Nefernefruaten, and, pulling Senet along with us, we ran against the force of the wind and the grit towards the further pylon. Nefertiti followed with Meretaten and Meketaten, pulling Akhenaten by the hand. He was struggling to hold his crown on his head as he hobbled against the storm that had brought him and his new world low.

We made it to the lee side of the eastern pylon. The storm had driven everyone else to the western end of the temple; the soldiers, too, had abandoned their positions and fled. But Khety and I could see shapes and silhouettes among the grey blur of the dust – armed figures advancing towards us, pushing aside the few aged or lost souls still stumbling about in utter confusion and despair, blinded by the violence of the dirty wind. I attempted to look around the corner, and saw that the worst was yet to come: the great wave of the storm was poised over the city. We were trapped.

'How do we get out?' I yelled over the screams of the wind.

'Inside the sanctuary!' Nefertiti shouted back.

I looked again and saw, running through the storm and pushing aside all who stood in his way, a familiar, hulking outline, with a close-cropped head of tight curls. Mahu. He would reach us in a very short time.

We ran into the forbidden interior of the sanctuary. At a point in the stone wall where a figure of herself was painted, Nefertiti pushed open a narrow, low door which I would never have seen. I looked back and saw Mahu enter the sanctuary; he called out but I could not hear his words. I had no intention of asking him to repeat them. I hurried everyone inside and closed the double door behind me, sliding across the strong wooden bolt to secure it. Suddenly the pandemonium of the storm seemed muffled. The glorious golden regalia of the royal family now looked fake, shoddy, something from a dressing-up box. Akhenaten had transformed into a confused old man, unable to look anyone in the eye. The girls were frightened, coughing and clinging to their mother, who smoothed their hair and kissed their dusty eyes. Outside, the wind and Mahu rattled, banged and shouted, trying to get in. Khety and I allowed ourselves the luxury of a quick grin at the thought of the chief of police hammering furiously on the other side.

There was almost no light at all. My head swam with dizzy constellations. Then someone was pulling a flint, and there was a spark. The little light hesitated, then leaped to life. We huddled around the flame. Akhenaten glanced at Nefertiti with fury. He was about to speak when she raised her fingers to her lips. Even now she was in control.

A newly lit lamp revealed steps disappearing down into darkness. Nefertiti, this woman of passageways and underworlds, led us down and we followed, grateful to be moving, glad of direction. No-one spoke, and when one of the girls started to cry with fatigue, Nefertiti calmed her. Where the passage divided she unerringly chose her direction. After what seemed a long time, we found another set of stone steps, half buried in sand, leading up to a wooden trap door. I pushed at the door, but it gave barely an inch. I tried again, struggling against some unexpected weight. It must be the sand, deposited above us: whole landscapes could change overnight after such storms, becoming unrecognizable. It was possible we would not be able to escape the Otherworld here. I looked at the lamp flame. It was diminishing. Khety joined me under the door; we both heaved our shoulders into place and pushed hard. The thing moved perhaps a cubit, then a torrent of cold sand poured in. We spluttered and coughed as the door slammed back down. We pushed again, grunting and groaning like

311

performing strong men, and the trap door creaked over our heads and gave way, bit by bit, as more sand poured over our heads.

Strong light blinded us. We had emerged onto the desert plain to the east of the central city, next to an altar. Luckily, no-one was near. I shaded my eyes. I looked back at the city and could see how the storm, vanished now as if it had never been, had blown off roofs and piled up slopes of debris against the walls of the main buildings. The real devastation would be in the streets, and I could imagine the chaos there. And here was its magus, Akhenaten, squinting and shuffling from foot to foot in the wilderness, his great dream, it seemed, blown away.

We could not remain standing here in the heat and light. We needed sanctuary, water, food and a plan. The city lay one way, but it promised great danger. All the opposition would be hurrying to take advantage of the disaster of the storm, with its implicit judgement of the god, the catastrophic failure of the Festival, and the blow to Akhenaten's prestige and power. I remembered the look of intent upon Horemheb's face. I could imagine he would be capitalizing on the situation immediately. The desert lay the other way, and it offered nothing but bad spirits and death. Our only choice was to seek refuge in one of the tombs in the cliffs, preferably one closer to the river, and then use the river as a means of escape. But to where? I stopped the thought. There was no time for such considerations at the moment. They could come later.

'The tomb artisans might keep basic supplies of water and food,' I said. 'We could rest, at least.'

Nefertiti nodded.

We began walking towards the northern cliffs taking as distant a route as possible from the limits of the city. Khety, Senet and I each carried one of the younger girls on our shoulders, while the older daughters walked. Nefertiti sang to them like a mother now, but their father continued to shuffle and mumble to himself behind us. Meretaten walked sulkily at his side. Such was the royal family on the evening of this strange day.

By the time we reached the tombs, the sun was once again descending over the far western cliffs. Our lengthening shadows trudged and stumbled beside us. The girls were desperate with thirst; they had all fallen silent, and the younger ones had nodded off to sleep. We stood at the base of the ramps of sand that led up to the tomb entrances, which were set perhaps fifty cubits up in the rock faces of the cliffs, some with their columns and doorways almost completed, others no more than low wooden gates guarding the laborious work in progress. Khety and I slipped the sleeping girls off our shoulders and quickly and silently ran up the ramp to check whether they were truly deserted. We moved from chamber to chamber, but there was no-one there. Just piles of tools and, luckily, pots of relatively fresh water.

'Pick a tomb,' I said to the Queen.

She did not smile, just pointed to one furthest to the west. Its entrance was knee-high with sand and grit. We stepped down into this little interior desert, under the as yet uninscribed lintel, and entered a grand, square chamber, perhaps twenty cubits high. So this was how the rich spent their wealth. It was very large and beautifully proportioned; cut from the rock, it must have required the labour of many skilled artisans over several years. The ceiling was supported by a forest of powerful columns, all white except where their middle sections bore painted carvings. The walls were painted with unfinished scenes and dominating every wall were carved images of the royal family worshipping the Aten, and of the family in turn being worshipped by two kneeling figures, a man and a woman.

I looked closely at the face of the rich man whose eternal resting place this would be. It was very familiar. And then I suddenly understood whose tomb we were hiding inside – Ay's. I looked at Nefertiti. Her face was turned away from the walls, towards the last of the golden evening light entering directly through the main door. She had chosen this place. She had wanted to come here.

41

The last of the light faded to black. The Queen sat outside watching, her arms around her dozing girls, her gold costume dulled and streaked with dust and sand. Senet sat near, frozen despite the heat of the evening. Meretaten was awake, sitting a little apart, staring not at the sunset but at the ground. Her mother glanced across at her, but seemed to decide to leave her alone for now. Akhenaten remained in the tomb chamber, huddled on a pallet in a dark corner.

Khety and I found lamps, and a small supply of twisted wicks.

'They add salt to the oil,' he said, whispering for no reason. Perhaps because we were in the presence of Akhenaten; perhaps because we did not want to hear our own voices in the dead acoustic of the chamber.

'Why's that?'

'To stop the wick smoking and spoiling the ceiling work. Look.'

He stepped up a ladder that was leaning against an uncarved column and revealed, in the light of his lamp, a great patterned pathway of gold stars – the celestial kingdom of the goddess Nut – against the serene indigo of the night. He looked for a moment like a dusty young god among his constellations, swinging a sun gently in his hand, his face touched with a smile of wonder at all he had made. I saw that Akhenaten, too, had turned and was staring up at the old vision of creation on the ceiling.

After a moment of silence, I said to Khety, 'Come down now.'

The glow descended to our mortal level and Khety became himself again.

'We've only got enough wicks to last a few hours,' I said. 'There's water and some bread, but I can't find anything else.'

Khety inclined his head towards Akhenaten's dark figure, which had turned again from the light to face the dark wall. 'What are we going to do about . . . ?'

I shrugged. I had no idea. It was too big a problem for me to solve.

'Bring me some water,' called Akhenaten from the shadows.

I took him a cup, and had to help him to sit up to drink from it, like an invalid. Something had snapped inside him. He was light and frail. He drank with little tentative sips.

'We must return to the city immediately,' he said suddenly, as if the thought had just occurred to him. His eyes, in the dark, looked haunted, as if he already knew this would not be possible, and that this knowledge of his powerlessness made it more urgent still. He struggled up, propping himself on his beautiful ceremonial staff. 'I insist we return *immediately*.'

Suddenly Nefertiti was beside him, talking quietly, persuading him to lie back down, making him comfortable. I moved away. There was something both intimate and dreadful about the way she calmed him, and the look of something like loathing hovered faintly in his eyes.

The girls were all lying on pallets now. Meretaten was staring at the scene of her mother and father carved on the wall beside her. She had a strange look on her face. 'That's me,' she said, pointing at the largest of the smaller figures gathered at the feet of the King and his Queen in the Window of Appearances to receive the blessing of the Ankh of Life. Then she looked across at the very different scene of her mother trying to calm and restrain her father. Suddenly she looked older and wiser, as if she understood too much too soon of the casual, lazy brutality of this battered world. I hoped my girls would never look like that.

'We're not going home, are we?' she said quietly.

'I don't know.'

'Yes you do. Everything's going to change now.' She spoke with all the fierce candour of an angry child. Then she turned haughtily away from me.

She is right, I thought as I looked at her, a child with the weight of the world upon her hunched shoulders.

I stood up. In the light of the lamps placed around the chamber the scene looked like a picture from a story. But this was no picture-book story. Where could we really go from here? The best we could do was try to hold out. But I no longer rated our chances. I went outside to try to think, and to keep watch. Khety was perched in a dark niche of the cliff, on guard. Nefertiti joined me, and we looked down over the plain spreading west and south to the city. In the clear night air we could see hundreds of tiny night-lights – sentries and soldiers congregating at the roadblocks. We also saw chains of lights approaching, gathering and spilling around them, heading for the passes out of the city's territory and into the surrounding desert.

'I don't know whether it would be better to move on from here by night or by day,' I said.

She did not reply. Had she heard me? I glanced at her. Silence extended like a great distance between us, although we were no more than a few cubits apart. I looked up at the great imperishable stars.

Then she spoke:

'The land is in darkness as if in death.
They sleep in their chambers, heads covered.
One eye cannot see the other.
Were they robbed of all their earthly goods

– even those that lie beneath their heads –
They could not awake.
All the serpents bite.'

'Thank you,' I said. 'That's very encouraging.'

She smiled and looked away.

'Which poem is that?'

'It is the Poem of the Aten,' she replied. 'It is written on the walls of the chamber. Did you not notice it?'

How could she think about poems now?

'It sounds like a warning,' I said.

'It is a wise one.'

We looked up at the stars again.

'Do you think perhaps there are many other worlds besides ours under the sky?' she asked suddenly.

'I can imagine a few better ones, especially tonight,' I said.

'I imagine one where the Red Land is turned into a great garden. The trees are golden, and there are many rivers, and beautiful cities built on hills.'

'You always see heavens. I see the opposite.'

'Why?'

'Perhaps because I live in a land where malignity rules, where fear and shame dwell. I see botched and corrupted lives, failed hopes, broken dreams, murders and mutilations. Injustices committed with authority. I see people with no souls doing the worst possible things to people with no power. For what? For nothing more than riches and power. There is no honour and no dignity in such things. But we're a rich, big, strong, tough, proud land now, so it doesn't matter at all.'

I looked away to the southern horizon, surprised by the ardour of my reply.

'I had a dream before I came here,' I continued. I realized I suddenly needed to tell her about it.

'You are quite a dreamer for such a sceptical man,' she said softly.

'I was in a cold place. Everything was white. There were dark strange woods. The trees looked black, as if they had burned. Everything was very still. I was lost. I was looking for someone. Then something impossibly light began to fall from a white sky. Snow. That's all I remember, but the desolation has stayed with me. Like a loss that can't ever be put right.'

She nodded, understanding. 'I have heard of snow.'

'I heard a story about a man who carried a box of it back to the King as a treasure. When it was opened, the snow had vanished.'

She looked interested in this. 'If I were given such a box I would not open it.'

'Surely you'd want to know what was inside?'

'You should never open a box of dreams.'

I thought about this for a moment. 'But then you never know if the box is empty or full.'

'No,' she said. 'You never know. But it is still your choice.'

Eventually my thoughts came back to the present.

'We could get to the river and find a boat,' I suggested.

She shook her head. 'And then go where? We must return to the city. All the night creatures are collaborating on their plots and betrayals. I imagine the serpents are sharpening their teeth and filling their mouths with poison. The world makes its claim upon us, and we must not say no.'

She was right, of course. More than anything else, the storm had damaged the family's prestige and opened it up to attack. If they were going to survive they needed to show themselves and reassert their authority. But at what risk?

'But let me ask you this: how are you going to do that? They'll say the storm was a divine judgement against you both.'

She laughed. 'The one thing you never think of is the thing that brings all the great dreams, plans and visions crashing down on your head.'

Her eyes glittered with something other than curiosity and amusement. Everything she had done seemed, now, to have been futile. Everything she had achieved had been destroyed by the storm, as if it had been clearing the playing board, making many new and unforeseen developments possible.

'Perhaps you could commission a poet to rewrite the story of today to make the storm seem like part of your grand plan after all. The Poem of the Triumph over the Storm. The Queen returns in glory from the Otherworld, the god of chaos tries to vanquish her, but all his might could not blow down the city of the Aten, nor frighten its Queen.'

'I'm frightened now.'

She looked at me for a moment. I wanted more than anything to hold her as she sat with her arms wrapped tight around her legs, trying to keep warm – or trying to stop herself shaking. My heart was suddenly inappropriately tripping and fluttering like a schoolboy's. She was so close. I could sense the warmth of her skin across the cool night air; I could see the potency of her eyes in the dark. She was distant and sad. I reached out and gently let my hand touch hers. I feared the mountains would rumble and the stars fall from the sky. But none of that happened. She did not move. I believe, now, her breath stilled for a moment. We sat like that for a long moment. Then, with something I hope was reluctance, she slipped her hand out from under mine.

It was then that I heard a very faint trickle of grit and tiny stones nearby on the slope below us. It could have been a desert rabbit, but it was not. I looked up to see Khety gesturing at something. I stood up slowly and backed towards the tomb entrance, trying to make no sound, trying to shield the Queen from whatever was coming up out of the darkness. Another faint trickle, then a clearly audible step being taken closer up the slope, a foot seeking purchase. But the stranger remained in the realm of the shadows. At least we had now reached the entrance to the chamber, which offered us some temporary sanctuary; we lacked the means, other than our daggers, to defend ourselves. I pushed the Queen back into the shadows of the chamber and waited.

A shadow rose up from the slope. It was somewhat out of breath. I recognized immediately the outline of the bulky, powerful body, the brutal shape of the head. I recognized too the dark panting bulk that followed him, faithful and dumb.

'This is a strange place to spend the night.' Mahu's voice was tense. He was trying to disguise his breathlessness.

'We were just looking at the stars,' I replied.

'You could use their help. Where are they? Are they safe?'

'Why are you asking me?'

Then Nefertiti slipped past me, holding a lamp. Mahu looked relieved, and immediately got down uncomfortably on his knees, like a monster before a child.

'I offer prayers of thanks to the Aten for the safe return of the Queen,' he said.

'Give me your report.'

'May I also report to our Lord?'

'He is resting.'

Mahu looked unhappy 'But—'

'He is well,' she insisted.

There was steeliness in her conduct. Mahu was caught out. There was a moment of silent tension between them during which she yielded nothing; and then he nodded. But he had not yet given in.

'That man must leave. I will take charge now.' He pointed at me, his eyes full of loathing. The encounter with Ay still smarted. Good.

'Why? He has protected and saved me, he has brought the royal family to sanctuary, he has performed well. What have you accomplished? What have you to say to us that he should not hear?'

It was hard not to smile. I did not try too hard.

Mahu's head moved about nervously on his bulky shoulders. He was like a baboon trapped in a cage, seeking an escape. He was still dangerous to me. He would savage me in a moment. But Nefertiti remained implacable and absolute.

'Speak,' she commanded.

'The city is in chaos,' he said. 'The Great River is jammed with traffic. All who can are leaving. The tent accommodations were blown away. Scaffolding has collapsed, killing citizens and blocking ways.

Many food stores have been ruined by the sand. Wells that were uncovered have been spoiled. The supply of sweet water is unreliable. There have been many deaths in the panic.' He hesitated. The harder part of the report was obviously yet to come.

'And what else?'

'There is disorder.'

'Meaning?'

'Authority has collapsed. My troops are few, and unable to control the situation. The temple stores have been ransacked, all the supplies of grain, wine, fruit – all dispersed among the mob. They have even butchered sacrificial animals in the temple precincts for food. The people have become barbarians overnight. There has been fighting on the streets between different nationalities for possession of food and shelter. The ambassador of Mittani and his family and followers were assassinated in the confusion. We suspect Hittite forces. We could not protect them. We accommodated as many of the important families and leaders as we could within the Great Palace, and we have set up temporary shelters in the Small Aten Temple.'

'Why have you failed to maintain control over the city in our name?'

His face darkened. 'Horemheb elected to take command, over my own authority and that of the Medjay. He has deployed his soldiers around the city and commanded the support of reserves. They arrive in the next day or two. He has won military control of the area, until such time as . . .' He paused again, having reached the moment of the unspeakable.

'Speak.'

'Until you return to meet with him.'

Her face remained impassive, but this was bad news.

'Has he sent you here? As his errand boy?'

Mahu glared at her, pride triumphing over respect. 'I am not now, nor have I ever been, other than a loyal servant. I am no errand boy. I came to warn you of his intention.'

She allowed a slight relaxation of her features. 'Your loyalty is greater than gold to us.'

It was strange to see the power of a few words of praise upon such a man. Mahu's fierceness melted away.

She spoke quickly now, alive to the imperatives of the new situation. 'I shall return. But to command, not to negotiate with Horemheb's army.'

This statement did not quite have the expected or desired effect on Mahu. There was something he was not revealing. An argument? Bad news? An assassin's knife, even? The Queen glanced quickly at me, having observed this too. I decided to move closer.

Mahu growled at me. 'Stay away from me.'

Nefertiti nodded imperceptibly, and I stepped back again.

'You must speak truthfully,' she said. 'Hide nothing. Otherwise I return to the city flawed in my knowledge and understanding.'

I glanced up to where I'd last seen Khety, but I could not spot him up there in the darkness. Surely he was listening though.

Mahu made up his mind and spoke with a hesitation I had not thought he was capable of. 'There is . . . another thing.' He paused, dramatically.

'Do not expect me to interpret silence. Speak.'

Then out of the silence and the darkness came a hissing sound, and a dull thud. Nefertiti and I stared out into the unknown. Mahu made no move. His expression changed to puzzlement, as if he could not quite remember the beginning of his thought. Then a dribble of blood appeared at the side of his mouth. He reached up and touched it slowly, surprised at the redness on his fingertip. Then he shook his head, and slowly fell forward like a beast with too great a burden, onto his face.

We crouched down and ran over to his body. An arrow had split his spine. It was lodged deep between his shoulder blades. I looked at it carefully; it bore a familiar hieroglyph: the cobra. My mind raced back to the memory of the charred arrow on the burning boat. The warning sign sent to me before I'd even arrived. And here it was again. Identical.

I turned him on his side as carefully as possible. He was still breathing, in shallow gasps, as if he were now in the wrong element, as if air were water. Some recognition of the irony that mine should be the last face he would look upon in this life dawned on him.

'Damn you.' He forced out each word through his bloody teeth from a gurgling throat. 'You were right.'

The Queen looked at me. I shook my head. Mahu coughed and spat, and a sudden shower of red drops speckled my clothes. This made him laugh, and more blood welled out of him, thicker, darker now. He noticed.

'Dying,' he said, almost with a shrug, as if mortality were nothing. The dog licked his face. I pushed it away.

'Right about what?' I said.

I sensed someone standing above us. It was Akhenaten, looking like an old man awakened from a deep sleep. He was holding a lamp, and in his white robes he stood out like an easy target for another arrow. I dragged him down out of the range of danger. He shouted with outrage. I held my hand over his mouth. The three of us huddled together around Mahu, whose eyes took in the sorry sight of his puzzled and shambolic Lord. Did I see disappointment pass across his eyes before death's hands slowed then stilled them and turned their topaz glitter to something more like misted bronze?

I grabbed Akhenaten by the arm and we all scurried, crouching like dogs, back to the mouth of the tomb chamber. He stumbled, trying to look back at Mahu's corpse, the dog sitting faithful and confused by its side, and I had to drag the King of the Two Lands behind me in the dust. Khety appeared as if from nowhere to help me.

We hid inside the chamber, our breath making brief clouds in the now chilly desert air. The lamps had burned down low, lending a flickering, feeble light to the painted figures and the forest of white columns. The girls had woken up and were huddling around their mother, who warned them in a whisper that they must be completely silent. We waited, listening intently. I knew these might be the last moments of our lives. We had trapped ourselves; there was no way out. Anyone could enter the chamber and slaughter us all like beasts in this dying light. As if to presage this, I heard Mahu's dog whine sharply, then fall silent.

'Please do not hide on my account.'

The words, spoken very quietly, seemed to come from nowhere. Then a long shadow slanted across the moon-silvered stones of the entrance, and moved along the wall into the chamber. The shadow was followed by a man's figure, slim and elegant. He had with him a lamp, which illuminated a bony face made gaunter by the flickering shadows.

Ay was accompanied by guards who stood back at the entrance. Their bows glinted in the moonlight. I noticed that their arrows were tipped with what looked like silver. I looked across at Nefertiti. She looked as if she had finally come face to face with her worst fear.

Ay nodded to the bowmen, who checked us for weapons, taking my dagger. I knew two of them. One had been on the hunting party; the other was the young architect from the boat, the one who was designing the temple latrines. So I had been watched from the start. He looked me in the eye, as if to say: we meet again. Then Ay ordered them to go outside, and he slowly approached us. The Queen and I split up, moving in different directions among the forest of white columns.

'How strange and yet how right that you came to my own tomb for sanctuary,' Ay said. 'I'm sorry to see you all accommodated in such inadequate surroundings. But perhaps there is a sense in which this incongruous setting amuses you, and so compensates for the discomfort.' He was toying with us. He smiled like a necropolis cat. 'We are all mortals. Except for those of us who have become gods. In their own opinions, at least. See, here it is, written in stone.' He read off a column of hieroglyphs: '"An adoration of the Aten who lives for ever and ever, the Living and the Great Aten, Lord of all that Aten encircles, Lord of Heaven, Lord of Earth. Lord of the House of the Aten in Akhetaten, of the King of the South and the North, living on Truth, Lord of the Two Lands, the Son of the Sun, Lord of Diadems, Akhenaten, great in his duration, and of the Great Wife

Nefer-Neferuaten-Nefertiti, who has life, health and youth for ever and ever." And so on and so on. Oh, here's my part: "the Bearer of the Fan on the Right Hand of the King, Overseer of all the Horses of his Majesty, he who gives satisfaction in the whole land, the favourite of the good god, God's Father, Doer of Right, Ay who says: 'Your rising is beautiful on the horizon of heaven, O living Aten, who gives life; when you rise on the eastern horizon you fill every land with beauty.'"' He paused for a moment, relishing the irony of it all. 'Well, hardly, as it turns out . . .'

Then another voice spoke out from the shadows, shaky and strange: ' "For you are splendid, great, radiant, uplifted above every land . . . You are the Sun, distant but on the Earth, and when you set on the western horizon the Earth is in darkness, and in the likeness of Death . . ." ' Akhenaten's voice grew in strength as he declaimed the lines, his thin arms raised up, mirroring his own carved image on the stone wall beside him, towards a sun that was not there. But then he stopped suddenly, as if he no longer wished to say the words that followed.

Ay looked at this spectre of failed power without expression. 'Yes, the likeness of Death,' he said. 'I commissioned this tomb at some considerable expense, but I have never had the time to visit it and inspect the progress of the work. They are quite expensive now, these Houses of Death, yet there is no time while we are alive to attend to the things that matter. We rush, we make mistakes, we hurry to correct them, we do not think enough about the past and the future.'

He paused. I had no idea where he was going with this. Nefertiti remained oddly silent.

'Would you like to hear a story about the past or the future?'

'Let us consider the future.' Nefertiti spoke at last from the darkness at the far end of the chamber.

Ay moved towards her, but she moved away again. I could not tell shadow from substance.

'Certainly,' he said. 'I will tell you what I see. I see a time of calamity. I see this world crumbling, collapsing. I see Priests attacking the Aten temples, I see the Treasury empty, I see hatred in the eyes of the people, I see our enemies conquering our great cities and destroying our gods. I see our great green and gold world drying up, the Great River denying its bounty, the land parched and the crops wilted, and the locusts consuming all in their path. I see our granaries full of dust. I see the wind of time sweeping in from the Red Land, bringing fire and destruction, razing our cities, turning all that we have made to ash. I see children instructing their parents in acts of barbarity and horror, and I see barbarians celebrating in our temples. I see the statues of the gods replaced by chattering monkeys. I see the river flowing backwards and Ra turning cold. I see dead children in unnamed graves.'

'You should not eat dinner so late,' Nefertiti responded, carefully. 'It disturbs the imagination.'

He fastidiously ignored her. 'I see things as they are, and as they will be. Unless we act decisively now. We must return to things as they were. We must return to the ways of the traditions. We must fold up this city and lock its god, this Aten, in a box, and bury it deep in the desert as if it had never been. Then we must be practical. We need troops and grain. We must negotiate agreements and compensations with the new army, and with the Amun Priesthood. We must restore to the Theban Priesthood some portion of control over their wealth and resources, and allow them back into their temples. At the same time we must show the world we, as a family and a country, are stronger than ever, and that the gods support us. And to do this we must have a figure of power who can say to the people and the gods: "I am yesterday and tomorrow; I see all time; my name is one who passes on the paths of the gods. I am Lord of Eternity."'

'There is no such person.'

'I think there is,' he said, quickly. 'I think it is time to reveal her.'

He let that hang in the air. An offer. A possibility. But who was Ay, for all his authority, to make such a proposal? Was he a king-maker, a god-creator, a director of what shall and shall not be?

Then Akhenaten spoke with a madman's futile conviction. 'This is treason, and I will have you arrested and executed like a common thief.'

Ay laughed in his face – the first time I had heard him make such a human sound. 'And who will hear this command, and who will obey it? No-one. You are a bankrupt, broken man. Failure and dissolution hang over you. Your power is departed. You will be lucky to be allowed to continue to live.' His voice was calm and ruthlessly severe.

Akhenaten moved quickly to the entrance, but was barred by two guards. 'Let me pass!' he ordered. 'I am Akhenaten!' They remained still and silent. His powerlessness was terrible to behold. He beat his fists against them like a child in a tantrum. His blows were light and they simply ignored him.

He turned to Ay, incandescent with rage now. 'The King will not be denied! You have stolen my kingdom. You have betrayed my trust. I curse you, and I and the god will be revenged upon you.'

'No. *You* have betrayed the trust of the Two Lands. *You* have betrayed me. *You* have mocked and destroyed the great inheritance of this world. Your curses have no power. How can you feed the people? You cannot. How can you restore *maat*? You cannot. How can you show yourself again under the sign of the Aten? You cannot. The people hate you, the army despises you, and the Priests are plotting your assassination. I gave you this world and all its riches and power, and what did you do with it? You made this fool's plaything of mud and straw. Can greatness be conjured from such materials? No. It crumbles, it decays, it falls apart. Soon there will be nothing left of this city and its mad King but shadows, bones and dust. Your father's spirit dies a second death of shame. You will give up the crowns. Fall to your knees.'

Akhenaten stared at Ay. 'To you? Never.' He had lost, but he remained defiant.

Nefertiti emerged from the shadows. My heart twisted inside me when I saw her face.

'You are God's Father, but you cannot be the King,' she said.

Something changed in Ay's expression. I had seen it before, on the face of a committed gambler about to double the stakes.

'You do not know who I am,' he said.

His words changed the currents running in the dark air. Nefertiti stood still, caught out.

'You are Ay, are you not?'

He moved among the columns, appearing and disappearing in the light and shadows, the conjuror of himself.

'You cannot remember?'

She said nothing, waiting.

'Memory is such a strange thing. Who are we without it? No-one.'

Still she waited.

He smiled. 'I am glad you do not remember. I intended it to be so. I wanted you to be pure of all associations of the heart.'

'That cannot be. The heart is everything.'

He shook his head gravely. 'No, it is not. I hoped that you would have learned the greatest truth. There is only power. Not love, not care. Only power. And I gave it to you.'

'You gave me nothing.' At last she sounded angry.

He smiled again, as if this were another little triumph, and then dealt his blow softly and quietly: 'I gave you life.'

He watched her face as she struggled to accommodate the implications of these few words. He was a murderer, his knife twisting expertly in the heart, observing the suffering of his victim. Then she spoke, her voice oddly calm, as if the worst had happened and nothing more could hurt her.

'You are my father?'

'Yes. Do you know me now?'

'I see what you are. I see you have a desert where your heart should be. What happened to your heart? What happened to your love?'

'These are soft words, daughter. Love, mercy, compassion. Strike them from your heart. Action is everything.'

She came closer to him, curious despite her obvious pain. 'If you are my father, who is my mother?'

He dismissed her with a wave.

'Do not turn away from me. Tell me who my mother is.'

'She was no-one. She is nameless. She died giving birth to you.'

This new fact did its quiet and terrible damage. She buckled under the pain of the loss, the loss of something she had never had except in dreams, her hands against her breast as if holding the broken pieces of her heart in her tight fists.

'How could you do this to me?'

'Do not try me with feeble words and arguments of care. You are not a child, to speak of childish things.'

'I was never a child. You took that from me too.'

She turned into the shadows and disappeared. Ay strolled casually among the pillars, waiting calmly for her to return. As he passed close to me I swiftly drew the knife from his belt and held it at his throat, touching the soft, chilly skin, almost cutting it open, my arm pinning his arms behind his back. It was like holding almost nothing, he was so still. The guards came running in, but I said quietly, 'Stay back, or I will cut his head off.' Khety disarmed them efficiently.

Nefertiti returned to the lit part of the chamber. I pressed the knife blade harder against the gently pulsing vein in Ay's neck and was glad to feel, at last, a tremor of uncertainty. 'I can kill him now, or we can hold him and return to the city. Arrest him; put him on trial for treason and murder.'

She looked at me sorrowfully, then shook her head. 'Let him go.'

I could not believe she meant these words. 'Who do you think had Tjenry tortured, mutilated and killed? Who do you think had Meryra burning in agony? He may not have committed the acts, he had his Chief of Physicians to do that; but he planned and incited them. And after everything he has done to you? This man has brought nothing but suffering and destruction, and you wish me to let him go? Why?'

'Because we must.'

I threw the knife away in disgust. Ay slipped free of my grasp, and with his red leather glove slapped me hard across the face. 'That is for having the temerity to touch me.' Then he slapped me again. 'And that is for having the temerity to make baseless and unprovable accusations.'

I stared at him, unmoved.

329

'My daughter is an intelligent woman,' he continued. 'She understands.'

And then he smiled. I loathed that smile.

'You have everything in the world,' I said. 'Yet some fury is raging inside you, eating away until you are a hollow man. Whatever it is, it will never be satisfied.'

Ay ignored my contempt. He bent down and scooped up a handful of dust, which he studied casually. 'I never liked this place, and I doubt now I shall be buried here. Why do we need all those pretty pictures of the good afterlife? See how we depict our desperate hope for more life; rich fields and many servants to work them; great honour and position; the acquisition of wealth and property – the best the world can give, or that we can take. Yet it is all nothing but paint. We both know what happens when we die. Nothing. We are bones and dust. There is no eternal life, no Otherworld, no Field of Reeds. The sweet birds of eternity sing only in our heads. They are all stories we tell to protect ourselves from the truth. Now, *if* I had everything I would be able to change this dust back into life. I would buy more days and years as if they were grain, and I would live for ever. But it cannot be done. We cannot survive time. Only the gods are immortal. And they do not exist.'

He let the desert grit fall from his open hand onto the floor and turned again to Nefertiti. 'There are more practical matters requiring our immediate attention. I offer you this: return to Thebes and I will negotiate a new agreement with the different parties. You will agree to return to the old ways. You will make a public worship of Amun in the Karnak Temples before a gathering of the Priests. This will be an absolute necessity. In return, your daughters will be allowed to live. Your husband will be allowed his life, and his crown, but he will have no authority. He may remain in this ridiculous city for all I care, worshipping the noon sun and the dust like the lunatic he has become. No-one will know. He will be granted sufficient attendants to care for him.'

'And you?'

'I am God's Father. Doer of Right. I will remain.'

'You are the society,' I said. 'The Society of Ashes. What an appropriate name. The men of ash.'

He smiled that calculating smile. 'It is another show. A ceremony, if you like. But it works well. Men love the power of secrets. It is interesting what they will do, and give, to know the great secret of power. Seven gold feathers from the bird of rebirth. I believe you still have one in your possession. Please pass it to its rightful owner now.'

'You left it there for me to find.'

He nodded, as if politely accepting a compliment.

I reached into my case, found the feather, and gave it to Nefertiti. She looked at it as if now she could see the future. As if now she knew the end of the story. And it was not what she desired.

'Good,' said Ay. 'I will prepare for tomorrow. The people love you, daughter. Your strategy in outwitting your enemies was admirable. You have returned from the Otherworld. We will of course make use of this. You must become co-regent. You are a star among us lesser mortals.'

'And if I refuse this proposal?'

He laughed quietly. 'You are my child. I know you too well. Let us not waste time. I will make the necessary preparations, and await you at the palace for a public ceremony of return tomorrow. The guards will remain here to escort you back, when you come to the right decision. If you do not, they will follow my other orders. You may well guess what they are. Tomorrow is another day.'

'You would kill your own grandchildren?'

'Remember: there is no love, only power. As your maid knows. Don't you, Senet? You should ask her about it. And about scarabs. I like to leave my mark, you know.'

He turned and left. No-one dared to speak. Senet shivered.

'He has such power,' she whispered, with loathing and misery.

'Let me tell your story,' I said, as gently as possible.

She nodded.

'You killed Seshat.'

She looked up, but did not contradict me.

'You brought her to her death. You brought down the blows upon her face. You left the scarab hidden on her body.'

She continued to stare at me.

'You wore gloves to hide the damage to your hands. You let me think something was missing from the Queen's jewellery. You let me believe the scarab belonged to the Queen. But the scarab was given to you by Ay. He told you to place it on the body. He said it was his mark, his sign. He was right. He is from the dung of the earth. The lowest of the low. Yet he pushes kings and queens like suns into the light of the new day.'

Senet glanced at the Queen, who gazed at her almost compassionately.

'You fulfilled his instructions. You ferried the disguised girl up the river and then, in the dark, when she was not expecting it, you hit her. She would have been badly wounded by the first blow, but it must have taken much more strength of mind, as well as body, to beat her face off.'

She looked directly at me now. 'It takes a long time to kill some-one,' she said. 'The first blow was simple. But she would not die. She kept making noises, even though she had no mouth left. I beat her until she was finally silent. It took a long time.'

The chamber was silent. I continued with the story.

'She dressed in the clothes you brought from the Queen's wardrobe. She was wearing a headscarf, as required by the instructions. But you did not know, until I told you, who you had killed. You only knew it was a woman. As far as Ay was concerned it did not matter who died and who lived. But it mattered to you. You murdered and mutilated an innocent woman. Her family loved her dearly.'

'So did I,' she said, proudly. 'I loved her with all my heart.'

They had been lovers. The simple words of truth.

'Please show me your hair,' I asked.

She nodded, slowly revealing a cropped head of auburn hair. Khety looked at me, understanding now.

Senet spoke again, this time to the Queen. 'He knew everything.

He could read my thoughts and dreams. He told me he would expose us, Seshat and me, not only to you, my Lady, but to the world. I could bear this. But then he told me he would have her killed if I did not do as he commanded. If I did not tell him everything. He told me what I had to do. He told me to take the sealed instructions and the clothes to the Harem as if they were from the Queen. A woman would be brought. And he told me what I must do. He told me we must not speak. He told me where to take her, and how to do what I was to do. What choice did I have? What would you have done?'

These last questions were directed at me, but all I could offer her was a look of understanding. She suddenly howled with grief, clutching and beating at her own head. 'Hathor, Lady of the Sky, Lady of Destiny, she who is powerful, forgive me. I have killed the woman I loved! I acted out of love and fear. Now there is nothing but death.'

Nefertiti touched her on the shoulder, gently. 'If you had come to me with the truth I could have protected you.'

The maid looked up at her slowly. 'He is greater than all of us. He is Death. Do you know he kissed me? On the lips. From that moment I was doomed.' She picked up the dagger I had thrown away, walked out of the tomb chamber and disappeared into the darkness. I knew no-one could save her, and I knew we would never find her. I hoped the goddess Nut would spread herself over the girl and find some place for her among the imperishable stars.

Khety and I walked outside for some fresher air. It was the darkest part of the night, and the moon had sailed low and deep on the horizon. We sat down like two glum monuments.

'I thought I knew Senet well,' he said. 'When did you work it out?'

'I knew there were strange and missing elements to her story. But her grief betrayed her.'

He nodded. 'That man is a monster.'

'I don't believe in monsters, Khety. That makes it too easy for the rest of us. Ay is one of us, in the end.'

'That makes it worse,' he said.

I had to agree.

Nefertiti came out from the chamber. Khety moved away respectfully, leaving us alone. I had things to say now.

'That was quite a story you told me, when we first met, about your father and your family. You fooled me well.'

She looked at me calmly. 'When you are born without parents, you spend all your time imagining them. You imagine them as perfect people. To make up for all the things that didn't happen you dream up all the stories, and the stories seem real. Until one day . . .'

'The truth.'

'Yes. I imagined my father as a good man, a wonderful, kind man. One day I believed he would come to rescue me. I believed he would take me up on his white horse and we'd ride away together, for ever. Safe.'

'I could have destroyed him for you.'

She paused, thinking. 'No. You could have killed him, but then he would still be inside me, inside my head, for ever. That is worse, perhaps. Perhaps all I can do is forgive him. For what he has done to me. For what he has done to others. If I can do that, then he has no power over me any more.'

I was again amazed and appalled. 'Forgive him? He's used your life, his own child's, as a means to an end, as a way to power, and he's threatened to kill you and your children. There is no love in him.'

'That does not mean I should not forgive him. Love begets love. Hate begets hate. Revenge begets revenge. The choice is mine.'

'So you will accept his demands? Will you keep the feather?'

'I must. There is no choice. This is the destruction of all we have worked for; it is the end of the dream of a better way. But I warned you: the world makes its demands upon us, upon me, and I cannot say no. I have enough power to save those I love, and to influence the course of the future. I have a responsibility to the future.'

Then a thought came to me very clearly. 'I will not see you again.'

She took my hand in hers. 'I will not forget you.'

We sat there for a long time, together.

42

Well before dawn, in order to return without being seen, we descended from the tomb chamber and began to walk across the chilly dark plain towards the city and an unknowable future. I glanced across at Nefertiti, the Perfect One, who walked beside me now. She looked calmer, resolute; her eyes were raised, looking ahead steadily. Perhaps knowing the truth was easier, for all its horror, than living with uncertainty. The older girls stumbled beside us, still half asleep, and Khety and I carried the younger ones on our shoulders, lolling in and out of their sweet, strange dreams. Akhenaten shuffled along looking down at the dark, arid ground. Ay's guardsmen followed behind us at a little distance.

Nefertiti chose to return to the North Palace, the family's countryside retreat set apart from the rest of the city and its suburbs. It was not well fortified, and it lacked a resident barracks, so the security would be weak. But she said she had her reasons, and besides, its isolation was an advantage. Then Meretaten and Meketaten chimed in, suddenly awake, insisting also on the North Palace so that they could visit their pet gazelles.

From a distance, all that could be seen of the palace was an endless high mud-brick wall which seemed to enclose a vast area of land running down to the bank of the Great River. There were no windows in the walls, and when we arrived we found the solid timber gates shut tight. I knocked as loudly as I dared. The sound seemed to travel far and unnaturally loud in the pre-dawn quiet. Eventually I heard a rattling and a groan, and then the small gate window opened. An old man blinked cautiously, then, recognizing the early callers standing in their dusty royal robes with a start of wonder and awe, began praying loudly. There was more fear than reverence in his eyes. I had no patience for this, and thumped on the heavy doors until he opened them. He prostrated himself and continued praying, so we stepped over him and moved into the palace precinct. He got up and followed us, telling us that the place was empty but being defended, single-handedly and with honour, by him alone. 'I am the only one remaining here, all the others have fled, but I knew, I *knew* you would return, and here I am waiting for you.' He looked like a waiter expecting a tip. Nefertiti thanked him quietly for his loyalty.

Sand had piled up against the walls in the courtyard, and all the internal doors and windows remained shuttered. The Queen walked ahead, opening doors and passing through columned reception halls, deserted and echoing. Khety and I kept ourselves alert, for I could not be certain there were no hostile forces here, perhaps Horemheb's. But we found no trace of anyone.

Ay's guards had stayed at the gates, so Khety and I stood guard in the main courtyard while Nefertiti took the children into their chambers to rest and prepare themselves for the coming day. Akhenaten sullenly followed them. We observed the last stars retiring, and soon dawn's high blue light began to fill the dome of the sky. Slowly the moon sank into the Otherworld. Dogs barked across the landscape, and the ceaseless chatter of the birds in the river-side trees began. Life was reasserting itself.

Then Akhenaten appeared at the door. He looked at his god, the Aten, now a sliver of red, as it appeared just at the rim of the eastern cliffs. But there was no jubilation or celebration in his expression. He raised his arms in silent adoration. It looked futile and mad. We averted our eyes, as respectfully as we could, hoping not to have to emulate him.

'Come, I wish to show you something.'

He turned and shuffled back into the dusty hallway, and I followed, leaving Khety to remain on guard. We walked for some time until eventually we came to a splendidly carved double door. He threw it open, and insisted I enter first. I found myself in a tall, square chamber. It was open to the sky, and had only three walls on which an artist had recreated a vision of the Perfect Life. Kingfishers were depicted in mid-flight, their black and white wings scissoring the still air as they dived in and out of the ringed, lucid water; or alighted, momentarily but for ever, upon the nodding heads of the great papyrus stalks twice as high as a man. And then a strange thing happened: with a brief shrill cry a shape darted, on a flash of brilliant wings, into the chamber and vanished, just as suddenly, into the wall. What had I seen? I could not believe my eyes.

Akhenaten clapped his hands and laughed with childish pleasure at my amazement. 'Nesting boxes, hidden in the walls! You see, even birds can be fooled by the greatest art. They believe they are in a real river!'

He was delighted with this make-believe world, but for me it was proof that his perfect city of paint and mud and light and shadow was just an illusion. I had seen the wrong side of it, I had seen how it worked, and I understood above all that it was built not for beauty or even for power, but for fear.

'This is not all, there is more,' he said, taking me by the arm, his eyes brimming like a lonely old man in an asylum.

The chamber opened on to a secret green world: a park full of fruit trees, plants and water channels. Like the Otherworld, it seemed to have no beginning and no end. In a penned area, young gazelles waited by long, carved feeding troughs. The troughs were empty. No-one was feeding these abandoned animals now. I found a store of grain and quickly filled the troughs, although to what purpose I had no idea. Surely these beasts would not survive for much longer amid this dereliction. I watched Akhenaten stroke the feeding animals with some deep need, talking to them quietly.

We moved deeper into his green world, and with his gold staff he pointed out all the beasts and the birds, reciting their names as if he were their creator. Then, suddenly, he was furious. 'I created this world,' he shouted. 'This city, this garden! And now they will destroy everything!'

I nodded. There was nothing to be said.

The sun was moving into the House of the Day. I bade him farewell. He gripped my arm, stared me in the eye, and said, 'May you breathe the sweet wind of the north and go forth into the sky on the arms of the Living Light, the Aten, your body protected and your heart content, for ever and ever.' It was a blessing from his heart, and I was moved, more than I expected. Then he waved me away and disappeared slowly into his green world. That was the last I ever saw of him.

43

Nefertiti rode ahead in her chariot of gold. The older princesses rode behind her in their own smaller chariots. Their red and gold scarves flared out, fluttering like rare birds in the soft morning breeze. Khety and I followed them, flanked still by Ay's guards and their silver arrows. The day, paradoxically, was exceptionally beautiful, as if the storm had polished the natural world, restoring it to its pristine state. The waters sparkled and the birds sang. The river glittered here and there beyond the trees. But as we moved onwards through the city, the human world looked very different. Fires had destroyed sections of the suburbs, leaving charred ruins. One area of storage buildings was still ablaze. People wandered aimlessly, their faces grey with ash. Dead bodies lay untended in passageways. I saw soldiers throwing corpses on carts, one on top of the other, without care or respect.

A troop of Horemheb's soldiers controlled access to the central city, and had set up barriers across the way. But when they saw the Queen, and Ay's men, they stepped aside, and we passed unchallenged.

Along the Royal Road, small crowds began to accumulate. People stopped what they were doing – sweeping up debris, or tending improvised little fires around which they had gathered against the terror and darkness of the night hours – to stare blankly at the sight of the Queen in her chariot. As she passed, some rose and made profound gestures of respect and worship; others cried out in desperation, their hands clenched in supplication. She acknowledged them.

As we approached the temples of the central city we saw Horemheb's troops in their uniforms standing guard on all corners, while others herded straggling groups of people – the uncertain remains of visiting parties from all over the Empire – from one place to another. Improvised encampments had grown up literally overnight. A well had been cleared, and long lines of people holding jugs and jars waited to receive fresh supplies. Some bread stalls were selling, no doubt at inflated prices, to orderly queues of people. Everywhere, people looked shocked and terrified, unsure about what was happening to their world, amazed and daunted by the swift changes of fortune. They stumbled about, or suddenly stopped walking, as if they had forgotten where they were going, and why.

But when they saw Nefertiti passing on her chariot, everyone's faces lightened, as if here at last was something they could believe in; something they had lost and now found again. She slowed her chariot and acknowledged the cries and calls of support and approval as they grew. The people, forgetting their fear of the soldiers, now pushed and surged to line the sides of the Royal Road. Theirs was not the well-orchestrated and insincere enthusiasm that had greeted Akhenaten in worship; their cheers were cries from the heart. Something in the Queen's spirit rose to meet their call. I too believed, at that moment, that she could, after all, save something from this. My spirits lightened a little. What surely lay ahead suddenly seemed less intractable.

To the overwhelming accompaniment of roars and prayers of support in a chaos of languages, and a fanfare of trumpets from the assembled troops, we turned through the gate and into the vast courtyard of the Great Palace. It had been swept and restored to order.

The great stone statues of Nefertiti and Akhenaten lined the huge open space, which was now packed to the walls with waiting dignitaries, ambassadors and leaders, their scribes and attendants, servants and fan holders and parasol holders, all of whom turned to observe the Queen's arrival. It seemed they had been waiting for some time. Everything suddenly went very quiet. All I could hear was the rustle of several thousand of the finest linens in the world as the gathering rose to its feet, waiting to witness the next move in the game of power. There was no sign of Horemheb or Ay.

Nefertiti came to a halt and, still holding the reins of her team of horses and looking magnificent in the double crown, addressed the people from her gold chariot.

'This night has been long and dark,' she said. 'But now a new sun has risen upon a new day. We are gathered together in witness and in celebration. The shade of our Great Palace offers protection, and comfort, and security, to all of you. We return to it. We invite you to join us.'

She was acknowledging, without saying so explicitly, that the cult of the Aten was finished; that Akhenaten was absent but that she was present and there had been a shift in power. She was the embodiment of this political change. She was the new sun. She was the new day.

There was silence for a long moment. Then, gradually, a slow murmur of approval and appreciation began to spread through the crowd. Men nodded, and turned to each other in agreement. This was what they had wanted and needed to hear. Applause and calls of praise began to ring out, growing from tentative beginnings into a long, loud, strong affirmation. So far so good.

Nefertiti descended from the chariot, gathered the princesses around her, and strode into the main building as if to say: we are a dynasty of strong women; we are in charge. The crowd of men followed her inside. I tried to keep up with her as we all struggled along the palace's overwhelmed corridors. Despite the clamour and activity, the petitions and prayers and calls for her attention, she was still able to make discreet acknowledgements of the respects paid by the waiting scribes, administrators, palace officials and overseers – fathers and sons standing together to witness her return – as she passed down the corridors.

Finally we entered a great hall, near the water's edge. I had never seen a chamber with so many graceful columns, hundreds of them, surmounted by red, blue and white chevrons, holding up a ceiling of heavenly stars. It seemed ironic to me now that the dirty business of power and politics required such beautiful chambers.

The hall was soon overflowing with dignitaries, and there were many more people crowding into the side passages and antechambers. Nefertiti, accompanied by her daughters, entered the Window of Appearances, turned, and looked out over the gathering.

'I am returned,' she said. 'I stand before you now not as a god but as a woman. I am heart, and spirit, and truth. Listen to what I say, and speak of it to your people. I come to restore truth. Let all know this: truth shall prevail. Any man who challenges or dishonours our peace with war or corruption or lies is guilty of a crime against truth and against the Two Lands. This is the Truth of the Gods, the Truth of *maat*, and the Truth of my House.'

The chamber was utterly silent. Everyone was attending to every nuance and each unspoken implication of her words.

'And now we shall reward, in the sight and witness of the whole world, those who we love and who have tendered us their love.'

Through the columns and the crowded heads of the world's men of power, I saw Horemheb approach the Window. He ascended the platform before her, bowed his arrogant head, and received a gold collar, which Nefertiti placed around his neck. He stood back, bowed, kneeled, and stepped down. He did all of this with an exact grace, but it carried with it no sense whatsoever of real commitment. Next came Ramose. He, too, received a collar, but his reaction was one of pride. He looked moved and relieved. Others followed as the herald called out their names, leading figures in the hierarchy whose loyalty she needed to ensure in public before she could move forward to the harder negotiations. She was bringing together the elements that had threatened to tear the land apart, making them acknowledge her authority and obey her rule.

Then I heard my name called. The room went silent. Surely it was a mistake. I heard it again: 'Rahotep, Seeker of Mysteries'. I was startled. My breath suddenly sounded loud in my ears, and my heart raced. As in a dream, I saw a pathway open up for me in the crowd, and I passed through it, past the rows of curious, shadowy faces, towards the Window. I stepped up onto the platform and looked up at her face, framed by the icons of her power. Everything seemed charged with detail: the clear light in her glittering eyes; the colours, red, gold, blue, in the Window; the red ribbons that hung below the frieze of fierce, protecting cobra-heads above us; even the expectant hush in the room.

I knew that I had found her, and I understood that I had lost her. I had always known it would be so. This was the end. Is it foolish to say I felt something like snow falling about me, as if these last moments with her had slowed and changed into the intangible, delicate and fast-disappearing flakes? There was a look of lightness on her face. She possessed her power once more. I felt a sadness welling in my heart. It was not a good sadness, clear as sweet water; it was darker and stranger, like some beautifully bitter, rich, blood-red wine. I thought of her then as that box of snow. My treasure. I would carry her memory with me, and I would never open it.

She reached down to me and placed a gold collar around my neck. I breathed deeply, needing to take in her scent. Already she was becoming distant, drifting away from me. She whispered one word: *goodbye*. Then I stepped away, the unaccustomed weight of gold and honour upon my shoulders – the gift of a better future, the one thing she could give to me. She had rewarded me with gold and with respect. And she had done it in front of the world. And she had spoken to me.

I walked back to my place, and this time I drew interested and sometimes admiring expressions and nods from these powerful men. Things had changed again. Status, that strange and fickle god, had smiled on me. I found myself standing next to Nakht. He gestured to the collar with a kind of 'well done' expression on his face.

343

I looked back to the Window, for Ay had appeared, carrying with him his peculiar cold atmosphere, his uncanny unearthliness. He stepped up onto the platform, the last to be acknowledged. There was utter silence in the room, as if no-one dared even breathe during the encounter of these two great figures. They stared at each other for a moment, then Nefertiti lowered the collar around her father's neck as if it were a chain not a reward. She was trying to yoke him to her intentions. She seemed to have succeeded. He made a light bow of respect, and stepped back. But then he looked up again and, with a faint smile I instantly mistrusted, clapped his hands together.

From a side door emerged a slight, strange figure – the young boy I had seen once before with Akhenaten. He shuffled forward with an exquisite gold staff tucked under his right arm. Its tapping on the floor sounded loud in the hushed room. His face was gaunt and charismatic, his body angled and thin. He looked as if he had been here among mortals before, many times. I shivered involuntarily. I looked at Nefertiti's face. It was shocked, as if a ghost were standing before her.

The boy arrived at the Window, and Ay invited him to come and stand next to him. Nefertiti seemed to have no say in the matter, and she honoured him with a collar as well. The three stood together, the Queen in her Window looking down upon the older man and the young boy. Something as yet unknown was framed here for the future.

'Who is that boy?' I whispered to Nakht.

'His name is Tutenkhaten.'

'Who is he?'

'He is a royal child. Some say his father is Akhenaten, some say not.'

'And who is his mother?'

'That I do not know. But it would be important to find out, for that boy has a role written for him by Ay in the Book of Time. If the time of the Aten is over, the Amun will be restored. He may yet be called by a new name. Tutankhamun.'

Then Ay invited the Queen to descend. She did so, with her

daughters. A large door opened at the far end of the hall. The chamber it opened on to was dark with congregating shadows. There was a sound of rustling and shuffling, as men made way for her. Nefertiti knew she must walk now, across this great hall, past these great men and into that dark chamber, with pride and dignity. She set off, followed by Ay, Horemheb, Ramose and the shuffling boy. I thought again of the Society of Ashes. I wondered who else held feathers. Who else was waiting in that room of shadows?

The Queen walked past me, her face proud and dignified beneath the great crown. I remembered all those glorious stone faces in Thutmosis's workshop, and it was as if the best of them had come to life now in her poise, balance and beauty. Her face was self-possessed and powerful. But I saw in her eyes, for a moment as she glanced at me, those gold flecks of pain. Then the door closed behind them, and she was gone.

As the hall burst into an uproar of controversial shouts and arguments, a breathless pain overwhelmed my heart. Nakht noticed.

'Let us go outside,' he said.

As we walked away through the crowds I tried to regain my breath. I needed to talk, to keep thinking, to move ahead, as she had done, into my own future. I needed to evade the pain of this moment.

'How is your garden coming on?' I heard myself say, astonished by the irrelevance of my question.

Nakht smiled, understanding. I had forgotten how much I liked him.

'Oh, it is struggling with the desert, as always,' he said. 'But I am returning to Thebes, now that all is changing. Why don't you join me?'

44

Khety and I stood together on the jetty while Nakht's boat was undergoing its final preparations. The city was emptying. The dock was a mess of boats and cargoes, but a new sense of purpose seemed to have taken hold. People knew, once more, what they could believe in. For my part, I could not wait to leave the terrible delusion of this place.

'Find your family, Khety. Go home. Stay in touch. I'm sure we'll meet again.'

He nodded. 'And you yours. That's what matters now.'

'Thanks. And keep trying for a child.'

'We will.'

He smiled. I liked him.

'We will look back upon all this one day over a good wine from the Dakhla Oasis.'

He nodded again, and embraced me. How strange these partings, when words will not suffice.

So I stepped away upon the Great River that carries us all to our different destinations and destinies. As the boat pulled off from this strange, unreal land, Khety stood watching and occasionally waving, growing smaller and smaller until, finally, as we sailed away around the great curve of the river, he and the city of Akhetaten disappeared. I wondered for a moment if I would ever return, and if I did, what I would find. Then I looked ahead, towards Thebes.

Of the journey home I have little to say except that it was too slow, the north wind helping us against the ever-opposing current. I had no patience, and I could not sleep. My heart beat too fast. I saw the unchanging world pass by: the long, luxurious light of dusk upon the marshes; the shadowy and magnificent papyrus groves; the cattle drinking at the water's edge; the women washing pots and clothes in the river; the children playing with nothing, using their imaginations, then waving and calling with open delight as we passed; the sky always the same great blue, the fields the same green haze, turning now to gold; the moving water with its endlessly changing hues – silvers, viridians, greys, ambers; and the blackness of the unknown depths below our passing keel.

I recalled sailing in the opposite direction all those days before, with this journal almost empty, and with no knowledge of how things would turn out. And as I sit here now, in the dawn light, as we approach the great and glorious chaos of the city of my life, with its familiar noises and cries, streets and secrets, smells and perfumes, beauties and catastrophes, I find I am glad but also afraid. The gods have granted me a safe return to the place where I started. But do we ever truly return from such journeys? Surely we come back to where we started, changed. We are not the same. 'How do you know what you know?' Nefertiti had asked me. There is only one answer: 'Because this happened. Because now she is gone for ever.' This is the truth of a true story. Something lost. Something found. Something lost again.

I bade farewell to Nakht. 'We will meet again,' he said. 'I am sure the future has something in store for us. Come and see me soon, and let's talk about the world, and its changes, and gardens.' I believed we would. I embraced him, a man I knew I could trust, with fondness and gratitude.

I walk up towards my street in the early morning light, back through the familiar passages and squares, past the expensive shops selling monkeys and giraffe skins, ostrich eggs and engraved tusks; past the familiar stalls of the Alley of Fruit, and the wood and metal workshops just opening for the new day; under the roofs where the children leap and the birds sing who have no knowledge of the dark world beyond. Back towards my life and my home.

I arrive at the wooden door. I offer a prayer to the little god in his niche who knows I don't believe in him, then push the door open. The courtyard is swept and tidy, the olive tree stands silver and green. I listen to the silence. Then I hear a girl's voice asking a question, and then another, in the kitchen. I enter the room, and there they are, my girls, my Tanefert, with her hair the colour of midnight, and her strong nose, and her eyes that brim suddenly with tears. And I hold them all, for a long, long time, hardly daring, yet, to believe that life could bring me now such happiness.

ACKNOWLEDGEMENTS

I would like to thank Broo Doherty, my agents Peter Straus and Julia Kreitman, and Bill Scott-Kerr and the superb team at Transworld, for making this book possible, and then making it better.

Thanks also to Carol Andrews, BA PADipEg, Lorna Oakes of Birkbeck College and Raafat Ferganie for sharing their expert knowledge with such kindness and generosity, and to Patricia Grey for her help with certain signs. As is always true, interpretation of the facts – together with any faults and errors – is my responsibility alone.

For advice and comments on various points of detail I would like to thank Walter Donohue, Mark Stuart and Bevis Sale.

And to the bright girls, Siofra, Grainne, Cara, and their parents Dominic Dromgoole and Sasha Hails: love and thanks for the inspiration and the happiness.

And, above all, thank you Paul Rainbow for going on this journey with me, and reading and rereading, and always saying the right thing at the right time; as a song from the New Kingdom says: 'You have uplifted my heart.'